Dear Readers,

BET books is proud to present the winners of BET's First Time Writers contest. This collection features the literary talents of our grand prize winner, Tracee Lydia Garner, and our three runners-up, LaTwaan Green, LaShell Shawnte Stratton, and Kendy Ward.

These young writers have done a wonderful job of producing stories that demonstrate their maturity and strength. The collection will showcase romantic comedy, romantic suspense, and classic contemporary romance at its best.

BET will be holding the First Time Writers contest annually to keep introducing fresh young voices into the marketplace. You may find submission guidelines for this contest posted on the BET Web site (www.bet.com).

We truly hope you enjoy this collection.

Best,
Glenda Howard
Senior Editor

All That . . . And Then Some!

Tracee Lydia Garner
LaTwaan Green
LaShell Shawnte Stratton
Kendy Ward

sepia

BOOKS

BET Publications, LLC
www.bet.com

SEPIA BOOKS are published by

BET Publications, LLC
c/o BET BOOKS
One BET Plaza
1900 W Place NE
Washington, DC 20018-1211

All Kensington Titles, Imprints, and Distributed Lines are available
at special quantity discounts for bulk purchases for sales promo-
tions, premiums, fund-raising, and educational or institutional use.
Special book excerpts or customized printings can also be created
to fit specific needs. For details, write or phone the office of the
Kensington special sales manager: Kensington Publishing Corp.,
850 Third Avenue, New York, NY 10022, attn: Special Sales
Department, Phone: 1-800-221-2647.

First Printing: September 2001
10 9 8 7 6 5 4 3 2 1

Printed in the United States of America

CONTENTS

Family Affairs

Tracee Lydia Garner

*For Momma and Daddy, who instilled in me drive,
determination, optimism, and a will to succeed,
despite the situation.*

And special thanks to:

Richard, who's always bugging me but is really all right.

Mrs. Sampson—the greatest kindergarten teacher in
Virginia.

Mr. Brennan, the master storyteller.

Falls Church High School English Teachers, Ms.
Singley, Ms. Bucco, and Mrs. Smith, who made the
Montagues, Capulets, and even Lady Macbeth, easier to
understand, exciting, and fun.

LaShaunda Hoffman at www.sormag.com, for providing
a place and forum for "us" to learn and get inspired.

Chapter One

The noise from the cafeteria was a slow drumming to her ears. Entrants and eaters chatted while her thoughts ran unleashed through her mind.

"Faye? Mind if I join you?" He looked at her with concern but also with something else. She had peacefulness about her, yet he knew inside a storm was raging out of control. She was always very calm, but he hoped to be there to comfort her when she finally broke down. The feeling was foreign to him but not unwanted. He knew what lay ahead for her, and he promised to be there if she'd let him.

"Dr. Cove?" Faye opened her eyes slowly, focusing on him. He held a large cup of steaming liquid in one hand, the other hand he held poised above the chair opposite her.

"Um, yeah. Yes. Okay," she replied to his question. He sat watching her, his gaze intense but friendly. She knew he had to talk to her, to prep her for what would come.

She'd been preparing herself and she believed she was ready. "I know what you're going to say," she said while he sipped his coffee.

Jacob scooted to the edge of his chair, waiting for her to talk. "Okay . . . Why don't you tell—"

"You're going to tell me that it's only a matter of time, that I need to be ready, and that there's nothing you can do to save him," she interrupted.

"Yes." He hesitated, "You're right. That's what I'm going to tell you, but also that I think you should talk to someone, a friend . . ." He stopped abruptly when she waved her hand.

"There is no one . . ." she said, her voice quiet and barely audible. She continued, gaining more strength. "I'll be fine, thank you. It's no concern of yours. I have to go." She began placing her unused utensils on the tray and wiping the space before her clean of nonexistent crumbs.

"At least finish your soup. It looks like you haven't touched it at all," he said.

She hated the way he made her feel. He was gorgeous, but his eyes were too knowing, too assessing. He was always there, solid as a rock. Around him she felt dependent, and she knew that if he gave an inch, she'd take yards, wanting and taking more until satisfied. He might be one of those one-in-a-million who'd give willingly without ceasing, but she couldn't let herself do that. She had done it before and been trampled.

"I'm not hungry," she replied, lifting her tray.

"You need to eat . . ." he said, pleading with her. She wasn't fat by any means, and he could tell she had lost weight in the last months. He knew that between her job and spending every day at the hospital she probably skipped more meals than was healthy. Her eyes looked fatigued. The light he'd seen in them was always bright and luminous. But the ordeal was taking a toll and slowly extinguishing her flame.

He reached out a hand to her, placing it gently on the hand tightly gripping the tray.

His hand on hers was hot. It singed her skin, warming her from the point of contact all the way up her arm. At that moment she knew she had to get away from this man. His presence, his being already caused her panic, but the touch was single confirmation of the growing attraction between them. If the circumstances were different, if there weren't such turmoil going on inside and around her, things could be different. But she couldn't think about that now. She couldn't think about him and her, or them together. It only confused her more.

Faye turned from him, hurrying to the trash receptacles. She deposited her items in their proper bins and headed for the elevator.

One week later . . .

The odors were acrid, all pounding her nostrils at once. The disinfectant cleaners of Pine-Sol. The lotion she'd recently applied to his arms and hands. The meatloaf dinner that sat on his tray table, cold as ice would go untouched. None of it mattered now.

"I'm sorry. Yes. He's gone," said Dr. Cove

Faye took her eyes from her father to briefly stare at the doctor. She knew her father was gone by the loose grip of his hand on hers. She didn't need the everconfirming statement from the everpresent doctor to inform her what was happening. Reality had yet to set in for her. The moment she knew would eventually come had arrived. She had prepped herself so much. The moment was here and she found she wasn't prepared at all.

She looked down at the frail body that used to be full of life. Once a big man, tall and thick, he had lost a lot of weight in the last months. The prostate cancer had taken over, eating everything he put into his body. *It is over,* thought Faye.

Over. Over. The words echoed in her head. The memories she had of him came back to her like slides in a picture show. They were vivid, colorful, and so full of detail. She felt each one assault her mind. Her breathing became labored, and her eyes rolled back. She closed them thinking maybe she could make the images go away. Even there, they remained, more pronounced on the black canvas of her closed lids. She opened her eyes frantically, and saw the memories etched everywhere as if being projected. She felt confined, and there was no escape. Quickly she let go of her father's hand. It fell limply back onto the bed.

Faye looked for an exit, any exit. Her hand splayed against her chest, willing it to cease its erratic pulsation. Maybe she could escape the pain if she left the room. Dr. Cove was immediately in front of her, his hands were on her shoulders, squeezing gently as she trembled. He became concerned regarding her reaction. They'd had lunch in the cafeteria just hours before and he thought his talk had prepped her for the reality he assured her would come. She seemed okay then. She knew the hours were small amounts of time. Even those, he'd said, had been rationed rather abundantly. Ultimately, her father would be gone. Dr. Cove's forehead creased in the middle as he studied her. She looked directly at him but nothing registered. Jacob talked gently and soothingly, but firmly as he brought his face closer to hers, willing her to see him clearly.

"You can get through this. It's okay. Breathe deeply," said Dr. Cove. She saw his lips moving, but no sound penetrated her ears. She wiggled free of his hold.

"Wait." He tried to hold on.

"Let me go. I have . . . have to get out of here," she replied. She stumbled through the electric doors of the cancer center ward and exited into the night. She ran as fast as she could, her heels clicking loudly on the pavement. The cold air swirled around her. Snow fell lightly, melting upon hitting the pavement, slicking the ground.

Her head began to feel light from breathing so deeply, and the world around her spun frantically out of focus. She heard cars but didn't realize she was in the middle of the street as she tried to catch her breath. One car came toward her, the blaring of its horn causing her to freeze. It swerved around her. She tried to regain her frame of mind, but the vi-

sions kept coming, and the realities of the last week continued their onslaught.

She began the review of her life. So much lay in ruin: the
aftermath of a disastrous quake. She felt alone. The father
who'd been a rock and a cornerstone of her stable foundation
was no more. Support from siblings didn't exist: She was an
only child. Her mother she never really knew: dead since
Faye was ten. Her career as a day school assistant director
was going nowhere fast. Marcus: Infidelity and lies were all
he conveyed.

The hospital bills continued to pile up while she worked a
nine-to-five and spent every last penny playing catch-up
with them. There was nothing left. What purpose, then, did
that leave her?

Lijah. Faye thought as if blinking lights went off in her
optic nerves. How could she forget her lifeline? The person
she spent day and night thinking of, taking care of, and giving all of her love to?

The night was pitch black. Another car sped toward her as
she turned to make her way back to the sidewalk. Her head
continued to pound, a fierce, numbing ache setting in between her eyes. The extreme cold raised the hairs on her
arms. She swayed, losing her balance due to dizziness and
the slippery pavement. Letting out a small shriek, she fell to
the ground. Slowly reorienting herself, she got up to continue her path . . . *back to Lijah,* she thought with renewed
determination.

Suddenly she was jolted. Her fingers scraped the hood of
the car as it impacted against her body sending her over it and
then propelling her away. Her fingers grabbed frantically for
anything that would give stability but encountered nothing. A
jarring thump to her side threw her across the street. Faye
rolled from the jolt. Everything hurt at the same time. Her
head hit the curb as an endless, black tunnel beckoned her.

Chapter Two

The driver of the black BMW spun the car around the side street and quickly exited. He ran up the street to find out what had happened. His swaying gait was an indication that he had not been fully alert. His mind raced. He hoped to encounter a stray animal, but deep down he knew otherwise. He staggered just a bit as he approached. The sight of the body sickened him, but not nearly as much as the intoxication affecting his motor skills did. He gawked at the long, slender, cocoa-colored legs leading up to a midlength skirt. One navy pump lay in the street a few feet from the body. Thick white flakes continued to fall, sprinkling her crimp, copper-colored hair.

A woman, damn, I can't take this crap right now, he thought. He continued to approach the body, his blood pressure surged while his heart beat wildly in his chest. He crouched down beside the body to feel for a pulse, willing his vision to clear. The pulse was there but slowing rapidly. He leaned his face closer to Faye's. Her breath was faint, but relief surged through him that it existed. The bruises were just beginning to turn a faint purple. Some oozed blood on her pecan-colored face, and her slender fingers with short manicured nails had scrapes on them. A small bruise began on her forehead, reddening with broken blood vessels underneath the skin. Her lips were deep red and pouted.

The driver ran back to his car and sped away. Ten miles away he pulled into the local gas station and made a call to 911. He informed them that there had been an accident and the location of the body on Georgia Avenue, Northwest Washington. He quickly hung up before the operator could ask any more questions.

Bolting as fast as the BMW could go from the gas station, he headed home. If only her face and the impending fate of the young woman he hit wouldn't niggle him for the rest of his days. It all gave him an excuse to drown more of his sorrows. The tempting liquid in the thick, colored bottles was an easy reach at the small bar in the living room. They sat waiting, eager to carry him away.

Faye lay still on the cold concrete. Her toes felt like heavy icicles. Her surroundings and the world around her were very distant, but she remembered some of the things that were happening to her. A mask filled with stale, frigid air was placed over her nose and mouth. Before the mask came she remembered a hideous odor and the thick smell of cigarette smoke and liquor, a raspy voice, and a rough, frantic touch jerking her wrist. Someone pleaded with her not to die before she heard heavy footsteps grow distant and the screech of tires grinding against the pavement. A stiff, cool board under her back and too-tight straps fastened around her were all that Faye could feel. She was terrified, but there was no escape even in semiconsciousness as visions of her father continued to enter her mind, and *Lijah . . . What would happen to Lijah?* This thought was even more troublesome to her than the state of her father. *"Lijah, I'm sorry baby,"* she whispered before losing the battle to remain conscious. The pains of her head, her physical body, and her heart were overwhelming. The only escape a dreamless sleep that pulled her down.

Chapter Three

Dr. Jacob Cove was finishing his rounds when the bustle of another emergency room entrant came in. He finished writing down some information on the chart, took a deep breath, and mentally readied himself for the newest arrival.

"Hit-and-run accident. African-American female, late twenties, head injury, broken left ribs, scrapes and bruises to the head. Could be experiencing comatose head trauma," the EMT said as he looked her over and continued to prepare the intravenous tube in her arm.

"Got a name? ID?" asked Dr. Cove, taking out his light to examine the patient's eyes. He immediately froze upon doing so, experiencing complete shock. *The eyes were* her *eyes*. He'd looked into them almost every day for what seemed like an eternity but was really just the last few months. He looked over the rest of her body to make sure. The short, blue, knee-length skirt with the sky-blue blouse confirmed. She always dressed so professionally, he assumed for her job. One foot clad in sheer hose showed perfect toes. One blue pump remained while the other, Jacob guessed, lay in the street, lost on impact. Over the past few months, every day, in her eyes he saw the hurt and pain, and he only seemed to add to the misery with his progress—or lack thereof—reports. He never had any good news to share, nor saw any happiness in her eyes. He felt somehow responsible. It seemed he was always her private bearer of bad news. His heart constricted a little bit further as he spoke with her about her father's condition.

He comforted her when she cried. Sometimes she pushed him away. Only now and again did she permit him to comfort her and he had cherished those moments. With her in his arms he felt like her protector, and enjoyed the small formal intimacies she allowed him.

At other times she was on the warpath, informing him about his bedside manner and how much work it had needed. She was never at loss for words to let him know what she was feeling. He knew it was because of the tragic ordeal she was going through. He was no stranger to the brunt of people lashing out at him. It was always somehow his fault for the pain they suffered. Deep down he knew it wasn't. In some way, however, he felt accountable. Maybe— the all-knowing doctors—never knew, learned or discovered enough about the human body in order to do more to save it, resuscitate it, cure it, and make it all better.

He often questioned his profession in times like these. The victories outweighed the tragedies, but tragedies did occur. They couldn't compare to what he felt, what the family felt. He, too, was once an outsider. He had been talked to by some know-it-all doctor. The utter loss outweighed any other emotion, perhaps even anger at those who tried, but ultimately couldn't help.

"Thanks. We'll take it from here," said Dr. Cove as he continued his routine ministrations in examining the patient.

"Abby, let's get her to X ray, CT scan, slow drip for pain three milliliters acetaminophen, and do a look at her legs, too, to make sure she didn't break anything else." Jacob took a deep breath and continued to speak to the nurse. He felt his anger rising. Taking out a small package from the table drawer, Jacob pulled out a swab, dipped it into some special brown, pasty balm that he used to attend to Faye's cuts. His large fingers felt awkward as he fumbled with the tiny, cotton-tipped stick spreading the paste on her cuts and forehead bruises. He then bandaged them. After the job, Jacob viewed his handiwork. The cuts and scrapes weren't something he usually attended to on patients. The nurses did what were considered the small jobs, but something compelled him to see to her needs, to be the one responsible for her, and the simple fact that he wanted to prompted his attention.

Abby eyed the doctor carefully, wondering why he paid such attention to her wounds when he hadn't done so with other patients. Jacob felt the nurse's stare and knew the question behind it. He couldn't, or wouldn't, go into his reasoning behind seeing to her care. He simply stated that he knew her.

"I want those orders done *now,* Abby," he said to her. Her curiosity would have to be set aside. More quietly and calmly, he said, "Her name is Faye, Abby. Her father just died here. I guess she just ran out and someone hit her, or she was delirious . . ." Jacob continued, his emotions a conflict of helplessness and responsibility for her present condition. He shoved them aside and tried to pull himself together. *Time was everything.* He told himself. "I should have stopped her, but I didn't know . . . I didn't think. I . . ." he said. Shaking himself back together, he realized it would do nothing for Faye if he continued to heap self-loathing and guilt on himself when Faye needed his alert mind, quick thinking, and clear head.

"Let's see she gets everything she needs, okay? Tell Davidson I want two heated blankets from OR. Then tell one of the nurses to go to where her father was. Her things are there. We should be able to get the name of someone, a family member, friend . . . anyone, from the contents."

Nurse Abigail Dixon began taking care of the things the doctor had ordered. She began the chart on Faye Hicks and had her placed on the list of urgent X rays.

"Yes, Doctor." Abigail left the room to get the necessary people.

Jacob hoped there may be someone, a family member, anyone to be here with her, but deep down he knew if there had been he would have known of it. At some point during the many hours she had spent at the hospital, no one came to comfort her while she comforted and took nurse-level care of her father. She bore the pain alone. This was the case now. She must've have been frightened, bearing the pain alone.

Jacob looked around the room as if he'd never seen it before. Everything seemed so white, bright, sterile, and impersonal. He looked back down at Faye and reached for her hand. Her body seemed small and childlike, but it was nothing compared to who she really was. The powerhouse in a beautiful package of five-foot-seven, 135 pounds came to his mind. In just a few short, but emotionally long months he had come to know her as the "in your face," strong black woman she was. Her fingers were like ice.

Pateon Davidson entered the room. His skin was the color of honey, his eyes small and assessing. He was almost the same height as Jacob. His moves were slow, calculated. "What's your problem?" he asked, swinging into the room as if he hadn't a care in the world.

"Where are the blankets, Davidson?" Jacob replied. He knew if he asked for anything directly from Davidson it would turn into an ego contest. He didn't have time and had long ago relinquished participating in the games of superiority that Davidson insisted on playing.

"You know we only give heated blankets to operating room patients," he replied.

"I don't give a damn. I want them and you had better damn well get them. Now!" Jacob yelled.

Davidson left, a smirk crossing his face. He enjoyed every opportunity he had to rattle Dr. Jacob Cove, but vaguely wondered why Jacob wanted the blankets for the patient.

Jacob's body vibrated with anger. Looking down at Faye, he grabbed her hand, rubbing and massaging it with his own, careful of the bandages. Her copper hair was damp from the melting snow as he brushed tendrils from her face. He knelt beside her bed. "You know, the body shuts down so it can heal itself. That's all," he whispered in her ear. He didn't know if the affirmation was truly for her. From it, he, too, felt comforted. His dad had once told him the very same thing at the inquisitive age where questions came endlessly. His deep voice came back to him. *After any kind of trauma to the body, son, the body shuts down. You know, "tunes out" so to speak. That helps it focus internally and heal itself. When it's finished, though, it sometimes takes a while, a week or even months, to wake up again.* He remembered that's how his dad had explained it to him. For the simplicity and how logical it sounded, Jacob was inclined to let it be of comfort.

"As soon as you're done healing you'll wake up. If I have anything to do with it, you'll be okay. I need a good 'tongue lashing' and someone tell me 'bout myself.' I missed the Bedside Manners 101 course and I need someone . . . " He cleared his throat. ". . . you to give me some pointers." He smiled to himself remembering that attitude. "I promise . . . Faye. I'm sorry about your father, but you will live. I'll make certain of it, but you gotta fight. No one can fight for you but you. I'll give you every possible aid I can, but ultimately it's up to you."

Jacob sat holding Faye's hand until two nurses came to take her. Letting her go, he silently prayed that there weren't more internal injuries. He also promised he would come down shortly if she wasn't back. For some reason he felt as if he were her caretaker now. Whatever happened, he was responsible to see to it that she was taken care of, that she was well and safe.

Chapter Four

Most of the personnel from the thirty-third district City Day School in Northeast DC had left for the evening. Cynthia Carter, the school's infallible secretary, paced the confines of the office. The telephone cord's reach kept her steps short.

A little girl sat on a small rug which had big, green letters of the alphabet around its edge, black Barbie clutched in one grubby little hand. The other made a small pile of crumbs on the floor with her half-eaten peanut butter cracker. The little girl was becoming restless. Cynthia eyed her while searching with one hand through the small card file box containing various emergency addresses and phone numbers. The other hand clutched the phone, switching ears as elevator music droned on the other end.

"Yes. Faye Hicks. Her father, Isaac Hicks, is a patient there . . . No! Hon. I can not hold another time. I'm looking for her and I need to speak with her as soon as possible . . . What? . . . Your records show what?"

Cynthia turned her back to the little girl, lowering her voice. "What did you say?" she whispered to the operator on the other end of the receiver.

She heard the news she knew would come. Over lunch Faye and Cynthia had discussed her father's condition, and Cynthia knew it was only a matter of time. Cynthia gave an inaudible "Thank you" to the operator as she replaced the receiver. She knew Faye was the type of person who maintained the calm aura that all was well, but in reality, the passing of her father was one of the very few somethings that could send her into a tailspin.

"Lijah . . ." she called to the little girl, pasting a composed, all-is-calm mask on her face. "Come on, baby gal," she said.

"Where we going, Aunt C.C.?" the girl asked as she got up from the floor to retrieve her Rugrats book bag, being sure to grab the Ken doll. She stuffed the items into her school bag.

Cynthia began packing up her own things. Smiling at the child's term for addressing her: aunt. She knew she was more like nanna, or grandmother. Despite her age in relation to the child or the child's mother, she refused to be deemed as such. It was agreed between the three of them. Faye being almost like a daughter, she would simply be called aunt. Setting aside her tote, she got on her knees ignoring the small popping sounds her bones made. Once in front of the little girl, she began to explain where they were headed. She bundled up the little girl for the cold November weather.

The drive to the hospital was really thirty minutes, but seemed like hours as Cynthia turned into the lot marked VIS-ITOR. She pulled a ticket from the booth and parked the car. She looked at the child thoughtfully, wondering if she was not truly more than a meager four years. She'd always told Faye she was smart, but just how smart consistently baffled her. By the time they reached the third floor of the Howard University Medical Center, Cynthia's nerves were frayed and she hoped Faye had pulled it together enough to take the child off of her hands.

Hospitals always gave Cynthia the creeps. She walked to the nurses' station holding Lijah's hand. She gave the woman that sat behind the counter the information she sought, only for a blank stare to be returned. She was asked to have a seat and proceeded to the waiting lounge already occupied by a couple of others. Some sat idly riffling through magazines, others' attention was diverted to the television hanging in the corner.

"I'm hot, Aunt C.C." Lijah said impatiently as her small hands tugged on the snaps of her stuffy winter coat. Cynthia turned to help the little girl remove the coat. She then riffled through her purse looking for change for Lijah to get a snack out of the candy machine.

Chapter Five

One person after the next seemed to roll into the emergency room and time slipped away. Here and there Jacob was able to get a few minutes away from his doctor duties to check on Faye. She still hadn't come out of her coma but was in stable condition and resting in the ICU.

He had asked two of the nurses to let him know of any change. As Jacob's shift ended, he found himself at Faye's bedside. He gave her a look-over to ensure she was okay, knowing in reality she was anything but. He held her hand and talked to her about various things. He wanted her to know someone was there who cared about her, and he truly did. He glanced at his watch and couldn't believe how much time had passed.

He would only be able to get a few hours' sleep before he would be back at the hospital. Before leaving, he gave her one last look. He didn't know what or from where had compelled him to kiss her. Moments ticked by. He found himself bending down, lightly brushing against her lips. They were soft and unresponsive, but nonetheless warm with the simmering fire he knew existed somewhere within. It was just hidden for the moment.

At the nurses' station, Jacob discussed information on a few of the patients' statuses. He made notations and other pertinent information changes on the dry erase board.

Just as Jacob left the ICU, one of the hospital volunteers, who happened to be helping out because the hospital was short-staffed, approached. Jacob knew her because her mother worked in the ICU, and she had spent a few of her summers off volunteering at the hospital. At present she wanted to be a doctor. Jacob was skeptical regarding her current chosen profession. She had changed her choices more times than he could remember and was certain they would change another ten times before she actually enrolled in her freshman year of college.

"Hi, Shelby," he said.

"Hi, Dr. Cove." She blushed before remembering her purpose for coming.

Shelby went on to discuss the woman sitting in the waiting area. Jacob gave a brief nod before heading to the area.

"Ms. Carter," he said gently.

Cynthia looked up at the gentleman. She knew immediately that he was the man Faye couldn't stop talking about.

Jacob gave Cynthia a once-over as she stood to greet him. Her hair was mostly gray. She had an older nature, he thought, but very vibrant and alert regardless. She looked rather grandmotherly with her antique jewelry. Small, tinted glasses hung from the silver linked chain around her neck. Her suit was almost as gray as her hair: a dressy jacket with crisp slacks. Her face was a light tan with deep lines around her mouth and smaller lines fanning from her eyes.

"Yes. Cynthia Carter. Dr. Cove, I presume? Can you tell me about Faye? Where exactly is she, dear?"

Jacob was taken aback at the woman's use of the endearment on him when they'd just met, as if she knew him personally. She reminded him of his mother.

"Ms. Carter, I'm afraid I have some very bad news," he

began, gauging her reaction. "Faye became very upset when her father passed, and she left the hospital frantically. She was hit by a car and now . . . she's in a coma."

He assisted Cynthia in taking a seat. One hand covered her mouth, the other was a tight fist in her lap. Jacob watched Cynthia's demeanor quickly change as a little girl approached slowly, her gaze down as she bounced over the lines in the floor.

"I've found what'd I like, Aunt C.C.," she said cheerily upon reaching Ms. Carter.

Ms. Carter cleared her throat, and gave the little girl a reassuring smile. "And what might that be, Missy?"

Jacob watched the exchange between the two. His heart seemed to pick up its slow pace as the little girl smiled at the woman. Something very familiar about her reached the corners of his mind but refused to let him recognize it. They chatted on as he continued to rack his brain to discover the familiarity.

Ms. Carter was talking; then she looked expectantly at him.

"The nice doctor here, Dr. Cove . . ." she was saying.

"Hello . . ." He came out of his musings about the girl long enough to introduce himself and pick up the conversation.

"Hi, I'm Lijah Hicks." She held out her hand, proud of her display of manners as Jacob reached to shake it. His large, hand completely closed around hers. She smiled brightly at him before removing her hand.

Lijah whispered something to Ms. Carter, and she gave the little girl knowing reassurances.

Again Lijah talked low as Jacob continued to eye her. Her skin was the same color as Faye's and her eyes, like Faye's, only large for her small frame. Little colored barrettes were attached all over her head at the ends of fat amber twists of hair. She wore jeans, a bright mulberry sweater with a small, yellow, big-headed bird on the front, and blue sneakers with neon laces.

"Potty, Aunt C.C. I have to go potty," Lijah said as she tugged on the hand of Ms. Carter. Ms. Carter gave the girl a placating smile before turning to Jacob.

"Point me in the direction of the rest room, dear?" Ms. Carter was saying to Jacob as she stood to take Lijah by the hand.

Jacob stood, too, but his eyes couldn't be taken from the little girl.

"Down the hall, first door on your left."

The little girl . . . Lijah, thought Jacob. She looked just like her mother. For such a young age, she was bright and impeccably mannered.

Moments later they returned. Jacob whispered briefly to Ms. Carter as the little girl went back to the snack machine.

"Why don't you go and see Faye?" he spoke low as he watched Lijah just over the woman's shoulder.

"What about Li—" she replied casting a worried glance in the child's direction.

"There's a supervised play area on the second floor," he interrupted, anticipating her concern. "I'll take her down there, and you can come and get her in a bit. Just ask Nurse Abigail or the volunteer, Shelby, they will tell you where it is. I'll keep an eye on Lijah. I really want you to talk to Faye—I mean really talk to her." Jacob crouched low so Ms. Carter could see the urgent pleading in his eyes. "Remind her about Lijah, Ms. Carter, and anything, I mean anything else you could think of that would help her break out of this. I have every reason to believe she will pull through, but not without knowing that there are people who need and care deeply about her."

"Do you, Dr. Cove? Care deeply about Faye?" she questioned. He patted her arm in reassurance before looking toward the little girl. "More than I realized," he replied.

Cynthia stuck her arm out to stop him before he left, following his gaze to the girl.

"You won't tell her about her mother? I'm not sure what to do or say. I just . . . she's so young."

Jacob took Ms. Carter's hand in his own. It was frail and bony, but her grip was strong.

"I won't tell her. I'm a stranger to her, but she'll have to know soon enough. Kids can sense these things, Ms. Carter."

Ms. Carter smiled as if she knew some secret. "I'm very aware. If you can keep her from asking you at all, Dr. Cove, I'll be very surprised. She's very attentive, endless questions at that age. If we don't tell her she'll figure something out. I just don't know how she'll take it . . . Her mother is all she has, Dr. Cove."

"Yeah." Giving her hand a pat, Jacob left to be with Lijah while Ms. Carter went to be with Faye.

Chapter Six

Jacob dug in his pocket for change as Lijah pointed to a package of vanilla crème cookies behind the plexiglass of the snack machine.

"Mommy taught me but I forgot. I think that seven is more than five," she said as she scratched her head, trying to remember what her mother had taught her about numbers. "That says 'seven.' " She pointed and proceeded to hold up seven fingers then began digging in her jeans pockets for the money. "But I only have two quarters and I think that's fifty cents," she continued, holding one in each hand.

"You're right," Jacob said to her, a huge smile crossing

his face. "Seven is more than five." He went on, "The cookies cost seventy cents, and you have fifty cents, so here's twenty more cents." He put the money in her little hand. She then put the money in the coin slot, waiting in great anticipation as he pressed corresponding buttons. She watched the package fall almost magically to where it rested in the collection pan. He held it open while her little hand dug anxiously for the treat.

On their way to the play area Jacob searched his brain for something to talk about. He wasn't aware of what the popular subject matter of four-year-olds was these days. Lijah ended his musing with her own questions that Ms. Carter had suggested would come.

"Do you know my mommy?" she questioned around a mouthful of cookie.

"Yes, I do," Jacob said. "Your mother, Faye, is a very nice person. She's pretty like you, too," he said, chancing a glance from the corner his eye, watching her giggle. "Why don't you tell me about her," he probed.

"She's busy a lot. My grandpa, he's sick, you know. Mommy says he might go to heaven to be with the angels."

"Yes, I know," he said quietly.

"But mommy is never mean to me. I love her very much," she said as if Jacob wouldn't know.

"She told me she'd never leave me." She paused as if pondering something. "Well, she said that if she had to leave, it'd never be for very long, and that she'd always come back."

Jacob couldn't believe it. The little girl was amazing. He was supposed to be of comfort to her, but her constant and endless babble about her mother's promises somehow made him feel unbelievably better.

"Except for Marcus," she continued.

"Who's Marcus?" Jacob asked with just a twinge of jealousy setting in his gut.

"He's a punk," she replied honestly.

Jacob almost doubled over in laughter but didn't think it appropriate. "Who taught you that?" He looked at her.

"Jason. He's older, first grade. Knows lots of words," she went on.

"I'm sure he does, but I don't think we should repeat all of them," he replied sternly.

"I know. But I don't like him. He's mean, and sometimes makes mommy cry."

Jacob's eyebrows shot up. *I could hurt him,* he thought, but didn't let the words leave his mouth. He simply nodded as if understanding the little girl's reasoning behind the descriptive name.

Jacob bent down in front of Lijah just outside the door marked PLAY AREA.

"Your Aunt C.C. will be down shortly. There're plenty of things to play with, and there are a few children in there, so if you need me just tell that lady over there that you would like Dr. Jake. Okay."

The little girl nodded enthusiastically before heading to the large, colorful dollhouse that had caught her attention.

Vondell sat in the corner puffing away one cigarette after the other. He couldn't get enough nicotine into his system. An empty Jack Daniel's bottle sat on the coffee table.

It was close to two A.M. as Jacob entered. Seeing the BMW parked in the driveway, Jacob knew his brother was home, and most likely in his usual state of drunkenness.

The entire place smelled of smoke and beer. The lights were off except for the small table lamp in the corner, giving the room a soft glow.

"Want me to set up a nicotine IV?" said Jacob to his brother, skeptically.

Vondell had yet to take his eyes off the pack of cigarettes on the table. Jacob noticed but was too tired to further comment on, or analyze the peculiar behavior of his brother. Vondell usually had a great comeback and their banter was cutting, mean, and sometimes comical. Vondell, had nothing, however, to say at present.

The ritual between Vondell and Jacob had become intense. He didn't know why he bothered trying to figure him out let alone make small talk. His brother had recently moved in because he couldn't pay his rent and keep a job at the same time. Over the years, they had distanced themselves more and more each day.

In his bedroom, Jacob sat on the edge of the bed as his mind became heavy with the happenings of the day. He thought about the scene with his brother briefly before his thoughts returned and were consumed by Faye and her present condition. He felt to blame for not going after her when she left in near hysterics. Her father had drawn his last breath, and that triggered her actions. He went as far as the hospital room's door calling after her. He figured she'd want to be alone with her thoughts. He'd informed enough families about their relatives' untimely passing to have seen all kinds of reactions. Much like Faye, they ran away frantic and overcome by grief, only to return moments later after calming down. The possibilities of the traumatic accident troubled him. Severe brain damage, memory loss, vision and/or hearing impairments were just some of the complications Jacob acknowledged. *And Lijah. What would happen to her if Faye didn't pull through?*

He'd made numerous calls to the police station throughout the day, giving them an interrogation of his own about the accident that had been called in. The information they had was scant. He knew hit-and-runs were often never solved, though he prayed this one would be different.

Standing, Jacob removed his slacks for a pair of cotton

shorts, he pulled the beeper off his pants and placed it on his shorts. His hand rested on the pager, knowing she would pull through.

Chapter Seven

After Jacob awoke, took a shower, and dressed quickly, he placed a call to the hospital to inquire about Faye's condition. Nothing had changed through the course of the night.

Downstairs, his brother stood clad in jeans at the kitchen sink with a cup of steaming black liquid. Jacob helped himself to the coffeepot, adding a spoon of creamer. He cringed at the thought of sounding like his Dad as he watched his brother. He realized it was what Vondell needed in order to pull himself together, "Did you find anything yesterday?" Jacob asked his brother as he nursed his coffee and sat down at the table of the eat-in kitchen.

"No," Vondell replied despondently. "Nothing."

"You only have the car for a few more days, that's all I agreed to loan it to you for and then that's it. You got it?" Jacob replied. His brother's responses always irked him. It was as if he didn't care about anything or anyone.

Vondell had been looking for a job for close to two weeks. Much of the time so-called looking was spent in his favorite bar, drinking away the hours.

"Clean up your act and maybe you'll get something damnit," Jacob said, clearly disgusted by his brother's nonchalant attitude. Twenty minutes ticked by slowly until Jacob heard the beep of the taxi.

*   *   *

Thirty-two hours had passed. Faye's condition hadn't changed. Jacob had spent more time with her than at any other place. When he was supposed to be at lunch, he was with Faye. When he was usually holed up in his office reviewing reports and responding to business related mail, he was with Faye. Each night, the time gained closer to morning when he went home. Faye was the last person he saw each night.

Ms. Carter had come every day after the center had closed, with Lijah in tow. They both had seemed to be growing restless of each other, and Lijah often looked as if she was on the verge of tears.

Jacob was at a loss of what to do. They had informed the little girl about what had happened with her mother, but she hadn't been allowed to see her. Jacob wondered if that was for the best. Children under the age of twelve were never allowed into the ICU. Jacob thought maybe it was time the rules changed. He would rather inflict harm upon himself than leave any permanent traumatic scars on a child. He'd spent nights at home researching information about the psychology of children. He'd consulted his friend about the idea. His research concluded that other hospitals let children at any age see their relatives in the hospital. There were still a handful of hospitals, however, that had yet to change.

He discussed his findings with Ms. Carter and could only do it if she, too, agreed.

"I just don't know," she replied. "She would see a child psychologist before and after the ordeal?"

Jacob assured her as much. The psychologist he'd called was a friend and colleague of his older brother Vondell. Vondell had also been a prominent psychologist before he allowed the drinking to dictate his state of mind thus ruining his practice.

Ms. Carter agreed and they set up Lijah to see a psychologist in Jacob's office for the next day. She felt comfortable there. She had spent much time chatting with Jacob and eating dinner while Ms. Carter talked with Faye and spent the needed break on her own.

"I think she'll be fine," Dr. Weston Benning was saying as Jacob sat in the chair across from his desk. Benning was an older man, head of psychology and acting director. He was a good friend of Jacob's father and was on the board of directors.

Benning was almost sixty years of age. His hair had yet to go completely gray as remnants of the black still lingered. Standing, he had yet to lose his height with his age, all of six feet two inches tall. His steel gray eyes always looked very serious. He never wore anything casual. His cheeks sagged and were loose, leading to a broad nose and big ears. His beard was completely gray and covered his thick lips.

Taking off his glasses he eyed Jacob. "This . . . Miss Hicks, and the little girl? Lijah?" he questioned, knowing the answer.

Jacob shifted in his chair. He hadn't had a lot of time to question his own feelings, let alone begin to convey them to someone else. Before Faye had been in the accident she was with her father most of the time. She asked questions about the best practices for his care, about the illness, and what she could or should do to take care of things. He felt drawn to her. Her caretaker ways, the little girl—everything about her attracted him. He was drawn to her strength and stability. He knew, had it not been for the unfortunate accident, they would be dating on a regular basis. In spending time with Lijah, the little girl tugged at his heart, reeling him in the rest of the way after her mother had him hooked. Even more than Lijah, he was able to get a glimpse of who Faye was through her eyes. He couldn't explain it, even *he* thought it weird that he would come to love her mother even more somehow through what the little girl shared with him about her.

Jacob relayed all this to Benning, having confidence that he would understand, at least the psychological aspects of it. He knew Benning could empathize and make sense of what Jacob couldn't understand.

Chapter Eight

Jacob held Lijah in one arm as he carried her to Faye's bedside. Once close enough where she could see her mother, she looked at Ms. Carter who stood on the other side of Faye's bed, and then back at Jacob, tightly clutching his shirt. Jacob whispered reassurances in her ear as he leaned closer to Faye.

"You gotta talk to her, sweetheart."

Jacob proceeded to pull up a chair, placing Lijah in it on her knees. He released the side rail, letting it down so Lijah could lean on the bed. Nodding to Ms. Carter, they moved past the dividing partition. Jacob gave one last encouraging nod to Lijah before leaving.

Lijah leaned closer to her mother's ear. "Momma . . ." she began. "I really miss you. I wish you would wake up so we can go for ice cream. Aunt C.C. can't cook, because the bottom of everything is black and crusty." Lijah chanced a look toward the end of the room to ensure no one was coming.

"Dr. Jake, Momma, he's nice. I think he likes you a lot. He spends time with me and never yells like Marcus."

Lijah ran out of things to say. Before jumping off the chair, she leaned in close to kiss Faye on the cheek, then ran from the room.

* * *

Ms. Carter took Lijah home for the night. She and Jacob eyed each other. They silently acknowledged that their attempt to revive Faye had failed. He'd run out of options and hadn't known what to do.

Jacob went back to Faye's room. Taking her hand he rubbed it against his face.

"Listen to me, baby. You gotta get through this. I know you can do it. I know you can. Lijah needs you . . . Hell, I need you."

Moments passed. Jacob's eyes grew round. Faye's hand began to move against the day-old stubble of his chin.

"Lijah . . ." she said breathlessly.

Jacob's heart sunk. "Faye. It's Doctor . . . " At that moment Jacob didn't want to be anyone's doctor. He wanted to be and had been her friend. With this realization he knew that he wanted to be even more. "It's Jake . . . cob. Jacob."

Jacob? she thought. The bright light assaulted Faye's eyes as she struggled to open them. Jacob was to her right leaning over her as recognition came to her. He looked different, she thought. His eyes seemed kinder, but they still held that sleepy look with the lids covering half of his pupils. They were eyes so dark the color was still to be determined. Ebony eyes. His thick hands were holding hers in a position she thought a little too personal for a doctor-patient type relationship. Every other finger belonged to him. His gaze was intense, steadfast on hers with his long, dark eyelashes. They swept up, pointing to bushy brows. His lips were thick and luscious, she thought. Probably made those moist, sucking sounds when he kissed. He didn't look like a doctor without the official white coat most doctors wore. The muscles in his arms were pronounced in the form-fitting, fuzzy, black sweater. The attraction coupled with the confusion etched on her face.

"Dr. Cove?" she asked.

"Yes, Faye. Call me Jacob," he replied.

Call you Jacob? What had happened? she thought. Her mind shoved away thoughts of want and desire to refocus. "My dad . . . gone?" she croaked out in a hoarse whisper.

Jacob simply nodded. His doctoring ways turning on as he looked in her eyes, halting the want and need he felt. But her eyes always pulled him in deeper with each glance. They were cloudy but she was alert. No sign of memory loss, recalling her most recent and tragic event. Reaching for the cup on her tray table, Jacob filled it from the larger pitcher of water. He bent the flexistraw and held it to her mouth.

Faye gulped thirstily. Her tongue was a log, heavy and thick in the desert of her mouth. Jacob refilled the cup as Faye continued to gulp.

"My baby?" she began to cry, her voice grew stronger. "God, how could I be so stupid. I almost orphaned her. Please tell me she is okay?" her eyes pleaded as the tears continued to fall.

Jacob's strong arms held her, sitting her up as he sat on the bed to face her. She fought him at first but soon welcomed the cocoon of his chest, the comfort he evoked and the solidarity his presence stood for. She stopped fighting and brought her arms as best she could around his neck careful of the IV, letting him hold her. His arms hugged her tighter as her trembling subsided. He rocked her back and forth, whispering soft gibberish in her ear. Assuring her that Lijah was safe and well. Jacob grabbed the box of tissues that sat on her bedside table. She took deep breaths to calm herself. He wadded up the tissue in his hand and began to dab at her eyes. Faye had never known such tenderness. She looked at him searching, and perhaps willing herself to understand how their relationship had changed without her knowledge. Their faces were so close she felt his breath as he continued to wipe the tears that fell. He leaned in, brushing her lips with his own, until he deepened the kiss. She didn't pull away. The fire of longing raged in her. Faye opened her mouth to speak. To resist him was a failed attempt. Jacob felt her lips part and air rushing to exit, but no words came out. He mistook her wanting to resist as a welcoming invitation, when his tongue entered, deepening the kiss. He was the first to pull way and regain control. He silently berated himself for his eagerness, but refused to apologize. He wasn't sorry.

Faye had calmed, her eyes were dry, but a different kind of pain now plagued her and that was the loss of Jacob and his hot mouth on hers. His arms continued to hold her and she was thankful, but his mouth, his sweet tongue dancing with hers, was lost. She didn't know the magnitude of the feelings that existed for him, or maybe she knew but hadn't wanted to acknowledge them. Jacob pulled away. Faye's eyes drooped with tiredness.

"Are you okay? Do you hurt anywhere?" he asked trying to focus. Her pain should be more pronounced now that she was alert and fully awake. Faye could not relay her real place of hurt. The heartache of loss, her father as well as what she viewed to be Jacob's lament from their passionate kiss. She simply shook her head. His hands cradled her back, he laid her down gently. Her eyes were intense upon him, but sleep called her to rest.

". . . Lijah to see me?" she questioned softly.

"Of course," he replied. "She'll be here when you wake up."

Chapter Nine

Jacob had strapped Lijah in his rented SUV as he headed for the hospital. He had phoned Ms. Carter at the school the day before, informing her about Faye's state.

The child was so anxious, bundling her up was a struggle. She was wiggling and refused to settle down.

"I can't wait to see mommy," she chanted.

"Your mommy will be very happy to see you, too, Lijah." *If only the traffic would let up,* he thought. Thanksgiving had yet to arrive, but already people were out in record numbers. He used his cell phone to call the hospital. If there had been an accident, perhaps the hospital was about to page him with the news of a multicar pileup. After confirming none, he hung up. Lijah watched Jacob using the phone and placing it back in his pocket.

"Can we call mommy?" she asked skeptically.

Jacob wondered why he hadn't thought of that. Pulling the phone back out he dialed the same number he had previously. Asking for the appropriate room, he handed the phone to Lijah.

Faye flipped through channel after channel seeing nothing of interest. If she ever got out of the hospital she was certain she would know how to put up drywall, install lighting fixtures, make a famous sushi dish, and reupholster her furniture.

The noisy ringing of the phone was a welcome interruption as Faye turned down the television. Her voice had not fully returned and she still felt weak.

"Hello," she said.

"Mommy!" The small voice replied cheerily from the other end.

Faye leaned her head back into the pillow. A smile of relief spread across her face. "How is my sweet baby?" she crooned.

"I fine, Mommy, but I miss you. We're coming to see you," she said.

"I know, baby." She had been counting the hours. They couldn't end fast enough as she looked at the clock wishing it later already. "I'll be waiting, baby. As soon as school is over, I know you'll be here."

"Oh, no, Mommy. *Now.* We're coming now," she replied enthusiastically. "Me and Jake stuck in traffic, but we'll be there soon, 'kay?"

Faye wondered, "Jake who, honey?"

Lijah gave an impatient sigh. "Dr. Jake, Mommy. Your doctor," she sang merrily, impatient that Faye didn't seem to remember who he was.

"Oh," was all she could say. "Can I speak with him, baby?"

Lijah held the phone out to Jacob. "She wants to talk to you," she informed him.

"Jacob, what are you doing?" she questioned before he could say hello.

"I'm bringing Lijah to see you. I know how much you want to see her," he commented.

"Yes, but Jacob," she replied. She pushed aside her befuddlement. "Thank you, Jacob."

"You're welcome, love," he replied, hanging up before she could respond. A smile tugged loosely at his lips at her state of confusion.

Chapter Ten

Faye and Jacob had grown quite close in the last week. She trusted him, cared about him, but that was as far as she would let herself go. She still couldn't believe he'd pick up Lijah from school and, sometimes before school ended, bring the little girl to the hospital for visits with her mommy.

Jacob took great care of her, of Lijah, seeing to their every need. Her father's care had consumed her life in the last few years, and with him gone, away went the roots and vestiges of her own foundation. Again Lijah was her savior. Lijah gave her the purpose she needed. Jacob however, he had fulfilled a different kind of need. He proposed a different type of stability she never knew could exist from a man. It had always been up to her in relationships to be the caretaker and emotional supporter. She gave and gave until it seemed she had nothing left.

Over time she had erected a wall she wasn't sure could be torn down. Outside, she projected a front of toughness and strength, when really all she wanted to do was lose herself. No one seemed to be a likely candidate for that role, until recently. *But in Jacob? Could I lose myself to him, in him? Two years ago, with Marcus, hadn't I done the same thing?* she thought with trepidation and agitation. Thoughts of Marcus came. The breathless woman, but they no longer upset her. Then and now, she would focus. Determined that she'd build the best life possible for her and Lijah, and maybe she could explore something with Jacob.

When no one was around, and after Jacob had left for the day, she grew destitute as thoughts of her father plagued her mind. She hadn't even gotten to say good-bye to him, and now he was buried. Faye sat up abruptly in her bed and winced at the pain it caused her, not to mention the dizziness. *But who had seen to his burial arrangements?* There wasn't a lot to do. His thoughtfulness in preplanning had removed much of the burden. There were, however, still some minor details she had needed to see to. *What about a memorial service or funeral?* she thought sadly.

Jacob entered her room with a large greasy sack. Noticing the sad look on her face, he deposited the bag on her tray table and went to her.

"What's the matter, baby?" he asked taking her hands in his own.

"My father's funeral? Is he buried already? He didn't get a service, and I didn't get to say good-bye."

Jacob knew of some provisions though he never thought further about what happened to the bodies after they died. He was usually the last one to attempt resuscitation, but after that they went to the morgue, never to return.

After letting her hands go from his own, he hugged her. "I'll find out, okay? It'll be all right."

She believed him and trusted that he was capable of taking care of things. He had been her savior thus far, that was all the proof she needed to know that anything she placed upon him would be taken care of.

"Well, I have some information in my purse about the funeral home. I can call them to see what's going on," she said.

Jacob got up, retrieving her purse from the closet. She rummaged through it for the necessary information. He reached for the phone and took the paper from her hand to dial the numbers.

"Let me?" he asked.

She nodded simply. He reached for the big greasy bag he'd brought in and placed it in her lap. A lopsided, devilish grin tickled the corners of his mouth.

Her elation showed as she began pulling out the contents. Her eyes widened at the two steaming foam trays with the imprint of lobster on them. Her mouth watered at the fried gulf shrimp before her eyes. The other container held collard greens and macaroni and cheese. She dug in as Jacob talked on the phone. He stared at her closed eyes, savoring the tangy cocktail dipping sauce and the meat of the shrimp. Jacob thought nothing of it when his thumb reached out, removing some leftover sauce from her lips, licking it off of his thumb.

Faye's eyes flew open, realizing what he had done. The brush of his thumb across her lips sent tiny fire darts down her spine, and she felt the buttons of her breast tighten with his intimate touch. They stared at each other for moments without words, but the messages from his—very personal— actions spoke volumes.

Jacob muttered some words into the phone before hanging up. "Listen, baby. Your father is buried beside your mother, just like you or . . . your dad had specified with the funeral director. They do need to finalize some paperwork with you as soon as possible."

She nodded. The shrimp box lay in Faye's lap as she thought about her father. "I didn't get to say good-bye, Jacob. I gotta go to the cemetery." Faye glanced toward the windows. The sun was high, and bright with the promise of more daylight hours. Closing the trays of food, she placed them on the tray table and began removing the bed covers. Her actions were slow because of her tender spots, but nonetheless purposeful.

Jacob rose to stop her. "If you think I'm letting you out of here, you got another thing coming. You were in a coma, Faye. Do you know how many people go into comas and don't wake up? Do you?" His tone was serious. He couldn't believe how fortunate she'd been. The statistics were more than stacked against her. "What are you thinking? You're still under the responsibility of this hospital. Until I see fit you cannot be released. You got that? I don't care what you say." His look was stern but her glassy eyes with unshed tears were his undoing.

Faye watched him incredulously. Her bottom lip trembled. If she didn't get out of the hospital she'd lose her mind. Just a few days had seemed like months.

"I can't take it here anymore. I just want to go see him for a little while, and what do you care what happens? *I'm* the stupid one. I got hit by a car, in a moment's hysterics. I hate it here, this place makes me sick," she wailed. "And the accident, as much as I regret it, it was my fault . . . What do you care?"

"I care more than you know. You just refuse to see how much, but I do. I care a lot," he said still standing in front of her. His thumbs reached out to wipe the tears that escaped down her cheeks.

Faye knew, and she regretted questioning him at all. She shook her head in affirmation. "I just want to say good-bye to him. That's all," she pleaded.

Jacob could deny her nothing, especially something so vitally important. He couldn't fathom what being confined to the four walls was doing to her. He knew she'd find some way to go, with or without him. He should make it with him, in the company of a skilled doctor who could foresee and be ready if anything happened. He wouldn't trust anyone to care for her other than himself.

"All right, listen. I'll take you to the cemetery tomorrow. But I still can't release you until your vitals are back to norm and stabilize."

Jacob helped Faye settle back into bed. He would once again see to things, and his promise to do so renewed her. She picked up the fork, digging into her food with vigor. He gave her a light brush on her cheek before leaving.

The entire walk to the Dr. Weston Benning's office, Jacob cursed himself. Thoughts of how he could agree to—let alone pull off—getting Faye out of the hospital and back again, all of it unnoticed, plagued his mind as even more daring thoughts came into light.

Chapter Eleven

Jacob mentally reviewed his "to do" list. Everything was coming together except for the most important detail as he reflected on his conversation with his colleague and confidant. "If you can take her and get her back by tonight, I'm sure everything will be fine," Jacob's friend Weston Benning was saying. "No one should pose a problem, it's Thanksgiving, Jacob. I feel sorry for anyone stuck in the hospital over the holidays. Everything should be okay, but if you are caught, it's my responsibility to report the happenings to the board.

"I guess there's no point in me trying to change your mind?" Benning asked skeptically.

Jacob shook his head when thoughts of Faye renewed his decision. He and Benning had been friends for some time, but Jacob knew he could never compromise his superior's position. Before leaving the office, he patted the older gentleman on the shoulder.

"You gotta do what you gotta do, man. I understand." Scratching his head, Jacob was thoughtful. "You're invited for dinner if you're not doing anything else," he continued, changing the subject, ensuring Benning that he knew when hospital business was just that, "hospital business," that in other matters they were friends.

Benning nodded at the invite. Both men turned heads as the door swung open and an older woman entered.

Going to the woman, Jacob gave her a brief hug and a small peck on the cheek. "Momma, what are you doing here?" he questioned, knowing she always came to visit the hospital around the holidays, but mostly to check up on him with his superiors.

"Emma!" Benning said, coming around the desk to embrace the woman. She returned his affection as Jacob stood back while the two chatted amicably.

"Weston. How are you?" she replied. "Jacob?" Emma Cove turned to eye Jacob disapprovingly. "I've need to talk to you. I'll come to your office in just a bit," she said before turning back to Weston Benning and taking the winged back, leather seat Jacob had occupied.

Jacob eyed his mother, anticipating. She'd always found something to nag him about. He had no doubt she'd make good on her promise to talk to him in a bit. It would be much too soon, as far as he was concerned. Nonetheless he'd wait. She always eventually hashed out whatever it was. Her stern mouth and set jaw meant whatever the issue was she was not happy about it.

"Mom, I invited Weston to Thanksgiving dinner." The guest list kept growing. He gave her a mischievous wink before closing the door without waiting for her reply.

Jacob replaced the receiver to the phone. His first call to Merry Maids, Inc., had been last minute, he knew. He hoped the one-hundred-dollar-tip was enough incentive. He called the center to discuss his plans with Ms. Carter, then had a brief chat with Lijah. She shared with him news of her recent tooth loss. He felt a secret surge of pride that she thought enough of him to share the information and wondered if she had had a chance yet to tell Faye. Replacing the receiver, he cleared his desk and packed away papers for the long Thanksgiving weekend.

Emma Cove entered the room just as he put on his coat. He had a few more errands to run. He sat back down with his coat on hoping to convey to his mother that he didn't have a lot of time and that she should make her comments quick.

Emma took her time approaching her son's desk, recognizing the features of impatience on his face. She moved across the room gracefully, dramatically, and had once dreamed of being center stage with her art. The times, however, when she was a young, lithe, and prominent black dancer, hadn't warranted an easy entry into the business. She settled with teaching instead. Opening her own studio, she taught adolescents in a small downtown loft for almost twenty-five years until her body could no longer keep up with the vigorous exercises.

Removing her coat, settling into the leather chair before Jacob's desk, she cut to the chase. "Where is Von?" she asked tersely.

Jacob rolled his eyes. He wasn't up to having another discussion about his brother's whereabouts. "Mother, we've been over this. Vondell . . . I have no idea. I'm not his keeper . . ."

"Don't get smart with me," she replied sternly.

Jacob slumped in his seat. "When you came earlier this week Vondell was gone, and he took my car. I don't think that when I do see him he'll be happy to see me. I loaned him the car for a specific amount of time, it's been up. I'm paying for renting a car while he has mine in God-knows-where. I couldn't care less about where he is, so long as my wheels are intact." Jacob stole a glance at his watch. He needed to get going.

"Do you need anything else from the store?" he asked,

changing the subject. "I want everything to go well with Faye, Lijah, and Ms. Carter coming."

Emma Cove returned Jacob's look. "Everything will be fine, though I don't understand why this girl is so important," she said dismissively. "It's not like your brother to miss Thanksgiving."

"If it makes you happy I'll visit the bar down the street, his favorite hangout spot." Jacob swore he'd agree to put out an APB or file a missing persons report if he thought his mother would stop hounding him. Their relationship ceased amazing him. His brother was almost five years older. Somewhere through their child hood they'd switched roles. Jacob became everybody's caretaker, "the older brother." His mother was always overly concerned only about Vondell. Years ago it hurt him deeply when he would get the sole blame for something both he and his bother had been equally guilty of. Vondell always did what he wanted to do forgetting to think about the consequences.

Concentrating more on medical school, Jacob distanced himself. His mother had supported him and encouraged him, but ultimately she imposed too many of her own ideals on him, relentlessly suggesting what she thought he should do with his life. Her thoughts, however, never stayed with him long before they ultimately returned to his no-good brother.

Getting up quickly, he pushed aside the thoughts that only angered and embittered him. "I'll see you tonight when I get home," he said removing the thick black scarf and sports cap from the rack by the door. Apologizing for his brother again, "The guest room should be cleaned up by the time you get back tonight. Sorry things were such a mess." Giving his mother a quick peck on the cheek he left the office.

Chapter Twelve

The Macy's Thanksgiving Day Parade reminded Faye about the time of year. Outside was overcast with dreary, cloudy skies, coinciding with her own gray feelings of gloom and sadness.

A new nurse she hadn't recognized had already come taking her vitals. With her she'd toted a large basket filled with knickknacks, a book of crossword puzzles, some worn out, once-best-selling novels, and magazines with raggedy edges. An "activity basket" their attempt to take the patients' minds off the fact that they were stuck in the hospital while others were at home enjoying family banter and tables spread with all the trimmings. She dreaded the approaching lunchtime with slices of processed turkey, a breaded mixture called stuffing, a white roll with the consistency of cement, and soupy mashed potatoes. She wondered what Lijah was doing, anticipating her visit. Wondered about Jacob, and thought of the holidays without her father.

Each day Faye walked around her room, slowly gauging her stamina. For lack of something better to do, she decided she'd wash up.

Jacob entered Faye's room around eleven o'clock. Her bed was empty and he heard the water running. He hung the garment bag in the closet and put the small duffel bag on the end of Faye's bed.

Faye opened the door, a skimpy, tattered towel wrapped snugly around herself. The steam spilled from the bathroom as Faye stepped out, creating a heavenly scene. The corner of the towel strained to stay tucked around her ample bosom, one hand held it tightly secure. Long mocha-colored legs glistened with the lotion she'd applied, leading up to the hem of the towel. His gaze continued up over her breasts until they reached her pouted luscious lips, her nose, and finally her eyes.

"Jacob?" she said.

Remembering where he was, Jacob retrieved the tote from the bed and the garment bag from the closet. After handing them to her, she disappeared back into the bathroom.

Faye eyed the items before shutting the door completely, "Where'd you get these?" she said to him.

Jacob had forgotten to come up with a ready excuse for how or why he got all the things she would need. Deciding the truth was the best answer, he said, "I had . . . Ms. Carter pack some things for you." He hoped that would be enough of an answer, giving a sigh of relief when the door closed after she nodded.

Faye managed most of her clothing, her shirt and bra. She cried out from bending down to put on her panties and then her pants.

Jacob heard her soft yelp. "Faye, are you all right?"

"Yeah. I just . . . " She slowly blew out her breath. Jacob was in the bathroom before she could finish.

"Are you sure?" His frame filled the doorway. Her clothes were just about on. The energy it took was draining.

"Yes. Just a little tough, that's all."

"I'm here if you need me, honey," he replied, noticing the slight perspiration beading her forehead. He wetted a cloth with cool water and wiped her forehead.

"Thank you, Jacob."

He bent to help her with her shoes and socks. The small space of the bathroom pressed them close. There was no escape from her fresh scent of soap and shampoo.

Jacob asked to take a look at her side as he helped her to stand. The bruise on her hip was still red with irritation. The high-cut underwear provided a good view. The hip didn't hurt, she said, but as he pressed lightly on her ribs, she winced with pain and he quickly withdrew his hand. He informed her about the healing of ribs. They would remain sore for a long while but in a week he would take another X ray to ensure they were healing properly. For now she would have to favor the other side as she continued doing. Faye brushed her tangled hair, periodically wetting the brush to make the possessed strands lay flat.

Everything was planned. They reviewed the order while he helped her into the ankle-length, all-weather coat and hat. Removing his own wool scarf, as if he were securing a small child, he tied the wrap snugly around her face to disguise her from the nurses. He couldn't resist when he finished the tie under her chin, stealing a light brush from her lips.

Jacob exited first and then Faye. He held the elevator door for her. Faye walked as fast as her bruised body would carry her to the elevator. She kept her head low but her eyes set firm on her path. Once inside, the elevator door closed. Faye, Jacob, and a couple of other persons in the elevator waited patiently for it to make the slow descent to the garage, with two stops on other floors allowing the personnel to exit. Each time the elevator descended, out of the corner of his eye, Jacob saw Faye grab the handle bar that lined the walls of the elevator. The elevator's descent and the fluttering stop at each floor caused Faye to become dizzy and mildly nauseous.

Grabbing the side of her head, she stifled small gasps as the elevator came to the garage level. Once the others had exited on the previous floors Jacob went to Faye, putting his arms around her. He kept her from swaying due to the dizziness. Reaching the SUV, she struggled to get up the height of the vehicle. It would have been easier and automatic if she weren't favoring her battered side. She was almost up when she felt Jacob's strong but gentle hand push on her bottom assisting her the rest of the way. After securing her seat belt, he shut the door.

Ten minutes down the road, she reached for his hand resting by his thigh. She must have sensed he was at constant war with himself. The ethics committee part of his conscious constantly hissed at him. Once again, he'd broken the rules. This time it wasn't administering aid to patients that had no money, the special charity fund established in most hospitals had covered that. It also wasn't giving medicine away for free that someone needed but really couldn't afford, or even writing more exaggerated symptoms that would warrant insurance companies pay for extended patient stays, or any of the other things he thought petty in the ethic handbook. This one was serious, the last straw that could put a glitch in his career.

Jacob eyed Faye periodically. Her hand on his was comforting and reassuring. All would be well. He had made the right choice. *That no matter what happened she would always hold me in what?* . . . he wondered. *Esteem? Thanks? Heck, a lot of people already hold me in that regard.* He wanted more from her than any other person he had ever met. *That she would always love me. Love? Perhaps, yes? Do I love her? What the hell am I doing: risking my career, questioning my ethics, if I don't love her?*

Jacob nearly missed the turn to the cemetery which sat behind a large church. The lawns were manicured and well kept, a respect to the loved ones now deceased. His thoughts continued to run rampant. He glanced at Faye. Her eyes were alert, watching her surroundings and periodically eyeing Jacob as he made faces of confusion lost in consuming thought. She wondered what occupied his mind, what he was thinking, and hoped that just maybe he was as confused about their relationship as she. *What had happened over the last few, emotionally charged months? One door closes another opens?* So she'd been told, but continued to weigh the truthfulness of the statement.

Jacob was around the side of her door, his hand reaching

for her as she grasped it. He helped her down, closing the door, walking slowly with her to the burial site. The wind whipped at their backs. The air was thick with cold and the soil moist under her tennis-shoed feet. She smiled through the silent tears that glistened on her face. Jacob helped Faye as she got on her knees. Before leaving her, he opened his coat, handing her a single rose. It was faded, but more than she had to give. Her mouth formed an O shape of astonishment as more tears streamed down from her eyes.

Jacob left her in privacy. He wasn't far and wouldn't let her stay long. The sun had yet to make an appearance for the day. The skies continued to become grayer and the November air grew more frigid.

Chapter Thirteen

"Oh, Daddy," Faye began, "I miss you so much." She continued, "But I don't want you to worry, okay? I'll be all right. I think . . ." She lowered her voice to a whisper. "I've fallen in love with your doctor. He's sweet and kindhearted. He's done everything for me and asked for nothing in return. Lijah is so taken with him, too, Daddy, and he's great with her.

"I will come back to visit you just as soon as I can. I love you." Faye began the Lord's Prayer, apologizing to her father for not being able to give more, and promising that when she was better she'd hold a memorial service.

Slowly she got up. Jacob was instantly beside her to help.

* * *

Faye sat silently, watching her surroundings, noticing the route they took, and glad to be going anywhere but back to the hospital, though her curiosity was piqued.

A beautiful house with a brick front, the door a plum wine color, and a two-car garage came into view. It looked every bit of the inviting single-family home she often dreamed of owning.

Jacob helped Faye from the car, his hands reaching into his pockets, searching for his keys. Once inside he removed the coat and scarf. Voices went on distantly. The heat the house gave off, surrounding and welcoming her, replaced the heat her coat held.

Taking Faye's hand, Jacob led her to the far end of the room where bright lights spilled into the dark hall.

Ms. Carter peeled potatoes, chatting with Lijah who shoveled a fruity-looking cereal into her mouth. An older woman was at the kitchen counter chatting as well when she saw Jacob enter.

All eyes turned to Faye. "Momma!" Lijah squealed from her chair. She ran into the open arms of her mother.

"Hi, baby," Faye crooned, hugging the child close. Jacob went to stand beside his mother as she continued to prepare one of the many Thanksgiving dishes. She turned when she felt his arm around her shoulder guiding her away from her task and toward Faye.

"Mother, I'd like you to meet Faye Hicks. Faye, this is my mother, Emma Cove."

"Mrs. Cove, it's a pleasure to meet you. Thank you so much for inviting us to your home and seeing to Lijah . . . I don't know what to say . . . Thank you."

"You're welcome," Emma said, pasting on a fake smile. She looked at Jacob briefly. "Go on into the living room and have a seat. Dinner will be another hour or two, but we have some breakfast pastries if you'd like some."

Jacob's mother was beautiful. She had to be at least in her

late fifties, but looked no more than forty. Her eyes were a deep dark color like Jacob's, only set in the loose flesh of a tan face. Her hair was the color of steel with a lustrous shine. Her scent was of talcum powder, perfume, and a hint of mint from the mentholated candy she shifted around in her mouth.

Faye was reminded about the wonderful smells running past her nostrils, and the Thanksgiving dinners she used to prepare in her own kitchen, a fourth of the size of the one she stood in now, but still functional. Her palate filled with juices. "Can I help you with anything?" she asked excitedly. She'd love to cook in a big country kitchen. She could imagine all of it. "I'd be happy to assist . . ."

Jacob cleared his throat loudly at her offer, announcing, "Faye is under doctor's orders to take it easy." He wouldn't elaborate any further about the circumstances.

He winked at Faye before excusing himself and exiting the kitchen.

Faye looked at Jacob, slightly perturbed with the limits he placed on her activities. His mouth was set and firm, indicating he was unmovable to any other notions she might have had.

Cynthia stood, taking Faye's hand. "Finish your cereal, sweetheart. We'll be back in a minute," she called to Lijah who was very contented gobbling the rest of her food. Cynthia pulled Faye along gently.

Entering the large bathroom, Faye sat down heavily on the commode lid.

"If you don't grab that man, I will. Not that I think he'll settle for anyone but you, my dear," Cynthia began, checking her hair and makeup in the mirror. Rummaging through her makeup bag, finding the right shade she was looking for, she handed Faye the lipstick tube.

Faye felt that she could talk to Cynthia about anything,

but could she really discuss something that had yet to make sense in her own mind?

"What are you talking about, Cynthia?" She kept her head down, focused on the floral-stenciled tiles.

"What am *I* talking about? Honey! Lord have some mercy on me. I was born in the morning but not this morning." She finished her own hair and began fussing with Faye's, "You are just confused, but I'm telling you don't take too long to figure this one out, or it will be too late. There has got to be some woman—shoot, a lot of women—just waitin' for the good Dr. Jacob Cove. The thing is, he don't want none of 'em. He want you."

"But why, Cynthia? That's the thing I don't understand. Why does he want me? Why has he invited me to his mother's house for Thanksgiving dinner? And why has he taken such care of Lijah?" Faye questioned, looking up to the elder woman.

"Gal, you a big ol' dummy if you don't know the answer to those questions," Cynthia huffed. "I know Isaac didn't raise no dummy. We can't stay in the bathroom all day while I explain all this to you." Taking out a bottle of perfume, she sprayed Faye before spraying herself. She was about to exit, when Faye's hand lightly captured her arm. "Thank you for taking care of Lijah, Cynthia. I can never repay you for letting my child into your home."

Patting her hand, Cynthia nodded, shutting the door behind her. Faye stayed in the bathroom looking at her reflection in the mirror. Clear lightbulbs decorated the huge square mirror. Faye rummaged through the makeup pack Cynthia had left, finding other shades to suit her. She applied water to her face before blotting it dry with tissue, then, using the tip of her finger, applied a hint of lipstick color to her lips and cheeks. She left the bathroom.

The living room held the greatest noise, as Faye made her

way farther down the hall. Laughter from adults and the giggles of a child made it seem homey. A full-projection television showed a football game on the far wall that no one paid
attention to. The large sofa and love seat, burgundies and
browns and other dark autumn colors, a fireplace crackling
with red and yellow flames, elaborate oak end tables resting
at each seat end, created a tight-knit space perfect for gathering. Lijah was at the large coffee table. Faye smiled knowingly that whoever had gotten the large fold-out coloring
book had found the one activity to occupy her daughter for
hours on end.

Cynthia and an older gentleman seemed engaged in deep
conversation. His eyes periodically crinkled at the end with
laughter. Faye couldn't remember Cynthia ever talking about
a man in a context other than acquaintance or relative. These
two engaged in banter as if they had known each other for
years.

Moments had ticked by when she smelled Jacob before
seeing him—the aftershave and fresh peppermint scent
alerting her. He'd taken a shower. His hands wrapped around
her waist, and he gave her a brief kiss just behind her ear before turning her around to face him. "I hope I was able to
make Thanksgiving somewhat special for you, Faye," he
whispered while his eyes searched hers and his arms cradled
her back.

Make Thanksgiving special for me . . . Her eyes filled
with tears, she blinked rapidly to remove them. Unable to
relay her feelings, she nodded. It had to be the best
Thanksgiving she and Lijah had had in a long time. He
kissed her lips before announcing that dinner was ready.
Taking her hand he led her to the table.

So much food was located in one setting. The substitute
for the turkey dinner she'd dreaded in the hospital would
turn out to be the best meal she'd had in a long time. The
turkey was golden and the brown-sugar ham had a crusted

glaze the color of caramel. Yellow pineapple rings and the reddest cherries decorated it. Green bean casserole, corn bread–sausage stuffing, potato salad, macaroni and cheese, baked apples, corn bread, white rolls, and the sweetest candied yams completed the side dishes.

Faye had been introduced to everyone as they gathered around the eight-seat solid oak table. Rev. Friendly, from the Greater Life Church, was the last to arrive for dinner. He was a young preacher about Jacob's age. They had been friends in school. He was shorter than Jacob, but built, wearing a contemporary style of glasses. He chatted with Emma and Jacob about this year's Toys for Tots campaign, trying to commit everyone at the dinner table into taking part. They also discussed Jacob's free bimonthly checkups for the elder care facility.

Dr. Weston Benning pulled out the chair for Cynthia before taking his own seat beside her. It was a job he clearly used to do for Emma. She took in their exchange before pulling out her own chair, sitting down heavily.

Jacob introduced Benning to her. The man seemed shocked once her name left Jacob's lips. Throughout the meal, Benning eyed Jacob so incredulously she wondered what had transpired between them to cause the tension. Rev. Friendly began the blessing over the food as everyone joined hands. Jacob's hand held hers in their familiar intimate position. Mrs. Cove noticed the intimacy shared between them. She sat directly across from Faye. She also witnessed the kiss Jacob touched to her hand as the prayer ended. Her eyes narrowed into slits, watching the two.

"I sure wish Von could be here, Jacob . . ." Emma commented, spreading butter on her roll.

Faye looked briefly toward the unoccupied seat at the end of the table wondering who Von was.

"Where is the man?" asked Rev. Friendly, looking at Jacob expectantly.

Jacob shrugged his shoulders, before letting out a sigh toward his mother. "I haven't seen him in a week. Vondell"—he looked pointedly at his mother before turning back to Faye—"is my older brother." Jacob said nothing more as he resumed eating his food.

The meal was almost finished when a beeper went off. Jacob held up his hands in concession. "Mine's upstairs."

Benning pulled out his own beeper, frowning at the number he read on its screen. He excused himself, directing the apology mostly toward Cynthia, as he headed to the living room where the cordless phone sat.

"How about a little rest before the trip back?" Jacob said to Faye, grabbing her empty plate and his own, taking them to the kitchen. Lijah had stuffed herself, clearing her plate of two helpings, as she, too, rose, following Jacob with her own plate. Faye couldn't believe how the child readied to help without being asked to do so.

Faye was reminded with Jacob's statement, however, that this setting was as unusual as they come. No matter how comfortable she felt, wishing this to be the everyday routine, she couldn't stay here forever. She knew she would have to go back to the hospital. If she weren't a patient she'd still have to leave, to return to her own home regardless of how much she felt a part of things. *All good things must come to an end,* she thought sadly. She rose slowly, grabbing the empty dish nearest to her, following the path Lijah and Jacob had taken.

Chapter Fourteen

The master bedroom was a secluded palace. He placed Faye on her feet. The king-size sleigh bed, with a walnut chest set at the foot, a wicker hamper in the corner with clothes hanging out of it, and end tables on each side of the bed made up the decor. It was cottagey compared to the modern style of the downstairs. The room was bare except for the functional furniture. The spread and curtains were drab beige with brown trim.

"I'll come back in a hour, or so, and we'll head back out. Get a little rest." Jacob needed to hurry and leave before he ravished the body of the beautiful woman before him. It was the very setting he saw every single night before he went to bed: Faye standing next to this very bed, his bed, waiting for him, or him carrying her up the stairs to it as he'd just done. He'd had a thousand different scenarios in his mind, each in living color. Her body lay sprawled on top of the feather bed in great anticipation of him and what he wanted to share with her. The starving need that woke him up painfully every morning, and again kept sleep from him at night, present in his mind.

Jacob turned to leave, his eyes never leaving Faye's as he backed away to the exit. If she said anything, if she even breathed the beginning syllable of his name he'd be back in front of her before she finished the word.

As if she read his mind, "Jacob. I . . . I . . ." she whispered. He stopped and slowly walked back to her, just close enough to reach if she so desired. Her hands traveled up the material of his sport shirt before winding around his neck. He came closer to her, planting his hands on each side of her waist.

"Thank you for everything," she breathed. Her tongue

darted out, moistening her lips. Jacob became a blur, leaning in to capture the pink snake of his torture. He sucked her tongue greedily back out of her mouth and into his. His hands traveled up and down her back, massaging and caressing, until they dared venturing to her sides just below her breasts. He teased her with the promise of touch, before they returned to her back, and lower. His hands cupped her bottom. His legs spread, bracing himself lest he fall down, but more to ease the ache of his rising hardness, giving it room to stir. His hands continued to knead her bottom, bringing her up the length of him and closer until she could feel his erection pressing and straining against her pelvis.

Standing on the tips of her toes, Faye could feel the muscles of her inner thighs, and higher contract. The kiss broke long enough for words to be spoken. "I want you, Faye. God, how I want you." His breath came in deep gulps.

"I know . . . I know . . . but . . . we can't. Not now," she said even as she allowed him to lay her down, his body on top, pressing her deeper into the mattress. His hands winding under her shirt, finding her nipples erect through the sheer material of the bra.

"Jacob . . . oh, God."

"Yes. Yes. I'm here, baby . . . I'm right here," he assured her.

Faye tried to sit up. "Jacob . . . Jacob. We've got to stop. This . . . this is your mother's house. We're not teenagers." Jacob rolled to his side bringing Faye with him, trying to put a lid on the boiling fire, remembering the guests downstairs.

"This is my house, Faye, my mother just visits for the holidays." He was thoughtful a minute before sitting up, shifting Faye to his lap. "You're right, though," He rested his forehead against hers. "There are too many people here right now." Reaching to take off her shoes. He climbed out of bed, kissing her soundly on the lips.

"Go to sleep." He whispered before heading to the door.

"Jacob? Are you . . . are you okay?"

Jacob chuckled before turning around. "I'm fine, baby, but other parts of me are a little worked up."

Faye felt the heat rush all over her body settling in her secret center. Her eyes traveled to his lower body where the jeans bunched in the middle of the zipped crotch.

Jacob looked into her eyes. "I'll make love to you, soon! Now get some rest," he commanded before closing the door.

Faye lay in the bed burying her face in the sheets. She felt utter frustration. Exceeding that, however, she felt like a woman. No one's caretaker or mother, just womanly and desired. She smelled remnants of Jacob. She grabbed the pillow, beating it in frustration before resting her head. This was his house . . . she thought, turning her head to the side. On the bureau rested a man's watch, loose change, and a beeper. *I'm in Jacob's bed,* she said to herself. *Get some rest?* she echoed his last words. *Impossible!*

Chapter Fifteen

Marcus Washington's blood was simmering to a slow boil as he paced the lobby of the third floor nurses' station. He'd been in New York attending to business matters for the last five months. Getting to DC proved to be a task only the crazy should try. He'd left close to midnight thinking most people would have gotten to their holiday destination already. When traffic slowed him an hour after leaving his Manhattan brownstone, he knew otherwise.

It'd taken him a great deal of time, and a phone book to

find out which hospital Faye's father was at, but he hadn't expected, once he found it, to hear the news of his death, let alone to find that Faye, too, was now a patient.

Marcus couldn't say he felt much for the old man, who had been a pain in Marcus's side since he'd laid eyes on his daughter. Everything about Faye, especially her body, turned him on. She had lost the snobby, I-can-do-all-by-myself attitude once he'd gotten to know her better. Marcus had dated enough gold diggers to spot one from a mile away. He knew Faye wasn't one of them. It was the little brat who constantly posed a problem for him at present. If it weren't for her, Marcus thought with agitation, he'd have been much farther along with Faye by now. She constantly claimed Lijah and her old man as reasons why she couldn't stay the night. His attempts to get her into his bed went unsuccessful, and he was getting tired of trying. Glancing at his watch, he wondered if Sherry was up for a little visit.

Dr. Benning walked briskly up to the black male. His finger smoothed the whiskers of his beard, a habit he did when he was mildly irritated. He'd been having a nice dinner with friends when he received the most unwelcome page.

Benning waved aside thoughts of Emma Cove's sweet potato pie, as well as the lovely Ms. Carter, whom he was immediately smitten with even before shaking her hand.

"Mr. Washington, sir? What seems to be the problem?" asked Benning.

"And you are who exactly?" replied Marcus. His eyes assessed and immediately dismissed the man before him.

"Forgive me," Benning went on. *Too bad,* Weston thought. He wasn't the bothered type. Washington's assessing and dismissing review did nothing to rattle him. He was too old, he'd often say, to be bothered by young, know-it-all boys like Marcus Washington.

"I'm Dr. Weston Benning, acting director here at H. U.

Medical Center. I was called because I was told there is a bit of confusion here. You're looking for whom exactly?"

"Her name is Faye Hicks, Dr. Benning," spewed Marcus with disgust. His irritation surging due to the fact that he needed to reiterate the story, the name, and the other facts for the umpteenth time. It was wearing his patience. Marcus read the recognition on Dr. Benning's face and found it mildly interesting. The man knew her, and in what capacity, Marcus wondered.

"I understand her father died not long ago, and then she too was admitted for a hit-and-run accident. Your nurse so kindly disclosed the details to me, without inquiry as to who I was. I find that disturbing, Dr. Benning, but I'm not here to critique your rules of procedure, staff training, or a lack thereof." Marcus removed his hands from his pockets as if waving them would pound home his point. "I'm here to see Miss Hicks, and it seems no one knows where she is. Now you or one of these nescient flunkies you have working here need to find Miss Hicks or face serious legal action."

Dr. Benning wasn't easily agitated, but he worried about the young and promising doctor the words would really affect. The name Hicks, however, was like gasoline to a small fire. Things were just waiting to explode regarding that woman, not to mention how much flack Jacob could receive. Benning knew it was Jacob she was with, and that it wouldn't be long before they finished dinner and returned to the hospital. Dr. Benning began to assure Washington that Miss Hicks was in good hands, when the elevator doors opened revealing Faye with Jacob by her side. Lijah also walked merrily holding her mother's hand as they exited.

Faye's perfect day took a turn for the worse when she saw Marcus. She moved slowly across the floor, her eyes lighting on him. Marcus rushed past Dr. Benning to her side, grabbing her up, planting kisses on her face. Faye backed up from his clutches and swung her hand across his face. Marcus was taken aback from her outburst and the sting of the slap. His hand went instantly to his face rubbing the spot where she had struck him.

"How dare you!" yelled Faye. The anger she had felt cooled, instantly reheated itself upon seeing his face. She was immediately reminded of the breathless woman answering his phone. Memories of his long trips, supposedly away on business, when she needed him here to support her, and the other ways he showed he cared about no one but himself, flooded her mind.

Faye leaned in closer, whispering so only he could hear. "I told you I didn't ever want to see you again. It's over between you and me." She cast an apologetic glance toward Benning, realizing Marcus's tantrum was the cause of his interrupted Thanksgiving dinner.

Marcus was stupefied. He'd known she'd be mad about his prolonged absence, but to embarrass him in front of people like that was truly uncalled for. "Faye, honey, let's just go to your room and clear this up . . ." He proceeded to take her arm and direct her toward the room.

"Did you hear what I said?" Faye interrupted, her frustration mounting when he continued on as if he hadn't heard her. "I don't want to hear it . . . I'm feeling . . . I feel . . ." Faye begun to sway on her feet. Jacob stepped forward helping her to a nearby seat.

"Look what you did, you punk!" Lijah, who'd been silent, watching the exchange, stepped forward yelling at Marcus, her eyes wide with outrage, before kicking him in the shin.

Howling at the pain, Marcus grabbed his leg. "You little urchin!" he spewed, reaching for the cause of all his problems with Faye. "You've been a pain in my side for longer than I care to remember!" His arms were outstretched just inches away from grabbing the little girl before Jacob reached out, propelling him backward.

"Don't ever attempt to touch her again." His eyes turned an arctic charcoal with anger.

He looked at Faye who spoke calmly through hazy eyes to Lijah. His concern for the both of them caused his jaw to twitch. He turned back to Marcus "I don't think anyone wants you here, Washington, so why don't you leave?" Jacob asked before grabbing Marcus, propelling him to the elevator doors, and pushing the button.

Marcus brushed his jacket clean, composing himself. He stared down Jacob, letting him know the issue was far from over. "Oh, I'll leave, but I'll be back, and you'll be sorry for it when I'm through." After the elevator doors closed, Jacob walked quickly back to Faye. She sat with Lijah's head on her lap, absently caressing the child's back. The nurse was taking her vitals, then noting the data on a clipboard. She handed the information to Jacob who gave silent thanks and read the data, eyeing Faye. Making his own notations, he spoke with the nurse.

He gave a wink to Lijah who held the door open as Jacob picked Faye up, carrying her to the bed where he begin removing her clothes. Once in her pants and shirt, he removed her shoes and socks. He did a double-check of her vitals with his own equipment. Her heartbeat was erratic, but not so much that it overly concerned him. She *was* a little worked up, and he concluded that the ordeal with *The* Marcus Washington he'd heard about from Lijah had upset her, as well as their outing, more stressful on her body than he had calculated. Nothing rest and a mild sedative wouldn't take care of. Her eyes closed when Jacob began to cover her with the blanket. He brushed her hair off her face. Faye's hand reached out from under the covers, catching his shirt lightly in her clutches, pulling him closer until his face was inches away from hers.

"Thank you, Jacob. Today was wonderful, and I'll always cherish it," she whispered. Her lips pouted, and he brushed them with his own. Her eyes narrowed into small slits as his tongue moistened her soft, supple lips. She moaned groggily before her eyes closed completely, drifting off to sleep.

Outside Faye's room Jacob took Lijah by the hand, helping her hop down from the chair. Together they headed toward the elevator. He picked up the little girl, gave her a peck, and tickled her. He turned serious momentarily. "You know that was wrong, don't you, Lijah?"

Lijah was thoughtful. "I know, Jake, but he made mommy mad," she defended.

Jacob shook his head. "I understand, sweety, but to call people names and hit them is wrong. Okay?" *I'll hit them for you,* he thought, smiling.

Lijah nodded, the elevator carried them to the top level.

Setting Lijah on her feet, he instructed her to go into his office and play with the gifts he'd bought for her. He waited seconds for the elevators to open again, knowing who and what awaited him.

Benning cleared his throat signaling Jacob. "My office." Benning turned on his heel, walking briskly away to the end of the hall where his own office was situated.

Behind the doors of his office, Benning didn't wait for Jacob to take a seat. "I hadn't known you were going to bring her to Thanksgiving dinner as well, Jacob. Washington blew everything to hell and will probably make a ridiculous case out of all this with a formal report. Once the report is filed, an investigation will be conducted. Do you realize you could be placed on suspension until the board reviews the information?" He was thoughtful. "I hope she's worth it, Jake," he said before waving a hand that Jacob was free to go.

On the way back to his office, various thoughts plagued Jacob's mind. *So this could be it,* thought Jacob. He had yet to feel the effects of all that was happening around him. If he could have Faye then he'd get through everything else. Thoughts of her made him happy, but how did she feel about him? She could move on with her life and care nothing about him. A simple gut feeling reigned down deep. He loved her. He understood her. Once he had gotten to know her, *really* know her, the walls she had erected crumbled whenever he looked into her eyes. He saw nothing but tenderness. He once thought he hated everything about her, only because her ways reminded him of himself. She was like him, everybody's caretaker. He knew that, just like him, she overcommitted herself. She took care of everybody and exasperated herself trying to be a superwoman, like people thought he was a superman. He wished at times to relinquish that type of responsibility, but kept getting thrust into the position. Ever since Faye's accident and spending time with Lijah, he realized how much he enjoyed his newest role.

Jacob picked up the pace back to his office with renewed determination and purpose. He was on a mission. In six months, and maybe before then, Jacob had come to know and love Faye Hicks. No one had ever touched him the way she did.

He never considered himself father material, but his sibling's void attempt at being a competent big brother had thrust him long ago into a fatherly role. In one week he'd taken Lijah to the kids' jungle gym center downtown, for cocoa with marshmallows and "extra" whip cream, and to the park. Everything Faye had done but wasn't able to now do, he did. Ms. Carter couldn't keep up with the energetic bursts of a child, and he stepped up not knowing what he was doing. Not realizing he was filling a type of void the little girl had, and filling a void existing in himself. Both feelings of need were equally important. Faye and Lijah unknowingly dragged him deeper and deeper into their world, and he had become comfortable, fit, needed, an intricate and vital part of it. If each didn't understand alone, together perhaps they would make sense of it.

Lijah had fallen asleep on the floor of his office. Flash cards, markers, and colored paper created an irregular circle around her. Picking her up, she stirred and was vaguely alert as he bundled her up for the return trip to Ms. Carter's house. She'd wanted to come along with him to drop Faye off, and he thought he'd give Ms. Carter a break, returning Lijah to her later that night.

Jacob was about to leave, tugging on his own coat and picking up the sleeping bundle, when the ringing shrill of the phone stopped him from exiting. Jacob looked down at Lijah in his arms. If it hadn't been Thanksgiving he wouldn't have answered it. In two strides he was behind his desk. Shifting Lijah, he picked up the phone on its third ring with his free hand.

"Cove," he said into the receiver.

"Jake," the deep, scratchy voice of his brother returned.

Chapter Sixteen

Marcus slipped into Faye's room when everything had calmed. Standing beside her bed, he took her by the hand. Her even and deep breathing slowed, her hand tightened on his, and a sigh escaped her lips before her lids opened slowly.

"Jacob . . ."

Marcus's eyes widened. His hand quickly let go of hers, startling her fully awake. Faye blinked rapidly at the image. Sitting up in her bed, her temper returned immediately.

"I told you to stay away from me."

"Yeah, I remember something like that," he replied.

"You remember? I should hope so, it was just moments ago. So what part didn't you understand? I specifically said I don't want you in my life, Marcus. I know about your affair, and God-knows-how-many other people you've been sleeping with."

"People I've been sleeping with? Faye, I'm not the one whispering names in my sleep . . ."

"No," she returned. "You just let them answer the phone while in the heat of the moment. Give me a break, regardless of that, Marcus, where were you when I needed you . . . My father died, and as much as I've been there for you, I can't say that you've been there for me, and that shows me where your concerns really are." Faye waved her hand, she berated herself for acknowledging the need she felt going through the ordeal with her father. Jacob had seen to everything, and anything Marcus offered couldn't compare.

"Your father, the man who hated my guts? Who warned you against dating me? Why should I feel anything for him?" His face was growing hot with anger with her constant diatribe.

"It doesn't matter, Marcus. The point is, I'm not in love with you, and even if I was, you killed that with the woman. You haven't even tried to deny that you've slept with other people."

"Why should I deny it? A man has needs, and if you weren't so damn frigid, always using that little wench and your father as excuses, we could have . . ."

Faye knew she made errors at times, but with what Marcus was saying she knew she had made the biggest blunder of her entire life. Something had changed in him. She didn't know what, or maybe she refused to see it, and it had been there all along.

"Don't you dare make this out to be my fault. Just leave me alone, Marcus. Please go. It's over, I have nothing more to say to you."

"You should have been glad someone even wanted you, Faye, with that brat of yours. Good luck in finding someone else who is willing to put up with you and Lijah. You should've been very thankful I looked twice when I saw you."

"Get out of here! Just get out right now!" Faye was yelling now. She shook with anger at each word, but more than that she was hurt. She closed her eyes, as the nurse entered with a stern look on her face directed at Marcus before he left. The nurse turned off the light before she, too, exited behind him.

Chapter Seventeen

Emma Cove wore an expensive floral-print caftan. A silk cap kept her steel-gray curls tied securely. She sipped the orange spice tea she drank each night before settling into bed. She eyed her travel pack and small Gucci suitcase by the door, mentally ensuring she had packed everything for her trip home to Maryland. She enjoyed the holidays, cooking in Jacob's expansive kitchen. The meals she prepared there were savory and reminded her of family gatherings. She went over the events in her head. The dinner guests, a bunch of people she'd never met, but she *had* enjoyed the rather smart little girl. But she wondered just how serious Jacob was about the relationship. She could see from their subtle exchanges that their involvement was further along that she would have hoped. She wanted Jacob to settle down, but not before he had gotten the medical fellowship in Chicago, and certainly not before establishing himself further and opening his own practice in a couple more years. She had had dreams for him and certainly wouldn't let some woman and her charming child defer them. She had had her own dreams at one time, but times and circumstances of unrelenting prejudice prevented them from being attained. She wouldn't watch a second life be wasted.

She made a mental note to discuss his feelings for the girl before leaving tomorrow. Her thoughts continued, moving on to Von. She wondered if he was yet again in some type of trouble and the extent of it this time before her lids drooped with sleep.

Vondell looked like a changed man from the weeks that had passed. His hair, once a wild and nappy fro, was now trimmed neat. His left ear held a silver hoop earring. Flicking a cigarette away, he dug in his pocket for the spare key. He wore a long-sleeved cocoa shirt with black jeans and black, thick-soled chukkas. His beard was gone, a goatee like his younger brother's in its place causing the two to look even more alike. His baseball cap shielded his ebony eyes as he entered. Removing his cap and leather coat, he entered the kitchen, opened the refrigerator, and looked over the many containers of leftovers from Thanksgiving dinner. He pulled out the largest container, and he pulled out the mayonnaise, deciding on a turkey sandwich.

Jacob was exhausted and glad to be home. He gave his brother a chastising eye. In the guest bedroom he checked on his mother, turning off the small television blaring the theme song to a popular talk show. His mother didn't stir when he left the room, quietly shutting the door behind him.

"Downstairs," Jacob said to his brother in passing on his way to the stairwell leading to the basement.

Vondell put down the half-eaten sandwich, no longer hungry. In the cool air of the basement, he sat on the worn out couch.

"So what is it this time?" Jacob put his hands in his pockets, leaning against the old cherry desk.

"A couple of weeks ago," Vondell began, sitting more toward the edge of the sofa as he braced his forearms on his thighs and clasped his hands together in front of him. "I got drunk."

Jacob chanced a glance at the ceiling. "You're always getting drunk!" he returned before Vondell could finish.

"Yeah, well this time something happened. I . . . I . . ."

"Just spit it out, for God's sake." Jacob rarely lost his patience with anyone, but his brother was the exception.

"I hit somebody, okay. I hit someone with the car," he rushed out.

"My *car?*" was Jacob's first question. His hands came out of his pocket. He desired something hard to strike. Jacob's eyes grew wide as a different kind of realization set it. *The bar. The bar Vondell frequented was just down the street from the hospital.*

"Where the hell was the accident, Vondell?" He dreaded the answer even as he posed the question, willing it to be anywhere but—

"In front of the hospital," he said in a low whisper.

Jacob was on Vondell before he could escape. *It couldn't be. Please, no.* His mind shouted, as his hands grabbed handfuls for Vondell's shirt. "Which hospital damnit?" he asked, his anger continuing to build.

"The one you work at. H.U.," he responded, trying to wiggle away from his brother's deathly grip. "Is she okay—I mean, she didn't die did she?" he asked as Jacob continued to eye him incredulously.

"Did she die? You're asking that now? Isn't it a little late, brother? Do you really even care? Did you stop to look or did you just flee like you always do when there's trouble?"

"Hey, I did care," Vondell replied, "I called the ambulance, and I checked her pulse." Vondell broke free of his brother's grip, stumbling backward, sending a wooden chair crashing to the floor.

"Did you now?" Jacob returned with a tone of disbelief. "I guess that just makes it all better. You should be excused 'cause you called the ambulance and checked her pulse. Let's see, African-American female, late twenties. She has a little girl about four years old. Her father was in for misdiagnosed prostate cancer." Jacob ticked off each item with his fingers. "Is that enough information for you?" he asked before continuing. "She experienced comatose head trauma. How's that for information? Makes her seem a little more real? Doesn't it? Like someone you know? A friend? But God forbid if you knew all that, you just might give a damn, huh, *huh?*" Jacob was now yelling at his brother. He hadn't noticed his mother standing in the shadow of the stairwell. She watched the encounter, trying to piece together what her ears hadn't heard.

Jacob turned on his heel at hearing the creak of the bottom step indicating another presence. His mother came into full view.

"What is the matter, for heavens sake?" Emma came forward to get a better look at her sons. She rubbed her arms from the chill of the basement.

Jacob turned to leave up the stairs. His mother's hand on him halted his steps.

"I want some answers," she said.

Jacob shrugged away from her grasp. "Ask him," he replied, before turning back to Vondell, pointing his finger. "And you, don't you go near her. I'll talk to her," he said before jogging up the stairs.

Emma looked at Vondell expectantly before he, too, got up to leave, silently acknowledging that he wouldn't be forthcoming with information, either. "Sorry, Ma," he muttered before bending to plant a kiss on her cheek. He left the same way Jacob had seconds earlier.

Chapter Eighteen

Jacob cruised the streets where he lived. The suburbs, low crime, not much nightlife, and complete silence had first attracted him as reasons for choosing the town. At times like these he'd wished for the camaraderie of his brother's type to get into.

Pulling into what looked like a bar, he entered the pub. He didn't care what kind of company surround him, just so he could be served a decent drink. Watching his brother and father in various states of drunkenness had curtailed any desire he had to travel their path. He nodded to the bartender, who approached him for his order.

Jacob took the drink willingly when the bartender returned. His face carried a knowing grin.

Jacob looked at the brown concoction. Vodka was the strongest drink he knew. Mixed with other things, however, he was sure it had the ability to become even more potent. He downed the liquid in two gulps, temporarily losing his voice. He felt as if he were having a heart attack. He stole a glance down his shirt to see if any hairs had grown in the last ten seconds. The bartender returned with the bottle. Jacob put his hand flat over the top of his glass preventing the bartender from pouring more. Leaving enough to pay for the drink and a sizeable tip, he left.

The recent days consumed Vondell with numbing thought. The accident had changed him, and he vowed to stop letting his brother clean up messes he made. He hoped it wasn't too late to start taking responsibility for himself and salvage whatever kind of relationship they could have. Strolling to the nurses' station receptionist desk, he hoped he was making a valid attempt. Vondell hadn't expected Jacob to get so upset, storming from the house before he was able to explain how he wanted to change and that he planned on telling the woman himself about what he'd done.

The head of the young girl behind the glass bobbed to the jams sounding from the small, black radio on the counter. Tiny microbraids covered her head, secured by colorful elastic bands. Vondell cleared his throat signaling her attention.

Slowly she looked up, the gum she'd been smacking bursting over and covering her lips in sticky pink blotches.

"Hi . . . Hi. Kin I hep ya?" she smiled sweetly.

"Hello there . . . Shelby." He noticed her nametag and the smile that split her face at the use of her name. "Mind telling me the woman's name that was brought in, say, two weeks ago, hit-and-run. She was an African-American woman, about five-foot-six, 125 pounds or so."

"Are you family of hers?" the girl inquired.

"I'm just a friend. I just want to make sure she's okay. You know." Vondell smiled at the young girl.

Shelby casually flipped through the book, scanning its contents. Looking around for any nurses or other personnel that might have been nearby, she turned back to the man, "I think you're asking about Faye Hicks." She read the name in the book; it seemed in the last few days a lot of people had wanted to know about her. "She came out her coma of a few days ago and is going to be released . . . today actually." The girl finished brightly.

"Thank you, sweetheart," replied Vondell.

He strolled casually through the halls, noticing the names on the charts hanging on the door, before finding the right room.

Faye rested comfortably on top of the covers of her made up bed. After packing her bags, she settled down for the waiting that seemed endless. On a notepad she scribbled her "to do" list, which included the items on Lijah's growing Christmas wish list. Her mind drifted sadly to presents she would no longer get for her father before moving on to presents she might get for Jacob and what he would like.

With thoughts of Jacob, she tried to make sense of their relationship. She was over Marcus and had been for some time. Their confrontation had more than sealed the envelope on their finale. But she wasn't so sure about jumping head-first into another relationship. She had feelings for Jacob, admittedly they were more serious than she had first thought. But what did that mean? She couldn't deny the nagging guilt she experienced over finding a possible someone in conjunction with losing her father. From experience and constant letdowns with other men, in this relationship she again waited for the pendulum to swing slicing her heart through the middle.

She wanted to believe that he was everything she'd waited for, that they could have something real together, but the reality of it seemed distant.

The tedious paperwork was all signed and finalized. Jacob's eyes still saw the material before him, but his mind was elsewhere. His own brother had been responsible for hurting the woman he loved. He hoped she could forgive his brother, and find it in her heart to forgive him for being related. Somehow they had to put this whole mess behind them and move on.

He went over the scenario again and again in his mind. Tonight after dinner he would tell Faye it was his own brother that hit her. He'd tell her first how much he'd come to love her and how much he'd like her and Lijah to be a part of his life. In some crazy way, he prayed that would soothe the other news that followed.

There was no way he could prolong the events. Release papers in hand, he headed to her third-floor room.

Faye hadn't realized when she dozed. She stretched lazily, unhooking her feet crossed at the ankles and arching her back off the bed to work out all the kinks.

A man she'd never seen before, but who looked vaguely familiar was just to her right, staring at her intently.

"Faye Hicks?" he said, his voice a hoarse whisper. Vondell pulled up a nearby chair and sat heavily in it before continuing. "Listen, I'm here because I have some things to tell you." His hands clasped together in front of him, his thumbs warring with each other.

"Yes," she said, wondering if the strange man in her room should alarm her. The rustiness in his voice alerted her to danger, and vaguely made her aware that she knew the man. Suspicion got the better of her, her hand traveled slowly under the covers for the nurses' call box.

"That night you were hit, It was me . . . I'm the one who . . ."

Before Vondell could finish, both sets of eyes traveled to the door as it swung open.

"You ready to go ba—" Jacob said, frowning at the look on her face. His eyes immediately left her, landing on the other person sitting in the chair beside her bed.

Faye sat up abruptly as she saw Jacob enter the room. Eyeing him, her eyes glanced back to the man beside her bed, noticing how they looked alike. The man beside her seemed older, rougher. His lips were blacker than the rest of his chestnut-colored skin, a small, silver hoop earring occupied one ear, and the goatee was the same, except Jacob's was smoother. The stranger looked like an older version of Jacob.

"I told you I'd handle it. Why couldn't you just wait?" he yelled at Vondell.

Horror washed over her, remembering what the stranger had said before Jacob entered. She took deep breaths to calm her nerves. The deep inhaling through her nose and exhaling through her mouth wreaked havoc on her ribs, but the recognition of what happened was screaming in her ear. As she continued to inhale, her nose wrinkled. The smoke, she could smell the faint, but surreal odor of smoke. Heavy smokers, the odors clung to everything, their clothes, and their skin.

"It was you," she said. Scrambling off the bed, she stood as fast as she could. "You hit me that night. Did you know if I died, or did you even care? You left me on the street, like some stray dog. How could you?"

"Listen I'm sorry," Vondell began. "That's why, that's why I came to make sure you were okay. I . . . I . . ."

"Just leave, Vondell. Just go," Jacob said. If he could talk to Faye alone, he might be able to salvage something, anything.

"Vondell? Vondell?" she repeated. "Your brother? Your brother hit me and you knew?"

"Yes, I knew and I was going to tell you about it when we were alone . . . but . . ." Jacob said, the papers wrinkling from the curling grip of his hand.

Faye's hand touched her forehead, rubbing back and forth. A slow ache pounded in her head, and if she could escape from this terrible nightmare everything would be okay.

Jacob put down the papers, walking to her. Vondell watched the exchange briefly before leaving the room. Jacob's arms went around Faye as a sense of déjà vu came over him. He kissed her and hoped she wouldn't resist. She didn't, but her lips were stiff and unresponsive. If she didn't at least hear him out, it would break him.

"Baby, listen to me. I'm sorry. I'm sorry for him and what he did, but I . . . damn . . ." He looked away before continuing. "I love you. Do you hear me? I love you and I never meant to hurt you."

"Is that a fact? Right now I don't know what to believe," she replied before fully thinking about what she was saying, "I think that you were so nice to me to ease your guilty conscious. Did that make you feel better? Make up for what you . . . your brother did? Guilt makes people go a long way, Jacob."

Jacob backed away from her, withdrawing his arms. She immediately felt nothing but cold and regretted what she'd said.

"I know you don't mean that," he said in disbelief. "Everything I did was for you . . . and Lijah. I just told you I love you, and if that's guilt talking, I'm getting in pretty deep, don't you think? I know you don't for one second, Faye Michelle Hicks, believe I did all I did to ease my guilty conscious. I'm not the one that hit you." Jacob ran a hand over his head before continuing. Constant blame, that's all he ever received and he was tired of it.

"I've been answering for my brother a long time, but I'm not him," he finished before leaving the room.

Once outside, Jacob's eyes immediately landed on his brother. "Always mucking up my life, aren't you, big brother? I hate you! You disgust me! I've tried to help you so much, Vondell, and all you do is piss on everything. When are you going to stop mucking up your life and dragging me along with you?"

Jacob took one last look at the door to Faye's room. His heart was in there with her . . . breaking. He looked at Vondell one last time before he left.

Chapter Nineteen

Faye's week sped by at rapid pace. She'd managed to clear up the chaotic confusion at the Center, that only her orderliness and quick thinking could do. Her skills had moved her to assistant director in the span of two years, when she'd started out as a lead teacher. Everything was moving at a smooth and orderly pace.

Cynthia filled her in on all the happenings over lunch breaks. Faye expressed again how much she was thankful to her for taking care of Lijah. Cynthia huffed and reminded Faye about the circumstances regarding Lijah's care.

"I'm too old to keep up with your daughter, Faye. You know very well I had a lot of help with her, and you know *who* helped me to do so," Cynthia had said, informing Faye about Jacob's relationship with Lijah. She knew some of the details, Lijah went on endlessly about their outings, but the subject was a sore spot. It seemed like the bulk of things had happened while she was sleeping and that was what bothered her the most. Her heart had already forgiven him. Her mind insisted there had been nothing to forgive, that the way he'd taken extensive care of her, everything he'd done for her and Lijah was testimony in itself of how much he loved her. Why she couldn't set aside the details surrounding the issue was beyond her.

With Jacob she had been able to forget her roles of mother, friend, teacher, confidant, and the many other responsibilities heaped on her, while he took care of everything. He was prepared for every minute detail, a planner, and one of the most thoughtful persons she'd ever met.

Cynthia however, went on about Dr. Benning whom she had been seeing on a regular basis, and that if it weren't for

Faye's accident they never would have met, reminding her, once again, how everything happens for a reason.

Faye's mind came back to the present when the buzzer on her desktop phone went off. She placed aside the magazines, scholastic periodicals, and promotional junk mail, pressing the answer button, "Yes, Cynthia?"

"Mrs. Cove is here to see you, hon."

Mrs. Cove? Jacob's Mother? her mind announced. "Uh, okay. Send her in."

Emma Cove walked into the office and took a seat in front of Faye's desk. She didn't remove her coat, indicating that she wasn't staying long, but settled herself in the padded, metal chair. She took her time, meticulously pulling each finger of her suede gloves, removing them. Faye watched the older woman before beginning, "Mrs. Cove, it's nice to see you. I want to thank you again for making Lijah and me so welcome over Thanksgiving. What can I do for you?"

Emma watched the sincere smile on Faye's lips, though she hadn't come to exchange pleasantries or even to be nice. Her family was at arms and it seemed the woman before her was the reason.

"I've come, Miss Hicks, to discuss my sons with you. It seems they aren't getting along very well, and whatever you've done has driven them apart." Emma leaned forward scrutinizing Faye for any kind of recognition behind how she figured into the scheme. When she saw the brief shadow cloud her face, she knew she was justified in her visit.

"If you think I have something to do with why they're not getting along, then you're probably right, but not in the capacity you think. I'm not responsible." She saw Emma's eyes light up before she continued, "How can you sling accusations at me when you don't know all the facts? You'll have to speak to them about it."

Emma was growing weary. No one wanted to give her any answers. She always had to obtain them by going behind others' backs, standing in shadows, and hanging on to everyone's words. "Tell me, Miss Hicks, are you also going to plead that you're an innocent behind Jacob's possible suspension from the hospital?"

Faye stood on her feet. "What?"

Emma couldn't understand her naïveté. She should know by now. She should have received notice regarding the action against Jacob filed by some New York lawyer. After all, it was because of her that he was in trouble. "It seems he took a patient from the hospital, Miss Hicks. Do you deny that that patient was you? Everything is your fault, and I don't know why you're claiming such ignorance." Emma was on her feet, too. With one hand on her hip, she leaned closer to Faye over the desk. "You could very well have ruined his career with your selfishness." Her eyes became small slits of ebony. "I don't know what you did or said to get him to take you from the hospital, but you and your little daughter have somehow wormed your way into my son's life. He is acting proportionately out of character. Jacob is a kind and caring person, but sometimes he allows things to sidetrack him. I have no doubt you knew this and used it to manipulate him," she finished, her finger pointing at Faye, while her bottom lip trembled nervously.

Faye was befuddled. Jacob was on suspension for taking her out of the hospital on Thanksgiving? He'd made a special day even sweeter for her and now he was being punished. It was all her fault, but how could she help him? What could she do to erase the mess she created?

The review? She wondered when the review would be. Certainly they'd wait until after the holidays to make a decision.

"Mrs. Cove, I'm sorry. You're right, this is my fault," she confirmed, waving her hand at the elder woman's look of triumph. "But the review, Mrs. Cove, when is it?" She looked at the woman expectantly.

Faye looked around nervously until she located her briefcase on the side of her desk. She had dumped a heap of personal mail into it to review on her lunch break. She now remembered receiving some official correspondence from the hospital days ago, but quickly put it aside thinking it another bill. Her hands searched frantically through the contents until she located the envelope with the official H.U. logo. Opening it frantically she scanned the information, searching for a time when the board would review the case. The words moved frantically past her eyes.

Pending Action: . . . Jacob Daniel Cove, M.D., H.U. Medical Center . . .
Removal: Recovering comatose trauma patient, Thursday, November . . .
Filer Suit: Williamson, Johnson & Washington . . . Attorneys At Law . . . Marcus J. Washington, Esq.
Board Action Review Committee Meeting: December . . .

"Oh, my God . . ." she gasped, glancing at the red numbers displayed on her desk clock.

Emma crossed her arms over her chest, watching Faye's reaction. The letter fell from Faye's hand, before she scurried to the coat rack, shoved her arms through the sleeves of her coat, and grabbed her keys and purse.

"Just what do you think you can do? Haven't you done enough already?" Emma said incredulously.

"I can go there and tell them my part of the story. I can let them know what an incredible doctor he is," she said, scribbling a note to Cynthia before hurrying from the office.

Emma, too, left, praying that just maybe she'd been wrong about Faye. Maybe she wasn't the manipulating gold digger she'd originally thought. The fact that she'd torn out of the school to try and save Jacob was cause enough for her to be viewed differently. Still, the questions she had no answers for, the nagging feeling of Faye's part in why Jacob and Vondell weren't getting along, bolded in her mind.

Chapter Twenty

The city traffic and the numerous repairs being made to the streets could turn the twenty-five-minute trek to the hospital into a forty-five-minutes-to-an-hour one. Faye thought vaguely about what she would say to the review board, vowing that when all was said and done she would finally tell Jacob her feelings. She'd been too stupid, and hoped she hadn't waited too long to come to the realization of how much she wanted him in her life. Emma Cove's visit was a needed catalyst for her wake-up call. The fact that Vondell and Jacob weren't getting along, and her part in it confirmed that she'd been wrong. He hadn't had an ulterior motive for taking care of Lijah, for caring about Faye, and ultimately falling in love with her.

She hoped Jacob would be present, so that when the meeting was over she could proclaim her feelings then and there.

The elevator took forever to get to the fourteenth-floor executive office suites. When the doors opened Faye rushed out, nearly colliding with the reception desk.

"Yes?" the woman said, not looking up from her magazine, and waving away the fly buzzing around the opened can of soda and bag of potato chips.

Faye composed herself, running a hand over her wind-rustled hair. Her face felt frozen, stiff from the cold air. She rubbed her hands together before speaking. "The review board meeting?" she rushed out. Looking around she searched for any sign that might identify the meeting room. The cherry wood doors lining the circular hall were all closed. No activity looked to be going on anywhere.

The receptionist took out a neon-pink clipboard, roving over the data contained on it. "Yes, there's only one meeting today, conference room C. Now, I'll just take your name and . . ."

"Thanks," Faye returned, running in the direction of the room. She ignored the woman hollering after her.

"Hey! Hey, Ma'am! You cain't get in dere, less yo name on da rosta!"

Faye swung the doors open and immediately felt the heat of stares on her as she walked in. The woman ambling behind her stopped at the entrance, composing herself. "You won't me call curity, Dr. Benning?" She addressed the oldest-looking gentleman seated at the table.

Before Benning could answer, Faye cleared her throat. Her eyes pleaded with Dr. Benning before turning her full attention on the group. "I'm Faye Hicks," she announced. "The patient that Dr. Jacob D. Cove is being reviewed about. I would just like a little of your time . . . Please!"

Benning turned from Faye in his swivel chair. The receptionist was a nerve shredder. If he allowed her to call security she'd probably end up dialing nine-one-one. The temp agency must have had the lowest rate they could find. She hadn't pronounced his name right once in the weeks she'd been working here. Waving his hand at the receptionist, he said, "It's fine. Thank you, Edna." The receptionist left in a huff.

The heavy doors closed with a loud thud, and all eyes returned to Faye, expectantly. The silence grew thick and heavy.

Benning hoped she had something prepared. He'd liked the girl upon meeting her at the dinner. It was because of her that he was introduced to Cynthia, and that certainly worked in her favor, but shouting words of a love grandiose for Jacob would not help him in the least. She would have to present some real evidence.

Benning tried to refocus and concentrate on what she was saying. It wasn't him she had to sell, it was the other hardnosed young bloods sitting with him, especially Jacob's nemesis whose mouth was salivating with thoughts of ruining him. The man was nothing but a tyrant with jealousy as his sole motivation. He had used every opportunity to discredit Cove, each attempt failing with Jacob coming out unscathed. It was him who caused a ruckus every time Jacob had gotten into the least bit of trouble.

Faye took a deep breath, shrugging off her coat, which, in conjunction with the heated stares, caused beads of sweat to trickle down her back and gather under her armpits. If Jacob had been present, she knew she could handle anything. His calm demeanor and sleepy but knowing eyes always gave her a comforting calmness. She had long scanned the room finding him nowhere in sight. She was on her own.

"It is my understanding that under hospital policy children are not allowed into the Intensive Care Unit, and Dr. Cove—"

"Since when did we start letting people come in here and speak for the person we're meeting about?" a good-looking gentleman about Jacob's age spoke, interrupting Faye. He tapped the table with his long, skinny index finger with each statement he made. "They can send written comment and call with information, but nowhere does it say they can barge in here and give personal testimony. No offense to you, of course," he smiled at Faye. His eyes traveled slowly down her body, before coming back to her face.

Faye walked to stand beside the man, though she was somewhat agitated by his interruption and his less-than-subtle devouring gaze of her body. "Maybe it's time your rules changed. You should hear every side of the case, Mr. . . . ?" she questioned laying on the charm.

"Davidson. Pateon Davidson," he said, as he stood to take her proffered hand. Her scent wafted directly to his nostrils, he recognized the perfume immediately, brazen and alluring. He wondered just how personal she and Jacob were.

Davidson sat back down, reluctantly letting go of her hand, his mind moving to more personal thoughts of her. The burnt-cinnamon skirt outlined the curves of her bottom, while her breasts strained against the rust-colored, long-sleeved blouse. He scratched the illusory itch in the palm of his hands, alerting him to the need for touch. He imagined stripping the clothing from her, and wondered if Jacob had had the chance to do so yet.

Pateon noticed the others gathering papers, his mind refocused on the situation at hand.

Faye grabbed her coat. "I've said what I have to say. I encourage you to think about the integrity and the prestige that Dr. Cove brings to the table. He has quite a few innovative ideas about the direction of the medical field. Thank you so much for your time."

Pateon rushed over to help as she shoved her arms into the sleeves of her coat. He reached for her purse and keys which remained on the chair. "What you said about Jacob was very nice. I'm always playing devil's advocate, you know. I hope you didn't take it personally," he said, smiling at her.

Faye reached out to take her keys and purse from his hands, "Well, no. Of course not. I understand," she replied, though she really didn't and sensed the twinge of underlying hostility the man harbored against Jacob.

"Say, you wanna grab some coffee in the cafeteria or the shop just down the street?"

"Thank you, but no. I have to be going," she replied, walking toward the door.

"Are you sure? My treat."

"I'm sure, but thank you again." She waved, exiting the room.

Pateon watched her retreating back. A look of annoyance crossed his face. His eyes concentrated on her swaying hips, and the stretching and contracting of her tight calves with each foot striking the floor.

At the receptionist's desk, Faye looked down at the woman. "Can I please use a pen, paper, and an envelope?" she asked, optimistic that the woman would oblige despite their earlier encounter.

The woman slapped the items on the countertop without uttering a single word. Faye went to the waiting area, sat down heavily. Her heart was so heavy and full she thought it would burst. She needed to jot down her thoughts while the emotions she felt were clear and fresh. The weight became lighter as she scribbled furiously. Sealing the envelope, she hurried to the elevator, and back to work where closing time approached, and Lijah waited.

Chapter Twenty-one

"I'm asking you to go. What's the big deal, Jacob? Cynthia asked Faye to attend . . . I thought you were in love with the woman."

I am, his mind screamed, but it was impossible to love someone who obviously didn't love him back. Jacob sat slouched in the leather chair. His eyes covered by his arm as he listened to Benning drone on and on about the big Christmas party held every year.

"It's obvious she loves you. What the heck is your—"

"She loves me? That is news to me! How do you know anyway?" Jacob retorted.

Benning raised his eyebrows in confusion. "How do *I* know? Boy, you need to wake up?" Pushing his chair back from the desk, Weston rested his ankle on his other knee. He rubbed the bridge of his nose where shiny indentations had been made by his reading glasses.

"Tell me, Dr. Cove, with as many reviews as the board has given you, don't you think the last straw would have been when you took a patient from under the hospital care? Do you think Davidson would have let you get away yet another time without a serious fight? I guess you're just the greatest black doctor to ever grace this hospital, and that's why you keep getting breaks when you let stupidity, or shall I say in your latest feat, *love,* rule your actions?"

Jacob looked toward the ceiling. His mind was too tired to truly comprehend what his friend was trying to say. "Can you just explain that in the simplest terms?"

"You are not the great untouchable doctor. I thought that this time, when you took Miss Hicks, that that would be it for you. A suspension on your record is mighty hard to get rid of, son. And you know Davidson was salivating with the juicy taste of victory, that you had finally done it," Benning said.

"Don't the rest of those crackers know by now how Davidson hates my guts, and that they should take everything he says with a grain of salt?" Jacob asked, sitting up straight in the chair.

"Yes, I'm sure they do. But he has a lot of valid points,

Jacob, the way he presents things his name should've been Johnnie Cochran. But that is not my point."

"So you're saying someone else stepped in? Who was that? My mother? She write up some hot testimony shouting silly threats if the issue wasn't overlooked?" He knew his mother was capable of doing something like that, if not something even more dramatic.

"Jacob, even if she did, we can't formally admit any comments from relatives. You're on the right track, though. It was a female. She barged into the conference room close to the end of the meeting with praises for your doctoring."

Jacob stood. His mind raced with hope at the possibilities. Glancing at his watch, he wondered where exactly Faye would be. School was just getting out and the traffic would be murderous.

Jacob gave Benning a parting look. "Thanks, old man." And headed for the door.

"Seven-thirty, Jacob. Get some rest before the party, you look like hell," he yelled to Jacob's retreating back.

Jacob was in the elevator, thinking about all he needed to do. Looking like hell was an understatement; he laughed momentarily at Benning's statements. He felt as if he'd been run over by a Mack truck. Since Faye had been dodging his calls, he submerged himself in work: pushing himself to the limit, taking on an extra patient load, and agreeing to cover for those who wanted days off before the Christmas holiday. Jacob pulled out his cell phone.

Chapter Twenty-two

Lijah sat in her room packing her kids' tote. Her mother had laid out the clothes she was to include, but Lijah couldn't figure out how to get the clothes in because it was already stuffed to capacity with toys. The phone rang and she jumped up, running to her mother's room to answer it.

"Hello," she said into the receiver.

Jacob had been anticipating Faye's voice. He hadn't known what'd he say. "Hi, Lijah. How are you?" Jacob replied, letting out a deep breath.

"Dr. Jake!" she sang. "I'm fine."

"That's good. How is your momma?" he probed.

"She's okay. She's in the potty. She's going to a big party, and I'm going to a sleep over at Kiera's."

"Wow . . . Have you lost any more teeth?" He loved talking to her, and she babbled endlessly without prompting.

"No," she said sadly, "but guess what? Mommy says when I start first grade I can take ballet," she cheered.

"Really? You want to be a dancer?" he asked picturing her pirouetting in pink tights and leotard. "My mother used to be a dancer. You should ask her to tell you about it sometime."

"Oh, cool. I will." She became silent for a minute before continuing, "Dr. Jake, are you coming to see us soon?"

"Well . . . yes, I think I will see you very soon," he replied. He was more than hopeful.

"Oh, great. I miss you, and I think mommy does, too."

A child's encouragement, it was all he needed, "I miss you both, too, Lijah. I'll see you soon. I promise." He would see Faye at the party, he thought with hope, and on Christmas they'd both come over.

"Okay," she replied. She said good-bye and hung up.

Faye stepped from the tub, wiping at the scented bath oil on her skin. She had never been the type for the big party scene, yet a nudge from Cynthia and thoughts of Jacob being there propelled her to say yes. She'd run out of options, and this was it.

With the one-stop shop to the Potomac Mills Mall in Northern Virginia, Cynthia and she had been able to find a reasonably priced dress that was perfect. The accessories and the knee-high suede boots had been a steal. Faye had also finished her Christmas list of items for Lijah, though she hadn't been able to afford the computer . . . maybe next year.

The bodice was formfitting, outlining and defining her soft curves. The scoop neck showing off what she vied her greatest assets was a bit daring, but Cynthia had told her, "God has blessed you, dear. Don't hide it." She didn't want to, but only with the eyes of one person in mind.

At her bureau, she dragged the small crystal with drops of perfume along her collarbone, the nape of her neck, and one final dip between her breasts. The action brought back memories of her mother. Her eyes turned to the floor where Lijah sat watching her. Faye had done the same as a little girl. Faye patted her knees, and Lijah jumped up quickly climbing into her lap.

"Are you going to be a good girl for momma tonight?" she asked, placing a small peck on the girl's cheek, then using her fingers to wipe away the berry smudge her lips had left.

"I'm always good, Mommy," she replied modestly.

"You sure are. Do you have all your stuff packed?"

"I think so," Lijah replied.

"Momma, can I ask you something?"

"You can ask me anything, baby," Faye replied.

"Well, do you think you and Dr. Jake could marry so I can have a daddy?"

Faye hadn't been expecting a question so blunt. She knew the child was fond of Jacob, but she didn't know how much Lijah understood the role or the want of a father. It was important, but it reminded Faye of how dumb she'd been, robbing herself of the love of a man, but equally robbing Lijah of the love two parents can give and the different kind of love the father gave. She honestly didn't know, however, where Jacob was. The letter she'd mailed to the hospital days ago had produced no response. Maybe it was too late. Maybe it took too long for her to get it together, and he realized he didn't want her anymore.

"Honey, I thought we were doing okay by ourselves," she questioned.

"Sure, Momma, but it's nice to have a daddy. Grandpa is gone," she said sadly before continuing, "but, Dr. Jake, he's nice and buys me things, and spends time with me. Marcus never did that. Dr. Jake says he misses us. Don't you like him?"

"Yes, I like him very much. But . . . When did he say he misses us?"

"While you were in the potty," she replied.

"He—he called, honey? Well, Wh . . . What did he say? Why didn't you come get me?" She was sorry she missed his call.

"I told him you were getting ready for a party, and that I was going over Kiera's house for a sleepover. He said he'd see us soon, Mommy, so maybe Christmas . . . you know?" the girl asked, looking up at her mother. Her large eyes filled with hope.

"Well, yes. I know. I guess if he said he would see us then he means it." she replied. Unfortunately, Faye wasn't a child, and things people said were often what they believed and not so much promises of what they would actually do. *But Jacob is different,* her mind whispered. She kept the negative thoughts to herself. After tonight, she'd know for sure.

Lijah nodded, before hopping off Faye's lap. In the child's little world, all was well.

Faye turned back around to the mirror, arranging her hair. She thought of Jacob. His touch, his kiss, and everything they'd shared, she recalled expertly to her mind. But feeling meant wanting the real thing, and until she was sure about him . . . She shook her head frantically to remove the images.

She checked the time, grabbing her bag, coat, and keys. She looked down at Lijah. Her large brown eyes and little nose were the only things visible through all the winter attire. "The day after tomorrow is Christmas, honey, and who knows what Santa will bring us. But . . ." she took a deep breath, beginning to feel a twinge of the child's optimism, " . . . but if we pray and believe just enough, maybe Jacob will be under our tree."

Lijah cast a glance at the small, pathetic fake tree in the living room. "I don't know, Momma," she looked doubtful, "that tree is kind of short, and Dr. Jake . . . he's tall," she said. Using her arms she demonstrated the comparisons of Jacob and the tree by spreading them wide then closing them together to illustrate the sizes. "I don't think he'll fit," she finished, turning back to her mother.

Faye laughed, though she felt like crying. Taking the little girl's hand, she grabbed the kid's tote and headed out the door.

Chapter Twenty-three

Jacob sat on the edge of his bed, rubbing the sleep from his eyes. He'd been to the stores he needed to go to. The tree was in the living room and the cleaners had gotten his clothes done early. Everything was going good. He turned into the bathroom for a quick shower. The clock caught his eye, reading six-thirty, and he felt at least somewhat renewed with the short nap. His black tie with small, shiny topaz dots brought out the color of his crisp, silk-blue shirt. His jet-black slacks finished the ensemble.

Looking in the mirror, he combed his puffy, thick hair into a neat heap. He hadn't had a cut in over a month and the growing fro would have to stay a few more days until he was able to do so. Splashing his face with aftershave, he placed the ring and watch that used to belong to his father on his hand. He checked the hands of the clock once more before grabbing his black suit jacket. The time hadn't changed since he'd gone into the bathroom. He muttered an expletive when he checked the time on his watch. The clock on the table was dead and it was really two hours later.

He rushed down the stairs, grabbing his leather bomber jacket before heading out the door.

The party was in full nightlifelike swing as Faye entered. Some men gathered in small groups on the outskirts of the dance floor discussing various affairs. The women waited patiently, seated and talking amongst each other, for their chance to be twirled and spun. The lights were dimmed and the pastel crepe paper hanging from the ceiling created a rainbow of shimmering colors across the walls. Two long tables lined the far side of the room, laden with treats of every shape, color, texture, and consistency. A small bar kept people coming and going as the bartender filled each request. Round tables with crisp, white linens sat opposite the dance floor sprinkled with green and red sequins, and gold foil stars. Two men behind loads of equipment operated the turntables with consecutive jams of various tempos.

Faye spotted Cynthia across the floor seated at a table with Dr. Benning to her right. Her eyes led the path to their table.

"Faye, dear," Cynthia said as she and Benning stood at her approach. Embracing Faye, Cynthia gave her a look of approval for pulling together the outfit.

"Miss Hicks, you look lovely this evening," said Dr. Benning.

"Thank you, Dr. Benning. It's nice to see you again," she replied, moving to accept the hand he held out. He nodded.

Not knowing what else to do, she took a seat next to Cynthia and watched the rest of the couples mingle, dance, eat, and chat amongst themselves. A slow song began, and Dr. Benning laid a light hand on Cynthia's shoulder. From her seat she looked up him, his hands moved to the back of the chair to remove it.

"Would you like to dance, Cynthia?"

Her eyes lighted with pleasure as she stood, taking his hand. Cynthia gave a parting wink as they left for the dance floor.

Faye's feet were hurting in the too-high boots an hour into the party. She had danced with Dr. Benning, who was light on his feet despite his burly size.

Faye contemplated leaving as she sat looking through the crowd toward the dance hall entrance for any sign of Jacob.

Faye walked toward Cynthia and Dr. Benning to tell them she was headed out for the night. Before reaching the end of the dance floor, she tensed, feeling arms around her waist. They propelled her like a skilled dancer back to the middle of the dance floor before turning her around.

Her eyes traveled up the tan suit coat, before meeting his eyes. "Mr. Davidson?"

Chapter Twenty-four

"Yes, Miss Hicks. Pateon," he corrected her.

"Pateon. Uh, it's nice to see you again," she lied.

"Are you enjoying your evening?"

"Yes." *No,* she thought.

"Good," he replied. Though he knew otherwise, she couldn't be without the good doctor, Jacob, nearby. He was about to ask when he felt Faye grow more tense in his arms, if that were possible. Faye was glad for the interruption, but hadn't realized how glad until she saw the tall man who had just tapped Pateon on the shoulder.

"May I cut in?" Jacob's voice carried, deep and rich, despite the loud music. Jacob gave Pateon a sly smile, leaving him stunned as he whisked Faye away.

The intrusion and the without-a-second-glance dismissal had Pateon fuming. He stormed off in the opposite direction.

"Hi," Jacob relaxed a bit now that she was in his arms. He'd been watching them briefly before he received a shoving nudge from Benning. "How are you?" he questioned, searching her eyes.

"I'm all right," she replied. *Incredibly better now that you're here,* she thought to herself. She noticed he looked tired, but didn't comment on her observations.. Of its own volition, her hand reached out to rest on the side of his face. Jacob pressed his cheek into her hand slowly moving his head back and forth causing her palm to caress him. His eyes closed savoring the feel of her soft hand against his face. She wrapped her arms completely around his shoulders, embracing him closer.

They became the only ones in the room. The world and activity around slowed to an oblivious hum. Jacob heard, saw, and felt nothing but the live, warm, welcoming heaviness of Faye's embrace. Everything about her rushed back in gushes to the front of his brain. She looked beautiful in her cranberry side swept hem dress. It swayed unevenly, in billowing falls almost to the floor on one side, exposing the leg with a see-through mesh on the other. Her skin was radiant, and she flushed slightly when he laid eyes upon her. The eyes he remembered were full, vibrant, and fiery. In his mind, he had never forgotten, but the present realness of her reminded his body.

"I've missed you."

"I . . . I missed you, too," she said. The apprehension that he might not have shown evaporated.

It was all the encouragement he needed as his arms held her more snugly. His head bent slightly to rest in the crook of her neck. The heels made her taller than he had remembered her being. He could feel her rapid pulse surging just below his lips as he feathered a light kiss there. He ran his nose lightly from her ear down to the strap of her shoulder, a trail of wonderful scent guiding him back and forth. She released a pent-up breath, relaxing even more into his embrace. His fingers drew light circles just at the base of her spine.

Faye's feet had left the earth and exited to rest on the clouds of Heaven she found in his arms. With the lightest of touches, she tumbled headfirst into a state of longing. When she looked into his eyes, she thought she'd see the blinding headlights of the car and smell its drunken and nicotined driver. She thought he'd have the eyes of his brother, guilt riding in the pupils, but none of that came to her. It wasn't his fault. "I'm sorry . . . I shouldn't have blamed—"

Jacob quickly brought a gentle finger to her mouth, silencing her, before he replaced the finger with his lips. "I've been trying to get here to do that all night." He smiled devilishly before continuing. "You have nothing to be sorry about. If I had any idea what he'd done, if I'd had known . . . Faye . . . I—"

"I know . . . it's okay," she interrupted. "I thought in seeing you, all I'd see would be him, but you're not him and I realize it was wrong for me to lump you into that." She took a deep breath before continuing, "I just realized how much I want and need you. If you still want me? I mean, I needed to close a chapter, Jacob. My father . . . I felt guilty about finding you with his death, and there are still twinges of that, and I don't know . . ."

She cut off her babbling when Jacob nodded as if he understood. She couldn't get the words out to make sense, but he continued nodding as if she'd put everything so simply.

She nodded too, smiling as they embraced again, mutually agreeing that whatever the reason, they both, equally, had wasted time.

Pateon stood at the bar as others came and went. They requested various amber and ruby concoctions with pungent odors made by the one bartender. Watching Jacob and Faye, their touches and kisses, he felt pangs of envy kicking him in the gut. He signaled the bartender for something stronger.

Ever since they were younger, it seemed Jacob got everything. The women flocked to Jacob who only ignored their advances. The same women wouldn't give Pateon Davidson a second glance. Jacob was prestige. His father was a great doctor before he'd drunk himself to death. Pateon's attempts to thwart Jacob's career since working for H.U. were unsuccessful. The man was untouchable.

Gulping down his drink, he couldn't remember the number he'd had, Pateon made his way across the dance floor. The effects of his intake had long since started affecting him. He staggered to the middle of the floor where Jacob and Faye were enjoying an intimate embrace.

The music ended, and Jacob and Faye took a few moments to separate. "I'll go get our coats. Tell Ms. Carter and Wes we're leaving," Jacob said.

Faye nodded as he leaned in for one more kiss then headed for the coat room.

Faye looked through the dark crowd for Cynthia and Dr. Benning. Spotting them, she headed in their direction.

"We didn't get to finish our dance," Pateon said from behind Faye. His arms grabbed her, roughly whisking her away from her destination.

Chapter Twenty-five

Pateon twirled her across the floor so fast she'd thought she'd faint as the room spun around her. His hands groped her, his body wiggled and rotated against hers. He kept moving as the crowd around them perked up with a loud ballad. His body was equally enthused by the fast beat.

Faye didn't want to be rude, but she moved slowly to the edge of the dance floor. She would leave him to make a fool of himself alone. As the song moved without pause into a different, but equally loud, fast-paced mix; he grabbed her up before she could turn to leave, bringing her uncomfortably close. She could feel his hips bumping and grinding against her own, and his hideous breath made her gag. His hands traveled across her back, grabbing and massaging sweaty palms of flesh, before they descended to her butt, squeezing and pulling her hard against him. Her pelvis pushed against the hard bulge in his pants. Faye's mind reeled with disbelief.

She backed up hastily from him. "What's the matter with

you?" she yelled, it came out like a hissing whisper, unable to compete with the music blaring about them.

Pateon lunged for her as she continued to back up to the edge of the dance floor. His voice was controlled as he said, "I just wanted some of the same lovin' you were giving the good doctor."

Faye was irate. "What? How dare you!" she looked around nervously. Just a few noticed their state, staring briefly, but continuing to dance as if nothing were going on.

Pateon kept coming toward her. His alcoholic intake was making itself known, affecting his vision and ability to walk normally. "That's right. You heard me. I just want you to share." He grabbed her and proceeded to try and kiss her. Her face turned away from him, and his lips landed a sloppy suckle on her cheek.

Faye's color deepened as heat rose to her face. Putting up her right hand, she quickly let it fall with muscled momentum against Pateon's cheek. He let her go to rub his burning and stinging face. She was quickly across the room and halfway to the door with Pateon following behind.

Jacob exited the door marked COAT CHECK, as Faye ran past him. With his free hand, he gently grabbed her by the arm to stop her before she could fully recognize who he was. Once she did, she wrapped her arms tightly around him. "Home," she said breathlessly. "Let's get out of here . . . *Now!*"

"Of course," he soothed. Jacob wondered what had happened since he had gone. It had taken a while for the German-speaking coat check woman to understand the information on the tickets that he gave her.

"You just a big tease, you little . . ." Pateon slurred, coming out of the ballroom into the lobby, when he saw Jacob.

"What the hell did you do?" Jacob pulled Faye behind him, directing her to the wrought-iron bench, and placing their coats beside her, his eyes never leaving Pateon's.

Pateon was hot. He loosened his tie. "I was asking your

woman here for the same lovin' she gives you." His coat began to come off. He threw it, missing the bench he'd aimed for just feet away.

Jacob shook his head as if he hadn't understood what was said, "You did what?" he snapped.

"I said . . ." Pateon continued.

Before he could finish, Jacob's fist went back contacting forcefully against Pateon's jaw. "That's what I thought you said."

The alcohol took a backseat as Pateon rushed forward, momentarily put off from the jab. He scrambled for Jacob, who stuck out his fist a second time. A few blows passed between them. Pateon struck air most of the time, his intoxication affecting his ability to properly coordinate his moves. Eventually, his face lay pressed into the cold tiles of the floor with Jacob's knee in his back. Faye had picked up Pateon's coat and was watching the encounter in a daze when a white envelope fell out, catching her attention. She bent to pick it up, recognizing her own handwriting, and rushed over to where they fought.

Tears that wanted to break free were pushed back. She leaned down. "You intercepted this letter for Jacob? You took it! How could you?"

Her eyes turned to Jacob, pleading. "Jacob, honey, let him up."

Jacob brought Pateon brusquely to his feet, keeping Davidson's hands held securely behind his back. Faye rose, too.

"This letter, Jacob, I had mailed it to you, but somehow *he* got hold of it and . . ." She checked the back. *It's still sealed,* she thought with relief. The words contained therein were meant for only one person.

Jacob understood. He dragged Pateon toward the exit, the glass doors automatically sliding open. Cabs sat waiting for guests who were ready to go home. The doorman recognized Pateon's drunken state, not to mention the swelling bruise across his lip and cheek, and his hand lifted, signaling a yellow car. The taxi sped up and stopped abruptly in front of them. The doorman opened the door before Jacob shoved Pateon inside.

"If you ever touch her again, make a rude comment, either under the influence or completely sober, I'll rearrange that pretty-boy face of yours. Your hatred for me is getting old, Davidson." Jacob slammed the door to the cab. It exited slowly into the traffic. The taillights winked and grew distant.

The electric doors opened back up and the gust of cold air caused Faye to wrap her arms around herself. Her eyelids closed, she leaned against the wall, resting her head. Jacob was in front of her, caressing her arms with his hands before wrapping her totally in his embrace. "You ready?"

Faye cleared her throat. "Yes," she replied. "Jacob?" Her pulse raced and the blood pumped through her veins.

Jacob retrieved their coats from the bench. "Hmm?"

Faye's nerves skittered around in her body, "I want to go home . . ." She took a breath, watching him nod in understanding, " . . . with you," she rushed out in a whisper. His hands slowed helping her into the coat. She changed the subject, looking toward the door. "He was drunk, you know?" she said evenly as if to excuse him.

"Yeah," was all he could say, her earlier statements foremost in his mind.

Chapter Twenty-six

They were silent in the gold Dodge Durango as he drove her to his home. Jacob didn't feel the need to tell her that once the BMW had been fixed he'd sold it to the first buyer; that he knew, despite the summons she'd received, she hadn't pressed charges against his brother; and that he hadn't seen Vondell since that day in the hospital. Their subtle glances and touches were a tacit communication as Smokey Robinson crooned a "Quiet Storm." Her hand periodically rested on his thigh, causing him to shift slightly in his seat at the growing discomfort and the tightness of his pants. He rested his own hand on top of hers.

He pulled into the driveway, pushing the button for the garage and entered to park the SUV.

"You want some coffee?" he asked.

She nodded as he backed through the door allowing her to enter. Hanging up their coats, he went to the kitchen setting the coffee maker. He left Faye in the kitchen.

At the entertainment center he selected the Teddy Pendergrass, Barry White, and Marvin Gaye CDs for the stereo. He returned to the kitchen. Faye moved knowingly, fittingly about the space, easily finding everything she needed. This is how he had wanted things. Lijah would watch from the high stool or sit on the counter, babbling endlessly. He could visualize it all. She placed sugar and creamer in the cup, while the water continued to gurgle and drip. He came up behind her to place his arms around her waist. He turned her around gently searching her eyes. "What was in the letter?" He cleared his throat.

"Some important things that I wanted to tell you."

He knew that, and she knew he knew it, but he smiled at her.

"Were they good or bad?" he replied.

"Good." The belching of the last drips of the water alerted Faye. She turned from Jacob's embrace, pouring the black liquid into two mugs.

"I care about you, Jacob, more than I knew. And I want . . ."

Jacob hadn't moved from behind her. He pressed himself closer. "What do you want, Faye?"

He expected her to answer, but his hands and his mouth were working against her ability to release any coherent thoughts formulating in her mind.

"Jacob, I just want you to know . . . I don't make a habit of sleeping with people."

He kissed her on her neck. "I never thought you did." He kissed her on the cheek, behind her ear. His tongue darted out to taste her skin.

"I'm here because . . . I want more with you than I've ever wanted with anyone else . . . but I also want to make the right choices, for me and Lijah."

He turned her back around to face him. "Faye, I want what's right for you and Lijah, too. I want you as mine . . . forever. If you can't handle that . . . if you aren't ready for that, you need to let me know."

Leaning into her, his hands traveled down her back and to the sides of her chest, lightly touching, squeezing, and caressing. Faye moaned into his mouth as she kissed him. She'd waited forever to hear the words he'd said.

He picked her up and carried her up the stairs. Laying her down gently, he brushed his lips over hers again and again. Faye opened her eyes, and her arms went around his neck. She brought his face back closer to her own to share another kiss.

She tugged on him but he was resistant, he wasn't through expressing what he had to say.

"Forever, Faye. I want a long time. I want to know if you can give me a long time."

She looked intensely into his eyes, questioning. *A long time? Forever?* There was no doubt, "Yes. Yes, I can give you that."

Faye leaned forward pressing her lips against his. Her

hands couldn't find any exposed flesh, and that wasn't satisfactory with her. She nervously sought buttons to loosen.

Jacob's body ran ahead, readying faster than his mind could follow suit. His hands mimicked Faye's, working the buttons just below her fingers in succession until his shirt was discarded on the floor. His arms were thick, his chest smooth with taut nipples. Faye pulled her dress in bunches up her legs and thighs, revealing a shiny, cambric slip.

He helped her remove the dress the rest of the way, wondering exactly how many underthings she was wearing. He began to push the slip up, revealing lacy underwear through the netting of her hose, above that, a matching lace bra. Jacob lightly pushed Faye back onto the bed as he too crawled more fully onto it. On his knees as she lay beside him, he leaned down to sprinkle kisses on her lips, trailing his tongue down the center of her stomach and kissing the remnants of a dark scar from a bruise that might never heal. The reasons behind the scar tried to enter his mind, but he pushed them back. Moving aside the elastic of her underwear and the hose he pulled them down to her boots, tugging them off as well. They landed with two loud thuds on the floor. He peppered kisses on every exposed inch of her, his mouth sucked on her outie belly button, trailing back to her neck. His hands slid her bra off each shoulder kissing the honey tan line it exposed. His fingers flexed as he reached under her to unhook the clasp keeping her full breasts from his sight. Faye lifted her arms as he removed the flimsy fabric. He inhaled deeply, releasing the air slowly through his nostrils when her breasts bounced lightly and her dark nipples tightened under his gaze. Jacob's hand rubbed from her side to her breast, watching her reaction. His index finger circled the dark patch around her nipple before pinching it between his thumb and forefinger. Faye let out a small gasp when his mouth and tongue replaced his fingers. His teeth bit lightly, scraping, then he used his lips to pull the taut peak. He paid equal attention to the other. His hands continued to massage her breasts until the core of Faye's ache throbbed with want. Her hands reached for him, tugging him down until he covered her fully. Her pelvis ground against him to communicate the place she wanted him most.

Licking her lips, she kissed him passionately, one hand traveling between them to unhook his belt. She feasted on his bottom lip, drawing it into her mouth, as her hands fumbled at the buckle without success. Jacob got off the bed at Faye's protest. She turned to watch his hands unhook the belt. He pushed down the pants along with his briefs, getting tangled, and clumsily removing his shoes and socks. The pants and underwear followed. His member sprang free. Faye's mouth gaped open, as the core of his desire bobbed, and twitched pointing directly at the reason for its state. Rejoining Faye on the bed, he kissed her inner thighs, moving higher. Faye panted when his tongue darted out to taste her. His thumb swirled around the pink butterfly of her womanhood. She writhed against his hand while her own hands grabbed handfuls of sheet on either side. Jacob inserted his tongue, entering and withdrawing it before closing his mouth over the small orifice to suckle. His thumb continued to apply light pressure. Her body jerked under his relentless ministrations.

"Oh, God, Jacob. Oh, please," Faye whispered. Her body singed into a raging inferno. Small beads of perspiration misted her forehead as Jacob's tongue continued to lave her. He climbed up her body, staring at her intensely until she slowly opened her eyes to return his gaze.

Chapter Twenty-seven

He kissed her softly, leaning to the side of the bed, opening the drawer, his fingers fumbling until they located what he was looking for. His hands tore the package, rolling it up his length. He looked down at her, wondering how she'd feel about more kids. Another girl or a boy, he didn't care, so long as she agreed to them.

"I need you to tell me, sweetheart," he said.

Tell him what? Her mind wondered. She'd missed the question. "Yes," was all she could muster. Her body was still vibrating and depleted of strength from the complete attention he paid to loving her. "I need and want you badly," she said, wondering what exactly he had asked of her and if her reply sufficed.

Jacob laid his weight more fully on her. His hands traveling down each side of her, skimming the back of her thighs, bringing her knees up. His tip was at the entrance.

Faye held her breath, anticipating. He entered slowly. Her breath came out with every inch he came in.

"Ugh, umm," she sighed.

Jacob stilled. "Are you okay? I'm not hurting you, am I?"

She brought her hips up to capture him and hasten his entry. She shook her head, tucking her bottom lip between her teeth. "No, no. It's just been a long time," she said breathlessly. The pinching and tension would ease once he entered her fully.

Jacob continued to ease himself slowly down, until he was buried deep within her folds. He continued to stare at her. Her eyes fluttered closed. He withdrew slightly before coming back again. "I love you, Faye Hicks."

Her eyes opened slowly, questioning, she hadn't heard him again. She wondered how he expected her to listen while he possessed her. He took her in mind, in body, and ignited her soul.

"Do you love me Faye?" he asked before picking up the tempo.

Faye was drowning. She never loved anyone the way she loved this man. Her eyes filled, and a tear sneaked down her temple and into her ear. "Yes," she said on a sob.

He became still for a moment before continuing. Leaning in their tongues matched the actions of their bodies.

Jacob reminded himself to take it slow and easy, to give completely and totally. He gave, and she met him with each thrust, giving back equally. He couldn't hold back. He moved more fiercely, harder, but purposefully and controlled. He came to the edge, looked over, then went back for more and kept reaching, eventually cresting toward a peak.

Faye's heels crossed at his back as he continued to pound. She felt the pressure building in her stomach, her lower back. She was falling, but he was there to catch her. He lifted before slightly withdrawing and plunging back in again. Faye let out a small cry of pleasure as the contractions began tightening and relaxing again and again. He wanted to give everything to her. He was a giver, like her. He went still and rigid, his own powerful release descended upon him, robbing his breath. He grunted with its force.

Faye's hand went up and down his back, slick with the sweat from their fierce lovemaking. Her other hand massaged the tense cords of his neck muscles. Her breathing had yet to calm down. "I love you, Jacob. With my whole heart, I love you."

Exhaustion upon them both, his arms went around her, pulling her with him as he rolled to the side. Covering them with the sheet, Faye snuggled into the cocoon of his chest. "I love you, too," he whispered into her damp hair. The feelings he felt were overwhelming. A part of him was inside her despite the protection he used. He couldn't comprehend the possessive feelings he felt. There would be no one else for him but her. His body was ready for her again, but only a few moments had passed. Looking down at her resting in his arms, he whispered, "We'll get married on New Year's Day."

Her eyes opened slightly revealing golden, fiery orbs with lovemaking remembrances.

Nothing of what Jacob said registered. "Okay," she replied unconsciously. She was sleeping. Jacob chuckled at her light snoring noises.

Chapter Twenty-eight

The light filtered through the blinds, creating sharp yellow lines of sun across Jacob's face. He awakened, his hands reaching and searching, finding nothing but the coolness of empty sheets. His eyes came open, squinting at the bright sun. He sat up. "Faye . . ." he whispered. Getting up, he rummaged around looking for underwear. Finding a pair, he shoved his legs into them. The aromas stirred his belly as he neared the stairs and then the kitchen. The different kind of hunger he thought would lessen after making love to Faye once only intensified.

Faye peeled the skin from steamy potatoes. A small platter of perfectly round sausages sat next to the stove, draining on paper towels. Eggs sprinkled with salt and pepper sat in the glass bowl. Faye turned to retrieve something, when Jacob came in wearing nothing but his cotton boxers.

His chest was bare and his gaze was already intense with the smoldering heat she'd witnessed not long ago.

She forgot what she was looking for and walked toward him.

The shirt she wore was his undoing. His cotton undershirt covered her, but the hem only reached to the blue lace of the underwear he looked forward to stripping from her derriere again. Her braless breasts bounced under his gaze as she moved. She gave him a kiss on his mouth. "Good morning," she whispered.

"That it is," he replied, his eyes never leaving hers. His hand grabbed hers. He placed it over his mouth, kissing her palm, before bringing it down the length of him, to his taut chest, rock hard stomach, and lower . . .

Faye gasped when he placed her hand on him, ready and erect.

"I'm hungry, Faye," he said huskily.

"I just have to scramble the eggs and fry the potatoes," she replied, smiling. The thumb of her free hand pointed over her shoulder to the stove.

He picked her up, her legs wrapping around him, his hands holding her securely under her bottom.

In the living room, he sat on the couch fumbling with the foil packet. Faye stood to remove her underwear when something in the distance caught her attention. She turned to gawk at the huge tree beside the fireplace. "Oh, my God, Jacob?" she said, turning to walk toward the tree. Her hand struck out, grabbing a branch, closing around it and pulling. The needles remained intact.

Faye sat on the floor, bringing her knees up to her chin and hugging them tight.

Jacob came to sit beside her. He'd hoped she'd be excited, but her being moved to tears had him a little worried.

"Daddy . . . he never got a real tree." She wiped at the tears in her eyes. "Said it was too much work. You gotta clean up from the needles it leaves, and the sap, and it cost too much, and just all these excuses," she said with emotion clouding her voice and heart. "I just wish he were here now. Complaining and all," she said waving her hands. "I don't care so long as he was here and healthy.

"It's beautiful, Jacob." She rested her head against the sofa watching him; the concern in his eyes was comforting. The tree had to be at least seven feet. Nothing like it would begin to fit in her small apartment.

"Well, I thought you, Lijah, and me could decorate it."

"She'll love it," Faye replied, knowingly. Lijah would love it, no doubt in her mind, and she wondered who'd love it more, herself or Lijah. It'd be a close tie, she surmised.

Jacob moved closer to Faye, bringing her legs across his thighs. "Your dad, Faye. He's here," Jacob said, laying a hand half on her breast where her heart was.

She nodded. "I know. I just miss him, and the tree reminded me of him . . ." she said, taking a deep, cleansing breath. "I love you, Jacob," she said, and bringing his face closer to hers, she kissed him.

"I'm ready to eat now," she said brightly.

Jacob began to get up, "Okay, I at least know how to scramble eggs, so I'll do that, and you can fry the potatoes." Her hand on him kept him from getting up. She pulled him back down to the carpet as she began removing her underwear before straddling his lap.

Jacob watched her climb onto him, and he understood what she meant. He quickly located the protection he'd dropped near the end of the sofa. He snaked his thumb between them, applying light pressure to the secret button of her desire.

Faye was lost. Her head fell back as her body arched, trying to expose more of herself to him. He sheathed himself in the condom before pulling her toward him, sliding himself deep. Faye cried out when he invaded her fully. His hands on her bottom assisted her in the thrusting motions.

Their moans and gasps echoed throughout the room until they were exhausted and sated.

Chapter Twenty-nine

Emma Cove toted in a mass of shopping and grocery bags before shutting the door. The table in the foyer held differently sized packages with shiny wrappings of various colors. Turning around, she stopped abruptly.

Faye stood at the sink with her hands in the soapy water. Her hair was tied securely in a towel, drying from a recent shower. The evening gown she'd worn the night before was wrinkled from a hasty discarding. Faye and Emma locked eyes before Emma resumed her task, carrying the groceries into the kitchen without a second glance at Faye.

"Nice to see you again, Mrs. Cove." Faye was the first to speak. She felt as if she'd been saying that a lot lately, though the last couple of times she hadn't meant it. "Do you need help?" she asked, removing the stopper from the sink and drying her hands on the dishcloth. She picked up a bag of groceries and carried them to the kitchen.

"No, I don't need help, Miss Hicks, and I thought I told you to stay away from my sons." She turned, looking straight at Faye.

Faye kept her eyes on her task, before stopping at the counter, her head bowed, "I love your son, and I would never do anything to hurt Jacob," she replied.

"If you love him so much, then why do you insist on keeping him from attaining his career goals?" She asked, briskly taking out the products, slamming each down onto the table.

"I'm not . . . I went to the hospital that day, and I apologized for getting him in trouble in the first place, and they agreed to drop the issue against him."

"I'm aware of your attempts and what you did, and that's commendable, but Jacob is on his way to a very prominent career. He will open his own practice in a couple of years and move to Chicago where he will head one of the biggest emergency trauma center departments," she replied triumphantly before continuing. "Do you think he can do that with you and child in tow? You'll weigh him down and I won't have that. You can either leave now, or . . ."

"That's enough, Mother!" Jacob entered the kitchen, straightening his tie. His hair glistened with tiny droplets of water.

She turned from Faye, following Jacob as he moved to Faye's side linking his hand with hers. Her eyes blazed upon seeing their display. "Isn't it enough that this woman split you and your brother up? What about Chicago, Jacob, and the practice? She'll only slow you in your dreams, honey. Listen to me," she pleaded. Everything she'd hoped for him was slowly burning away, and she felt powerless to stop it. She felt the fleeting years ago with her dreams of being a dancer only different circumstances had prevented her success then.

"Now you wait just a minute," Jacob began. Jacob had tolerated all that his mother had imposed on him for long enough. Before, he had nothing to lose, so he pacified her. But Faye was in the picture now, and he wouldn't lose her because his mother couldn't understand all he'd been saying for some time. "Faye won't slow me in anything I want to attain, *if* I indeed want to attain it. I've told you that I don't want the Chicago position, but you can't seem to understand that," he continued.

"As for Vondell and me, we've been distant a long time. Faye isn't the cause of our problems, and I hate to tell you why, Mother, but . . ." He paused, drawing strength from Faye. Her hand moved up his back and was a comfort on his shoulder.

He begin the awful details of the night, "The son you love so much, the prodigal one, Vondell James Cove; he got drunk one night, but that's no surprise it's his favorite pastime . . ." He finished the story but felt horrible for having to be the one to bear such news. But it was time she knew the truth, and he would no longer cover up his brother's doings to save his mother grief.

Emma placed a shaky hand over her mouth. "That's not true. She's just lying. Is that how you turned my boys against each other, with hideous lies?" she yelled at Faye, her eyes wild with anger.

"It is true, Ma." The deep voice came from behind her. All eyes turned to face Vondell as he fully entered from the hall.

"Yeah, it's true," Jacob continued without looking at his brother. "You just refuse to see it. You've never believed anything he did. It was always me who got the blame. I could have gotten it this time, too. You know why?" He didn't wait for a reply. "I loaned Vondell my car. I would have gone to jail. I could be, once again, paying for something he did. We're grown men, and you're still covering for him just like when we were kids.

"You gotta wake up, Momma, or you'll lose both of us. If you can't handle Faye . . . I love her. And she's going to be my wife."

Emma's head jerked back, looking at Faye.

Jacob walked off, returning with their coats. He held Faye's coat while she hurriedly pushed her arms into the sleeves and secured the belt.

Emma was stunned at the revelations. She never understood how much she'd imposed her views and thoughts onto him, until now, as he threw them back in her face. And

Vondell, he brought her to shame. She pacified and coddled him so much, and now he was good for nothing.

Faye and Jacob left through the laundry room to the garage. She watched their retreating backs and heard the garage door. She turned back around to Vondell. His eyes, his height, everything . . . looking at him, she saw his father, her husband. The man who drunk away his life, died of kidney failure, and left her with two teenage boys to finish raising on her own. She did the best she could.

She walked to him, her eyes filled with disgust and contempt, but also harboring her own guilt for the how she'd played into the way he turned out. Her hand landed one stinging slap across his face before she walked to the guest room. She slammed the door and collapsed on the bed, her emotions a clashing eclipse before gathering and spilling down her face in tears.

On the way to the hotel where Faye's car was parked, she'd been silent. Her thoughts amuck with various aspects of all that had happened, not to mention that Jacob had informed her she'd said a very drowsy "okay" last night when he stated they'd be getting married on New Year's Day, and thus that locked her into it.

Her heart was full, but things were moving so fast. There was little doubt she wouldn't say yes to his proposal, but his mother and their relationship remained torn and in question. She valued family, and it was because of her that things were so discordant. It was his mother she thought of as they talked.

"But your mother, Jacob, if you resolve that, then we can talk about . . ."

"No," he said firmly, interrupting her. He pulled into the parking lot beside her car. A few cars littered the otherwise empty lot.

"Stay here a minute," Jacob said, and before exiting the car, he pried away the keys she held clutched in her hand. In her car he turned the ignition and switched the heater dials on high before returning.

In his seat he turned to face her. "No matter what happens, Faye, I want you and Lijah at my house. We're getting married. Tomorrow's Christmas and I want to spend it with my future wife and daughter. Do you understand?

"There's been tension between us a long time. Even without you, things were cresting, Faye, and were bound to break. I won't let it ruin what you and I are trying build," he finished.

"Lijah . . . your daughter?" she whispered looking out the window, thinking back to what he had said. Her mind stuck on the words.

It took Jacob a minute before he understood what she was talking about. She barely whispered and he had to lean in closer to hear. "If she wants it, Faye. You're not the only one who'll get Cove as their last name."

Her mouth dropped open in astonishment. Lijah had no trouble. The child never wondered, fretted, or obsessed over what it was she wanted. It was her mother who had all the issues. "She loved you before I realized I loved you, too."

"I know. I love her. But I'm *in love* with her mother." He said.

They both exited the car. He removed the rest of the packages from her trunk, transferring them to his. Settling in her car, Faye rolled down the window as Jacob leaned in to place a sweet kiss on her lips.

"I'll see you tonight," he said, brushing her lips again, flicking out his tongue. Faye nodded. Her thoughts a puddle of confusion, her life before her, if she would just grab hold of it.

She started to put the car in gear when Jacob leaned in, "Put your seat belt on," he said, smiling, before he was gone.

Chapter Thirty

Lijah sat amidst tons of wrapping paper. Her eyes glued to the funny-looking animated character on her new computer screen with its purple hardware. She and Jacob had worked endlessly half the day setting it up. He was overjoyed watching her and glad he could find the machine at the last minute. She delved into it, clicking the mouse and her little index fingers, pointing to and searching for the letters of her name. She typed it in the designated slot of the new game. All of it, she did skillfully as if she were a computer programmer.

Faye whipped the topping to the cake while humming to the Christmas CD. Luther Vandross sang for all to "Have yourself a merry little Christmas," and Faye agreed it was. The dinner was almost ready. Jacob had tried to help, but he ate more than he made and she'd sent him away. Lijah, too, had helped, but her whining about the toys that waited for her to play with them had also taken her away.

Faye stopped a minute to look at the exquisite ring on her left-hand ring finger. Jacob had formally proposed in front of her and Lijah and she had, without a second thought, agreed.

Faye remembered her mother and how she wished she could be there to help while she made what was supposed to be a masterpiece into a disaster. She tasted the icing for the tenth time, about to gag from consuming so much of it. The bitter, salty taste to it remained and she set it aside threatening to dump it.

Mrs. Cove entered, as Faye was about to dump the contents of her ruined efforts into the trash. Placing a gentle hand on hers she took the bowl from her. "Just needs a secret ingredient," she said. Her eyes were still slightly puffy from yesterday's crying stage. She'd gone on a last-minute shopping spree, and had bought a new perspective and attitude in the process. Some soul-searching she did in the midst of all her digging, gave her a new lease on life. She realized something had to give, and since she hadn't done any giving in a while, it was time she made more of an effort. If she didn't, the son she loved dearly but was so imposing upon because she didn't want him to be anything like his father or brother, would leave her. She couldn't make him choose, because she'd be the one to lose.

Faye watched Emma in complete surprise while she added generous amounts of the various ingredients before her.

Emma took a deep breath before turning back to Faye. "I'm sorry," she said finally, releasing the breath she held. "I've realized a lot and I hope you can forgive me . . . I hope Jacob can forgive me," she finished, looking down at the icing.

Faye nodded. Jacob had forgiven her long ago. Faye herself held nothing against her and already understood more than the woman thought she did.

Faye began turning the cake plate while Emma spread the icing with patient adroitness.

Lijah wandered into the kitchen and watched the two women work and move respectfully around each other with precision and synchronism.

"How are you, Missy?" Emma asked Lijah as the little girl climbed up onto the high stool. She removed the hot cookies from the cookie sheet, placing them on the cooling rack directly in front of the child.

"Fine . . ." Lijah replied. Her eyes grew large at the huge, buttery sugar cookies before her. Lijah reached to take a cookie, when her mother's fast hand and faster approach smacked it away. "Not till after dinner," she said sternly.

Lijah removed her outstretched hand, frowning. Faye turned back around to her task, then went to the opposite side of the kitchen to retrieve an item from the pantry.

"Momma and Dr. Jake are getting married and he's going to be my daddy," she said to Emma before continuing, "Since you're his mommy, that will make you my grandma. Right?"

"Yes, I suppose you're right," she said, not realizing the new role that would result.

"When I'm in the first grade, I'm going to take ballet," she continued. "Dr. Jake said you used to be a dancer, and that I should ask you about it. Will you tell me about it sometime?"

Emma stared at the child. The dreams she'd had, now latent and dusty in the corner of her heart and mind, sprang again with new life. It was a new era. Times were different, and her dreams could gain life vicariously through someone else.

Emma nodded her head. "Sure I will tell you about it. I had grand dreams about dancing, once, but they changed. And yours might, too, but whatever you wish to do is your choice." She realized she had imposed her own visions on Jacob and Vondell long ago. For a millisecond she was about to do the same thing with Lijah, and eventually it, too, would backfire, exploding in her face. With each new pressure she put on them, it further drove a wedge between the three of them, creating a heavy and deafening drift of her family. She was a wise woman and she would not make the same mistake twice.

Reaching around her neck, she removed the link chain that held tiny silver ballet slippers and fastened the chain around Lijah's neck.

"You don't have to . . ." Faye said, coming over to admire the piece. She didn't finish her statement when Emma returned a stern look. "What do you say, Lijah?" she finished.

"Thank you, Grandma," Lijah replied sounding out the new word.

"I have new dreams now, for myself, my family." She looked at Faye, her gaze softening. "Sometimes things change . . . for the better."

Jacob watched from the kitchen entrance. His mother never parted with the piece she had held so dearly. He remembered it around her neck even as a little boy and knew she'd had it forever. He was surprised by her ability to part with it.

Faye walked toward Jacob. He held out his arms, letting her walk into them. She hugged him close and felt at home.

Emma watched them for a brief moment before turning back to Lijah. Her hands reached for one of the cookies she'd transferred to the cooling rack earlier. It was still soft and gooey with warmth as she broke it in half. Placing an index finger over her lips, she handed it to the child. Lijah slowly grabbed the cookie, shoving the entire piece into her mouth, chewing nosily while trying to suppress her giggles.

"Grandma" hmm? . . . I'll be a hip one at that! She thought to herself, warming to her new role. Winking at Lijah, she broke the rest of the cookie into a bite size portion and popped it into her mouth.

Epilogue

Rev. Friendly stood in front of the pulpit decorated with poinsettias of red, burgundy, and even a rare crème color. Lijah Hicks made her way down the crinkly paper of the aisle in the church. Her ivory chiffon dress made her itch, but her mother said when the ceremony was over she could change.

She smiled up at her mother, who gripped her hand. Faye's dress was ivory, like the child's but the top, a long-sleeved, beaded, crystal chemise, gave it more maturity and elegance. In her right hand Faye carried a cascading arrangement of gysophila, ivory gardenias, chrysanthemums, and gold-crusted leaves tied securely with brocade.

Faye looked at Lijah encouragingly, as they marched down the aisle to a beat they'd practiced just moments ago in the hall. The "Wedding March" was surprisingly mellifluous even though it wafted from a Panasonic keyboard containing numerous preprogrammed tunes.

Her eyes left the angelic face of her little girl to rest on the smoldering ebony eyes of her soul mate and future husband.

Jacob stood orgulous, watching and waiting for his girls to meet him in front of the pastor. He'd agreed to wait a whole two weeks when his mother and fiancée had ganged up on him expressing the need for more time to find the proper wedding attire and arrange other matters for the event. He couldn't have cared less and would have agreed to marry her in jeans and a T-shirt, but they would hear none of it. He couldn't believe the development of their relationship. Things had changed dramatically. He looked back over his shoulder. His brother stood behind him, alert and sober.

Their relationship was sketchy and still on shaky ground, but slowly he was taking his rightful role as big brother.

Faye and Lijah arrived. Lijah stood between them holding both their hands, while they exchanged words of love and hope for the future. They also made pledges to Lijah, who would be their big, little girl, the adoption papers close to completion and in hand. As far as Jacob and Lijah were concerned, however, he was her daddy.

Jacob turned his eyes from the pastor to focus deeply on Faye. The ring and wedding band, a two-carat solitaire with small opal birthstones around it, slid up her finger. Lifting her hand he placed a kiss just above the ring.

Jacob bent down, placing a small kiss on the child's hand to do the same. Lijah's ring was a miniature of the one he gave Faye, but the diamonds were replaced by her birthstone.

The pastor uttered the final words of joining and prayer. He expressed that Jacob was free to kiss his wife. The kiss: long, sweet, and a small token reminder of whispered promises they would reciprocate for each other in the lifetime that lay ahead.

The reception hall was full with close friends and family. Weston and Cynthia danced intimately together. Lijah nestled comfortably in the lap of her grandmother, yawning from all the activity and consumption of the endless food and sweets that existed. The older Mrs. Cove, also known as *Grandmother Extraordinaire,* filled the child's imagination with fairy tales and stories of mysticism. They also discussed their minivacation with plans for gooey fudge brownies, crafts, and endless cartoons. Just some of the many things they would do while Faye and Jacob went on their honeymoon.

Vondell danced and charmed the abundance of women in attendance from the hospital and the school, in between sipping a less-than-bubbly soft drink.

Jacob and Faye danced to the slow songs drifting over the chatter. Romantically, he dipped her, gliding fluidly to "Endless Love" by Lionel Richie and Diana Ross.

At their home, amidst the boxes filled with Lijah and Faye's things, they moved them aside just enough to permit space where they christened each room with their love.

Together they left the earth in a blissful haze. When they returned to the earth, they rested, decided they needed nourishment, but only momentarily took a reprieve before slowly beginning the journey to ecstasy again.

Ties That Bind

LaTwaan Green

ACKNOWLEDGMENTS

I would like to thank my mother Susan and my Aunt Shirley for all of their words of encouragement. Thanks for pushing me when I was down, never letting me give up on my dreams, and believing in me when I didn't believe in myself. I give the two of you my love and sincerest thanks.

I would also like to thank my two darling children, Bryan and Jasmine, for being so good while Mommy sat down at the computer.

Many thanks to my brothers Oscar and Tony.

To anyone I may have left out, I give my love and thanks.

Chapter One

"The laptop has to stay here," Claudia Marshall said as she sat down on the edge of Jasmine's desk. "I forbid you to even think about bringing it." Jasmine looked up and cracked a smile.

Her best friend and partner, Jasmine Hayden couldn't have asked for anyone more devoted to her than Claudia. With her dark auburn hair, mocha-colored skin and chocolate-brown eyes, she had men falling at her feet for her attention. She'd always enjoyed the attention until a year ago. For the past year, the notorious party girl had been spending a lot of evenings at home. Jasmine was convinced she was seeing someone special, but she never inquired. Whoever the lucky man was, she took her hat off to him for getting Claudia to slow down.

"I'm the boss. You can't tell me what to do," Jasmine said smugly as she threw her raven black hair over her honey-colored shoulder. "Besides, if I don't work we don't eat."

Claudia rolled her eyes. "I understand that you have to work, Jasmine, but you do it obsessively. You never take a break. If anyone needs this vacation it's you, and you're acting like you're being put in a torture chamber."

"That's an interesting viewpoint," Jasmine said as she clicked away at her computer. "I'll have to remember that one."

"Two whole weeks of sunshine and fresh air. How could you not enjoy it?"

Jasmine shook her head as she looked at Claudia. "You've never been home with me so you have no idea what you're talking about," Jasmine said as she briefly looked over her work. She smiled with satisfaction as she hit the print button.

"Does this have anything to do with Trevor?" Claudia asked. Trevor was Jasmine's late-husband. He was killed in a car accident on Christmas Eve two years before when a drunk driver hit him head-on. He was killed instantly. The other driver was able to walk away without a scratch.

"I've gotten over his death for the most part," Jasmine said softly. "Holidays just don't hold the same appeal they used to."

"It's hard to believe Christmas is here again. It seems like yesterday we were ringing in the New Year," Claudia said as Jasmine picked up her proposal and smiled.

"Can you believe that a whole year has come and gone already?"

"No."

"Neither can I."

"At least I won't be spending Christmas alone this year," Claudia said. Jasmine could hear the excitement in her best friend's voice.

"Is it just me, or are you really excited about this trip?"

"I'm excited because I haven't been anywhere in ages, Jasmine."

"Are you trying to make me feel guilty because you work all the time?"

"No," Claudia said as she shook her head. "You give me vacations. You're just the one who never takes one."

"Vacations leave too much time to think," Jasmine said as she put her proposal, two disks and several poster boards in an oversized envelope. "Now Martin will have this before he leaves for the holidays."

"He could have waited for that, Jasmine."

"He called me to ask if I could have it ready for him today. He's going to Paris for the holidays, and he wants to take it with him," she said as she shut down her laptop. She unplugged it and put it in the leather case.

Claudia shook her head. "I meant what I said, Jasmine. No laptop."

Jasmine couldn't resist the smile that crossed her lips. "Have you been talking to Jonathan?" she asked. Claudia shook her head in innocence. "It's funny that he told me that very same thing a few days ago."

"Listen to your elders." Claudia said, leading the way to the outer office.

"Maybe one day I will," Jasmine said as she retrieved her coat from the closet. "All I have to do is drop this off and we're ready to go."

"I can't believe I'm going to spend Christmas on the beach."

"One thing I can guarantee, this is going to be one vacation you will never forget."

Jasmine and Claudia headed out of Boston two hours later. Jasmine's mind was full and her heart was heavy. When she told Claudia this was going to be a vacation she'd never forget, she meant every word of it.

She wasn't happy to be going home. There were too many painful memories there for her. She hadn't been back in three years and she wouldn't be going this year if it weren't necessary. Home was not a place she loved to visit. She would much rather spend Christmas the same way she had for the past three years, sitting in front of the television watching sad love stories.

After spending the night in a hotel, Jasmine felt a little better about the trip despite her misgivings. Claudia played around with the car's radio as she watched the scenery slip by. As soon as they hit the Daytona Beach city limits, Jasmine felt the melancholy settle over her once again. Despite having talked herself into this trip, she knew it was not a good idea.

"Are you okay?" Claudia questioned as she put a hand on her arm. "You don't look very happy about this."

"I'm fine," Jasmine said as she flipped on her blinker. "I just haven't been home in a while."

"Are you sure that's all it is?"

"Positive," she said reassuringly. "We're here." She turned off the road and drove up the long, winding driveway. The moment they passed the trees, her parents' home came into full view. The look of awe on her best friend's face was priceless when she saw the huge estate tucked discreetly away from prying eyes.

Jasmine hadn't been home in so long, she'd almost forgotten how breathtaking her home could be. It was a white brick two-story home with four pillars that seemed to reach to the clouds. Dark green shutters framed every window while a huge oak tree kissed the roof every time the wind blew. The grass was so carefully manicured it looked as if someone had laid a carpet down and forgotten to take it up. Hedges of all sizes covered the front lawn, not a branch disobedient.

Christmas lights and ornaments of all sizes littered the house and the front lawn. Everywhere you looked there were figurines of some kind. Jasmine shook her head. Her mother always went overboard when it came to the holidays.

Claudia whistled softly. "When you described your home to me, Jasmine, you never said you lived in a mansion," Claudia said as she got out of the car. "How many rooms does this place have?"

"Twenty-seven."

"It's beautiful, Jasmine. A far cry from the modest home I grew up in," she said as she gathered her bags from the backseat of the car. "How did you bear leaving all this behind?"

"When I left here the last thing I was thinking about was how beautiful it was. I only wanted to escape," Jasmine said softly. "Besides, if you think this is something, wait until you see the view of the beach from your room."

"Is the beach really that close?"

"The house is only about two hundred feet from the ocean," Jasmine said with a smile. "I'll have to give you the grand tour when we get settled in." She walked up to the door and rang the doorbell. Her brother, Jonathan, swung the door open.

"Her majesty has arrived at long last," he joked as he picked her up and swung her around. "How good of you to grace your family with your presence."

"Very funny," she said with a laugh as he placed her down on the floor. "It hasn't been that long since I've seen you."

"It seems like a lifetime," he said as he stepped aside to let her enter the foyer. "I can see you brought the lovely Claudia along with you."

"It's good to see you again, Jonathan," Claudia said as she extended her hand. Jonathan took her hand in his and held it for a moment. Jasmine saw something pass between the two of them, but it passed so quickly she couldn't put a finger on whatever it was.

"The pleasure is all mine," Claudia replied. Jasmine raised her eyebrows slightly. Despite their cordial greeting there was definitely something there.

"Where is everyone?" Jasmine questioned.

"The adults are in the den. All of the children have been dumped into the playroom. I'll go grab your bags and you can join everyone in the living room. Unless you think you want to join the children," he said with a snicker. Jasmine punched him lightly on the arm before she handed him the car keys. He disappeared out the front door.

"This way," Jasmine said as she inwardly braced herself to greet the rest of her family. She hadn't told Claudia the specifics about them, but she was about to see the hate they had for Jasmine firsthand. She opened the door and stepped inside.

"The princess is home," her father, Howard, said as soon as she walked in the door. He set his champagne glass down and went over to hug his daughter.

"You're embarrassing me, Daddy," she said as she hugged his neck.

"If you were still a little girl I would swing you up into my arms," he said with a huge smile. Jasmine felt better. At least her father was glad to see her. "Besides, it's been almost two years since I've seen you."

"Hello, Mother," she said softly.

"Hello, Jasmine," her mother, Roslyn, replied coolly. "How wonderful of you to grace us with your presence this year," she said before she returned to her conversation. Jasmine smiled to hide the disappointment she knew was on her face at her mother's cold welcome. Even though her mother acted the way she'd expected, she wanted so much more from her. She smiled as brightly as she could manage. She turned to Claudia.

"Let me introduce you to the rest of my family. This is my sister Charlotte and her husband Michael. This is Alexis and her husband Seth. This is my sister Nicole and her husband Sean. Everyone, this is Claudia." Her family greeted Claudia with open arms. It wasn't long before she was engrossed in a conversation with Nicole.

Jasmine took a seat on the sofa while her sisters and their husbands laughed amongst themselves. Her heart felt heavy. It was exactly what she'd expected. Three years had done nothing to change the way her family felt about her.

She took the opportunity to look around the room. Nothing had changed in the past three years. A twelve-foot Christmas tree was in the corner by the fireplace. Presents of all sizes looked as though they were about to burst from underneath it. There was tinsel and stockings for the children hung next to the mantel. Ribbons and bows were attached to every piece of furniture in the room. Jasmine smiled. Every year since she could remember her mother paid a fortune to make sure the house was decorated for the holidays. This year was no exception.

It saddened her to realize just how little had changed in the past few years.

She saw Claudia approaching and smiled. "I see you were able to get away for a minute," Jasmine said with a laugh.

"Your sister is wonderful, but she talks entirely too much," Claudia said with a wicked grin. "Care to show me the rest of the house now?"

Jasmine shot her a grateful smile. "Sure," she said and she stood up and led Claudia out of the den into the foyer. She could hear Jonathan laughing with someone as he walked in the front door. When she laid eyes on his face, Jasmine felt as if the world had stopped. She saw him staring at her in equal astonishment.

Cameron Todd had changed a lot over the years. He was now well over six feet tall with the same baby-smooth, caramel complexion. His body was so toned and muscular that even his polo shirt and khaki pants did nothing to hide his physique. His black hair was slightly waved along the top. She could see his sable-colored eyes roam over every inch of her body. Despite her heavy sweater and jeans, he made her feel naked under his gaze. She could see the dimple in his left cheek as his lips curved into a smile.

As their eyes locked, she wondered to herself what he was doing there. It had been five years since she'd laid eyes on him and suddenly it seemed like only yesterday. She tore her gaze away from him and looked at Jonathan. Her brother's eyes skipped away guiltily. In that moment she knew she had been set up.

"Jasmine," Cameron said softly.

"Cameron." She felt as if someone had thrown her into the lion's den. How could Jonathan do this to her? Despite her cool exterior, she was on an emotional roller coaster. When had the boy she knew grown into such a handsome man? It seemed like only yesterday he was a skinny boy with no muscles anywhere. Now he had a body that would put any bodybuilder's to shame. "What are you doing here?"

"Jonathan invited me to spend the holidays here."

She turned back to Jonathan. "How nice of Jonathan to inform me that you would be here." No matter how hard she tried, Jonathan refused to meet her gaze. She turned back to Cameron. "You had no right to come here."

"I thought you'd gotten over this," Jonathan intercepted. "He didn't have anywhere to go for the holidays, so I invited him here."

"You should have told me," she said as she turned and left the room. Claudia stood there with her mouth open.

"What in the world was that all about?" Claudia questioned as she looked at Cameron.

"I take it you didn't tell Jasmine I would be here?" Cameron questioned as he looked over at Jonathan.

"Do you think she would have come if she'd known?"

"Is anyone going to answer me?" Claudia questioned impatiently.

Jonathan turned to face her. "I'll explain everything to you in a minute. I have to go after Jasmine." He started in the direction Jasmine had gone when Cameron put a hand on his shoulder.

"This is my battle. I'll go after her." Jonathan nodded and stepped out of the way as Cameron headed out of the room.

Chapter Two

Cameron blinked as he walked out the back door and into the blinding sun. He already knew exactly where he would find Jasmine. She was in the one place where she'd always been able to think clearly. The pier, as everyone called it, was their place.

He walked as slowly as he possibly could. He wanted to give her a chance to calm down and think with a clear head. He didn't want her emotions to get in the way. He knew she was pissed because Jonathan had tricked her. There was no way of knowing how pissed she was until he actually talked to her. He wondered if Jasmine would say anything to him at all. He couldn't believe he'd been stupid enough to think all the hurt and pain she felt had gone anywhere. If anything, the time that passed had only caused it to manifest.

He saw Jasmine sitting on the edge of the pier. Her arms were folded around herself as the wind whipped her raven-black hair around her face. She was still as gorgeous as she'd always been The red sweater she wore only enhanced her beautiful honey-colored skin. Her hazel eyes still turned dark gray whenever she was upset about something. He approached her cautiously.

She was still petite. He guessed she was about five feet tall, if that. She looked so small and fragile as she sat there staring out at the water. She must have heard him coming because she whipped her head around and stood up to face him. The pain he saw in her eyes caused his heart to swell with grief. It hurt him to know that he was the one responsible for her pain. He was the one who'd broken her heart into a million pieces.

"Why did come here, Cameron?" she questioned softly.

"Jonathan invited me here."

She shook her head. "That's not what I meant, and you know it."

"I wanted to see you," he replied honestly.

"Why?"

"Things have to be set straight between us, Jasmine."

"I can't believe this is happening to me. Neither one of you had the right to keep this from me. You knew I would be here, and yet you came anyway. Despite that you had to know the way I felt about you. You continue to inflict pain on me after all these years."

Cameron's eyes skipped away. He couldn't bear to see the pain in her eyes. It was almost more than he could endure. "I never realized just seeing me again would cause this much pain."

"What did you think it was going to do?"

"I didn't know exactly."

"You certainly seem to be in denial about a lot of things," she said as her gaze raked over him. "How could you possibly think this wouldn't cause me pain? You married another woman, and you didn't even have the courage to tell me the truth."

"There is a lot about that situation that you don't have a clue about, Jasmine."

"Let me tell you what I think about the whole thing in a nutshell," Jasmine said as she looked him straight in the eyes. "I think you were a coward not to tell me what you had to do to save your father's company. You never told me it involved you marrying another woman, and yet you knew. You were leaving me forever, and you didn't even have the decency to tell me."

Cameron looked away. He couldn't deny that what she said was true. He'd known that he was marrying Melissa, and he'd never told her. At the time he thought it would ease her pain if she heard it from someone else.

"You're right, Jasmine. I was being a coward not to tell you. At the time I thought you were too young to understand why I was doing it. I was trying to spare your feelings."

Jasmine laughed. It was a small, bitter sound. "Spare my feelings? Do you expect me to believe that, Cameron? Learning from my parents that you were marrying Melissa was supposed to benefit me in some way?"

"I figured you would take it better, yes."

"Guess what? I didn't. It hurt me even more to realize that you didn't even think enough of me to tell me the truth. Especially when you made promises to me that you knew you would never be able to keep."

"Jasmine, I . . ." She held up her hand.

"The bottom line is that you made promises to me that you knew you couldn't keep. You told me that we were going to spend the rest of our lives together, and you ran off to Atlanta to marry someone else. How am I supposed to feel?" She turned away from him.

"I never made a promise to you that I didn't intend to keep, sweetheart. My father—"

" 'My father' this, 'my father' that," she interrupted. "Every time you make a mistake you blame your father. You can't blame him for everything that has gone wrong in your life, so stop trying. Stand up, be a man and accept when you make a mistake." Despite the flatness of her voice Cameron was impressed. Jasmine had grown up to be a strong black woman. She wasn't about to let him make excuses for any of his actions.

"I'm not making trying to make excuses, Jasmine. At that time my father was still very much in control of my life. The way your mother kept you on a tight leash, my father did the same to me."

"And you expect me to believe that the only reason you married her was because your father wanted you to marry her?" She laughed dryly. "What kind of fool do you take me for?"

"It's the honest truth. My father needed financial security for his company. He'd been going broke for years. The only way he could get the money to keep his company afloat was through Melissa's father. Her father said he would only help him if I married Melissa and took her off his hands."

"And you had to agree or it would never have happened." Her voice was soft. She turned to face him with unshed tears in her eyes. "I loved you more than anyone else in the world, Cameron. I loved you so much I gave you my virginity the night before you left. I gave you something I'd never given to anyone else, something I can never get back, only to have you run off and marry someone else. How do you think that feels?" The pain in her voice broke his heart.

"I never meant to hurt you, Jasmine. At the time I thought I was doing the right thing."

"Well you hurt me," she said as her eyes locked with his. "You betrayed me, and I don't forgive you."

He watched as she turned away from him. As he stood there staring at the back of her head, he realized that he'd hurt her deeply. Probably much deeper than he had ever realized.

"You asked me to marry you that day," she said so softly he almost didn't hear her. "I didn't understand the concept of marriage at the time but I knew it was important to you, so I agreed. Then you turned around and stepped on me."

"There is no excuse for my behavior, Jasmine. I was wrong and I know that. I feel like such a fool now when I think back. Especially when I found out the reason Melissa's father wanted me to marry her."

"Why." It wasn't a question. It was more like a statement.

"Melissa's grandfather left her a trust fund. The only way she could receive it was to be married for two years. Since she couldn't seem to find someone on her own, her father did it for her. I was a pawn in their game. As soon as she was able to collect her trust fund, she crushed me like an ant beneath her feet. She divorced me and moved to France." He was bitter. He still hadn't come to terms with what they'd done to his life.

"At least now you know how I feel," she said as she walked over to him. "You can understand my pain."

"I didn't love Melissa the way I love you."

"Maybe not, but at least you know what it feels like to have someone betray you."

"How many times do I have to say I'm sorry?"

"You can never say it enough to make me forgive you," she said as he grabbed her and gently kissed her. For a moment she was so surprised she forgot to push him away. He relished in her kiss until she pushed him away roughly. She gasped in an attempt to catch her breath. He could see fire dancing in her eyes.

He couldn't help the smile of satisfaction that washed over his face. She'd pushed him away but he could tell by her lack of composure she was as shaken by his kiss as he was by hers. Despite the bitterness she felt towards him, she still loved him. All he had to do was find a way to heal her heart and mend her broken spirit. He reached for her hand.

"Don't touch me," she said as she backed away from him. "The last time I let you touch me you ran off and married someone else. You broke my heart in two and I can never forgive you for that. Stay here and enjoy your vacation, because I'm leaving first thing in the morning," she said as she brushed past him and headed back to the house.

Cameron reached down and picked up a seashell. He threw it into the water and watched as the waves swallowed it up. Jasmine still loved him whether she would openly admit it or not. She was just in pain because he hadn't told her about his marriage to Melissa, a mistake that would haunt him for the rest of his days. It amazed him to think how strong Jasmine's love for him was.

He cursed his father a million times over for ripping him

away from Jasmine, the only woman in the world he would ever love. His life would have been so much different had he remained here with her. If only he had defied his father and married the woman he really loved.

What he told her was the whole truth. His marriage to Melissa was a sham of a marriage. It was a marriage of mere convenience for Melissa. As soon as she was able to sign her name on the dotted line for her trust fund, she couldn't divorce him fast enough. They'd been divorced for three years now.

He'd never forgotten about Jasmine. He thought about her so much in the beginning of his marriage that he often called Melissa "Jasmine." Something Melissa took personally. As hard as he tried, he could never get Jasmine out of his mind. She was burned into his soul, and she wasn't going anywhere.

"I can't believe she's still pissed with you after all these years," Jonathan said causing him to jump.

"Don't sneak up on me like that," Cameron said as he turned to face his friend. "I'm not as young as I used to be."

"If I had known she was going to act like this I never would have invited you here."

Cameron shot him a smile. "Liar," he said with a laugh. "Why *did* you invite me here, by the way?"

"I think fate dealt you two a lousy hand. You two were made for each other, and destiny cheated the two of you. I thought it was time to make things right."

Cameron shook his head as he looked out at the water. "When you asked me to come here I thought it would be simple. I would come here, Jasmine would forgive me, and we could start over again. I can see that's not going to happen." He turned to Jonathan. "I really hurt her and she's not going to forgive me that easily."

"You hurt her, but you were doing what you thought was right, Cameron. You had no other choice."

"I had a choice, but at that time I didn't know it. I didn't realize until today just how deeply I hurt her, Jonathan."

"You were a pawn in someone else's game. That's why I brought you here."

"She has every right to feel the way she does, Jonathan."

"She'll come around. She can't hold a grudge forever."

"She's held this one for five years."

"She's stubborn, Cameron. You of all people should know that."

Cameron smiled. His spirits were lifted just a little. "You're right. No one knows that better than me."

"You know her inside out. Use that knowledge to win her over," Jonathan said mischievously. "If anyone can do it you can."

"I used to think so "

"I have faith in you. All you have to do is do whatever it takes to get her to forgive you. After that the rest is child's play."

"You've really thought about this haven't you?" Cameron asked. Jonathan nodded. "There is one thing you haven't thought of."

Jonathan frowned. "What?"

"What if she decides to go home?"

Jonathan laughed. "I have it covered. All you have to do is handle your end and we'll be good to go." He paused for a brief second. "I guess I don't need to tell you that the road will be long and tedious."

Cameron shook his head. "I've lived without her for too long already because I had no other choice. I'm not going to let her slip through my fingers when she's this close to me. Whatever it takes, I'm willing to do that, and more."

Jonathan slapped him on the back. "Then you shall have her, my friend. You shall have her."

Chapter Three

Jasmine could almost feel the steam drifting up from her skin by the time she reached her bedroom. She felt as if someone had dropped her into a pot of boiling water. She'd been set up, and she didn't like it one bit. Cameron had betrayed her, and she never wanted to lay eyes on him again, much less have him in her home. She threw the stuffed animals that adorned her bed to the floor viciously.

It wasn't the fact that he was there that upset her so badly. It was the fact that he was still able to evoke such strong feelings in her after all these years. Just when she thought she was over him, she discovered that she wasn't. Time had done nothing to lessen the passion she felt for him; it only succeeded in intensifying it.

She shouldn't love him so much. She'd given herself to him heart and soul only to have him run off and marry someone else. She should hate him but she didn't. It wasn't fair that he was back after all these years disrupting her life again. She turned around when she heard a soft knock on her door.

"Who is it?" she snapped. In the back of her mind she hoped it was Jonathan. She wanted to give him a piece of her mind.

"It's Claudia. Open up." Jasmine opened the door and let her in. "What's going on?" Claudia questioned as she walked over and sat down on the edge of the bed.

"I guess I could pretend not to know what you were talking about, but that isn't my style," Jasmine replied as she paced the floor.

"All I surmised was that Cameron is the enemy in some way." Jasmine threw her a weary smile.

"Whatever gave you that idea?"

"You saw him and ran like a bat out of you-know-where out of the room. I would have to be blind not to see the tension there."

"There's nothing I can tell you that would make you understand what having him here means to me," Jasmine murmured as she walked over to her bedroom window. She could see Jonathan and Cameron talking to each other out on the pier. If there was even a smidgen of doubt that those two were plotting against her, it was gone in that instant. They'd planned the whole thing.

"What did Cameron do to you that was so bad, Jasmine?"

"Let me give you the abbreviated version of the story. Cameron and I were childhood sweethearts. We spent all of our time together. One morning right before my seventeenth birthday, Cameron told me to meet him at the pier. I met him there and he told me that he was moving away. His father's company was in trouble and he was the only one who could save it. What he neglected to tell me was that he was marrying someone else to do it."

Claudia gasped. "Who did he marry?"

"The daughter of the man who could save his father's business."

Claudia's mouth dropped open. "You can't be serious, Jasmine."

Jasmine nodded. "As serious as a heart attack."

"I'm so sorry."

Jasmine put up her hand. "Don't be. It's over and done with now no matter how much I hoped it was all a bad dream."

"Do you think you'll ever forgive him?"

Jasmine paused for a moment before she spoke. "I don't know if I could or not," Jasmine said as she turned away from the window. "So much has changed in the past few years. I thought I was finally over him, but one look at his face and I knew I wasn't. All the hurt and pain I've tried to bury resurfaced."

"That's understandable."

"He only told me about it a week before he married her. I gave up my virginity to him the day before he left. I wanted him to always remember me. I loved him so much, and I knew I was ready. I wanted him to be my first and only. Imagine the pain I was in when I found out he was marrying Melissa Douglas two days later." Claudia remained quiet.

"Do you believe he loved her?"

"I don't know if I believe that or not, Claudia. All I can say is that he knew what was going to happen before he left and he never told me. I find that suspect."

"Maybe he was afraid you wouldn't understand why he had to do it."

"I would rather have heard it from him and not from my mother. Then, to make a bad situation worse, my parents took me to the wedding! Can you imagine what it felt like to watch the man you love say vows to another woman?"

Claudia shook her head. "That's deep, Jasmine," she said softly. "What are you going to do now?"

"I'm heading out first thing in the morning."

"Why are you going to cut your vacation short?"

"I'm not," she said as she ran her fingers through her hair. "I'm just not going to stay under the same roof as Cameron Todd."

"So you're going to be the coward Cameron was."

Jasmine stopped in her tracks. "What are you talking about?"

"If you leave things like they are you're being the same coward he was all those years ago. I know that's the last thing you want."

"So what are you suggesting?"

"That you stay here and finish things with him once and

for all. Let Cameron know just because he plotted against you he hasn't won."

"You think they plotted against me too?"

"There's absolutely no doubt in my mind," Claudia said with a laugh. "Jonathan and Cameron planned this whole sad episode. Think about it. Jonathan persuaded you to come here conveniently forgetting to tell you Cameron would be here. You were set up, Jasmine."

"Why in the world would Jonathan do this to me?" Her anger resurfaced quickly. "He was the only one who really knew why I was coming home this year. Why would he do this to me?"

Claudia threw her a questioning glance. "Does this have anything to do with Rafael?"

"This has everything to do with Rafael."

Understanding caused Claudia's eyes to light up. "You don't mean that . . ." She didn't finish her sentence. Jasmine nodded.

"Can't you see it now that you've seen Cameron?"

"There was so much commotion it didn't even register."

"That's why I don't understand how Jonathan could do this."

"He knows you still love Cameron."

Jasmine stopped to stare at her. "Is it that obvious?"

"As the nose on your face. You haven't had a chance to get over him. You still love him, but there's so much pain there you'll never admit it."

"And if I leave I'll be a coward in the lowest sense."

"Exactly," Claudia said with a smile. "This is your final opportunity to get over Cameron and move on with your life. It's time to let go of all the hurt and pain you feel. Do whatever you have to do to get over him and put this whole situation to rest."

"Do you really think I can do this?" Her smile was hopeful.

"You can do anything you set your mind to. You've come this far haven't you?"

"You're right," Jasmine said with the first genuine smile since she'd walked in the front door. "I can finally get on with my life and stop living in the past." She linked her arm through Claudia's.

"Well you were right about one thing, Jasmine."

Jasmine raised a perfectly arched eyebrow. "What was that?"

"This will be a vacation neither one of us will ever forget."

Chapter Four

Cameron and Jonathan returned to the house to find everyone seated at the dining room table. At the sight of Jasmine in her short, red dress, Cameron felt his heart leap in his chest. His feelings for her were still as strong as they had been five years before. Time had done nothing to dampen the intense passion he felt whenever he looked at her.

"It's about time the two of you joined us," Roslyn chastised lightly. "I thought I was going to have to send the patrol after you."

"We got caught up in the memories of yesteryear," Cameron replied as Jonathan took a seat in his usual position. He nearly froze when he realized the only seat left in the room was beside Jasmine.

He walked over as slowly as he possibly could. As he sat down he shot a look of surprise at Jasmine. She didn't even look up at him. He'd expected her to throw a fit because he was sitting next to her. It was unusual for her not to make her opinion known. In light of the fact that she'd lashed out at him earlier, he expected something.

For the first time since his arrival, Cameron was unsure of something. Up until this moment everything had happened pretty much the way he'd anticipated. Now she was throwing him off and he was unsure of what to do next. He realized for the first time that she was different now. He had no clue of what she was thinking any more. It scared him.

"It's quite all right," Roslyn assured Cameron with a smile. "We'll say our grace before we begin eating all of this wonderful food."

"Heavenly Father we thank you for this food you have placed before us. We thank you for bringing us all home again. We thank you for the many blessings you have bestowed upon us. Amen." Howard's voice boomed through the huge house.

"Amen," everyone around the table murmured. Cameron remained quiet as everyone passed food around the table. Casual conversation emerged as dishes of food were passed and people began eating. Jasmine passed food his way without so much as a glance.

"Cameron, how is your job coming along?" Roslyn queried as she began eating.

"It's coming along fine, Roslyn."

"We heard about your promotion to partner in your law firm. Am I correct in saying that was quite an accomplishment?"

"You would be," he said with a smile. "There were several other lawyers with many more years of experience ahead of me. I was honored they chose me."

"I'm sure it was an honor that was well deserved." She smiled. "How are your parents?"

"They're doing quite well. In fact they went to Paris this year."

"That's somewhere we haven't been in a while, Howard," she complained. "You know how much I love to shop there."

"We'll have to do it soon, then." Howard remarked.

Roslyn smiled and turned back to Cameron. "I was very sorry to hear about your breakup with Melissa."

Cameron nearly choked on the water he was drinking. He coughed loudly as he shot a look at Jasmine. Her face remained as calm as if she hadn't heard a word her mother said.

"I wasn't surprised our relationship didn't last. It was doomed from the very start because I never loved her, and she definitely didn't love me. Melissa was the type of woman who was only capable of loving herself."

"Why did you marry a woman you didn't love?" Claudia blurted out. Cameron saw the corners of Jasmine's mouth curl slightly.

"It had nothing to do with the two of us, in a sense. It was all a business arrangement between my father and hers. My father wanted to save his company, her father wanted her to get her trust fund. In the end it worked out for both of them. As for Melissa and I, our lives will never be the same." There was an uncomfortable silence that followed his revelation. Roslyn broke it with a nervous laugh.

"That's enough talk about the past," she said quickly. She turned to Jasmine. "Jasmine, are you still bringing Rafael here for Christmas?"

"He'll be here."

"The last time I saw him he was a baby in a blanket."

"He's grown a lot since then."

"Who is Rafael?" Cameron questioned curiously.

"Trevor's little brother," Roslyn supplied.

"I thought Trevor was an only child."

"When you left he was. Marvalette gave birth to him about eight months after you left for Atlanta. Rafael is four years old. I imagine he's a great joy to her, although for the life of me I can't understand why Marvalette would want another child when she's so up in age."

"You have nothing to do with that," Howard said sharply. "She's a grown woman. I'm sure she knew what she was doing."

"You're right," she said quickly. She laughed to cover her embarrassment.

"Rafael is a wonderful little boy. I go to visit him often. I think he bears a lot of watching. He's going to be a heartbreaker when he grows up," Jonathan offered.

"Just like his father," Jasmine said softly. Cameron saw a look pass between Jasmine and Jonathan, but it passed so quickly he couldn't distinguish what is was.

"How are your roses, Roslyn?" Cameron questioned hoping to get everyone's mind on something else.

"Actually, they're doing extremely well this year," she replied as she launched into an animated conversation about her favorite topic.

Jasmine listened to the conversations floating around her with disinterest. She was too aware of Cameron sitting next to her to contribute to any of them. She could kick herself for feeling the way she felt about him. Out of all the people in the world, why did he have to be the one that held her heartstrings. Even after all of the anger and betrayal, she felt all he had to do was smile at her and her heart would start to pound and her knees grow weak.

What was it about him that caused her to react the way she did? She asked herself for the millionth time. It had nothing to do with the fact that he was drop-dead gorgeous or that he looked good enough to eat. This was the man who broke her heart into a million pieces. This was the man who betrayed her in the worst possible way. There were so many things between them that needed to be settled, and yet they probably never would be. There so many things she wanted to tell him but how could she in light of the current situation?

How in the world was she supposed to survive being in the same house with him for the next two weeks? Emotions were high, and she was no fool to the concept that emotions could screw you over every time. She knew for a fact she hadn't gained enough control over her emotions. Her reaction to him earlier had proved that theory to be null and void.

"How is your business coming along, Jasmine?" Cameron queried softly. She turned to face him. He was testing her and she knew it. Since she was ignoring him, he was going to call her hand. He wanted an outburst from her, and she wasn't about to give him what he wanted. She smiled inwardly as she turned to face him.

"To be honest with you, my business is doing much better than I anticipated it would when I took it over. All it really needed was a different approach to management and a few fresh ideas. Once I smoothed over the rough edges, it's been smooth sailing since then."

"You've increased your client base well into the hundreds. You're being too modest, Jasmine. Considering what you had to work with when you took over, you've done an excellent job. Advertising is a hard business."

"I see you've done your homework," she said as her eyes locked with his. "Many of the clients headed for the hills when Nicholas took sick. Since most used him for daily jobs I can understand their reasoning. Quite a few of his clients hung in there to see where things were going. They were greatly rewarded for their loyalty."

"I can admire your persistence and determination. Like you, I have set certain goals and I don't plan to stop until I reach them." Jasmine caught the double meaning and glared at him. It took everything in her not to slap the smile off his face. He was sending her a message that he was determined to get her back, and, like her, he wasn't going to give up without a fight.

"Thank you," she said as she took a sip of her drink.

"Jasmine stepped up to the plate and accepted the challenge. I'm so proud of her," Howard said with a broad smile. "Not everyone has the ability to do what she did."

"I agree completely," Cameron said with a smile. Jasmine smiled along with them even though she was far from feeling at ease.

Cameron was too close to her. His very presence closed in around her and smothered any other thoughts she may have had. As hard as she tried to fight it, just sitting next to him caused a heat to stir in her stomach that hadn't been there since they parted five years ago. She felt the passion flowing through her veins as if it were only yesterday when they'd made love. In an odd way she wished that it were.

She managed to make it through dinner without any further verbal confrontations with Cameron. After dessert, her mother suggested everyone continue their conversations in the living room, but Jasmine had other plans.

"I'm going to take a quiet walk on the beach. It's been so long since I've been home." She was baiting Cameron. She knew he wouldn't miss an opportunity to come after her again. She had to get some things out into the open and try to call a truce. It was the only way she would be able to get through the next few days without losing her sanity.

"Is anyone else planning to do anything else special?" Her mother asked.

"I think I'll just go up and try to catch up on some sleep," Cameron replied. "It's been a long day." He shot a look at Jasmine. She tried her best to keep from smiling. He was lying and she knew it. Her plan worked. As soon as he was sure everyone else was out of sight, he was going to make a beeline for her.

"I thought I would show Claudia around the house,"

Jonathan offered. "That is if she doesn't have any objections."

"Of course not," she said as she turned her gaze to him. "That is if Jasmine doesn't mind." Jasmine shook her head. She'd caught the look between the two them and this time it didn't escape her. She wondered just how long **it** had been going on. It was surprising to her that Jonathan was the one who'd finally gotten Claudia to settle down. That explained all of her nights at home. Jasmine couldn't resist a smile. The two of them were good for one another.

"I'm heading out then," Jasmine said as she got up and left the room.

"I guess it's up to the rest of us," Howard said as he waved his hand to Jasmine's sisters and their husbands. "We'll have a cozy night by the fireplace and catch up on everything that's been going on."

"Are you sure you won't join us, Cameron?" Roslyn questioned again. He shook his head.

"I have a couple of cases that I should look over tonight. And I really do need to get some sleep."

"Very well then," she said as everyone got up and left the room.

Cameron remained at the dining room table until he was sure everyone had gone off in their own directions before he got up and walked out the back door. He had to find Jasmine and talk to her again. No matter what the cost he had to make her understand that what happened between them was not his fault.

He walked slowly down the beach. He let himself become absorbed in the memories of the past. He remembered the first time he looked at Jasmine and really saw the young woman she had become instead of his best friend's bratty little sister. He still remembered the first time he realized he wanted to make love to her. It was the day she told him she could outswim him.

It was about one hundred degrees in the shade that day. The only thing he wanted to do was stay in the cabana under the air conditioning when Jasmine walked through the door.

"Are you going to stay in here all day?" she questioned, her hands on her hips.

"I'd planned on it."

"Coward. You just don't want to be out in the sun."

"You're right, I don't."

"How about a race then?"

"Are you crazy? It's a hundred degrees outside."

She shook her head with a laugh. "I meant swimming, you idiot."

"Swimming?"

"Yes. I bet that I can beat you to the pier."

"Yeah, right," he said with a laugh. "I can beat you with my hands behind my back."

"Wanna bet?" The mischief was evident in her voice.

"I'll bet you ten dollars." He stuck out his hand. She shook it.

"You're on. There is no way you can beat me," she said as she stripped off her T-shirt to reveal a black two-piece bikini he knew her mother had no idea she owned.

"What makes you think that?" he questioned as he turned his head away from her. "I'm much bigger than you."

"That doesn't mean you're quicker," she said with a mis-chievous glint in her eyes. "Let's find out."

"Fine," he said as he took off his shirt and followed her out of the cabana. He followed her down to the edge of the water and went in up to his waist.

"Ready, get set, go," she said as she dived into the water and began swimming away. Cameron followed behind her.

She climbed up the ladder to the pier a full thirty seconds before he did. He could only shake his head and laugh. "You've been practicing."

She shrugged. "You didn't ask if I had before we started so don't think I'm going to let you out of the bet."

"I wouldn't dream of it." He forked over a soggy ten-dollar bill. She smiled. "Now that we've come all this way what are we supposed to do?"

"We lie out in the sun to dry off." She lay down on the wooden planks and closed her eyes.

Cameron felt every nerve in his body grow hard as he stared down at her. She was only fifteen, but Jasmine was gorgeous. Her raven-black hair was damp from the water and her skin glistened with droplets of water. Her breasts moved gently as she breathed in and out. She had curves in all the right places. In that moment he saw her as the young woman she was becoming instead of as Jonathan's younger sister.

It was in that instant that he realized he wanted to make love to her. That during all the teasing and kidding around he was in love with Jasmine. Her age didn't matter to him. He was head over heels in love with her and he wanted her. He shook his head to clear his thoughts. What was he thinking?

Jasmine opened her eyes to stare up at him. He could see the questions there but she didn't speak. She merely looked at him as if she, too, was seeing him for the first time. As she stood up and his gaze locked with hers, he knew their relationship would never be the same. She laughed nervously.

"I think it's time to go," she said softly. She didn't wait for his reply. She dived into the water and headed home. Cameron was left standing there with his mouth open.

He would give everything he had to go back to those days. The days when they were just discovering how much they loved one another. The days when they belonged to one another and nothing and no one could change it. He quickened his pace. The memories were just too painful for him now that she wasn't in his life.

He could see her silhouette as he approached the pier. He walked over to her and sat down beside her. He stared out at the horizon. He'd expected her to complain and leave but she remained quiet. She didn't even acknowledge his presence. He could feel the disappointment well up in his throat the longer she sat there in silence. He was thinking of something to say when she finally spoke.

"I really think that we should call a truce." Cameron snapped his head around in surprise. Was she serious? "Don't look at me like that. I just think that since we have to be here with each other for this vacation we may as well get used to the idea and try to be civil."

"It wasn't what you said, Jasmine. I'm just surprised that you want to call a truce with me after what happened earlier."

She took a deep breath. "After thinking about it, this is the only way. I really don't have much choice in the matter. And I really want to apologize for the way I acted earlier," she said as she turned to face him. "Seeing you caused all the anger and hurt I felt rise to the surface. It was immature and childish, and it won't happen again."

His eyes widened in surprise. Jasmine had grown up even more than he'd given her credit for. The Jasmine he'd left behind would never have apologized for anything she felt was justified. It was just another startling revelation about how much she had changed.

"I can understand that it was a shock to see me after all this time, Jasmine. You don't have to apologize for that."

"I want to apologize because I was wrong. I should have known better than to speak with my emotions and not my brain. It won't ever happen again." Cameron was even more puzzled by her sudden change in attitude toward him. Her anger made sense. This made no sense at all and he was completely baffled. Had he missed something between then and now?

"I want you to know I truly am sorry for everything that's happened," he said softly. Jasmine remained quiet for a moment before she spoke.

"Why are you sorry?" ·

"I hurt you, for one thing. I never realized how much until tonight. At that time in my life I thought I had no control over the situation, but I was wrong. It was my life and I had every right to refuse what I was told to do."

She turned to face him. "At the time I didn't understand. Now I think I do. Your whole family was dependent on you. You had to do whatever it took to protect your mother and sisters. You had every right to do what you did, but you went about it in the wrong way."

His heart skipped a beat. "What do you mean?"

"If you'd told me the truth I would have been able to forgive you. You left me in the dark, and that hurt the most," she paused. "I needed you, Cameron. I'd always been able to depend on you for anything and you were always there. The time when I needed you the most you disappeared. I resented Melissa because she had you and you belonged to me." There was pain in her voice. His heart felt heavy. It was because of him that she'd suffered such unbearable pain.

She still loved him. It was as plain as the nose on her face. She even understood his reasons for doing what he did. If he had handled the situation better it would have made things so much easier on everyone involved. His heart swelled up when he realized just how much he loved her. No amount of time and space had been able to erase her from his heart. Maybe she felt the same way. That thought gave him the hope he'd fought so hard to cling to. Maybe they could make it after all.

"I know now that I handled the entire situation wrong, Jasmine. I just didn't know how to make you see that marrying Melissa was the right thing at the time. I loved you too much to tell you, so I didn't say a thing about it before I left. That was dead wrong. I should have gone to you and did whatever it took to make you understand."

"All I've ever asked of you was for you to be truthful with me, Cameron. I would rather have heard it from you than from my mother, who couldn't wait to rub it in my face." Cameron hung his head down. He could only imagine what that must have done to her.

"Life would have been so much easier for both of us had I only been willing to tell you everything." He watched her expression closely. "You don't know how many nights I've lain awake thinking about you and the way I left things. I prayed so many nights that I could go back and undo the damage I'd done, but I never got my wish. I would change everything if I could, but I can't. That's something I'm not happy with, but I have learned to accept my limitations."

"As have I."

Cameron paused for a moment. "Why did you marry Trevor?"

There was a small smile on her face. "I know you think I married him to get back at you, but you're wrong. I did love my husband."

"Did you?" He didn't try to hide the sadness in his voice. He didn't want to think that another man had touched her intimately. It was almost too much for him to bear.

"Trevor was there for me when I needed him the most. For that I was always grateful. I'll always love him for that."

"Do you miss him?"

She nodded. "Every day."

"I guess a lot really has happened in our lives since we last saw one another."

"Both good and bad," she agreed. That was one thing he couldn't argue with. His life had been filled with a lot of ups and downs since the last time he'd seen her.

"There were more bad times than good on my end, but I think my luck is about to change." He couldn't tell her that his bad days were filled with his regrets of losing her. He would give anything he had in the world to get back what he'd lost, but he knew that he had to bide his time. He couldn't rush her into anything. He had to regain her trust in him before he could ever hope for her forgiveness. If only he had a time machine he would go back and undo the damage.

"I'd better head back to the house," Jasmine said as she stood up. "It's getting late." Cameron nodded as he glanced down at his watch. He was surprised to see that almost two hours had gone by since he sat down.

"I didn't even realize it was that late." Involuntarily he looked over at her bare arm where the gold watch he'd given her all those years ago had always been. He wondered when and why she'd taken it off. It made him wonder even more about her personality now. What had given her such a big change of heart? Was she really sorry that she'd blown up at him earlier or was it something else that made her want to call a truce?

As he watched the wind whipping her hair around her face, he no longer cared what her reasons were. She was talking to him now and that was all that really mattered to him. It was a major accomplishment in his book.

"I'm going back," she said as she started down the stairs. Cameron watched her disappear behind the dunes. He wanted nothing more than to make her understand she was the only one he had ever wanted in his life—then and now. He wanted to take her in his arms and erase any doubt she ever had in her mind about him. He wanted her to know she was the one who held the key to his heart.

"It's going to take patience," he scolded himself quietly. It would take time and infinite patience to undo five years of pain. He couldn't just walk back into Jasmine's life and expect her to welcome him with open arms as if nothing had ever happened between them. Time and distance had changed them both in ways they could never have imagined. If he rushed her now he could risk losing her forever. The thought of losing her wasn't a thought he wanted to entertain, but he had to consider the possibility. What if it really was too late for them?

He looked out at the moon that seemed to be smiling down on him. It wasn't too late, he said to himself. It couldn't be too late. If it meant he had to fight for her the rest of his life, then so be it: fight he would. He'd always been told you had to be willing to fight for whatever you wanted, and Jasmine was worth the fight. Jasmine Hayden was going to be his again if it was the last thing he did.

Chapter Five

Claudia glanced over at the clock on the nightstand as she paced the floor. It was almost two o'clock in the morning. What in the world was taking him so long? Moments later, she heard a soft knock on the door. She opened it quickly and beckoned him inside. She closed the door behind him.

She met him at a time in her life when she didn't think she'd be able to trust another man. A string of bad relationships had dampened any hope she'd ever had of finding someone of her own to love. Of finding the one man out there that wasn't afraid of commitment, a man who wouldn't make promises he couldn't keep.

Claudia thought she was a party animal, but she was just the opposite. Going to the clubs was her way of avoiding the silence and loneliness she found at home. Then he'd walked in the door and her life changed forever.

They'd been seeing each other for a year and a half. Since the moment they laid eyes on one another, they were destined to become lovers. Claudia loved everything about him, from his stocky, muscular physique, to his devilish sense of humor. She loved him more than life itself. If only they were able to take their relationship public, it would be perfect for her.

"I was beginning to think you weren't coming," Claudia said as she wrapped her arms around his neck. He kissed her gently.

"Wild horses couldn't keep me away from you," Jonathan said as he folded her into his arms. "I just wanted to make sure everyone was asleep before I came."

"No one saw you, did they?" The concern in her voice caused him to smile.

"No one saw a thing." Her sigh of relief was audible. "I don't really care if they did, though. Our relationship will become public very soon."

"What in the world are we doing sneaking around?" she questioned as she looked up into his chocolate eyes.

"We're both consenting adults," he said softly. "I just don't want my family in my business."

"Do you think anyone suspects anything?"

Jonathan shook his head. "Maybe Jasmine, but I've never tried to really hide it from her. I love you and I don't care who knows it."

"What will everyone say when they find out? You're still a married man."

"A soon-to-be-divorced married man."

"When is the divorce going to be final?"

"I hope in three weeks."

Claudia looked up at him. "Is she still contesting?"

"She was trying, but I don't think she'll be very successful. I can't believe this has taken almost two and a half years to straighten out."

"I can't believe that she doesn't want to let you go." She smiled. "I don't really think I can blame her."

"If she hadn't cheated on me we still would have been together. That was the one thing I couldn't accept."

"Am I glad she messed up. I never would have known what a wonderful person you are if she hadn't," she said as Jonathan kissed her forehead gently. "Do you think we did the right thing?"

"What are you talking about?" He twirled a piece of hair around his finger.

"I'm talking about placing Cameron and Jasmine under the same roof."

"Do you have doubts?"

"Of course I have doubts. Did you see the look on her face when she discovered he was going to be staying here? My heart really went out to her."

"We did the right thing," he said as he massaged her shoulders. "Jasmine still loves him, but she's too stubborn to admit that."

Claudia remained silent for a moment. "I know that she still loves him, Jonathan, but you also have to take into consideration that there is a lot of bad blood between them," Claudia said softly. "She feels that he abandoned her when she needed him the most. Now that I know the whole situation, I can see why she feels that way. It wasn't an easy thing to accept."

"That's true," he said softly. "The way I see it is either way they get a resolution. Either Jasmine stops being stubborn and admits that she still loves him, or she finally gets a chance to close that chapter in her life. I vote for falling in love."

"I hope you're right about this."

"I know I am. I know the two of them better than anyone else does. This will work."

"Will it?"

"They have to have some type of relationship. What's going to happen when she brings Rafael here? I would rather she get this thing settled with Cameron first. Marvalette is not going to be around that much longer."

"The resemblance between Rafael and his father is remarkable. I just wish that this whole thing wasn't so painful for her. Jasmine is a wonderful friend."

Jonathan smiled. "That's what I love about you. You're always considerate of other people."

She looked into his eyes. "If not for her I never would have met you."

"Don't worry so much about Jasmine. She will be fine and so will we," he said. Claudia kissed his shoulder gently. "I don't know how much more of this torture I can take."

"I have no idea what you're talking about," Claudia said innocently.

"I want to know why we're standing here discussing Jasmine and Cameron," Jonathan said as he scooped her up and took her over to the bed. "You're the only one I want to talk about now."

Claudia stuck out her lip. "I was hoping you were going to do more than talk about me."

"Your wish is my command, sweetheart."

"Oh really?" she purred as he ran his fingers through her hair.

"Really."

"Now that's something I can definitely live with." She reached over and turned out the light.

Chapter Six

Jasmine awoke early, before sunrise the next morning. Even though she'd had a full night's sleep, she felt as if she hadn't slept at all. All night she'd been plagued by thoughts of Cameron and the memories he conjured up. Why couldn't he have stayed away from her? For five years she'd been able to press him into the back of her mind, because she didn't have to see him on a daily basis. Now that he'd popped back into her life without any warning at all, the memories of the way they used to be refused to remain dormant.

After he moved away, it was hard not to think of him at first, but she knew she had to forget about him. For years she'd tried to bury him with the unwanted memories of her past, but every now and then he would creep back into her thoughts. Now it was like a giant wave engulfing her. She had no control over anything anymore. She hated the vulnerability she felt whenever she thought of him.

Claudia was right. She needed to finish things with him once and for all so she could move on with her life. It wasn't helping her to keep everything bottled up inside, it was only delaying the inevitable. She had to do this now. She had to release the anger she felt.

She pushed memories of Cameron as far away from her mind as she could as she headed to the bathroom to take a shower. As she let the hot water wash over her skin, she could feel her tension slipping away. Everything looked better now that it was morning.

She finished her shower, wrapped a towel around her body and headed back into her bedroom. She paused at the mirror to brush her hair before she dressed. She was brushing her hair in the mirror when she saw it. She spun around quickly. On her nightstand next to the bed was a beautiful red-and-gold Chinese vase filled with white roses, her favorite flowers. She immediately turned to the bedroom door. It was still locked. Jasmine couldn't contain the smile that erupted. She didn't know how he'd done it but somehow he had.

She walked over and picked up a rose. It was still wet from the morning dew as she put it up to her nose. As she breathed in the soft fragrance, her thoughts drifted to Cameron. He was willing to go to any lengths to get her to forgive him.

She opened the doors leading to the terrace. The tiles were cool beneath her feet as she stepped outside. In the distance she could faintly see Cameron sitting on the pier. She knew what he was waiting for. He was waiting for her.

God, how she wished things were different. She wished she could forgive him and hand her heart over to him on a silver platter. For a moment she even wished that nothing had changed between them. Her heart felt heavy when she realized that everything had changed. They were two different people now. No matter how much she wished or how hard she tried, nothing would ever be the way it was.

She stepped back inside. She'd picked out a pair of jeans and a T-shirt to put on, but she decided against it. Instead she dressed in a blue-and-white sundress and white sandals. She brushed her hair back into a chignon and put on lipstick.

She looked out the window. The sun was going to rise soon. The sky had the murky, black look it always had before the sun brightened the horizon. She smiled as she headed out the door.

As she took the stairs two at a time, she reminded herself that her parents couldn't ground her anymore for sneaking out to watch the sun rise. She was a grown woman now. She could do whatever she wanted to do. She laughed softly as memories of being grounded for sneaking out crept into her mind. It amazed her how being home could bring back the smallest of memories.

Once outside she quickened her pace. She had to hurry or she would miss it. She walked as quickly as the soft, wet sand would allow her.

As she approached the pier, she could see Cameron sitting there staring out at the water. Even though her impulse was telling her to run away from him, she ignored it. How was she ever going to get through this if she just avoided him?

"I thought you weren't coming." She almost jumped out of her skin. His voice startled her as it cut through the mist. She smiled softly as she went over to sit down beside him.

"How did you know I was going to come?"

He smiled at her. "I just happen to know that you love sunrises more than anything else in the world." She didn't say a word, she just smiled. Cameron knew her a lot better than she would ever admit. She watched as the sky turned a dusty blue color.

When it came to things in the past, Cameron knew just about everything there was to know about her. They'd shared everything together. She still couldn't explain how her feelings for him changed, but they did. The moment when she'd stopped viewing him as Jonathan's friend who teased her and took her dolls and saw him as someone she was deeply in love with it had taken her by surprise. It was like she woke up one day and her feelings for him had changed.

"Did you love Melissa?" she questioned softly. Even though it was the last thing she should want to hear, she had to know. He shook his head.

"She couldn't hold a candle to you," he replied. "Melissa was a spoiled brat who was used to having everything handed to her on a silver platter. There was no time for anyone else. Melissa was all Melissa needed to make her happy."

"Was your life miserable?"

"Yes. Our marriage never even got off the ground. We went through the motions, but for the most part she remained in Paris with her father and I remained in Atlanta." He turned to face her. "I missed you so much in the beginning. I'd lost the love of my life and my best friend all in the same breath."

"I felt the same way, Cameron. You were my best friend and my lover. We'd spent our entire lives together. I wasn't afraid of what you thought because you'd teased me my whole life."

Cameron laughed. "I saw you through every new pimple, every new hairstyle. I've even seen you naked," he said as his eyes locked with hers. They were only inches away from one another. All he had to do was lean forward just a little more.

She laughed nervously. "You were the first one besides my parents."

"I know," he said softly as he reached out and touched her face. Jasmine closed her eyes at the moment of contact. It felt so good to have him touch her again. She never wanted that feeling to end. She felt as if she'd traveled back through time. "I was the first one to make love to you," he whispered as his warm breath caressed her face. She shuddered involuntarily.

Why did he have such a strong effect on her? He had the ability to make her heart melt just by looking at her. She felt the heat start in her stomach. She wanted him so bad she could almost taste him. The passion between them was still there. She was attracted to him like a magnet.

Cameron stared at her for a moment before he pulled her into his arms and kissed her. All thoughts of the past were pushed out of her mind the moment his lips met hers. Nothing else in the world mattered except her and him. This was where she belonged.

Jasmine forced herself to pull away from him. She could tell from his deep breaths that he'd been as affected by the kiss as she had. No matter what happened, she couldn't allow herself to fall in love with him all over again. She had to keep her distance or she would never be able to get over him. She didn't miss the look of disappointment in his eyes as she turned away.

"I can't do this, Cameron."

"Do what?"

"Pretend that nothing has happened between us."

"Neither can I," he said as he turned her head to him. "I know you feel it as much as I do. You're angry with me because I betrayed you, but you still love me. If you didn't you wouldn't be here right now."

"What do you want from me?" she questioned softly.

"I want you to give us another chance, Jasmine. I want you to be able to forgive me. I want another chance to have what was taken away from us. I want you in my life." She looked into his eyes. He was sincere. He really wanted her back in his life. She turned her head.

"I can't," she said softly as she stood up. "I think for a moment I can, and then I remember what happened and it makes me angry all over again. I can't sit here and pretend that I can trust you. What if Melissa comes back tomorrow? What will happen then? I can't pretend nothing happened, because something did," she said as she turned and walked away from him.

"Strike two," he murmured to himself as she walked away.

Claudia rolled over and peeped at the clock. It was seven o'clock in the morning. She stretched and sat up. It was then that she realized Jonathan was still in her bed. He'd never left her room. Panic sank in as she gently shook him awake.

"Umm," he moaned as he opened one eye.

"Would you wake up already?" she questioned with a laugh.

"What do you want so early in the morning?"

"Have you forgotten where you are?"

Jonathan sat straight up. "You mean I didn't . . ." He let his voice trail off.

"That's right, you didn't." He fell back on the bed with his eyes closed. Claudia couldn't resist the giggle that escaped. He opened his eyes and peered up at her.

"And just what is so funny?"

"You."

"What did I do?"

"You're the one who's always telling me that you don't need an alarm clock, and I always end up waking you up."

"Ugh," he moaned as he put a hand on his head. "I can't believe you let me do this."

"I let you do it?" she questioned as she put her hand to her chest. "I have no idea what you're talking about."

"I'd better get out of here before the rest of my family wakes up." Footsteps on the other side of the door told him someone was already up. Claudia hid a smile.

"To make a bad situation worse."

"You're telling me," he said as he stood up. "I guess I may as well take a shower in here since I can't very well go out there with no clothes on."

"I should say so," she said as he headed into the bathroom. She heard him turn on the shower. She laid her head down on the pillow.

This was the way their lives had gone for the past year. After a night of lovemaking she would wake him up so he could go to work, and she would get up to fix breakfast. The only thing different this morning was that someone else was cooking. As the smell of bacon drifted under the door, she felt her stomach growling.

She went over to her suitcase and pulled out the black velvet box. She opened it up to look at the two-carat ring inside. He'd asked her to marry him as soon as his divorce was final. She smiled. It was hard keeping it a secret from Jasmine. She wanted to shout it from the rooftop, but she knew she had to be patient. It was only a matter of time before she married the man she loved.

"Claudia, could you come wash my back for me?"

"Sure," she said with a devilish grin as she put the box back in her suitcase and headed to the bathroom. Washing his back was the last thing on her mind.

Cameron sat on the pier watching the waves toss and turn. It was like watching his soul. He was torn up inside and it was no one's fault but his own. What in the world was he doing? The last thing he needed to be doing was rushing things between them. It was unbelievable to him that he'd done something so stupid.

He cursed himself for being so weak. The sight of her sitting there, looking so vulnerable, had gotten to him. He'd allowed himself to get caught up in the moment. He spun around when he heard footsteps behind him. He was surprised to see Howard approaching him. He started to get up when Howard put out a hand.

"Sit." Cameron sat back down. "I was hoping I would find you here," Howard said.

"You were?"

"Yes. I came out here for two reasons," he said when he reached him. "One was to tell you that breakfast is ready. Two was that I wanted to talk to you about Jasmine."

Cameron's eyes widened in surprise. Howard had never said more than two words to him on any given occasion. He wondered what was up.

"What about Jasmine?"

"I know that you came here hoping to win her over."
Cameron nodded. Howard continued, "I just thought I would
give you a heads-up."

"You mean you're going to help me?" The shock was evident in his face and in his voice.

Howard smiled. "I know you might think this is strange,
but I do like you, Cameron. I've always liked you because I
knew you truly loved my daughter."

"I never knew that."

"My wife has always been dead set against you, not me. It
hurt me to my heart when your father forced you to marry
Melissa, because I knew what it would do to you and
Jasmine. I even offered to help your father out of the mess he
was in so you could remain here, but he refused." Cameron
was dumbfounded. He had no idea Howard had done something like that.

"I wonder why he refused."

"Whatever his reasons, he didn't share them with me. His
mind was obviously made up about what he was going to
do."

"He never said a word to me about this."

"I'm not surprised he didn't." Cameron looked away so
Howard wouldn't see the anger in his eyes. What made his
father do what he did? Why did he lie to him about the
choices he had to save the company? Why?

"You would do all of that for Jasmine?" Cameron asked.

Howard nodded. "By now I'm sure you've already
guessed that I love Jasmine more than the rest of my children combined. Anything that hurts her hurts me." He
paused. "Nothing hurt her more than losing you, Cameron.
She's never really bounced back from that."

"Is that why you agreed to let her marry Trevor?"

Again he nodded. "I thought he would help take her mind
off of you, but he didn't. Sixteen was a young age to marry,
but she was mature enough to handle it. It worked for a

while. I think she grew to love him, but she could never love him completely, because he wasn't you. He couldn't fill the void in her life that you left behind."

"At the time I thought I was doing the right thing for everyone. Now I can see that I only made things worse."

"Don't blame yourself, Cameron. It wasn't your fault."

"I should have refused him."

"There are so many things that should have been done and weren't." There was a brief pause before Howard continued. "She may not admit it, but there's a light in her eyes that hasn't been there since you left, Cameron. It's like she was living only half a life. She was frozen, and now she's starting to melt. Whatever you do, you can't give up now. You have to do whatever it takes to get her to forgive you."

"Is it that important to you?"

"Her happiness is the most important thing in the world to me."

Cameron stood up. "Then I won't let you down."

Howard patted him on the back. "Thank you," he said as he turned around and headed back to the house.

Chapter Seven

Jasmine felt like a fool. Why in the world had she shot Cameron down when it was the last thing she wanted to do? She groaned inwardly. She already knew the answer to her question: She was afraid.

She searched through her bags until she came across the bag of toys she'd bought for Rafael. She took the bag and car keys and headed out the door. The only way she would ever be able to think clearly would be to get out of the house. She was headed out the front door when she bumped into Jonathan.

"Do I need to ask where you're off to so early in the morning?"

"I'm sure you already know the answer to that question."

"Off to see Rafael?"

"Of course," she said with a huge smile. "I promised him that as soon as I got here I was coming to see him."

"I went up to see him about a week ago."

Jasmine smiled. "I'm not going to ask what you got him into."

"Me?" An innocent expression was painted on his face.

"Don't play dumb with me."

"We didn't get into anything if you must know." He paused for a moment. "Are you going to tell Cameron about him?"

"Cameron already knows about him."

Jonathan shot her a look of annoyance. "You know exactly what I meant, Jasmine," Jonathan said softly. "Are you going to tell him that he has a son?"

Jasmine closed her eyes. She spoke very softly. "There's too much going on right now. I hadn't planned on telling him yet," she said as she took a deep breath and opened her eyes.

"And may I ask why not?"

"No, you may not."

"Why aren't you going to tell him? He has a son and I think he deserves to know about him."

"Since when did you become an advocate for the Cameron Todd campaign?"

Jonathan looked away. "I'm not on anyone's campaign here. I just think you're trying to punish him for what happened. I just think it's time to let bygones be bygones."

"Easy for you to say," she shot back. "He didn't ruin your life . . ." She stated before she stopped herself. Why was she being so defensive? She wasn't trying to punish Cameron.

"You have to tell him the truth sooner or later. I think you should do it now."

"I'll tell him the truth eventually," she said as she fumbled with her car keys. "Would you like to go along?"

"As much as I would love to, I can't. Dad invited me to go sailing with him."

"That sounds like a lot of fun. Perhaps I'll join you guys when I get back."

"We'll be waiting."

"See you in a little while," she said as she walked out the door and down the stairs.

"Jasmine?" She heard Cameron call as she was getting in her car.

"Hum?" she questioned as she turned to face him.

He jogged up to her. "Where are you off to so early in the morning?"

"I'm going to visit a friend."

"Oh." She could hear the disappointment in his voice. "I was hoping I could tag along."

"Not today," she said gently.

"It's cool. I understand." She could tell he was lying. She wished he could go with her but there was too much at stake right now. She felt guilty for what she was doing.

"I'll see you when I get back," she said as she slid behind the wheel.

"Sure," he said as he watched her drive off.

Jasmine took one last glance in her mirror as she drove away. She could see him standing there with a look of rejection on his face. Her heart went out to him. He was trying so hard and she was being so difficult. In that instant she wanted to turn the car around and tell him he could go with her. It was just a wish. There was no way she could take him to the house where he would come face-to-face with his son.

Jasmine flipped on the radio as she drove to Marvalette's house. There was no reason to deny her feelings any longer. She still loved Cameron with all her heart and soul. She'd never stopped loving him. No matter how hard she tried to hate him, she never could.

As R. Kelly's *12 Play* filled the car, she felt her desire growing stronger than ever before. It had been five years since a man had touched her. That man had been Cameron Todd.

She'd married Trevor, but like Cameron's, it was only a marriage of convenience. Trevor had been her knight in shining armor. The one who rescued her after Cameron left her high and dry, pregnant with his child. And while she grew to love Trevor, she never experienced the intense passion she felt with Cameron.

Trevor was sweet, handsome, and did everything in his power to make sure she was happy, but it wasn't enough. He wasn't Cameron. At times she felt as if she was cheating Trevor out of someone who could really love him the way he deserved, but he protested every time she mentioned the idea to him. He didn't want anything from her; he just wanted her by his side.

And even though the time she spent with Trevor was priceless, Jasmine still pined away in her heart for the only man she'd ever loved.

The love she felt for him now was even stronger than it was before. She longed to be able to run into his arms and let him make everything right, but she knew she couldn't. His betrayal was still too fresh in her mind. Maybe in time she could find it in her heart to forgive him.

The drive to Marvalette's house flew by quickly. Before she knew it, she was pulling up in the driveway. She cut the ignition and went up to the front door. She rang the doorbell and waited patiently. Moments later, Marvalette opened the door.

"Jasmine," she said as she opened the door. "I wasn't expecting you until later."

"I wanted to see Rafael as soon as possible. You don't mind, do you?" she questioned as she walked in the house.

"Of course I don't mind," she said as she pulled Jasmine into her embrace. "It's been too long since I've seen you. Besides, I love when you come to visit. Life seems to get so much better as soon as you walk through the door."

Jasmine laughed. "You tell me that every time I walk through the door."

"Do I really?" she questioned with a laugh.

"Yes."

"I only say it because I mean it, Jasmine."

"Where is the little monster?"

"He's upstairs dressing. He's so independent now." Jasmine could hear the pride in Marvalette's voice.

"Just think, he'll be starting school next year," Jasmine said as the tears misted in her eyes. "My baby is growing up so fast."

"Don't you mean my baby," Marvalette said with her hands on her hips.

"*Our* baby." She saw Marvalette's face grow serious. "What is it?"

"I'm glad you're early. This will give us an opportunity to talk in private," she said as she shooed Jasmine into the living room.

"What's wrong?" Jasmine questioned with concern. "How have the treatments been coming along?"

"That's what I wanted to talk to you about," she said as she sat down in the rocking chair by the fireplace. "The prognosis is not good, Jasmine. The chemotherapy is not helping anymore. The cancer is too widespread. The doctors give me less than six months to live."

"Oh, my God," Jasmine said as the tears sprang to her

eyes. She walked over to where Marvalette was sitting and wrapped her arms around her. Marvalette stroked her hair.

"Don't cry, sweetheart. We knew this day was coming when they told me I had cancer."

Jasmine looked up at her through her tears. "I never thought it would come this soon. I thought we would have more time together."

"So did I, honey. You know everything happens for a reason."

"I can't think about this that way. You're like a mother to me. How am I supposed to accept that?"

"You don't accept it, you deal with it," she said softly. "That's why I wanted you to tell your parents the truth about Rafael. He knows you're his mother and he should know who the rest of his family is."

"That's why I agreed to this vacation. The time has come for the air to be cleared. Everyone has to know about him including his father."

Marvalette's gaze locked with hers. "How does it feel to have him back in your life?"

"Did you know about this?" she questioned as she sat up. Marvalette nodded her head.

"Jonathan told me about inviting him to your parents' home when he was here the last time. He wanted my thoughts on the subject."

"What did you tell him?"

"I told him I thought it was a good idea."

"Why? You know how I feel about him."

Marvalette smiled. "I hear what you say, but I know something different. You'd never admit it to anyone, but I know you still love him. You never got over him and you never will, so you may as well stop fighting it. No man will ever be good enough for you because that man can never be Cameron."

Jasmine dried her tears. Marvalette was absolutely right

and Jasmine knew it. It was easier to deny it than to admit the truth. She didn't get a chance to reply.

"Grandma, I need help!" Rafael called from upstairs.

"My job is never done," Marvalette said as she headed up the stairs.

Jasmine watched her as she climbed the stairs. She was more concerned about her than ever before. She'd lost a lot of weight in the past few months. The chemotherapy caused her normally pecan tan skin to look washed-out and pale. Her hair was completely gone now. She wore wigs to cover up her baldness. Her hazel eyes had lost their spark. It was as if she wanted to give up, but she was waiting for something.

Jasmine could feel the tears well up in her eyes. Marvalette was the mother she'd always wished she'd had. She'd taken her in and done things for her she didn't have to do. For that Jasmine was eternally grateful. She could never repay her enough for her kindness. She thanked God every day of her life for Marvalette.

As she sat down in the living room, Jasmine allowed her gaze to focus on the room around her. Like her parents' home, Marvalette's home was decorated for Christmas. In the corner was a small Christmas tree with presents under it for Rafael. There were stockings next to the fireplace. Tinsel, lights, and bows were everywhere. Jasmine smiled. Unlike her own home, there was a lot of love in this house.

"Are you okay?" Marvalette's voice broke through her thoughts. Jasmine blinked away her tears before she answered.

"I'm just taking a trip down memory lane."

"Rafael will be down in a minute."

"Thanks," she said softly.

"Thinking about Cameron?"

"A little."

Marvalette smiled. "Stop fighting it, Jasmine. You'll never win."

"Won't I?"

Marvalette shook her head gently. "He's a part of you, Jasmine. No matter what, you'll never get rid of him. Stop trying."

"I will," she said softly. "It's just hard to forgive him."

"Do what your heart tells you to do. Let it lead the way and it will never lead you wrong. I was in love with a man once. I let my heart carry me and to this day I've never regretted my decision. I only wished that I had the chance you have, honey."

"Thank you for giving me that kick in the butt."

"You're welcome," she said as Rafael came down the stairs.

Jasmine felt her heart swell with pride and joy. At four, Rafael already showed the size promised to him at birth. He was almost four feet tall with dark, wavy hair, almond-shaped eyes the same sable color as his father's. He even had a dimple in his left cheek. He was a miniature Cameron. The ache in her heart grew stronger when his eyes lit up.

"Mommy," he said as he ran into her arms.

"Hello, darling," she said as she hugged him tightly. "You grow bigger every time I see you."

"Grandma says I'm going to be seven feet tall when I grow up," he said as he threw a glance at Marvalette.

"She's right, you know."

"How do you know that?"

"Grandma is usually never wrong, is she?" He shook his head. "Okay, then."

"Where are we going, mommy?" he questioned as he looked up at her.

"We're going out for ice cream."

"Yea!" he screamed as she took his hand and led him to the door.

"Bye, Mom," Jasmine said as they walked out the door. "Get some rest."

"Bye, Jasmine. Bye, Raphael," Marvalette said as she waved good-bye. Jasmine strapped Raphael in his car seat and got inside. Marvalette waited until they drove away before she let the tears slide down her face.

Marvalette went inside and closed the door behind her. She released all the tears that were welled behind her eyes. She was losing everything at once and it wasn't fair.

She wondered how she could give Jasmine such good advice on her life when her own life was screwed up. Unlike Jasmine, her secrets would destroy an entire family if they were revealed. She had so little time to do anything anymore. She was knocking on death's door, but she was trying to hold out as long as she could.

She went up the stairs and into her bedroom. She had to make things right, finally. She couldn't wait until after her death, she had to do something now. She took out a pen and a few pieces of stationery. She wrote two letters. One was to Rafael to read when he was old enough to read it. The other letter was to Jasmine.

There was a lot she needed to tell them both. So much that needed to be said. She wanted to be able to go to her grave with a clear conscience. She wanted all of her secrets revealed, no matter what the cost. It was time for everything to be brought to the light.

She smiled with satisfaction when she finished. She'd told Jasmine everything she needed to know. The only thing left for her to do was to wait for death to claim her.

Life wasn't fair sometimes. Just when she thought she had time to enjoy life, she was slapped with a death sentence. She wanted nothing more than to be able to watch Rafael grow up and become a man. It made her happy that Jasmine would be there to see it. That's what counted the most. Family was all that really mattered.

The writing she'd done made her tired but the weight of the world had been lifted from her shoulders. She wiped the tears from her eyes and picked up the telephone that sat next to her bed. She dialed the number to his private office and listened as the phone rang.

"Hello?" his voice called into the telephone.

"It's me." She could visualize him smiling through the telephone. "Are you busy?"

"I'm never too busy for you."

"I need to see you. Can you come now?"

"I'll be there in as soon as I can," he said softly.

"I'll see you soon," she said as she hung up the phone. A smile played at the corners of her mouth. No matter what, he was always there for her when she needed him the most. She wiped her face and headed down the stairs to await his arrival.

Chapter Eight

A thunderstorm was threatening to erupt when Jasmine dropped Rafael off for the night. As she headed home, she prayed the rain wouldn't fall until she got there. Lightning flashed through the night sky illuminating everything around her.

Now that she had a moment to herself, she had a chance to think about everything she and Marvalette talked about. As usual she'd been right about everything. It was time for her to get over being angry with Cameron and start acting like the mature adult she was. She couldn't wait to get home. She decided to take the shortcut home. If she didn't she would never make it home before the rain started. She picked up speed. The road she was taking had a lot of sharp twists and turns. At first she didn't think anything unusual was happening until she rounded a corner. Her brakes squealed right before they went out. She hit them as hard as she could. Nothing happened.

Panic clawed at her throat. There was a sharp turn coming up. At a normal speed it was nothing special. She didn't know what would happen traveling at almost sixty miles per hour. She prayed to God that she would be okay as she neared the curve. She hit the brakes one last time in an attempt to stop the car. She had to do something before she reached the curve, if she didn't she wouldn't make it.

Her attention turned to the bushes at the side of the road. Maybe if she hit the bushes they would be enough to brake her speed. She said one last prayer before she turned the car toward the bushes.

"Something's wrong," Cameron said to Jonathan when Jasmine hadn't returned home by seven o'clock. Jonathan looked up at him in alarm.

"What are you talking about?"

"Something's wrong with Jasmine."

Jonathan smiled. "She just went to visit Marvalette."

Cameron wasn't convinced. Something deep down inside of him told him Jasmine wasn't alright.

"Will you call her and find out for me? I'll feel better if you do."

Jonathan dialed Marvalette's telephone number. Cameron only heard his end of the conversation, but from what he could tell it wasn't good. Jonathan thanked Marvalette and hung up the telephone.

"You're right. Jasmine left there over two hours ago on her way home and she hasn't got here yet."

Cameron was already putting on his coat. "I told you something was wrong."

Jonathan slipped into his jacket and zipped it up. "You're right. I just have to find her now and hope that nothing has happened to her," he said as they headed out the door.

"I'm coming with you," Cameron said as he followed Jonathan to his car.

"I'm not sure if that is a good idea, Cameron."

"Whether it is or not, I'm coming with you."

"Why does no one ever listen to me?" Jonathan mumbled as he got in the car. The lightning lit up the sky.

"What way would she have come home?"

"Considering the way she hates to drive in the rain I'd stake my life on U.S. 1."

"Then head there first."

As Jonathan followed U.S. 1 through the winding curves, Cameron held his breath. They just had to find Jasmine. As Jonathan neared a curve Cameron gasped when he saw Jasmine's car on the side of the road.

"Right there," Cameron shouted as Jonathan coasted his car over to where Jasmine's car lay on its side. He was out of the car before Jonathan could stop completely. As he approached the car he could see Jasmine lying on the ground next to it.

In that instant Cameron felt his heart stop. He ran over to her limp, lifeless body and cuddled her close to him. It wasn't fair that just when he found her again, fate was ripping her away from him. He stroked her face gently.

"Jasmine, please be okay," he pleaded. She stirred slightly.

"I will be okay once you let me go," Jasmine said softly. Cameron released his tight grip and looked at her.

"You're okay?"

"I'm just fine. Just a little shaken up."

"How did this happen?"

"I was driving and my brakes went out," she frowned.

"This is a brand-new car. I don't see how it could have done that."

"Maybe it was a freak accident," Jonathan offered. He'd just inspected the car. "I'll have a mechanic come out and tow it away. I think the damage will be minimal."

"Are you sure you're okay?" Cameron questioned softly.

"I'm fine," she said as she broke away from him and stood up. "It's made me realize a lot of things, though."

"Such as?"

"I've been a fool, Cameron. I love you. I always have and I always will. I forgive you." Cameron grabbed her and hugged her so tightly she felt like an extension of his body.

"You don't know how much I've longed to hear you say those words," Cameron said.

"Now that I've said them I think things are finally going to be okay."

Cameron looked at her with passion on his eyes. " I think everything is finally going to be alright. Let's get you home."

Just when they thought everything was finally alright, they found out just how wrong they were.

Chapter Nine

The day before Christmas Eve a huge storm hit the coast. No one left the house. Everyone stayed inside and did various things to amuse themselves until the storm passed. Jasmine and Cameron opted for a game of pool in the family room while the rest of the family watched videotapes. Jasmine had just shot the eight ball into the corner pocket when the doorbell rang.

"Who in the world would be out in this weather?" Howard questioned as he looked down at his watch. "And at this hour? It's well after eleven o'clock?"

"I'll get it," Jasmine said as she cast a smile at Cameron before she dropped her pool cue and headed out. She went into the foyer and opened the door. The rain was blowing harder than ever before. It was blowing so hard she barely saw the woman standing there with the small child in her arms. Without a word, the woman pushed past Jasmine and stepped inside the foyer. Puzzled as to who she might be, Jasmine closed the door behind her.

"May I help you?" There was something familiar about her, but Jasmine couldn't put a finger on it. She was sure she should know her, but the memory escaped her.

"I'm looking for Cameron," she said as she put the little girl down and began to remove her wet raincoat.

"What in the hell are *you* doing here?" Cameron questioned as he walked into the foyer. Jasmine looked up at him. Had she missed something?

"How nice to see you, too, Cameron," she said as she dropped to her knees. She began removing the little girl's raincoat.

"Answer my question," he demanded. She stopped what she was doing to glare up at him.

"Can I at least finish what I'm doing?"

"No, you can't, Melissa." Jasmine blinked for a moment. Surely she hadn't just heard Cameron call her Melissa. That's why she looked so familiar. She was Cameron's ex-wife. "You are supposed to be in France with the rest of your family."

"I had to come to the States for a few days, and I thought I should get this over with now. I'm sure you can understand that," she said as she dropped the wet raincoat on the floor.

For the first time Jasmine finally got a clear look at Melissa. She was about five-feet-eight with peach-colored skin, dark brownish-auburn hair, and soft, delicate features. She was dressed in a Louis Vuitton cream pantsuit with matching shoes. Her hair was an array of soft curls framing her face. There was no denying that she was beautiful and well put together. Jasmine glanced down at the jeans and T-shirt she was wearing.

"I don't even pretend that I understand anything you do," Cameron said to Melissa. Jasmine could hear the anger in his voice. "There is nothing in the world that is so important you had to come here. You have nothing in this world that would require my immediate attention. I can't believe you had the nerve to come here."

"I only came here because I had something important to tell you, Cameron. I was in the States and I felt now was the right time to tell you."

"Tell me what?"

Melissa glanced over at Jasmine. "I would rather tell you in private."

Cameron shook his head. "Anything you have to say to me you can say in front of Jasmine."

Melissa narrowed her eyes at Jasmine. "Are you sure about that, Cameron?"

"Of course I am. Now, spit it out."

"Fine. This is Isabelle," she said as she gently pushed the child in Cameron's direction. "Isabelle, say hello to your father."

Jasmine felt as if the floor had fallen out from beneath her. She closed her eyes. Surely she had to be dreaming. She wasn't standing in her parents' home listening to Cameron's ex-wife tell him he had a daughter. How much crueler could fate really be? She opened her eyes slowly to discover it was not a dream. She'd really heard what she thought she'd heard.

For the first time since Melissa walked through the door, Jasmine let her eyes focus on the child. She couldn't tell her exact age, but she guessed she was no more than two. She had Melissa's auburn hair and facial features. The eyes belonged to Cameron—Jasmine would know them anywhere.

For a moment Cameron stared down the tiny version of Melissa. Jasmine could tell he was searching for any features that could belong to him. The child looked up at him without saying a word. His eyes locked with Jasmine's before he spoke.

"I have no idea what the hell you're talking about," he said as he clenched his fists. "What kind of stunt are you trying to pull this time?"

"For the first time in my life I'm trying to be honest with you, Cameron. I'm not trying to set you up or be dishonest. I was pregnant when I left you. I didn't find out about it until I got back to France. By then it was too late to tell you, because you'd already moved away without a forwarding address. I ran into Stacy the other day, and she told me you were still living in Atlanta. I got in contact with your secretary, and she told me where you were, and I came straight here."

Jasmine felt everything from sympathy to anger. Was Melissa really telling him the truth? Just looking at Isabelle it was hard to believe she could be his, but once you looked at her eyes, the truth was evident. Jonathan, Roslyn, and Howard walked into the foyer.

"What in the world is going on out here?" Roslyn questioned as she walked over to where they were standing.

"What are you doing here, Melissa?" Howard questioned as he approached them.

"I came here because I needed to talk to Cameron."

"About?" Jonathan questioned as he folded his arms.

"His daughter," Melissa said with a smug smile.

"His daughter?" Roslyn queried softly as she stared down at the child.

"Cameron and I have a daughter. Her name is Isabelle, after my grandmother."

"What a beautiful little girl," Roslyn cooed as she dropped to her knees beside the child.

"Thank you," Melissa said softly.

"She's an absolute doll. All of my children have given me grandchildren but Jasmine," she said as she shot her a look. "I'm beginning to think she's sterile." Jasmine's face remained emotionless as she turned and left the room.

"I can't believe you just did that," Howard said as he left the room.

"Was that necessary, Mother?" Jonathan questioned as Claudia joined him. "You had no right to say that to her."

"She'll get over it," Roslyn said as she stood up. Jonathan was about to say more, but Claudia put a hand on his shoulder.

"I don't know what's going on here, but I do know that if you don't calm down you're going to say something you'll regret," she said softly. "Let's take the little girl to the kitchen and give her some hot chocolate while all of you work this out."

"That's fine with me," Cameron said through clenched teeth. "What has to be said here is not appropriate for a child to hear."

"Let's go," Claudia said as took the child's hand. Jonathan looked as if he was going to argue before she shot him a silencing look. He looked as if steam was going to come out through his ears, but he followed Isabelle and her to the kitchen.

Cameron stood there staring at Melissa for a moment. He was so angry he wanted to pound her to a pulp, but he held his composure. The last thing he needed was to lose his cool over this.

"Why are you standing here lying to me like this, Melissa?" he finally questioned. "Isabelle is not the reason you came here, and you know it. You wouldn't have burst in here like this to tell me something like that. You're up to something and I want to know what it is."

Melissa frowned. "I'm hurt that you think I would have some ulterior motive. I'm leaving the country in a couple of days, so I had to tell you now."

"You've had two years to tell me about her and yet you haven't. You knew what this would do to me. You're just trying to ruin my life all over again."

"Why in the world would I be trying to do that? You were the one who moved away and didn't leave a forwarding address. I wanted to tell you about her, but I couldn't find you."

"Was this really so important? You could have kept her to yourself, Melissa. Why did you have to do this now?" He could see Melissa's eyes light up.

"Because she's your daughter. I figured you would want to get to know her. Forgive me for assuming incorrectly."

"I don't have any emotional ties to this child. Why would knowing anything about her benefit me? You live in another country, for crying out loud. When would I ever get to see her?"

"I hadn't thought about that," she stammered as she took a step back.

"Well, I can tell you what I think," Cameron said as he brushed past her and opened the door. "Now that you've told me, you can be on your way."

"I don't believe what I'm hearing," Roslyn said as she went over to the door and closed it. "You can't possibly consider sending Melissa and Isabelle out in this weather. She'll just have to stay here for tonight." Cameron turned to stare at Roslyn like she was an alien from another planet. How in the world could she suggest something like that to him?

"Do you expect me to agree with this?"

"Whether you agree or not, this is my house and I say Melissa stays for the night. If you don't care about her fine, think about your daughter."

"A hotel would be the best thing for Melissa. I'll even drive her so she won't have to go alone."

"Melissa stays for the night and that is final."

Cameron clenched his fists. "Since you're so insistent she stay here, would you mind leaving the two of us alone?"

"Of course not," Roslyn said with a smile as she left the room.

"You never answered my question, Melissa." Cameron fired as soon as they were alone.

"Which question was that?"

"What in the hell are you doing here?"

"Don't speak to me like that."

"I apologize for speaking to you that way, but the question remains the same. I want an answer from you and I intend to get one."

"I've all ready told you why I came here. If you can't accept it, oh well."

"You're right I don't accept it based on the evidence." Melissa laughed as she threw up her hands.

"What evidence?"

"The fact that you waited two years to tell me about her for one."

"I've been out of the country, Cameron. She wasn't born here in the United States. There were a lot of legal issues that I had to deal with before she could even be allowed to come here. I thought a lawyer of all people would know those things." Cameron wanted to hit her but he restrained himself.

"I'm going to have a big talk with Maxine when I get back. I don't appreciate her telling you where I was and how to get here. That information was for emergencies only, and this was not an emergency." He threw her a look of contempt. "I can't believe you had the nerve to show your face here."

"Why not?" she questioned, her eyes flashing red with anger. "I have every right to come here to tell you about your own flesh and blood. I apologize if you feel I am stepping on Jasmine's toes by coming here but I don't care. She is not the concern here."

"I plan to marry her, so this *is* her concern."

Melissa's mouth dropped open. "How stupid of me to forget about your precious Jasmine. She was always a huge rift in our relationship."

Cameron nodded his head. "You could never get over the fact that I loved her instead of you."

"If anyone deserved to have your love it was me. I was your wife, the one you married. The one your loyalty should have been with, but *no*. You pined away for some tramp who married someone else before your signature was dry on our marriage license."

"As long as you live you will never again speak about Jasmine that way," Cameron said as he took a step towards her. "She is ten times the woman you could ever hope to be."

"Forgive me for stepping on the queen's feet," Melissa said sarcastically. "I should have known better."

"Despite what Roslyn said you will spend the night in a hotel. I don't want you here and I'm not going to stand for it."

"I will do no such thing," she said defiantly. "Mrs. Williams invited me to stay here and that's exactly what I intend to do."

"You will regret it if you stay here. You and your daughter are not welcome here."

"She's your daughter too, Cameron," she replied smugly.

"Are you sure about that?"

"Just what are you implying, Cameron?"

"I'm not implying anything. All I'm saying is that Isabelle could belong to anyone."

"She's your child, whether you want to admit that or not."

"First thing in the morning I'll take darling little Isabelle down to the hospital and have a few tests run. I want to know for certain if my blood runs through her veins."

"Do whatever you want, Cameron," she said as she placed a hand on her forehead. "I'm tired. If you'll excuse me, I'll let Mrs. Williams show me to my room." Without another word she turned and walked into the dining room. Cameron was right behind her.

"Mrs. Williams, I do want to thank you for your hospitality. Apparently someone knows how to treat guests," she said as she ignored the daggers that Jonathan and Claudia threw her way with their eyes. "I'd like to go upstairs now. Isabelle and I are very tired."

"Right this way, my dear," Roslyn said as she led them out of the dining room.

Cameron watched as Melissa left the room with Isabelle in her arms. He was so pissed off with her he couldn't see straight. Where did she find the nerve to come here? He glanced over at Jonathan and found a matching scowl on his face.

"Melissa is really a piece of work." Cameron could almost see the steam coming from Jonathan's skin. "I can't believe she had the nerve to come here, or that my mother had the nerve to insult Jasmine and invite Melissa to stay here."

"I was thinking the same thing after Jonathan told me what your mother said to Jasmine in front of Melissa," Claudia said as she put a hand on Jonathan's shoulder. "I can't believe that your mother was so insensitive to Jasmine. She knew that having Melissa here would hurt her even more."

"If you'd been around this family as long as I have, Claudia, what Roslyn did tonight would come as no shock to you. She's always trying to hurt Jasmine in one way or another."

"I can't believe that a mother would do that to her child," Claudia continued. "Melissa knew that it was raining cats and dogs when she showed up here. It wouldn't have killed her to stay at a hotel for the night."

"Melissa is a spoiled brat who thinks she can have anything she wants," Cameron said angrily. "When you've been married to someone any length of time you begin to know them inside out. She has a reason for being here. She wants something from me."

"What could she want from you?" questioned Jonathan.

"I don't know yet, but I'll find out soon enough. She didn't just come here because of some child she claims is mine. And she didn't come here out of the kindness of her heart."

"Could Isabelle be your child?" Jonathan questioned.

"It is a possibility. Melissa and I were together a couple of times before we broke up completely. I'll call the hospital tomorrow and set up an appointment to have blood drawn. I'm not going to just take her word for it. I want proof. To be honest, no, I don't think Isabelle is my child. I've never really felt that I could have kids."

"Are you sure about that?" Jonathan questioned curiously.

"No. That's just always been a feeling that I've had."

"If the child is yours what are you going to do about it?"

"I don't know yet. Melissa travels too much for me to really be a part of her life. I would make whatever effort I had to see her. If she isn't my child I can kick Melissa out of my life forever."

"I thought you'd all ready done that."

Cameron turned to Jonathan with a pained expression on his face. "I thought I had, but I guess I was wrong. Every time I think she's gone, she pops up again to cause trouble."

"Get rid of her for good this time," Claudia said firmly. "I'll go up and check on Jasmine."

"Go ahead," Cameron said as he watched her leave.

"Just when things seem to be going fine with Jasmine, Melissa shows up here to start trouble."

"She wouldn't be Melissa if she didn't cause trouble."

"I don't buy her story. This is just too convenient."

"Meaning?"

"Is it possible someone could have contacted her and told her to come here?"

"No one here would have had a reason to keep up with her."

"Someone did, and I'm not going to rest until I find out who," Cameron said as he turned and left the room.

Chapter Ten

Jasmine slumped down on the bed. As much as she wanted to cry, the tears refused to flow. She should have been used to her mother by now, but she wasn't. She just had to accept the fact that no matter what she did, it was never good enough for her mother. Roslyn had a deep-rooted hatred toward her that she couldn't explain or understand.

Ever since she could remember, Roslyn had always treated her like a stepchild. No matter what she did or how hard she tried to please her, it was never enough. There was always something wrong with everything she ever tried to do. It was as if Roslyn was punishing her for something she knew nothing about. It puzzled her at times.

How could her own mother hate her so much? The only thing she'd ever really wanted was for Roslyn to show her even a small amount of love. She loved her mother and all she ever got was a knife in the back. Life just wasn't fair.

Jasmine was always the one who bought her mother presents for her birthdays and holidays. She was the one that sent her mother gift baskets filled with her favorite perfumes. She was the one who called her every night to talk to her. And yet, she was the one who never got any credit. She was the one Roslyn stepped on at every opportunity.

She only wanted her mother to look at her and acknowledge that she was her daughter and that she loved her. She was twenty-one years old and her mother had never even said "I love you" to her. It hurt.

A soft knock on the door interrupted her thoughts. Jasmine turned over and sat up. She tried to put on a smile but it was halfhearted. She couldn't let anyone know how much her mother hurt her.

"Come in," she said softly. Her father walked in the door. He sat down on the edge of the bed without saying a word. Jasmine smiled. It was her father's way of letting her know she could start talking.

"Why does she do this to me?" Jasmine questioned sadly. "She's on a personal vendetta against me and I don't know why."

"To tell you that you misunderstood her would be lying to you." The smile on his face matched her own.

"I should be used to it by now, but I'm not. How can you face the fact that your own mother hates you?"

Howard took a deep breath before he spoke. "It's not you she hates, it's me."

Jasmine blinked as she looked at him. "What are you talking about?"

"Your mother is taking out the frustration she feels against me on you, and it's not right."

"What could you have done to make her hate you so much?"

"It was something that happened a long time ago. I'm not proud of it, but it happened. Your mother has hated me ever since that day and nothing will ever change that. She's grown even more bitter lately."

"What's wrong with me, Daddy? Why does she find it so impossible to love me? What have I done so wrong that she can't even bring herself to care anything about me?" Jasmine questioned as the tears began to flow down her cheeks. "The only thing I've ever really wanted was for her to show me half the love she has for the others."

Howard hugged his daughter closely. How he wished he could tell her the truth and make her understand. There were so many things he needed to tell her. There was so much at stake it prevented him from telling her the truth. It prevented him from revealing what she really needed to know.

"I'll get to the bottom of this, Jasmine. This is the last time Roslyn will treat you like a stepchild. I promise you that." Someone knocked on the door.

"Come in," Jasmine said as she wiped the tears from her eyes. Claudia walked in the door.

"I came to see if you were okay or not."

Jasmine smiled. "No."

"Everyone else has already gone to bed."

"Everyone was anxious to get out of the line of fire."

"Have you seen Roslyn?" Howard questioned as he stood up.

"The last time I saw her she was in the living room."

"I need to speak with her." He leaned down and kissed Jasmine on the cheek. "I won't break my promise."

"Thank you, Daddy," she said as he walked out the door.

"Is this what you meant when you said you never enjoyed coming home?" Claudia questioned as soon as Howard closed the door. Jasmine nodded.

"My mother has always been this way. My family in general treats me like I don't belong with them. That's why I haven't been home in so long."

"I had no idea this is why you never came home," Claudia

said softly. "Now I wish that you'd never come here for vacation."

Jasmine smiled. "I came here because I had to, Claudia. It's time to tell my family about my son. All the secrets have to be revealed."

"I guess you're right." They remained in silence for a few minutes.

"Maybe one day I'll get what I want from her," Jasmine said.

"Maybe you will," Claudia said with a smile.

"I can dream can't I?" The smile on her face was small and sad.

"You need to get some rest," Claudia said as Jasmine fell back on the bed. "Things always look better in the morning.

Jonathan ran his fingers through Claudia's hair. He loved the way it felt when it was damp from their lovemaking. He trailed his fingers down her back before he kissed her shoulder. She turned over and kissed him on the nose.

"Did you tell her Melissa was staying here?"

"I couldn't do that to her," Claudia said softly. "Whether she wanted to admit it or not, she was broken up over the way your mother treated her."

"Can you really blame her?"

Claudia shook her head. "No. I just can't understand why any mother would hate her child so much."

Jonathan remained silent for a moment before he spoke. "Right before Jasmine was born, my parents broke up for a while. My mother went to her aunt's house and we remained here with dad. When my mother came home she had Jasmine and nothing has ever been the same between my parents. It's like mother hated my father for something. No one ever mentions it, but the tension is still there to this day."

Claudia smiled. "Jasmine was right when she said there was always drama here."

"She told you the honest truth. You should have come with her a few years ago. This is just child's play."

"Poor Jasmine. She's getting flack from every end."

"If anyone can handle herself, its Jasmine," he said as he kissed her gently. Claudia smiled at him. "I have good news for you."

"What?" she questioned lazily.

"My lawyer called today. My divorce is final tomorrow."

Claudia sat straight up. "Did you just say what I thought you said?" Jonathan nodded his head and smiled. "I'm so happy," she said as she wrapped her arms around his neck.

"You and me both. Now all we need to discuss is when the wedding will be."

"So soon?" she questioned softly.

"It's been too long already," he said as he kissed her gently. "And if you don't mind, I would like to take my fiancée to bed again."

She looked up at him and smiled. "I don't mind at all."

Chapter Eleven

Howard went into the living room to pour himself a drink. He really needed one to calm his nerves. He fixed himself a Black Russian and took a sip before he realized he was not alone. Roslyn was staring at him from her position on the sofa.

"Is your precious daughter okay?"

He could hear the hate and bitterness in her voice. "She will be," he said as his eyes narrowed. "She should be used to you by now, but unfortunately, she doesn't possess your ability to ignore it."

"How unfortunate for her."

Howard stopped in his tracks. Her words were slurred. "Why did you embarrass her tonight, Roslyn?"

"She'll get over it."

"Whether she will or not, you had no right to do that to her."

"I'm not in the mood to be generous tonight," she said as she downed half the drink in the glass. "And I'm definitely not in the mood to argue about Jasmine, so drop the subject."

Howard felt his blood boil at her careless attitude. In the past he would have done what she asked, but this was one time he couldn't ignore her any longer. He refused to let her get away with hurting his child.

"You're not getting away with it this time, Roslyn. This is the last time you attempt to make Jasmine's life a living hell."

"I'm glad you have some compassion for someone in this family. Where is your compassion for me? What about what you've done to my life, Howard?"

"What in the world are you talking about?"

"I'm talking about the fact that *you* are the reason I'm the way I am. You have no one to blame but yourself."

"There is nothing I could have done to make you this vindictive and envious, Roslyn."

"Oh, really?" she questioned with a laugh. "To everyone on the outside, I guess that would be hard to believe. I know much better than that."

"Meaning?"

"Just look at your track record and you have your answer. You are the one responsible for the woman you see sitting in front of you."

"I did nothing to make you the monster you are, Roslyn. Don't blame me for what you've become."

Her shrill laughter rang through the room. "You destroyed my life, and yet you stand there with your self-righteous attitude. I loved you more than life itself, and look at the way you repaid my love. You destroyed our marriage."

"If our marriage was destroyed, I wasn't the only one who had a hand in it. You were the one who never had time for me. There was always something better to do. Your family, your friends, or some charity you just had to participate in. Didn't it ever occur to you that I was going to get sick of it after a while?"

"And that's your excuse?" Roslyn questioned as she took another sip of her drink. "Then again, the past is the past, and we should leave it at that."

"That's the only thing you've said tonight I can agree with," Howard said as he downed his drink. "Is Melissa gone?"

"No."

"What do you mean no?"

"Exactly what I just said. I invited Melissa and Isabelle to spend the night here."

"You did what?" Howard shouted across the room.

"I invited Melissa and her lovely daughter to stay here for the night."

"What possessed you to do something so stupid?"

She glared at him. "It's raining cats and dogs outside, and it's late. Since she came all this way I thought the least I could do was be hospitable."

Howard was so angry he was shaking. "She was aware of the rain before she came prancing in the door. You had absolutely no right to ask her to stay here."

"Why wouldn't I have the right?" Roslyn questioned as she glared at him. "It's my house as well as yours, or have you forgotten that, too?"

"You know exactly what I mean, Roslyn. Haven't you grown up yet? You continue to lash out at Jasmine every chance you get, like a spoiled child."

"You really have an overactive imagination, Howard."

"Do I really?"

"Of course you do. Why in the world would I have any reason to treat her any differently than any of our other children?"

"You know damn well why you have a reason, Roslyn. Don't play dumb with me and pretend that you don't treat Jasmine like a stepchild."

"And why do I do it, Howard? Could it have anything to do with the fact that she *is* my stepchild?" Howard wanted to grab her and shake some sense into her, but he knew that if he touched her at that moment he would kill her.

"We agreed that we would never speak about this again, Roslyn. What was done was done, and that was the end of it."

"Maybe it was the end of it for you, but I still have to live with it."

"That was why we agreed never to discuss this again."

"You wanted it that way so you could pretend none of it ever happened."

His smile was bitter. "As if you would ever let me forget."

"I, for one, wish I *could* forget."

"If you did, it would force you to act like a normal human being. Every day of my life you make me regret that I agreed to go along with your plan. You've done nothing but treat her like a second-class citizen since the day she was brought into this house. Why should you punish an innocent child for my mistakes?"

"She's the result of your mistake, Howard, not mine. Jasmine is a physical slap in my face," she said as she took another sip of her drink. "How do you think I felt when I discovered that you'd gotten another woman pregnant? How do you think the situation affected me? Or did you even stop for a minute to think about that? Then again, I guess my feelings weren't important to you."

"How can you say that?" he questioned in utter disbelief.

"You were only concerned with bringing your child here to live with us. You wanted her here, and that was the bottom line. No matter how I felt, it wasn't going to be enough."

"Have you forgotten that you are the one who approached me with this suggestion," Howard replied. "You were the one who was so worried about what our friends would think if they found out. You didn't want anyone to know about this, so you begged me to bring the child here. I would have left Jasmine with her mother. She would have led a life that was filled with love and compassion, not one filled with hatred and envy."

"You still provide for her mother to this day, or have you forgotten that, too?" There was no denying the bitterness in her voice. "She'll be taken care of for the rest of her life. How fair is that?"

"Considering the fact that she gave me a beautiful daughter, I felt the least I could do was make her life comfortable."

"And to hell with your wife, right?"

"It was never that way, and you know it."

"You and your precious daughter."

Howard stared at her in disbelief. "If only you had seen it in your heart to treat Jasmine with love and compassion, you would have received so much from her."

"Yeah, right."

"Don't you think I've noticed how hard you are on her? You were always harder on her than on any of the others. You've always found some fault with everything she's ever done. What you never took the time to realize was that Jasmine loves you so much more than the rest of our children. The rest of them could give less than a damn about you, but Jasmine will go out of her way to please you."

"Your daughter can't do anything right. Whose fault is that?"

"You've never given her a chance."

"Haven't I? She hasn't done anything right since you dumped her into my lap."

"I can't believe you just said that to me," Howard said as he shook his head. "My daughter has accomplished more than all of our children combined. She has her own company, and she's doing well for herself. You should be happy you raised her so well, but instead you're too bitter to even see it that way."

"You can see it any way you want," Roslyn said as she downed the rest of her drink. "You can be as proud of her as you want. I raised her, and that's all Jasmine is ever going to receive from me. If you want her to experience love and compassion, take her to her mother."

Without another word she stood up and left the room.

For a few minutes after Roslyn left Howard stood there staring at his reflection in the mirror. How had he screwed up his life so badly? For the first time in his life he allowed himself to feel the impact of what he'd done. He never should have done it. He should have never taken his daughter away from her mother.

A noise behind him caused Howard to spin around. He came face to face with Cameron. The moment he saw the look of confusion and shock on Cameron's face Howard knew he'd just heard his conversation with Roslyn.

"How much did you hear?"

"I heard everything."

"Now you think bad of me."

Cameron shook his head. "Never. Everyone makes mistakes, Howard. We're all human."

"My wife doesn't see it that way."

"She's a fool."

Howard laughed. "You can say that again."

"Why did you keep this a secret?"

"It would have destroyed our family."

"Everything makes a lot more sense to me now," Cameron said as he sat down. "Roslyn has been taking out her frustrations with you on Jasmine."

"I never intended for this to happen. I only wanted the best for Jasmine, Cameron. When I did this, in my heart of hearts I believed I was doing the right thing."

"At the time it may have been the best thing," Cameron offered. "You were doing what you thought was best."

"If only I had known back then this would be the worst mistake of my life."

"Is her real mother still alive?"

"Barely. She has cancer. She's dying."

"Don't you think Jasmine has the right to know that?"

"I wanted to tell her, but her mother refuses. She doesn't want her to know now," Howard's voice trailed off. "I can still remember the first day I saw her mother. She was so young, beautiful, and innocent. From the moment we met I knew we were destined to be lovers.

"That was the year we had interns for the first time. When I first laid eyes on her I remember thinking how beautiful she was. She could brighten up the room with only a smile. I was hopelessly in love with her from the moment we met.

"I tried to avoid her as best I could, but fate had other plans in mind for us. She was assigned to the team I was working with to develop a new fragrance. She was so eager to learn everything I had to teach her. One night we both stayed late to work on a project. I tried to be strong, but I couldn't take it any longer. I kissed her." He held his head down. Cameron looked at him with compassion. He understood completely.

"What happened next?"

"Our relationship evolved from that kiss. We began to see each other regularly from that day forth. Our relationship went on for about a year before she got pregnant. And while I never meant for it to happen, I can't say I'm sad it happened. I had strong doubts at first.

"On one hand, I was happy beyond belief. The woman I loved more than anyone else in the world was having my child. On the other hand, this child could ruin my marriage. Roslyn and I were already having problems. This child would be the end of our marriage for sure.

"I was still trying to decide what to do when Roslyn confronted me about Jasmine's mother. Like a fool I admitted to everything. It was the worst thing I could have ever done. Roslyn wanted to take the child in. She was so worried about our position that she would do anything to protect it. I went to Jasmine's mother and talked to her. She was upset, but she agreed to let me have the baby. She wanted Jasmine to grow up with me in her life."

"So Jasmine came to live with you when she was born?"

"Yes. What we told everyone was that Roslyn went away so we could work things out between us. What really happened was that she went away so no one would know Jasmine wasn't really her child. I thought my problems were solved, but they were just beginning for Jasmine."

"You thought Roslyn's heart was in the right place."

"Little did I know she was going to take her anger out on my beautiful little girl. Jasmine has always been the light of my life. She was born out of love."

"That's why you always took up for her and made sure she had whatever she wanted?"

"Yes. It was my way of burying my guilt for taking her away from the one person who would have loved her. This family has never really accepted her. Everyone treats her like a stepchild. It's as though everyone feels that she is not a real part of this family."

"Everyone except Jonathan."

Howard smiled. "You're right." His expression grew serious. "Are you going to tell her?" Cameron shook his head.

"It's not my place to tell her. I leave that up to you."

"Thank you," Howard said softly. "I feel a hundred times better now that I've gotten that off my chest. I'd better get to bed. It's getting late."

"Good night."

"Good night," Howard said as he walked out of the room.

Cameron stood outside Jasmine's bedroom door. He needed to talk to her so badly. There were so many things he needed to clear up, but he was unsure if it was the right time. His mind was still reeling with everything Howard had just told him, but he needed to talk to her and tell her how he felt about the whole Melissa situation. After debating for nearly ten minutes, he knocked on the door.

"Come in," she said softly. Cameron walked into the room. She was lying on the bed with her head hanging off staring at a magazine. She looked over at him but she didn't say a word.

"I need to talk to you."

"About what?" she questioned casually.

"About Melissa."

She sat up. "What about her?"

"I'm sorry she showed up here on your doorstep."

"That was one of my issues with you, Cameron. You know how I feel about the whole Melissa situation."

"I had no idea she would ever come here."

"And what about the child?" she questioned, as she looked him in the eyes. "Could she be yours?"

He nodded. "The time frame fits, but that doesn't mean anything."

"You lied to me," Jasmine said as she turned away from him.

"What are you talking about?"

"You told me that you only had half a marriage. You told me that you weren't really husband and wife in any real sense. If you slept with her and Isabelle could be your child you lied." The pain in her voice was almost tangible.

"That wasn't what I meant."

Her laugh was small and bitter. "I was married to Trevor and I never slept with him because I didn't love him. Obviously we both have two different meanings when it comes to the concept of marriage." Cameron was shocked. He'd been jealous when he thought of Jasmine in Trevor's arms, and she'd never even slept with him. He felt like such a traitor.

"Jasmine . . ."

She put her hand up. "I don't want to hear anything else you have to say."

"Your mother invited Melissa and Isabelle to stay here."

Jasmine's eyes widened as she threw up her hands. "As if my day could get any worse. Thank you for putting the icing on my cake, Cameron. Remind me to thank you for it someday."

Cameron heard the finality in her voice. "What do you mean someday?"

"Just what I said," she said as she brushed past him and opened the door. "You and I are finished. Get out."

Cameron wanted to say something to her but he was at a loss for words. He walked over to the door and stood next to her. What could he say to make things right?

"Jasmine . . ."

"Get out," she said as she turned away from him. "I don't want to hear anything you have to say."

Cameron walked out the door. She slammed the door behind him.

Chapter Twelve

The sun shining on her face woke Melissa up. She sat up and rubbed the sleep from her eyes. It was then that she realized Isabelle hadn't awakened for her morning feeding. She looked down at her tiny daughter sucking on her thumb. Perhaps Isabelle was just as tired as she was.

She got up and went into the bathroom to take a shower. By the time she'd finished her shower, Isabelle was awake and looking for her mother. She smiled softly as she scooped her up into her arms and took her into the kitchen. After feeding her oatmeal, she put her in the playroom and set out in search of Cameron.

She walked around the house for a bit before she headed out the door. She breathed in the fresh, salty air. She knew she would find him out there somewhere. No one loved the beach more than Cameron did. She wasn't sure of where she was going, she was just walking along. As she approached the pier, she saw Cameron sitting there staring out at the water. She walked over to him.

"I figured you would be out here somewhere," she said with a smile as she sat down next to him. He moved away from her as if being next to her burned him.

"I hope you don't think I've forgiven you for that little episode last night."

Melissa threw up her hands. "What do you want from me, Cameron?"

"I want to know the truth. I want to know why you're here."

"I was looking for you, Cameron," she said as she reached out to touch him. He moved just out of her reach.

"Why? You were the one who took your trust fund and headed for the hills. Why didn't you just stay there?"

"I needed to talk to you."

"Everything that needed to be said between us has already been said and done."

"Not everything," she said as she shook her head. How could she make him understand what she was feeling? She decided to be as honest with him as she could. "There is a lot more I have to say to you. I want something from you, and if you never know what that is I'll always wonder."

"Wonder what?"

"Would you and I still be together if I hadn't divorced you?"

Cameron shook his head in disbelief. "Does that matter?"

"It does to me."

"I don't know why it would."

"No matter what you may think, it matters a great deal to me."

"What is it that you want from me, Melissa?" Cameron questioned as he faced her. "I don't have anything to say to you anymore. You've ruined my life enough."

"I've done a lot of thinking since I've been gone," she said as she touched his arm. "You tried to make our marriage work but I was too stubborn and blinded by what I thought I wanted to realize it at the time. I could only see that I was forced into a marriage I didn't want."

Cameron's eyebrows rose. "How do you think I felt? I was forced into it the same way you were."

"There were a lot of things I thought at the time," she said softly.

"Have any of those thoughts changed?"

She nodded slightly. "I've done a lot of growing up since I had Isabelle, Cameron. I've come to realize that I handled everything wrong. I was being stupid and childish," she said softly. "My life hasn't been the same since we broke up. I've missed you something awful and I want you back." She saw his mouth fall open in disbelief.

"Have you lost your mind? After all the hell you put me through I can't believe you have the nerve to say this to me. Just when I thought I could make the relationship with you work you crushed me like an ant beneath your feet."

"Why didn't you end our marriage?"

"You had to end it. It was part of the agreement between our fathers. We had to remain married for at least a year. Now that I know about the trust fund the rest of it makes sense."

"When you left I had no idea what you really meant to me, Cameron. I'm not perfect; you, of all people, know that. The one thing I can admit is that I made a mistake when I divorced you. I never meant to hurt you. At the time I thought I was doing the right thing, but I'm able to see now that I wasn't."

"You did what you intended to do, Melissa. You knifed me in the back without a second thought. There is nothing in the world that makes me think you won't do it again."

"I've changed, Cameron," she said softly as she stared into his eyes. "I've realized what a fool I was and the mistake I made. When we first got married I resented you because I knew you didn't love me. After I got to know you I discovered I had feelings for you and that scared me more than I cared to admit."

"So that's your excuse for taking your trust fund and heading for the hills?" He questioned in a condescending voice.

"It's not an excuse, Cameron," she said softly. "I'm just trying to tell you what I felt in my heart."

"You aren't supposed to hurt the people you love, Melissa."

"I understand that now," she said as she looked up into his eyes. "I want more than anything for you to forgive me. Maybe we can start over from the beginning. We have Isabelle to think about now." She could see Cameron's jaw clench. His eyes clouded over for a moment before he once again maintained his cool gaze.

"Until I have proof she's my daughter, you know how I feel about that situation," Cameron replied.

"I can understand your doubt, Cameron," she said as she touched his face. "You can have whatever blood test you desire. I just wanted you to know that I want you back and I'm willing to fight Jasmine for you." Cameron stared at her in disbelief. She could see the questions in his eyes.

"You don't have a chance against Jasmine," he warned. "You're fighting a losing battle, Melissa."

"How much do you want to bet?" She could see Jasmine round the dunes out the corner of her eye. "Despite what you claim, I know you were close to falling in love with me."

"Call it whatever you like."

Without a second thought, Melissa kissed Cameron softly on the lips. For a moment Cameron was so shocked he forgot to pull away. Melissa could see Jasmine stop dead in her tracks out of the corner of her eye. Melissa wrapped her arms around his neck. Jasmine turned around and headed back to the house. Cameron pushed her away roughly.

"What in the hell are you trying to pull?"

"I'm trying to get my husband back."

"*Ex*-husband," he said firmly. "Your husband is gone and you're never going to get him back. Never. The sooner you get that through your thick head the better." Cameron glared at her as he turned and walked away.

Melissa was hurt he'd refused her but was content with her actions. She'd done what she'd set out to do. There was no way Jasmine would have anything to do with him after her little scene this morning.

"You can run to Jasmine all you want," Melissa said bitterly. "You won't be hers for long." She vowed as she stood up and headed back into the house.

Chapter Thirteen

Cameron walked back to the house slowly. Where did Melissa find the nerve to tell him something like that? Why in the world did she have to come here and mess everything up? Why couldn't she have stayed where she was?

By the time Cameron got back to the house, Jasmine was already gone. He needed to talk to her badly but she wasn't around, so he was willing to settle for the next best thing. He went up to Jonathan's door and knocked. He could hear scrambling on the other side of the door before Jonathan came to the door with a crooked smile on his face.

"What took you so long?" Cameron questioned as he walked into the room.

"I was busy," he said as he glanced at the bathroom door. Cameron caught his gaze and a smile erupted.

"So there *is* something going on between the two of you."

Jonathan nodded. "My divorce will be final today and I've all ready asked Claudia to marry me."

"Good for you," Cameron said as he sat down on the bed. "If only my life was going as well as yours."

"Melissa has wreaked havoc on your relationship all over again, hasn't she?" Jonathan questioned as he sat next to Cameron.

"I just don't understand what she thinks she'll gain from this little stunt."

"She doesn't expect to do anything but ruin your relationship with Jasmine all over again, Cameron. Melissa could care less about you and anyone else."

"I know but Jasmine doesn't know that. She hasn't given me a chance to explain anything."

Jonathan gave him a look. "You know how Jasmine can be."

"I want her to understand my position."

"Have you had a chance to talk to her?"

"Briefly."

"What did she say?"

"After I told her Isabelle could be my child, she threw me out and slammed the door in my face."

"Can you blame her?" Claudia questioned as she walked out the bathroom door.

"No."

"She's been pining away for you all these years, and you've been out sleeping with Melissa. Of course she's not going to understand."

Cameron felt miserable. He knew Claudia was right.

"I need to make her understand she's the one I want. Melissa means nothing to me. She never has and she never will."

"Give Jasmine some time," Claudia suggested. "She'll come around."

Cameron shook his head. "I think I've gone too far this time."

Claudia smiled. "Then you've underestimated Jasmine's love for you."

"Meaning?"

"She's hurt, but she'll come around."

"I hope you're right," he said as he stood up. "I hope to God you're right."

Jasmine did everything she could to avoid Cameron. She couldn't believe he had the audacity to come to her the night before and try to explain things to her, then be out on the pier kissing his ex-wife the next morning. All the hurt and betrayal she felt before was nothing compared to what she felt now.

She'd stopped in to visit Rafael and play with him for a

while, but her heart wasn't in it. Marvalette had inquired about her mood, but she refused to talk about it. To talk about it would conjure up the pain she was trying to smother.

She returned to the house well after sunset. The rest of the house was dark and she guessed everyone was asleep. She went up to her bedroom and changed her clothes. She got in the bed and closed her eyes. Her mind was filled with the events of the past few days. She didn't know when she fell asleep, but the sound of the telephone ringing awoke her.

She sat up and ground the sleep out of her eyes before she reached for the telephone. She glanced at the clock and saw it was three o'clock in the morning. She wondered who could be calling her at this time of morning.

"Hello?"

"Mommy?" came Rafael's voice.

"What's wrong, honey?

"Grandma fell down on the floor. I tried to get her up but she's not moving. I'm scared."

"Have you called 911?" Jasmine was wide-awake now.

"I called when she fell. I'm scared, Mommy. I don't know what to do." Jasmine could visualize the tears running down his face.

"I'll be right there, Rafael. Hold on, honey. I'm on the way."

"Okay," he said as he hung up the phone.

Jasmine slipped into a pair of jeans and a T-shirt as quickly as she could. She felt like she'd been run over by a truck as she pulled on a pair of sneakers and opened the door. She was surprised to discover Cameron standing outside her door with his hand poised as if to knock.

"Jasmine?" The surprise was evident in his voice.

"Why aren't you with Melissa and your daughter?" Her voice was dripping with sarcasm. She brushed past him and headed for the stairs.

"You're being unfair, Jasmine. Just because Melissa claims that child is mine means nothing to me."

"Her mother is your ex-wife. You said the time fits. That's all the evidence I need."

"My relationship with Melissa has been over for ages. I've already ordered DNA tests at the hospital today. I want positive proof whether that child is mine or not."

"Hooray for you, Cameron but I don't have time to debate with you on the subject," Jasmine said as she took the stairs two at a time. "I have somewhere I have to be."

"Where in the world are you going at three in the morning?" Cameron questioned as he followed her.

"Why should anything I do be of any interest to you?" she questioned angrily as she turned to face him. Her eyes had turned dark gray. "You should be upstairs worrying about your responsibilities."

Cameron remained silent. "Can we not get into that again?" he asked softly. "You're already convinced that I'm guilty, so can we discuss this later?"

"I really don't have the time for this," Jasmine said as she let herself out the front door.

Cameron finally stopped thinking about what he wanted for a second and focused on her. Why hadn't he noticed before how upset she was? He felt like a fool as he ran out the front door.

Cameron caught up with her as she was about to open her car door. He took the keys from her. She glared up at him as she attempted to snatch the keys from his hand.

"Let me drive you to wherever you're going."

"I am quite capable of driving myself," she said as her hand closed around his.

"The roads are too slippery, and you're clearly too upset to drive." She didn't answer him but she released his hand. He could see the fire burning in her eyes. "Please?"

She knew he was right, but she would never admit that.

Despite her anger, she felt her heart melting. He was going to find out about Rafael now, but he would have found out tomorrow anyway. She closed her eyes before she nodded her consent. She could hear his sigh of relief as she took a step back and allowed him to open the door for her. He took his seat behind the wheel of the car and started it.

"Where am I going?"

"Marvalette's house."

"Trevor's mother?"

"Yes. And please hurry," she said anxiously. Without another word Cameron backed out of the driveway. Jasmine felt a rising sense of panic as the minutes slipped by. She knew Cameron was doing the best he could on the slippery streets, but they just weren't getting there fast enough for her.

Twenty minutes later he pulled up to Marvalette's house. Jasmine could see the rescue squad in front of the house. She was out of the car before he could stop it completely. She ran up to the front door without so much as a word to Cameron.

What she found inside nearly broke her heart in two. The paramedics were working on Marvalette while Rafael huddled in the corner watching them. Without anyone saying a word, Jasmine knew that Marvalette was already dead. Jasmine's heart nearly stopped. There was no way she could hide the truth any longer.

"Mommy!" Rafael cried as he ran into her arms. "Grandma fell down on the floor and she never got up." Jasmine hugged him to her chest tightly. His tears soaked the front of her shirt.

"She's gone." The paramedic closest to her confirmed her worst fears. "She was gone before we got here." Tears began to slide down her cheeks.

"She's not gone," Rafael murmured softly. "She's right here."

"That's not what he means, honey," Jasmine said gently as she wiped the tears from his eyes. "Her body is here, but Grandma is gone up to Heaven with Grandpa."

"No!" he screamed as he clung to Jasmine. Jasmine held him as if she never wanted to let him go again. Her heart lurched in her chest. "It's not true," he said as he pulled away from her and ran up the stairs.

"We'll take her body to the hospital now. You can handle whatever needs to be done later." Jasmine saw the sympathy in the paramedics' eyes, but it was far beyond her to accept it. Her heart was filled with too much pain. She couldn't find her voice to reply to his statement, so she merely nodded her head.

Her throat was tight as they lifted Marvalette from the floor and eased her onto the stretcher. She watched as they placed the white sheet over her head before they wheeled her out. She brushed past Cameron and followed them out of the house.

Moments later, they drove off into the night. Jasmine felt tears slipping down her cheeks. Her heart felt hollow inside. It was as if her own mother had died. In a sense she had. Marvalette was the mother she'd never had. She walked back into the house and closed the door behind her. She leaned against the door and closed her eyes. It was hard to believe everything had happened this fast.

She opened her eyes slowly. Her eyes met Cameron's. She didn't have to ask him to know what he was thinking. She could see the shock and amazement etched into his handsome features. What could she say? That he hadn't seen her hugging his son.

"Why?" he queried softly. He didn't have to say more. She knew what he was talking about. There was no need to play dumb and prolong the inevitable any longer.

"I don't want to talk about this now," she said as she turned to head up the stairs. Cameron grabbed her arm.

"Don't think I'm going to let you get away that easily, Jasmine? I want to know why you never told me I had a son."

She took a deep breath. "Do you really want to know the real reason I didn't tell you?" He nodded. "I was pregnant when you ran off and married Melissa. What was I supposed to do? You had Melissa and a new life. All I had was my baby, our baby." She swallowed hard. "He was the only part of you I had left. I couldn't share him with anyone, not even you."

"Did you really hate me that much?" His face mirrored his shock.

"It wasn't about hating you, Cameron. I was sixteen years old. My mother would have made my life a living hell for embarrassing her. You know that. No one would have cared that you'd gotten me pregnant. You were already married and shipped away. All the blame would have been placed on me."

"If only you had told me. If only I had known," he murmured softly.

"You don't know how much I wanted to tell you," she said as the tears filled her eyes. "There was no way I could, so I swallowed it and came here to have him."

"So no one in your family knows about him?"

"Jonathan knows."

"He told me there was a lot I didn't know about what happened. This has to be what he meant."

She shrugged. "Perhaps. "

"Your parents never suspected anything?"

"I don't think they did. My father came to see Rafael when he was born, but I stayed carefully hidden. My mother ignored Rafael and Marvalette for the most part. She never would have come anyway."

"And Howard couldn't tell?"

"If he could, he never said anything to me."

"And now?"

"Everyone has to know the truth. Rafael is coming to live with me."

"I see," he said as Rafael appeared at the top of the stairs.

"Mommy," he called as he stared down at Cameron.

"I'm coming, sweetheart," she said as she turned and walked up the stairs without another word.

Chapter Fourteen

Cameron stood in the living room staring up at the staircase. His emotions were in an uproar. He felt everything from shock to anger that Jasmine had kept his son away from him. There was no mistaking that the boy was his. Rafael could have been his twin. He wondered how Jasmine had managed to keep him a secret from everyone, including him. How could she do this to him?

The man that promised to love her forever ran off and married someone else, his mind told him. Then, to add salt to the wound, she had to watch him say vows to a woman that she knew he didn't love. He knew, given the circumstances, she'd had no other choice. She'd done what she had to do to take care of herself and her son, their son. Cameron felt his heart swell up. How could he ever fault her for giving birth to his child? For protecting that child, even if it meant making a supreme sacrifice.

He struggled with his emotions for a few minutes before curiosity about his son got the best of him. He crept up the stairs and stood just out of Jasmine's view. He wanted to see her with his son. He wanted to be near them both.

"She's not coming back is she?" Rafael questioned softly. Cameron felt his heart leaping in his chest. His son was feeling pain no child should have to feel.

"No, she's not," Jasmine confirmed. "Your grandmother is dead." Rafael burst into tears. Jasmine held him while he cried. Cameron saw the tears in Jasmine's eyes as she held him. Suddenly, Rafael stopped crying and looked up at her.

"Am I going to come live with you now, Mommy?"

"Yes," she said as she nodded her head. "You're going to come live with me."

"I'm glad," he said softly. "I've always wanted to live with you."

"We'll talk more about it in the morning," she said gently. "You need to get some sleep."

"Will you hold me until I fall asleep?" he questioned softly.

"Of course I will," she said as she wrapped her arms around him. She began to sing to him softly but gently. Within minutes exhaustion kicked in and put him to sleep.

She laid him down on the bed gently and stared down at her beautiful son. As she looked up, her eyes met Cameron's. Her eyes showed her anger that he'd intruded on their private time together. Cameron saw the look in her eyes and turned to walk down the stairs before she reached him. They had so much to talk about and so little time.

He sat down on the sofa in the living room. He braced himself for the argument he knew was coming. He watched her as she walked in the room. She stared at him for a moment before she spoke.

"Did you see what you wanted to see?" she asked. He could hear the bitterness in her voice.

"I just wanted to be near Rafael. I'm sure you can understand that."

"You don't even know him."

"I don't know him because you never told me about him," he fired back. He could see Jasmine wince slightly. He felt an immediate sense of guilt. He shouldn't be taking his anger out on anyone but himself.

"I did what I had to do," she said as she sat down in the rocking chair next to the fireplace.

"I'm sorry, Jasmine," Cameron apologized. "I just can't make myself understand why you denied me the right to be in his life." For a moment she dropped her head and didn't reply. When she looked up and her eyes met his, he could see the pain and hurt lying just beneath the surface. It hurt him to know that he was the one responsible for that pain.

"I found out I was pregnant after you'd already married Melissa. There was nothing I could do about it then. I thought about an abortion but I knew I couldn't do that. Trevor found out about the baby and offered to marry me. What else could I do? I was sixteen, about to have a baby by a man who was already married. What was I supposed to do?" The pain in her voice was almost tangible.

"I married Trevor and hid out here until after Rafael was born. Marvalette helped me in more ways than I could ever repay. She allowed me to leave Rafael here with her so I could go back to college and get my career off the ground. Rafael has always known from the beginning I was his mother. I don't even know why you insisted on coming here with me tonight, Cameron. You have Melissa in my home claiming a child she has is your child. Isn't that enough?"

"I don't believe that Isabelle is my child, Jasmine. I want the DNA test to prove it."

A bitter smile touched her lips. "Then how can you be so sure about my child?"

"He looks exactly the way I did when I was his age. I don't know how no one ever recognized that."

"That's why I don't take him home. Jonathan comes to see him only because he already knew the truth. Rafael lives with me in Boston most of the year, but I've never taken him home to my parents'."

"But your mother asked about him. She said you were

bringing him home. I assumed this was something you did often."

Jasmine shook her head. "I was going to tell the rest of my family the truth tomorrow. I wanted him to meet them." Her eyes narrowed as she studied his face. "Why am I telling you any of this? It's not your business."

"I have every right to know, Jasmine. I am that child's father. From this moment on I think we should work together to decide what's best for him. You should be embracing me, not trying to keep me out of his life.

"Why do you keep twisting this around? I wasn't the one who left you. You left me, or did you forget. You weren't around when I needed you the most." Cameron hung his head. He couldn't deny that what she said was she truth. He wasn't there when she needed him the most.

"If only I had known," he said softly as he stood up and went to kneel before her.

"It's too late to think about that now," she said softly. "Get over it." The next thing he knew he grabbed her and kissed her gently. For a moment he thought she was going to pull away but to his surprise she didn't. She kissed him back slowly.

He smiled with satisfaction when he felt her go limp in his arms. She would never admit it, but her walls were slowly crumbling. She wasn't as bitter and resistant as she was a week ago. Despite what her words said, her heart was saying something else.

He groaned when Jasmine pulled away from him. He could see the emotions wash across her face. Her eyes were sad as she reached out and touched his face.

"You and I both know that if Isabelle is your child, Melissa will do everything in her power to use that against you. It's a hopeless situation. We may as well face that now."

"I can't," he said as he wrapped his arms around her. "For

five years I have lived without the only woman I've ever loved. I can't just turn my feelings off. It doesn't work that way. I'm not giving you up without a fight."

"In the real world you have to cut your losses and move on. Living in Boston has taught me that you have to depend on yourself. I can't sit here for the rest of my life waiting on you to make up your mind. One minute you want me the next minute you're stuck in Melissa's face. You can't have the best of both worlds." Confused, Cameron released her from his hold.

"What in the world are you talking about?"

"Are you going to deny kissing her yesterday on the dock?"

Cameron laughed. "Melissa came to me with some crap about getting back together for Isabelle's sake. I laughed in her face. She kissed me and told me she was willing to fight you for me. I told her only in her dreams." Jasmine stared at him for a moment.

"I don't have time for games, Cameron."

"Neither do I."

"At least we can agree on something," she stood up and headed for the front door. "Good night." She held the door open for him. Cameron felt his mouth fall open in shock.

"I'm not going anywhere." He closed the door.

"I have to stay here with Rafael so you have to go alone."

"I'm staying as well."

"There's no reason for you to stay."

"I want to stay here with you, Jasmine. I know you have a hard time believing me because of my track record, but I do love you. Now that I've seen you with our son I know beyond a shadow of a doubt I'll never love anyone as much as I love you."

"Don't you dare try to do this to me," Jasmine said as she wiped her eyes with her sleeve.

"Tell you what's in my heart? You know as well as I do that I'm telling you the truth. Don't let anyone try to destroy what you and I have. We still have a chance to make it."

She looked into his eyes. "What do you want from me?"

"I want a chance to be in your life, and Rafael's. I want us to be the family we should have been since the day you found out you were pregnant. We have a chance to make all the wrongs right. You can deny it if you want to, Jasmine. If the time and space we've spent apart weren't enough to change the love we felt for each other it had to be true love. I'm not asking you to pick up where we left off, I'm just asking you to give me a chance."

"You don't know how much I want to, Cameron. I just don't know if I can forget everything that has happened. Things aren't the way they used to be. I don't know if I can just forget the past and start over."

"I don't want you to do it tomorrow, Jasmine. I realize that it is going to take a lot of time and effort but I'm willing to try. I only ask that you be willing as well." She nodded.

"I can try, but I can't promise you anything."

"Thank you," he said as he kissed her forehead.

"I'd better go check on Rafael."

"Go ahead. I'll be here in the morning when you wake up."

"Thank you," she said as she hugged him gently before she turned and went up the stairs.

Jasmine was willing to give him another chance. Cameron stood there for a moment basking in the glory of what Jasmine had just told him. How lucky could one man be? He had a chance to have her and his son in his life? Did he dare ask for more?

He may have missed five years of their lives but he vowed that he wasn't going to miss another second. Jasmine could count on that.

Chapter Fifteen

The next morning everyone in the Williams household was up and about by eight o'clock. The children were opening their presents while the adults sat around the fireplace sipping coffee and reminiscing. Jonathan was surprised when he didn't see Cameron or Jasmine wander in. He knew how much both of them loved Christmas morning.

"Has anyone seen Jasmine or Cameron?" Roslyn questioned.

"They left about three o'clock this morning," Melissa offered as she sipped her coffee.

"Do you know where they were going?"

Melissa shrugged. "As if Jasmine would ever say anything to me."

"I can't believe she did this," Roslyn said with a look of anger. "She left without a word to anyone about where she was going."

"You know how Jasmine is," Melissa said with a smirk. "She's always been so irresponsible."

"That is enough," Howard said loudly. "I will not have any of you speaking ill of Jasmine. She is a grown woman. She doesn't owe any of us an explanation."

"Who cares about what Jasmine would do?" Roslyn questioned flippantly. "She took Cameron with her knowing he has a guest in this house." She shot a look a Melissa. "Two guests to be exact."

"Like Jasmine, he is a grown man. He can do whatever he wishes. I'm sure if Melissa was a concern for him he would have been here. And if I can recall, you insisted Melissa stay here, not Cameron. In fact I believe he was against the issue." Howard retorted.

An important message from the ARABESQUE Editor

Dear Arabesque Reader,

Because you've chosen to read one of our Arabesque romance novels, we'd like to say "thank you"! And, as a special way to thank you, we've selected four more of the books you love so well to send you for FREE!

Please enjoy them with our compliments, and thank you for continuing to enjoy Arabesque...the soul of romance.

Karen Thomas
Senior Editor,
Arabesque Romance Novels

Check out our website at
www.arabesquebooks.com

SPECIAL OFFER!
4 FREE BOOKS

ARABESQUE ®

A PRODUCT OF

BET BOOKS™

3 QUICK STEPS
TO RECEIVE YOUR "THANK YOU" GIFT
FROM THE EDITOR

Send this card back and you'll receive 4 FREE Arabesque novels! The introductory shipment of 4 Arabesque novels – a $23.96 value – is yours absolutely FREE!

There's no catch. You're under no obligation to buy anything. You'll receive your introductory shipment of 4 Arabesque novels absolutely FREE (plus $1.50 to offset the costs of shipping & handling). And you don't have to make any minimum number of purchases—not even one!

We hope that after receiving your books you'll want to remain an Arabesque subscriber. But the choice is yours to continue or cancel, anytime at all! So why not take us up on our invitation to receive 4 Arabesque Romance Novels, with no risk of any kind. You'll be glad you did!

Call us
TOLL-FREE
at 1-888-345-BOOK

THE EDITOR'S "THANK YOU" GIFT INCLUDES:

- 4 books absolutely FREE (plus $1.50 for shipping and handling)
- A FREE newsletter, *Arabesque Romance News*, filled with author interviews, book previews, special offers, and more!
- No risks or obligations. You're free to cancel whenever you wish... with no questions asked.

BOOK CERTIFICATE

Yes! Please send me 4 FREE Arabesque novels (plus $1.50 for shipping & handling). I understand I am under no obligation to purchase any books, as explained on the back of this card.

Name _____

Address _____ Apt. _____

City _____ State _____ Zip _____

Telephone ( ) _____

Signature _____

Offer limited to one per household and not valid to current subscribers. All orders subject to approval. Terms, offer, & price subject to change. Offer valid only in the U.S.

AN041A

Thank you!

Accepting the four introductory books for FREE (plus $1.50 to offset the cost of shipping & handling) places you under no obligation to buy anything. You may keep the books and return the shipping statement marked "cancelled". If you do not cancel, about a month later we will send 4 additional Arabesque novels, and you will be billed the preferred subscriber's price of just $4.00 per title. That's $16.00 for all 4 books for a savings of 33% off the cover price (Plus $1.50 for shipping and handling). You may cancel at any time, but if you choose to continue, every month we'll send you 4 more books, which you may either purchase at the preferred discount price. . . or return to us and cancel your subscription.

THE ARABESQUE ROMANCE CLUB: HERE'S HOW IT WORKS

PLACE
STAMP
HERE

ARABESQUE ROMANCE BOOK CLUB
P.O. Box 5214
Clifton NJ 07015-5214

"He was downright rude to Melissa and I wasn't going to stand for it." Roslyn hissed.

"I wouldn't want *my* ex-wife hanging around me if she caused me as much grief as the one sitting here has."

Melissa shot Jonathan an angry look. "And just what is that supposed to mean?" Melissa fired. "You don't know a damn thing about me, so I would appreciate it if you kept your comments and your opinions to yourself."

"I know enough to know that you ran off and left him high and dry as soon as you signed on the dotted line for your trust fund. You spent money like it was water on other men, fancy clothes, and expensive vacations. You slept around on him during the last year of your marriage. Let's see if I'm missing anything . . ."

"You don't have a clue about my relationship with Cameron," she said angrily. "Your sister was the one who ruined my relationship with him. He would wake up in the middle of the night and call me Jasmine. He never tried to make our relationship work; he was too busy worrying about what Jasmine was doing. So don't blame me for your sister's unhappiness. My life wasn't exactly a bowl of cherries, either."

"And my heart really bleeds for you."

"I will not sit here and listen to this another moment," she said angrily as she stood up and stormed out of the room.

"You will apologize to her at once," Roslyn said as her eyes bulged with anger. "She is a guest in our home and you will treat her as such."

"He will do no such thing," Howard countered. "You had no right to ask Melissa to stay here when you knew how much it would affect Jasmine."

"We've been over this before, Howard. It would have been wrong for me to turn her out into the streets."

"She would have survived, I'm sure."

"You always take Jasmine's side over mine. When are you going to start thinking about me for once?"

"I couldn't care less about your feelings, Roslyn. You don't seem to care about mine," Howard relied sharply. Roslyn's mouth dropped open.

"How dare you speak to me that way!"

"How dare you go there with me."

Jonathan held up his hand. "Can we have a moment of peace here?"

"Fine with me," Roslyn said as she stood up. "To hell with Christmas altogether," she shouted as she left the room leaving everyone with their mouths open wondering what was wrong with her.

Jasmine woke up early. She looked down at Rafael and kissed him gently before she stood up and stretched. She headed down the stairs to fix him something to eat before he woke up. She went into the living room to see Cameron lying on the sofa with his mouth hanging open. She smiled. It was nice to have him here with her even if she didn't want to admit it.

She wanted to start over with him. Last night had been a wake-up call to her. Life was too short to spend it without the ones you loved. She was going to take Marvalette's advice. She was going to let the past go and focus on the future. With a smile, she went over to him and gently shook him awake. For a moment he seemed to be confused about where he was until he saw her smiling at him.

"Good morning," she said gently.

"Good morning," he said as he sat up.

"I was just about to start breakfast. Are you interested?"

Cameron nodded. "Anything that interests you interests me," he said as he got up and followed her into the kitchen.

He took a seat at the kitchen table while she rummaged through the refrigerator.

"I'm going to take Rafael home today."

"How do you think they'll react to him?"

She shook her head. "I have no idea but I can't hold back any longer. I have to do this now."

"I agree."

"I don't know how they'll take it, but there's one way to find out," she said. Cameron shook his head in agreement.

"After breakfast?"

"After breakfast," she said as she broke two eggs into a bowl.

Jasmine packed Rafael up into the car. She handed the keys to Cameron and got in the car. He backed out of the driveway and headed to her parents' house. For the first time she wondered if she was doing the right thing. Perhaps Rafael was better off not knowing the rest of her family. What if she was making a big mistake?

"You're making the right decision," Cameron said softly. She smiled at him.

"How did you know what I was thinking?"

"I can see it in your eyes."

She let out a huge sigh. "I can't help thinking this is going to be a big mistake."

"Why would it be?"

She turned to look at him. "You know how my family is, Cameron. Things haven't changed at all."

He smiled at her. "You're doing the right thing. If they don't accept it, then so what? I think you're doing what you have to do."

She smiled at him. "Thank you. You've just given me the strength to do what I need to do."

Chapter Sixteen

Cameron pulled the car into the driveway and cut the ignition. He took Jasmine's hand and squeezed it softly. She smiled at him but she didn't speak. His heart leaped with joy. He was so glad she'd forgiven him.

"Let's go," she said as she took Rafael out of the car.

"Ready?"

"No," she said as she unlocked the front door. She walked inside and turned to go into the living room. He took her hand. He wanted her to know he was there for her no matter what. She smiled up at him as she opened the door.

Everyone was gathered around the fireplace. The children were playing with their presents, and the adults were laughing and talking, until they walked in the door. All at once you could hear a pin drop in the room as everyone turned to face them. Rafael broke the silence.

"Grandpa," he said as he got down from Jasmine's arms and ran over to Howard.

Jasmine's mouth dropped open. "How do you know him?"

"He comes to visit me all the time," Rafael said as he hugged Howard's neck. Jasmine turned to her father.

"Is that true?"

Howard nodded his head. "I've always known about him." He confirmed as he hugged his grandson.

"Known about whom?" Roslyn questioned as she walked into the room. She stopped short when she saw Rafael in Howard's arms. Her eyes widened when she saw the resemblance to Cameron. "How?"

"I was pregnant with Rafael when Cameron got married," Jasmine said softly. "I never told anyone here about him because I didn't think they would understand."

The veins in Roslyn's neck stuck out. Her eyes looked as

if they had turned into two flames as she turned to face Howard.

"And you knew about this?"

Howard nodded his head.

"Wasn't it enough to destroy my life once?" she sobbed. "You keep doing it over and over again." She turned to Jasmine. "This is the last time I let you ruin my life," Roslyn said as she pulled a gun.

Jonathan dropped the receiver on the floor. It wasn't possible that what he heard could be the truth. There was no way. Jasmine's accident had been no accident. Someone had tried to kill her.

"Who was on the phone?" Claudia questioned when she saw the look of concern on his face.

"The mechanic at the garage."

"And?"

"He just told me that someone cut Jasmine's brakes. Someone tried to kill her."

"Oh, my God. Who would do something like that?"

"Roslyn," Melissa said as she joined them. Claudia and Jonathan turned to her in surprise.

"What are you talking about?" Jonathan replied.

"Roslyn called me in Paris and told me to get over here as quick as I could. She told me that she'd tried to cut Jasmine's brakes and that it hadn't worked. Cameron saved the day once again. She told me that if she couldn't kill her, she would make her life as miserable as possible. She threatened Isabelle if I didn't do it. I was scared of her. What was I supposed to do? I jumped on the first plane here. Roslyn is dead set against Jasmine. Nothing would surprise me."

"If my mother would go . . ." He didn't get a chance to finish his thought. His sister Charlotte ran up to him with a look of fear in her eyes.

"Jonathan, you have to come quick. Mom pulled a gun and told us to get out of the room. She's holding Jasmine, Cameron, and dad hostage. You have to go and talk to her. You're the only one she'll listen to."

"Call the police," Jonathan said as he cut her off. He turned and fled the room with Claudia and Melissa right behind him.

Jonathan approached the living room with caution. From what he'd just heard he didn't know what frame of mind his mother would be in when he reached her. He opened the living room door and walked inside with Claudia and Melissa close on his heels.

Roslyn was standing there with a gun to Howard's head. Tears were flowing down her cheeks as she stood there.

"Mom," he said softly as he approached her. She turned to look at him. The look in her eyes told him he had to be careful. "What are you doing?"

"Your father ruined my life and I have to make him pay for that. He's done nothing but take and take and take and I'm tired of it. It's time to end this once and for all." Jonathan said a prayer to himself before he spoke to her.

"Mom, you have to think about this rationally. If you kill him you'll go to jail. Don't you want a chance to see your grandchildren grow up? Do you want him to win even more? He'll win if you go away for the rest of your life. You have to let this go."

She shook her head gently. "I only wanted the best for us, but he destroyed that when he had an affair. My life has never been the same since then. *He* did this to me." Jonathan approached her slowly. He had to keep her talking until he could reach her.

"What did Jasmine and Cameron do?"

"Jasmine is the result of that affair and Cameron is the man she loves. That's why I helped Douglas bankrupt Cameron's father. I wanted to hurt her and that was the perfect way. *I* was the reason he married Melissa. I wanted to make Jasmine pay for coming into my life and ruining it."

"All I've ever tried to do was get you to love me," Jasmine said softly. Roslyn shook her head and laughed.

"You're even more a fool than I thought you were. Didn't you ever wonder why I treated you differently? Your father had an affair with Marvalette and it resulted in a child. That child was you." Jonathan could see the shock in his face mirrored in Jasmine's. That explained a lot.

"I probably shouldn't have taken it out on you, but I couldn't help it," Roslyn continued. "Now to punish you even more I'm going to shoot Cameron first." She turned the gun to Cameron. Jonathan was close enough to act. Just as Roslyn fired the gun, he ran over to her and knocked her off balance. Melissa jumped in front of Cameron at the last moment. The bullet hit her in the chest, knockings her backwards in Cameron's arms. Roslyn hit the floor head first with a thud. She was knocked unconscious. Jonathan grabbed the gun and ran over to Melissa.

She lay there on the floor with her blouse soaked in blood. He took one look at her and knew she wasn't going to make it. She held out her hand to Jasmine. Jasmine took it and held it.

"I never meant to hurt you, Jasmine," she said softly. "I only did this because Roslyn threatened my child. I love Isabelle more than anything else in the world." She looked up at Cameron.

"Don't talk anymore. An ambulance will be here shortly."

Melissa shook her head. "I have to do this now. Isabelle really is your child. I couldn't tell you about her because I was so ashamed of what I did." She turned to Jasmine. "Please look after her for me. Don't let her forget me," she said as she slumped over. Jasmine screamed as Jonathan knelt down on the floor. He shook his head. Melissa was dead.

Epilogue

Cameron closed the trunk on the car. Everything they could fit in the car was packed away. Jasmine walked out the door holding Rafael with one hand, Isabelle with the other. A smile was on her face, but he could tell she wasn't as happy as she had once been. Too much had happened. The doctor said it was normal for her. In time she would heal.

A lot had happened in the past few days. Roslyn had been sent to a sanitarium. She was finally going to get the help she needed. Howard had finally confessed everything to his daughter with the hope that she would forgive him. Jonathan and Claudia had gotten married and went on a trip to the Bahamas. Melissa's parents came back to the States to bury her.

Isabelle's DNA test proved Cameron was her father. Jasmine wasn't upset like he thought she would be. She had taken his daughter under her wing, and Isabelle was already responding to her. They'd taken care of everything, all that was left to do was to pack whatever Jasmine wanted from Marvalette's house.

Howard had given Jasmine Marvalette's letter—a letter that was etched in Cameron's memory.

> *To my dearest daughter,*
> *If you're reading this letter it means your father has told you the truth. You know that I am your real mother. I wanted to tell you so badly in my last days, but I knew what complications that would bring. I talked it over with your father and we agreed this was the best way to handle the situation.*
>
> *I loved your father more than life itself, but it was a bad situation from the start. I never should have had anything to do with a married man, but I was young*

and foolish. I listened to my heart and not my head. I never once regretted that decision.

I wanted you to live with your father because he could give you so much more than I could. I never wanted to give you up, but at the time I felt it was the right thing to do. That was when I married Sigmund and adopted Trevor. Trevor was my replacement for you. Of course you can imagine my surprise when, years later, you came into my life as my daughter-in-law. I was ecstatic. Since Trevor was not my blood son, there was no risk if he married you. Howard and I had already discussed it in great detail before it actually happened. I wanted to be near you so much I was willing to take whatever I could get.

I know you may hate me now for what I've done to you but I hope you understand why I did it. I love you, my darling daughter, and I've enjoyed the time I spent with my grandson. I wish you the best life has to offer now and forever more.

Love Mother.

"To think all this time I was here with my mother and I never even knew it," she said softly. "I feel like a fool because I had no clue who she was."

Cameron smiled. "You shouldn't feel that way, honey. You had no reason to suspect anything."

"I think I knew deep down inside, but I was too afraid to let myself believe it."

"Don't feel bad, Jasmine."

She smiled at him. "I don't."

He leaned down to kiss her. "Did you tell Howard we got married?"

She shook her head. "I told him last night. He was happy for us, but he's still shaken up about my mother and Roslyn."

"I can imagine," Cameron said as Jasmine strapped Rafael

in the car. She stood up and smiled up at him. "Are you ready to go, Ms. Todd?"

"As ready as I'll ever be," she said as she got in the car and closed the door. Cameron took one last look around him before he got in the car with his family and drove away.

The Troubles of Meddlin'

LaShell Shawnte Stratton

To Great-grandma and Godmother Rachel—two perfect images of vivacious elderly women who have no problem interfering when they are concerned about me. They have been and will probably always be my literary inspiration. And a great thanks to my Aunt Debra—I could write a dedication three pages long, and it wouldn't do you justice.

Chapter One

Janelle Howard leapt from sleep with the desperation of a passenger leaping from a sinking ship. She had been drowning in that recurring dream and was thankful to be pulled out of it, but when she awoke to the noise that surrounded her, her thankfulness quickly turned into irritation.

The pounding on the wall behind her bed was starting to make the framed pictures over her headboard rattle. If she guessed correctly, this seismic quake would be a six-point-eight on the Richter scale. Her beagle, Jazz, lifted her head and gazed warily at her from the bottom of the bed. The poor dog already had to deal with her frenzied turns and kicks while she slept. Now this? Janelle was sure Jazz was growing to hate their new roommate Sharon's nightly escapades just as much as she did.

"Hey, Sharon," Janelle called with a yawn as she turned, raised her hand, and banged her clinched fist against the wall. "Could you keep it down? I'm trying to sleep."

She doubted they heard her. The tempo of the pounding increased and the soft moans quickly developed into yells. Her Harlem Renaissance–inspired painting of Zora Neale Hurston, Countee Cullen, and Langston Hughes fell from its perch on her wall and bumped her head. She rubbed her crown wearily. Jazz began to yelp and do a crazed dance around Janelle's ankles, leaving her with little else to do but grab two of the pillows her eighty-year-old grandmother had embroidered with painstaking care and arthritic hands, and shove them both over her ears.

"Yes! Yes!" a female voice yelled.

"Oh, baby. I'm coming! I'm coming!" a male voice answered.

"Then just come," Janelle screamed, banging her fist on the wall again, "and shut up!"

That scream must have been the crescendo of their nocturnal performance, for immediately afterward the pounding and moaning stopped, and Janelle sighed deeply. She shook her head and closed her eyes but opened them again several minutes later when she heard a knock at her door. Janelle's door was slowly pushed open.

"Um, excuse me," said a baritone voice. She looked toward the entrance of her bedroom and blinked. He licked his full lips and curled them into a smile.

His chest and shoulders were still covered with sweat. He was breathing as if he had just emerged from the gym, taking a momentary break from the treadmill. There was no look of embarrassment on his face, even though he only had a bed sheet loosely draped in front of himself, and Janelle had heard his guttural moans of delight barely five minutes ago. She wasn't sure if he was about to introduce himself or ask her if she wanted to join in the fun.

"Sharon asked me to get her some Kool-Aid. You got some left?"

"Kool-Aid?" Janelle asked vaguely and then frowned. *What? No Cristol?* she thought, raising her eyebrows cynically.

"Yeah, Kool-Aid. She's thirsty," he said while fluffing the light hairs on his chest with pride.

Janelle frowned again.

"I guess there's some left. It should be in the refrigerator . . . top shelf."

He nodded and turned to walk down the hallway, giving her a full view of his brown backside. Her cheeks began to burn and she averted her eyes.

"Hey," he said while turning back and pointing toward Jazz. "Is there something wrong with your dog? Why is he jumping around like that?"

"*She* doesn't react well to strange noises in the middle of the night."

"Oh," bed-thumper said, drawing out the word with a smile. "Didn't know we were that loud. We'll try to be more quiet next time."

She watched him until his shadow disappeared from the doorway and then shook her head.

Janelle was the typical soft-spoken introvert: boring life, boring job, and small bank account. Sadly enough the only excitement she experienced were moments like this one, when her roommate Sharon, the "don't depend on me" secretarial temp, hedged into Janelle's mundane life with her wild sex, loud parties, and general impoliteness.

"You're lucky you got me, girl," Sharon remarked one day at the kitchen table, after she had been late paying her half of the rent the second month in a row. "If it wasn't for me, you'd have nothing to complain about. All you'd have is that damn dog to fuss at."

"We'll try to be more quiet next time," he had said. She could hear bed-thumper's voice echoing in her head. Next time? Next time? They weren't done for the night? Janelle gazed at the digital clock on her night table and shook her head. The neon letters read 3:00 A.M. She would have to wake up and prepare for work in three hours, and she wasn't looking forward to the endeavor. Bad dreams and loud noises equaled no sleep, and no sleep equaled another listless, tired day of sitting in front of her computer terminal editing others' works as an underpaid copyreader.

Janelle did not hate her job, but only because she could

not work up the effort to hate it. As far as most journalists were concerned it was not even *real* copyediting. It wasn't like she was working for a newspaper or a journal or a magazine.

It was her job to edit travel agency brochures, to edit others' lies about places that did exist, but places where none of the writers had ever been and had only seen on the Discovery Channel. She knew that the stories of treks along the Amazon and caravans to Egypt were merely from research gathered from articles and books, not from actual experiences. She had seen the company's travel volumes, though it wasn't like anyone could draw inspiration from anywhere else in the office. For in their spacious ninth-floor suite, in front of those volumes were just plain, gray cubicles. Wall-to-wall cubicles and few windows. The windows that were there were better suited for the bottom portholes of a ship. There was the predictable gurgle of the water cooler and clatter of computer keys. There was the smell of coffee and printer ink. Posters of Paris, Japan, and Senegal (a sad attempt at inspiration) were tacked along the walls, and occasionally she would stare at them and sigh and wonder what it would be like to be there.

"Anywhere but here," she would think while clinking her spoon against the inside of her coffee mug.

Janelle now gazed down at her feet and saw that Jazz had fallen back to sleep. She closed her eyes and tried to meet her there, but her mind was fully awake, wallowing in self-pity. She could hear the creak of Sharon's mattress through the walls and a soft murmur erupted again. The bed-thumper had returned to Sharon's room a while ago with a cold glass of grape Kool-Aid. Janelle could only assume that they were going to work up another thirst soon. She gave up on the possibility of getting to sleep, grabbed her flannel robe and headed downstairs to the living room.

With the flick of a switch the stairwell and dark room

were suddenly illuminated, revealing a strewn pile of clothes tossed over the railings. Sharon's skirt draped lazily over a pair of men's slacks. The legs of her panty hose entangled themselves with dark socks. Janelle huffed while gathering the articles of clothing, and she hurled them at the couch before she walked into the kitchen and swung open the cabinets. With a box of cereal under one arm, a carton of milk in one hand, and a bowl and spoon in the other, she stomped to the dining room table, pulled out a chair, and sighed.

Outside her dining room window the city was quiet, but then again it was the early hours of the morning. Relative silence could only be expected of Washington, D.C., on this side of three A.M. She closed her eyes and began to eat her cereal, but the sensation of being crushed in her dream was still haunting her.

The dream always started the same way. She would lie in bed silently, then open her eyes to find someone on top of her—whether it was a man or a monster, she never knew—but it would squeeze and squeeze. The tight grip of the person holding her would be so terrifying, and the laborious tempo of their breath against her ear would cause her to panic so much that she would scream. But then it would squeeze her even tighter, as if the further suffocation was a punishment for her screams, for her attempts to escape. Then she would hear the brittle crack of her bones, and suddenly she would awaken.

The dream made intimacy with men impossible. Janelle could not stand to have any of them on top of her or holding her in bed. A few years ago she had given up on sex completely, no longer wanting to have to stifle the need to panic when she was in a man's arms, no longer wanting to explain why she didn't want him to touch her. But she *had* taken one of their suggestions. She saw a psychiatrist for her problem after her last boyfriend jumped out of bed, gathered his things, and stalked out the front door one night when she refused to have sex with him for the umpteenth time. Janelle had even undergone hypnosis in order to determine if it was some dark memory of childhood abuse resurfacing, but the doctors concluded that this was not the case and chalked her fear of intimacy up to "acute anxiety."

Acute anxiety, Janelle thought lamely as she crunched her cereal and shook her head with the same skepticism she had had in the doctor's office the day she received the diagnosis. "I've lost four boyfriends because of acute anxiety?"

According to the doctors, her acute anxiety could be best described in layman's terms as extreme shyness. Janelle was shy of people, shy of the opposite sex, and extremely shy about freeing herself sexually. That left her little leeway in a world dispersed with men and women who dated and had sex as often as other people shook hands.

Janelle sighed, wanting to shake herself hard.

Get out of this funk, Janelle, she told herself.

The wee hours of the morning always did this to her. It made her think too hard. It made her sad. Damn Sharon and her noise!

Janelle wanted to call her grandmother to hear her words of comfort. She would have been just as happy with merely hearing her grandmother's voice, period, but it was too late for something like that. The elderly woman wasn't exactly a night owl.

She walked over to the television and turned it on, flipping channels until she arrived at a silly comedy on one of the cable channels she rarely viewed. She wasn't much of a television watcher—she spent most of her time reading or writing while listening to jazz music. But now she was in need of something brain-numbing, like watching a comedy where a man played the song "La Bamba" by slapping his hands on his bare stomach. She squinted at the screen and shook her head.

In less than a half an hour, Janelle was fast asleep.

* * *

Terrence Boyer, or Tory, as his friends called him, managed to open his apartment door even with the five-or-so cumbersome suitcases dangling from his hands and shoulders. His muscles tensed against the strain of the heavy bags and he gritted his teeth. Terrence kicked the door closed and let each case fall to the floor in a series of thuds. His four-year-old bulldog, Sven, that he had rescued from an abusive master while in Switzerland, skidded into the foyer, meeting Terrence with pants and barks. He quieted only once Terrence leaned down and rubbed the dog's sagging cheeks affectionately. After that, Sven returned to his perch on the couch and fell back to sleep.

"Is that it? No hug?" he called to Sven with a chuckle.

Terrence had initially balked at the idea of finding a "dog sitter" according to his sister's advice. But now that he saw that Sven was well fed and happy and noticed that his apartment smelled just as fresh as he had left it, Terrence was glad he had changed his mind.

He took off his coat and draped it on the back of the sofa before walking over to a table and glancing down at his answering machine. He pressed one of the enameled buttons and heard a loud beep.

"October twenty-third, 12:20 P.M. . . ." the automated voice said.

"Hey, Tory," a male voice called out from the machine's speakers. "It's Steve, man. Just calling to see what's up about the game tomorrow. They're good seats, Tory. Second row. Hope you can make it. Call me if something changes."

"October twenty-third, 4:49 P.M. . . ."

"Tory," a sultry British accent purred. Midtown New York traffic blared in the background. "I've called your cell several times today, and I've yet to get a call back. Needless to say, I'm very angry. I understand that you may be busy, but the very least you could do is return my calls. So am I to assume that our date is canceled . . . *again?* Make a left here. Here! Just pull over! Idiot!" He could imagine her taking a puff from her cigarette as she shoved her money into the hand of the cab driver. "Tory, you promised me we would celebrate my new cosmetic contract. Jean-Paul asked me again if I would like to go to dinner . . . if you don't want me to say yes, you *will* call me in the next hour."

"October twenty-sixth, 6:18 P.M. . . ."

"Hello? Hello? Tory, baby? You know Mother don't like these machines," his grandmother said, making him smile. "Oh, well . . . I was just checking to see if you got home safely. Give Mother a call when you settle in. Remember we supposed to have dinner tomorrow. I'm making all your favorites with sweet potato pie for dessert. So bring that big appetite of yours. Bye, baby." There was a long pause. "Now am I suppose to hang up or is the machine supposed to hang up for me?"

Terrence smiled again, but he grew solemn when he listened to the echoing silence of his living room. He stared down at his luggage, deciding to not unload them at that minute but to instead take a few calming breathes and reassociate himself with his apartment. With the removal of his shoes and socks and with remote control in hand, this was at least partially achieved.

Terrence hated transcontinental flights. He had left Tokyo with the sun brightly shining and the streets teeming with people, only to come home to DC to find a city still asleep at three A.M. and a dog too tired to greet him with much enthusiasm. But it was still good to be home.

He had hopped across Europe in shows for various design houses—from London, to Paris, to Madrid, and then to Milan—only to have his agent call him to say that she had booked him a photo shoot in Japan. Because of that, he had to delay going home for another few days *and* had to cancel plans to meet his girlfriend, Kara, for their dinner date *and*

had to tear up his ticket to the Wizards game he was supposed to see with his boys. More canceled plans. More in-
conveniences. This whole modeling thing was growing more
and more irritating the longer he stuck with it. And though
he had heard the suggestion from Kara plenty of times before, now even his agent was advising that he move on . . .
literally.

"Because you're obviously taking your modeling career
more seriously, Terre, maybe we should consider maximiz-
ing this opportunity by moving you here to New York. There
are absolutely fabulous lofts in the Meatpacking District.
Once-in-a-lifetime opportunity here, Terre," the bespecta-
cled woman had rambled into the mouthpiece of her headset.

"Capitalize, Terre. Maximize," she sang.

He could only cringe at the suggestion. Rude cabbies,
way too many people, a pace that was so fast it made his
head spin—New York was a fine place to visit for a few days,
but he could never imagine himself living there, even if Kara
would only be a few city blocks away.

Terrence shook his head and stretched, resisting the urge
to look into any mirrors. He had seen enough of himself already.

He never would have guessed that he would one day grow
tired of looking at his own face. It had been fun initially, flipping open a magazine and finding a picture of himself in a
sales advertisement wearing a two-thousand-dollar suit, a
gorgeous woman on his arm. Not to mention the fact that de-
signers were willing to pay seven hundred dollars an hour
just for his mug and physique. But the luster and awe had
faded quickly. It just didn't seem manly to be so obsessed
with his looks, to spend so much time sculpting his muscles
in gyms filled with mirrors, and to get facials and manicures
and pedicures once a week. He could feel himself softening
on the inside, and the guy he was two years ago, who would
scarf down a three-tier cheeseburger and a milkshake without

a thought and who would not give up his Saturday mornings on the basketball court for *anything,* was slowly disappearing. He even missed his low-paying job. He missed the community center where he once worked. He missed the kids there. He missed a lot of old things. But his transformation to a highly paid model suited Kara just fine.

He lifted her framed photograph from his bookshelf and ran his finger over the cold glass. A honey-complexioned woman with beige eyes, flowing auburn hair, and a lithe frame (with the exception of her full bosom which made her a favorite pick for lingerie catalogues), smiled at the camera enticingly. He placed the picture back in its original position, furthest forward in a long line of photos of his friends, ex-girlfriends, and family. Conspicuously, there were no pictures of him.

Raised in a poor village in Ethiopia, Kara had gone without a great many things when she was a child and was desperately trying to make up for that now as a twenty-year-old model. Nothing ever cost too much for her, and if it did, she had, without shame, used her beauty and body to get it.

There were many things about Kara that irritated him. The fact that she often judged a person's worth by how much money they made, the British accent she used when she spoke to people even though she had only lived in England a few months and was as British as Terrence, the way she screamed at Sven when he nicked his claws on her parquet floors—all of this drove Terrence crazy.

But she had a way about her that still made her irresistible . . . well, sexually at least. He would hear a little voice in his head repeating his best friend Steve's mantra of "Good sex, good time, move on," after an argument with her, or after she pulled another one of her hissy fits in public. But she would always turn to him with full, pouting lips, unzip the dress she was wearing, and only whisper, "Are you still angry at me?" Then after a good twenty minutes of lovemaking, he would answer that very question with a loud and definite, "No." She could manipulate him easily, and they both knew it.

Terrence looked down, pulled at the uncomfortable leather pants he was wearing, and shook his head. She had even managed to manipulate his wardrobe.

"You are one whipped brother," he muttered to himself.

He sat down on the couch, glanced down at his dog, and gave a wary smile. He petted the bulldog's side, but the animal only gave a few grunts before filling the room with his loud snores. Terrence's stomach growled, too, and he rubbed it absently. He decided that he was too tired to rise from where he was sitting to make himself something to eat. He had sampled paella, escargot, and sushi in the past week, and the garden-variety late night snack just would not do at this moment.

"Besides," he told himself as he turned on his television, "you're saving up your appetite for some sweet potato pie."

He licked his lips at the thought.

Chapter Two

Mrs. Howard crept up the stairwell of the five-story apartment building with a glass dish filled with macaroni and cheese. The eighty-year-old woman worriedly glanced over her shoulder when she heard the main door leading to the street open. She waited to hear her granddaughter's footsteps, prepared to hurl the food out the hallway window if necessary. There was no need to draw any suspicion to her "mission." Good macaroni and cheese be damned.

But, to her great relief, she was greeted by the smile of a

friendly Mexican janitor instead of her granddaughter. He tipped the brim of his baseball cap, lifted his broom, and waved. She sighed and returned his smile.

"Would you like any help carrying that, Mrs. Howard?" he asked.

"No, Felipe, honey. I'm fine. Thank you," she replied as she began to climb the stairs again.

"You visiting Mrs. Boyer today?"

She turned to him and narrowed her eyes. "Why you asking?"

"I don't know." Felipe frowned and then shrugged. "I just thought. . . ."

She cradled the dish to her bosom, hunched, and whispered, "Well, if you must know I *am* going to Mrs. Boyer's today, Felipe. We havin' a dinner party. But if you happen to run into my grandbaby, I don't want you to tell her a thing about it. It's a surprise."

"A surprise?"

"Yes," she said with a nod. "A surprise. Promise me you won't tell her."

He frowned again, wondering when he would ever have the opportunity to tell her granddaughter *anything*. Whenever he did see the attractive young woman, she would only give him a shy smile and a "good morning" or "good evening," before she quickly walked toward her grandmother's apartment, always laden with grocery bags or gifts from department stores.

But he did not voice any of this aloud. To patronize the elderly woman he merely said, "Okay, Mrs. Howard. I promise." She nodded and walked up the steps with the spryness of someone much younger than her age. When she knocked on the front door of Mrs. Boyer's apartment and glanced back at him, he pretended to be engrossed with sweeping the dirt from the stairwell corner and only looked up again when he heard the door close.

"Where have you been?" Mrs. Boyer called out from the kitchen as she wiped her hands with a dishtowel. She wobbled into the living room under the weight of her heavy frame—a visible product of good Southern cooking and happy living. "Annie, I was about to call the watch out on you. Told you we ain't need no macaroni and cheese. We got too much food as it is."

"Gertrude Boyer, no meal is complete without macaroni and cheese. You know that and I know that. It is just as important as biscuits and gravy," Mrs. Howard said as she set her dish down on the dining room table triumphantly. She scanned the arrangement of china, silverware, and table linen for a mistake but nodded with approval when she could not find one. "Besides, it ain't my fault we're up to the last minute getting this whole thing ready. Told you we should have started sooner."

Mrs. Boyer mumbled her reply before returning to the kitchen while Mrs. Howard sighed and smiled. She was so excited she could actually feel butterflies fluttering in her stomach. Visions of chubby, brown great-grandchildren tipping over candy dishes and crawling around on carpets were bringing a twinkle to her eye. It was going to work. She knew it was. What those "two children" (as they affectionately called them) needed was a little push in the right direction, and she and Mrs. Boyer were going to give it to them.

This dinner had been a project long in the making. They had started off normally, simply sharing pictures and stories of the young man and woman with one another. They quickly came to the conclusion that each child had something about them that could complement the other. Plus, Terrence was one handsome devil. She couldn't deny that. The moment she saw his picture, she nodded her head and smiled. He reminded the widow of her late James, Janelle's grandfather. But of course, there was the small glitch of Terrence currently having some "snotty girlfriend" as Mrs.

Boyer called her, but she had assured Mrs. Howard that with the right urging from her and his mother, "that Kara girl won't know what hit her."

They could have launched a shuttle with the amount of planning they had put into the occasion, though it wasn't like either of the children made their plans easy. Between Janelle just wanting to "spend a quiet evening at home writing" most nights and Terrence's spur-of-the-moment modeling trips to God-knows-where, the two grandmothers were starting to think that they would never get them together. But everything was falling into place, and Mrs. Howard could smell victory in the distance, just as easily as she could now smell the corn-on-the-cob burning on the stove.

"Gerty! You better open up that oven and let me help you," she said as she tightened the strings of her apron, "because you are burnin' up the food!"

Janelle drove slowly down the street toward Desmond Oaks Apartments, though that was not her intention. Her foot pressed the accelerator down nearly to the floor of the automobile, but still each cherry blossom went by at the pace of a trot. She looked over at a jogger who breezed past her ancient Chevy and she flushed with embarrassment. But she could not stay embarrassed for long. The car's alignment was off, so Janelle kept drifting to the side, though she was trying her best to stay in the right lane. She had to continue to hold her arms at an awkward angle in order to control the steering wheel, which took all her energy and concentration.

"Come on, baby," she muttered. "Just get momma to her grandma's and back and she'll put you to sleep. I promise! Come on, please!"

But she had made that promise plenty of times before, and her car knew it. It answered her angrily with a loud backfire from its rusted muffler, and then the truck behind her blew its horn, making her jump in her seat.

Was his hand glued to it? The steady blare was starting to grate on her nerves. She rolled her eyes and fought the urge to slam on her brakes, but that BMW truck had been kissing her bumper for the past five blocks. It wasn't her fault that her car would not go above thirty miles per hour! It would serve him right if he smashed his luxury truck into the back of her car. She hoped he destroyed his personalized plate *and* his expensive rims while he was at it.

Janelle glanced in her rearview mirror again and grumbled, seeing that he had not pulled back an inch. "Look, just go around me if you're in such a hurry, buddy!"

But the fellow in the SUV behind Janelle could not hear her. She couldn't even hear herself. Her motor was too loud. It finally hiccupped and then chugged into a steady cough as she pulled into one of the complex's visitor parking spaces. Janelle yanked the keys out of the ignition and sighed.

The gleaming SUV pulled into a parking space not far from her. In contrast to her car, it glided between the two white lines as smoothly and as quietly as a seagull over a sandy shore. Janelle shook her head when the driver opened his car door. Until now, he had been no more than a shadow looming against the afternoon light that she figured had to be that of a man.

"Typical," she muttered.

He was handsome by most standards, even better looking than last night's bed-thumper. Though his lips were now drawn into a tight line as he glowered at her, she could tell that they were full. He loudly zipped up his leather jacket, which draped over his tall frame with ease and slammed his door closed. Needless to say, he was not very subtle in expressing his anger. Hell, she could see the tic along his jawline even at this distance.

He used his index finger to push his sunglasses up the bridge of his nose. Janelle could not see his eyes behind the dark lenses, but she knew he was glaring just as hard at her as she was at him. She squinted. She could have sworn she had seen him somewhere before. If only she could remember where.

She blinked, feeling a slight rush of fear flood over her as he began to walk to her car. She reached for her purse though she knew there was nothing in there that could help her. She couldn't very well lipstick him to death. So she sucked in her breath and sat up as if a steel rod had been shoved into her back. She stuck out her chin and forced herself to raise an eyebrow. What was he going to do?

Mr. BMW stopped inches away from the door of her Chevy and leaned down.

"Before you get in a car, kid, learn how to drive," he said in a low voice before breezing down the sidewalk and opening one of the buildings' heavy doors, not giving her a chance to respond.

She sputtered for quite a few seconds. Janelle's chest heaved with anger and she pouted. She flipped down the vanity mirror and stared at herself.

She really didn't look like a kid, did she?

Big doe eyes gazed back at her, set in an oval nutmeg-toned face. She brushed her fingertips over the spray of dark freckles on her button nose, one of the many physical traits she had inherited from her Cherokee great-grandmother. Even with her grimace, a deep dimple could be seen in Janelle's left cheek, and both cheeks were as plump and rosy as they had been when she was five years old. On her ears hung delicate gold hoops the size of quarters, and her hair, which had taken her literally over an hour to tame, was pulled back in a pillowed bun at the nape of her neck.

Janelle flipped up the mirror and sighed warily. She *did* look like a sixteen-year-old girl. But she gritted her teeth and shook her head. It didn't matter what that guy thought. He was rude ... period. People like that always had opinions, but they mattered little in this world.

She reached over into the passenger seat and lifted her purse and then a heavy toolbox onto her lap. Her grandmother had called her in a frantic state about an hour ago, saying that something in her bathroom had broken, water was spilling everywhere and she needed it fixed right away. Not having any grandsons, and Janelle being the most mechanically adept of all her granddaughters, Janelle was often the one called upon when her grandmother wanted something fixed. She felt it was too inconsequential to concern the superintendent, but too important not to concern Janelle.

"Honey, you were just going to sit around the house anyway," the older woman had cried into the phone.

Janelle had rolled her eyes with irritation and flexed her toes. She was still wearing her coat, having just arrived home less than five minutes earlier. She had just removed her shoes, but because of this, she had to put them on again. Despite all that, she had tugged her heels back onto her feet and sighed. "I'll be right over," she had mumbled into the receiver.

So here she was, walking up the three flights of stairs to her grandmother's apartment, licking her lips as the smell of a big, enticing meal of greens, chicken, and biscuits wafted down the hallway. Janelle hoped her grandmother had cooked dinner. She was starving.

The door sprung open just as she raised her hand to knock. The next thing she knew she was being tugged inside and had a kiss firmly planted on her cheek.

"You're here, baby," her grandmother exclaimed with a wide smile.

Janelle frowned. "Yes," she said slowly. "You told me to hurry over, Grandma. Remember? The leak in the bathroom . . ."

"Oh, that!" Her grandmother shrugged. "Well, you know, it was just the darndest thing. Water was spraying everywhere and I called you. I knew you had just settled in for the evening and wasn't in a hurry to go out again so your grandmother went on up and decided to try to fix it herself. Water stopped and everything was okay. But by then, I figured you had already left your house so . . . I just decided to wait until you got here to tell you it was fixed. I haven't seen you in a while, anyway."

The sentences came out in a hurried rush. Janelle stood in the middle of the living room, bewildered.

"Um," she finally murmured. "Well, if it's fixed, then I guess I should head back home. I have to take Jasmine for her walk. Sharon refuses to do it, but she doesn't like it when Jasmine uses the bathroom in the house."

"Baby," her grandmother said in a small, pleading voice, "can't you just stay awhile?" I haven't seen you in so long."

Janelle smiled. "Grandma, you saw me last week."

"Well, when you're my age, Janelle," the elderly woman began, "every week passes like a day, every month like a week. I never know which day is my last so . . . I'm kinda selfish when it comes to spending time with the people I love. But if you have to go, baby, I understand."

Janelle flinched, feeling as if her chest had been peeled open. She hated when her grandmother talked like that, like her death could happen at any moment, like she could collapse on the floor at any second. But she *was* eighty years old. Janelle supposed that her grandmother's death should always be considered a likely possibility, even if neither of them wanted it to happen. She blinked and bit her lip, lowering her toolbox to the floor. Janelle forced a smile and shrugged out of her coat.

"Sure. Of course, I can stay."

"Good," her grandmother said, her voice perking. "Then you can have dinner with me and a friend of mine."

Dinner? Janelle sighed. "Okay, but do we have to drive there? My car's been acting funny again and I don't know how many trips I can get out of her."

"Nope, she's one floor up. Apartment 428." Her grandmother paused and narrowed her eyes. She scanned Janelle's face and frowned. "Are you wearing makeup, baby? Because if you are, it doesn't look like it."

"Grandma, that was the point," she began. "It's a light application. I didn't want anything dark or heavy or noticeable. It's just for work."

"Well, baby, you're not at work anymore. Maybe you should fix it up a little. You got some more in your purse, right?"

Janelle slowly nodded, a little confused.

Her grandmother walked away from her and headed to her bedroom down the hall. "The lady who we're having dinner with is always boasting about her pretty granddaughter," she said over her shoulder. "She's always boasting about this chile though I don't see what the big deal is. She showed me a picture and I thought the girl looked fine, simple enough, but not real pretty. So I decided I should show her what real pretty was. I wanted her to meet you." She returned to the living room with a bottle of perfume in her hand.

"Put some of this on, baby. I bought it at the store this week 'cuz it smelled like something you would wear. And while you at it, take your hair down. It looks so pretty when its down."

Janelle shook her head, starting to feel overwhelmed. She furrowed her eyebrows as her grandmother sprayed some of the contents of her bottle onto Janelle's wrist and neck but she drifted out of her daze and grabbed at her head when she started to feel the pins being pulled out of her bun.

"Grandma," she whined. "Stop! It took me forever to get it up."

But her grandmother only smiled and continued at her

task as if Janelle had not said anything. "Baby, it looks so pretty full." She let the mass of dark waves and curls fall past Janelle's shoulders and fluffed them with her fingers.

Janelle caught a glimpse of her reflection in the china cabinet and shook her curly head.

"That's not full. That's big."

"Oh, chile, stop acting silly and go in that bathroom and fix yourself up," she said, tapping Janelle on the bottom. "You got five minutes and we don't wanna be late."

Janelle had her purse shoved into her arms and the bathroom door firmly shut behind her. She blinked and looked around the small room. It was decorated with the same ugly pink fluff that it was decades ago. To her dismay, the brilliance of the blinding shade had yet to diminish with time. She inhaled deeply, taking in the familiar scent of Ivory soap and air freshener. Janelle slowly shook her head.

"What is she up to?" she thought with a weary smile.

A tale of a spouting faucet, then an invitation to a dinner with a "friend," and now her urgent need for Janelle to touch up her makeup just to show someone what "pretty really was"—Janelle wasn't buying any of it. She shook her head again as she began to quickly apply mascara to her already dark lashes. Something was rotten in Denmark and it wasn't the cheese. She wondered who this mysterious friend would be. Perhaps it would be the son of Reverend Williams whom her grandmother had been raving about for the past six months. Or maybe it was the guy from apartment 206 with the three kids.

Janelle dug through her purse until she found a tube of lipstick. As she finished the last of her makeup, she rolled her eyes and sighed. One thing was definite. She would have to brace herself for anything. A loud knock tore her from her thoughts.

"You finished in there, baby?" her grandmother said through the door.

Janelle leaned her head back and closed her eyes. If she clicked her heels three times, could she magically send herself back home?

"Baby? You okay in there?"

"I'm fine," she called out weakly. "I'm coming out."

Janelle opened the door with a slow creak to find her grandmother gazing at her, smiling broadly.

"Now, don't you look pretty? Mrs. Boyer will definitely be surprised."

They quietly climbed the flight of stairs to apartment 428, and the pleasurable fragrance of the impending dinner intensified. It definitely smelled good.

Janelle's spirits began to brighten. She glanced over at her grandmother who nodded for her to knock on the front door. She forced herself to smile and waited patiently until they heard the turn of a lock and then the sound of the chain being removed. When the door swung open, her smile instantly faded.

There he stood but without his jacket and his shades. The same expression of shock that she now held, registered on his face. Funny, he was still quite tall but he seemed a lot less intimidating now in just a gray wool sweater and jeans.

She blinked and suddenly realized that the first time she had seen those eyes, that chin, and that mouth was well before her brief encounter with him in the parking lot. Janelle slowly nodded as the recognition settled. She had seen him on at least three billboards. How could she possibly forget that face? *He* was the guy in the Salik cologne ad.

Chapter Three

There she was, giving him that "deer caught in the headlights" look again. It was the same expression she had given him when he walked toward her car in the parking lot.

Terrence had been prepared to berate her, knowing that his temper had only gotten the better of him, but on his list of *Things Terrence Boyer Hates,* bad drivers and slow drivers ranked high. She had the unfortunate coincidence of being both. But the moment he looked into the girl's stricken face, his anger went away, and he chose to give her a quick lecture instead.

"But she's no girl," Terrence thought as he smiled to himself. That was pretty obvious now as he let his gaze subtly wander up the length of her. He had become accustomed to tall and somewhat thin women. They came with the business. He had grown to like their firmness and sleekness. He preferred the way the spaghetti straps of a silk dress fell over their slender shoulders and how the fabric draped instead of clung and pulled along their bodies, but every now and then he yearned for something a bit . . . meatier. At medium height and with a curvy frame, this woman with the black curls had hips and thighs that more than filled out the slacks she was wearing. She folded her arms (a self-conscious habit, he would imagine) over her full chest and pursed her lips. Terrence gazed at her with admiration until his focus settled on her saucer-sized eyes.

Does she always have to look like that? he reflected with amusement. *I'm not going to hurt you, sweetheart.*

He smirked to himself as he saw her being less than gently eased through the doorway of his grandmother's apartment by the matronly woman behind her.

He had been just as surprised as she when he viewed her

through the peephole. Well, perhaps "surprised" was too mild a word to describe what he had felt at that moment. In a matter of seconds he had switched from shock, to anger, to amusement, and now to interest. Terrence had been less than happy to find that the "girl" from the parking lot was the one his grandmother had intended him to meet, for he had known he was meeting someone. No, his grandmother had not come out and directly said it, but the instant Terrence saw the extra table settings, he had quickly come to that conclusion.

He now shook his head. How many times had he told his Mother, the woman who had practically raised him, that he was already involved with someone? How many times? *How many times does she usually listen to you?* he asked himself warily. But he wouldn't be rude. He would just have to grin and bear it. Besides, from the look on the woman's face, she seemed less than happy to find out that he was her mystery date, too.

"You came right on time. Glad you could make it, baby," his grandmother called out as she walked toward the young woman and embraced her in a friendly hug. Terrence supposed she knew the routine of openly affectionate black women from the South. She did not flinch when his grandmother hugged her but gave a genuine smile.

"Supper will be ready in five minutes," his grandmother continued while turning to him. "Terrence, this is Mrs. Howard and her granddaughter, Janelle. Janelle's a writer."

He took his cue and held out his hand for a shake but was only given a less than firm grasp from Janelle. In contrast, when he turned to her grandmother, he received a bear hug and a loud kiss on the cheek.

"Why don't you all take a seat on the couch? Get to talking," his grandmother said as she headed toward the kitchen. "I'll finish up."

He guided them toward the living room in silence, shoving his hand in his pockets before turning to them with an awkward smile. He gestured toward the plastic-covered couch, implying that they should sit down. He was forming his lips to comment on the weather just as Mrs. Howard suddenly burst out, "Well, I think I'll go and help Gerty in the kitchen."

The older woman rushed away, stopping momentarily to give a more than obvious wink to Janelle and a grin to Terrence. When the kitchen door closed behind her, they both stood in the quiet living room, each growing more and more uncomfortable with the lengthening silence.

This is dumb, he thought to himself as he watched her gnaw on her lower lip and slowly sit down. He wasn't an inexperienced thirteen-year-old boy, and he no longer intended to act like one.

"So, you're a writer," he began softly, stretching an arm across the back of the sofa.

She looked up, stared at him blankly as if she hadn't heard him correctly and shrugged. The flowery fragrance of her perfume wafted toward him.

"Actually, I write, but I'm not a writer. Not published anyway. I wish grandma would stop telling people that." She smiled. "I'm a copyreader."

"A copyreader?"

"Well, I think most people would call it a proofreader, actually. I edit brochures for a travel agency."

Janelle looked down at her hands as she said that, like she was embarrassed. She smirked, tucked a lock of hair behind her ear, looked up again and held his gaze. Her brown eyes glowed with amusement.

"I guess I'm the poster child for why kids shouldn't major in liberal arts in college."

She laughed softly at her joke and he smiled. Terrence could remember making similar jabs at himself before he started modeling. Unfortunately, with the exception of Mother, his family had not taken his decision to study social work in college instead of business quite so humorously. His father refused to pay the university's tuition if Terrence went through with his choice. But stubbornly, Terrence did it anyway, earning his own way through school.

Janelle began to nervously gnaw on her bottom lip again, grabbing his attention. Terrence eyes focused on that bottom lip.

It had been covered with a vibrant shade of glossy red a few minutes ago, but with her constant gnawing the color had disappeared and now its natural pink was showing. He wondered if he could bring back its flush of red if he leaned over and kissed her . . . hard.

Where the hell did that idea come from? he thought with surprise. He supposed his silence and intense staring was starting to irritate her. She shifted uncomfortably and started to speak.

"So," she began, "what do you do?"

Good move. Now he was in the spotlight. Terrence cleared his throat. "I'm a model."

To his surprise, Janelle let out a loud snort and smiled.

"What's so funny?" he asked, his eyes narrowing.

"I thought I had seen you on a billboard somewhere. But then I thought, 'No, it can't be him.' You know, every time I drive down the highway and see it, I have to stop myself from laughing? I mean, that commercial . . . what were they thinking?" She leaned her head back and laughed again. "All those violins, and naked people running through fields, and floating bottles of cologne—it was so crazy! 'I want to smell you, my love,' " she mimicked in an exaggerated French accent. "God, I'm all for artistic expression, but don't make a mockery of it. It was just so . . . stupid." She shook her head. "Did you feel weird doing that stuff?"

Janelle leaned over and tapped her hand on his knee as she spoke.

It wasn't an act of flirtation. She seemed rather naïve, unaware of how the smallest gestures could arouse the opposite sex. If it wasn't for the streamline of slaps she had just given to his ego, Terrence may have felt a perk of excitement at the sensation of her hand through the fabric of his jeans. But right now, all he could think about was her mention of the word "stupid." She had the gall to call his commercial stupid. He gritted his teeth and smiled.

"Well, I'm sure you could have written a much better commercial," he said blandly, "having all that experience proofreading brochures and everything."

Her laughter fizzled. She cleared her throat and crossed her legs. The friendly hand was removed quickly from his knee but he could still feel the heat of the warm palm as if she had seared it to his flesh.

"I'm sorry. I put my foot in my mouth, didn't I? I do that all the time." She shook her head and smiled awkwardly. "Look, I wasn't insulting you. I was only talking about the commercial. I didn't know you liked it. It was . . . different, I guess. It's just that every time I see it I—"

Terrence glanced down at his watch and yawned. "You don't have to repeat it. I heard you the first time."

At that instant, she shrank back into herself and all warmth and friendliness left her eyes. She began to fidget with a figurine on the coffee table.

He knew she hadn't meant to insult him. He knew he was only being rude. To be honest, Terrence had thought the commercial was stupid, too, but just the sight of her laughing infuriated him. When the director had given him instructions on what to do, he had stared at him as if he were crazy. Symbolism was one thing; pointless footage was another. But he decided as long as he received his paycheck on time and in full, he could roll around naked for an hour in daisies. It hadn't killed him. It was just that modeling already made him feel awkward. He hated when people, especially people whom he was finding himself attracted to, made fun of his work. He hated it, even if they weren't making fun of it directly.

"Collard greens still stewin' but everything else is done," he heard his grandmother call from the doorway of the kitchen. She held a dish in her arms filled with chicken drumsticks. "You two children gettin' to know each other?"

When neither of them answered her with more than a cold nod, she frowned. She turned to Mrs. Howard who shrugged and placed the gravy boat in the center of the dining room table.

"Well, once we all get to eatin', I'm sure the conversation will start up."

But it didn't. With the exception of words between his grandmother and Mrs. Howard, the dinner was carried out in relative silence. He would peek up occasionally from his plate to look at Janelle. Terrence would find her looking back at him but she would quickly break her gaze when their eyes met. He flicked his food around his plate with his fork and drank his lemonade quietly. The big appetite he had an hour ago had disappeared and now he wanted nothing more than to get out of his grandmother's apartment. He shoved the last of the food in his mouth and rose from the table.

"Well, I guess I better get going. It was nice meeting you, Mrs. Howard . . . Janelle." He leaned down to his grandmother and pecked her on the cheek. "Mother, I'll give you a call sometime this week, okay?"

She furrowed her eyebrows and slid back her chair. "You not going to stay for dessert, baby?"

"No, I really should get going."

"Wait. Wait." She said, shaking her head and shuffling toward the kitchen. "Let me cut you a slice a pie and wrap it up for you."

"Really, Mother," he insisted while waving away the food with his hands. "It's okay. I'm full. Anymore and I would burst."

"Well, you don't have to eat it now," she pleaded. "And you can't leave yet anyway. Janelle needs someone to walk her to her car. You wouldn't let her walk by herself, would you, Terrence?"

Janelle shook her head and forced a smile. "Oh, I'll be okay. Don't worry about me."

Mrs. Howard caught Mrs. Boyer's pleading glance and joined in. "I won't hear of it, Janey. It's too dark outside and this neighborhood isn't as nice as yours. Plus, you have that big toolbox to carry. You could strain yourself with that thing. Don't be stubborn, Janelle. Let Terrence help you."

Janelle and Terrence for the first time that night openly gazed at one another, silently waiting for the other to provide some cue that could give them a way out of this situation. But none was given. Terrence finally sighed gruffly and shrugged his shoulders.

"Well, if you want me to walk you to your car, we should do it now." He felt a hard hand smack his shoulder. He turned to find his grandmother glaring at him. Terrence sighed and gritted his teeth. "That is, if you're done eating, Janelle."

Janelle pasted a grin to her face. "No, I'm finished. I should be getting home, too."

"Well, then," his grandmother said a little too loudly, "problem solved. I'll pack you both dessert in some aluminum foil and you two can get going . . . together."

Terrence and Janelle left the apartment building with not only a slice of sweet potato pie for each, wrapped in aluminum foil, but two sealed plates each of that night's dinner.

"Just in case you get hungry later," his grandmother said with a wink.

He tried his best to balance the food and the toolbox in his arms as he was hugged and kissed by the two older women. Now as he stepped into the crisp fall night, he felt as if he was taking his first breath of fresh air. Their not-too-subtle attempts at matchmaking and endless hint-dropping had been stifling.

"Where's your car again?" he asked briskly, ready to bolt to freedom at any moment.

"Over there," Janelle said as she pointed. "Not far from yours, actually."

He took long, quick strides to the automobile and waited until she pulled out her keys and opened the car door. He set the toolbox in the seat beside her before muttering, "Good night. Drive safely."

He didn't wait for her reply. Terrence quickly walked to his car, dug into his pocket and retrieved the button that automatically unlocked his car doors and almost tossed the plates into the backseat.

He had just slammed the driver's side door closed when he heard the noise. It was a loud wheezing at first and then one clink and then another. It sounded like an engine trying its best to turn over but with little success.

"Come on," he heard her say as she slapped her hand against the steering wheel. "Come on. Please!"

It chugged for a few more seconds before dropping to dead silence, making Terrence roll his eyes and sigh. *What more?* he thought.

He slowly climbed back out of his car and walked over to her. He leaned down and knocked on her car window, motioning for her to roll it down. She obliged him but pouted as she did it, not meeting his gaze but only staring stubbornly out the car's windshield, her face flushed with embarrassment.

"Having trouble?" he asked. He tried his best to keep the laughter out of his voice.

She closed her eyes, bit her lip, and opened her eyes again.

"My car won't start."

"Yeah, I figured that. Well, do you want to pop open the hood? Maybe I can take a look at it."

She puffed her cheeks and slowly blew air out of them. "Don't bother. The only way you could fix this engine is if you installed a new one. It should have died a long time ago. It's a miracle she lasted this long."

He stood there crouched, listening to the night air whip past his ears until he finally asked, "So what do you want to do?"

She shrugged. "I don't know. Call Triple-A, I guess. Then maybe a cab."

"No need for a cab. Why don't I drive you home? You can call someone to tow this, uh," he paused to glance at the rusted exterior and battered tires, "car away at your place."

She shook her head. "I don't think that's a good idea."

"Look," he began, "both you and I know we haven't hit it off well. But *I'm* willing to put all that aside because I don't want to hear my grandmother a year from now talking about how I let a woman call a cab rather than drive her home. Save me the torture and let me drive you."

She turned to him then and studied his face quietly though he wasn't sure what she was looking for. Reassurance? A promise that he wouldn't try to jump her if she climbed in his BMW? Whatever it was, she seemed to find the answer. Janelle finally pulled the keys out of the ignition and Terrence stepped back to let her climb out of the automobile.

The directions she gave him were simple and, to his surprise, he discovered that she lived barely twenty minutes from his neighborhood. The drive was carried out in silence for the most part. It would have been a lot more pleasant if it weren't for the fact that he had to fight off strange impulses the entire time. If it wasn't her becoming profile under the streetlights of the highway grabbing his attention, it was the smell of her perfume. He had to battle the urge to lean over and smell her neck, to place his nose in the crevice behind her ear and nibble on her earlobe. When he finally couldn't take anymore, he lowered his window, letting the cold air whip across his face but making her hair toss around her as if they were caught in a storm.

She rubbed her shoulders and shivered.

"Could you please roll the window up? I'm freezing."

"We're almost there," he muttered, deciding that she would rather be cold than to have him pull to the side of the road and kiss her senseless.

His car skidded to a stop in front of her house and he tried his best not to look her in the eyes. For some reason she wasn't opening her door. He turned to her and saw that she was pursing her lips again.

"Thank you," she muttered softly.

"No problem."

He could feel a knot forming in his stomach as he waited for her to leave. An ambulance roared past his car and he looked up. When he saw it make a right at the corner and disappear from view, he turned back to Janelle to find her standing outside his car, closing the door. She looked as if she were going to climb up the steps to her house but then she faced him again and smiled.

"Do you always call your grandmother 'Mother'?" she said

His eyes narrowed. He could feel his anger perking.

"Why? Is that stupid too?" he asked icily.

She shook her head. "No, I don't have a problem with that. In fact, I thought it was . . . sweet."

He let his gaze follow her until she mounted the steps and closed one of the green French doors behind her.

Kara stretched her long limbs and lifted her behind from the cushion. She sighed gruffly, looked at the clock on the wall and took a sip of red wine from her glass. So much for coming off as spontaneous and sexy—the Italian leather of the couch was sticking to her naked body as if it were taped to her. It made the most irritating burping noise as she tried to slide her feet unto the armrest.

She fanned herself with her hands. It was hard being alluring when she was sweating like a pig. Well, not sweating like a pig exactly but she certainly did not feel attractive. She did *not* feel like herself. Kara Djibutar did not perspire under any situation where perspiration was not required, whether it be under the blazing lights of a runway or posing with a celebrity during a photo shoot. If the occasion needed a beautiful mystique that seemed more than human, she could give it full force.

Absolutely, she thought as she took another sip from her glass, affirming her own thoughts.

She wiped at the trickle of sweat that ran down her back and grumbled. God, it was hot! She considered rising from her enticing pose long enough to turn down the thermostat but she figured, why bother? Terrence would be home at any moment and the drops of sweat pouring out of her now would be nothing compared to the ones that would flood out of her later, after she and Terrence "made up." The very thought made a tingle of anticipation travel from the tips of her toes to the top of her head and back again. It radiated from a spot that caused her to cross her legs tightly and give another anxious glance to the front door.

Kara wanted much but needed little in this world. But with that in mind, Terrence had managed to take her to levels of pleasure that made her crave him like a drug. She needed her fix and she needed it now.

Kara didn't know who had given Terrence his "skillz" or if it just came naturally, but that boy was talented. She could vouch for that. He was talented enough to have a woman like herself lying buck-naked on his sofa, offering her body to him like an entree.

She glanced at the wall clock again. It was almost half past ten. Where the hell was he?

She sighed and laid her head back. She listened to the jazz music playing softly on his radio and began to hum while letting the wine tumble down her throat. Kara twisted a gold-streaked lock of hair around her finger and eyed a split end.

Suddenly, she stopped. The scratching grew louder. What was that noise? She gave a soft chuckle to herself when she realized what it was.

"That bloody dog," she mumbled and swirled what was left of her wine in her glass before finishing it all with one gulp.

She didn't know why Terrence bothered with the ugly thing. As far as she was concerned, that mutt could stay in the bathroom all night.

Kara had tussled with the bulldog for about an hour. She dragged him out of the living room and down the hall between growls and barks and nips at her hands, breaking an acrylic nail in the process. She finally managed to shove him into the master bath, and slam the door firmly behind him. She left him to charge his muzzle like a battering ram into the door over and over again. But Sven grew tired at his failed attempts to pop it from its hinges. He plopped down on the cold tile and whimpered. Every now and then he would give a few pitiful scratches at the door but she had no problem ignoring him.

"Why a bulldog?" she now thought irritably. Out of all the dogs Terrence could have chosen to get, he chose a bulldog. Why not a Pomeranian or a Bichon Frisc? They were so small and cuddly and not to mention more fashionable. All the other girls had one. Kara couldn't very well walk down

Fifth Avenue wearing Christian Dior, traipsing behind a bulldog. She would look absolutely ridiculous.

She shook her head. "One for money, one for love," she reasoned aloud.

That was the motto she lived by. It was the affirmation she clung to when men and their reasoning bewildered her. To Kara, men fell into two categories. Some men were meant to be lovers, others were meant to pay their paramour's rent and finance romantic trips to the Canaries or São Paolo. Now Terrence—he was definitely a lover. When they weren't in bed, she found him mildly amusing, but for the most part their biggest fire sparked on a sexual level.

Jean-Paul was her "financer," a doting patron of the young, beautiful, and female since 1978. She had not only accepted Jean-Paul David's invitation to dinner (as she had many times before though Terrence had been none the wiser), but she also accepted his invitation to his chateau, obliged his offer of a tour of his spacious vineyard, and did not refuse his invitation to bed. But the Frenchman, almost forty years her senior, lacked Terrence's prowess between the sheets. When he was without his wallet and standing naked before her in his pale and wrinkled glory, the attraction she had for him quickly faded. She could only stand a week with Jean-Paul, even with his army of servants waiting on her hand and foot. After five days, she leapt on a plane and headed for the U.S., heading straight for Terrence's apartment.

Kara leaned over, refilled her wineglass for the fourth time, and sighed. But she was still considering Jean-Paul's proposal. The velvet box containing the five-carat engagement diamond he had given her was tucked neatly in her purse.

"What is it with old men?" she asked aloud. "Do they just want to *give* their money away?"

Well, if she married him, she could at least keep on a few

men as lovers. There was no reason to sacrifice them completely.

Kara considered the possibilities until she heard a key being placed in Terrence's door. Her first instinct was to jump on him as soon as he stepped inside the foyer, but she checked it and lay back as if him finding her naked on his couch was the most natural thing in the world. Besides, she was *supposed* to be mad at him. She could at least act aloof.

Terrence threw his keys onto a table and began to remove his coat. She could pinpoint the exact moment when he noticed her for his mouth instantly dropped open.

"Well," she said smugly, "you're checking in late, aren't you?"

He frowned, shook his head, and then smiled. "But I see you had no problem making yourself at home."

"Yes," she said as she raised her arms, stretched and tucked them behind her head, "you could say that."

When he continued to gaze at her and she began to think it would be years before she felt his hands on her flesh again, she murmured, "I'm angry at you, Tory. Very angry."

"Well, you certainly have an odd way of showing it." He looked around and frowned. "Where's my dog? You didn't kill him, did you?"

"He's fine. Don't worry." She rolled her eyes. "Now stop being a smart ass," she ordered as she sat up and kneeled on the leather cushions. She felt a little dizzy under the spell of the wine, but she offered a hand to Terrence, beckoning him toward her. "Let me show you how angry I am."

He walked over to her slowly, making her knees weak with impatience. As he lowered his mouth to her, she saw a level of intensity in his eyes she had never seen before. She was sure it was the sight of her naked body that sparked the fervor. She wrapped one arm around his neck and let the other slide up his back, rubbing her torso and pelvis against the wool of his sweater, feeling his washboard stomach through the thick fabric. A moan pealed from the back of his throat and she answered it with her own. He then grabbed her with a ferocity that took her breath away.

Kara gazed up at him with awe and smiled. *What the hell has gotten into him?* she thought. Whatever it was, she hoped it happened more often.

Chapter Four

Janelle turned away from her computer screen and sighed loudly. She rubbed her eyes and gnawed on the end of the pen she was holding. If anyone walked past her cubicle at that moment, they would find her gazing at the calendar tacked haphazardly to the gray cloth wall. They might think she was skimming over the office meetings for the month of October or planning her schedule around the doctor's appointment written in black ink under Thursday, but she was doing neither. Her gaze was blank, completely devoid of focus, and her mind was lost in thought.

Janelle had been that way all week, lost in a daydream. She caught herself daydreaming in the kitchen as she squeezed dishwashing liquid into her milk instead of chocolate syrup. She had even locked herself out of her new rental car at least a half a dozen times because her mind was somewhere else. But these slipups, no matter how ditzy they seemed to her, went unnoticed by everyone else . . . thank God. It wasn't until she did the laundry that someone else began to realize that something was not right. She had accidentally washed colored clothes with the whites and had ruined Sharon's silk-and-lace negligee. Sharon had been forced to (horror of horrors!) entertain one of her nightly guests in just a bra and panties.

"I guess I'll just wash the clothes myself from now on," Sharon had remarked with a haughty lift of her chin before shutting her bedroom door.

"Maybe you should. We maids mess up sometimes, Ms. Sharon," Janelle replied, shocking them both.

Janelle gave up nibbling on the end of her pen and pulled a box of crackers from her desk drawer. She glanced at the desks around her. The constant telephone chatter and clatter of keyboards was starting to annoy her. Was the office always like this? Why did everything suddenly seem so loud?

Janelle sighed again. She had no idea what was wrong, but whatever it was, it seemed to be getting worse. Her mind was stuck in a haze, and the only thing that seemed to penetrate it was his face.

Of course, it didn't help that her drives outside DC always included passing his billboard at least once. Janelle would try to fight the impulse, but she would find herself looking up, gazing at the face that gave her the same expression of smugness and derision that he had given to her that night.

Don't go there, she thought.

Every time she reflected back to that night's dinner she wanted to smack herself . . . hard. If she hadn't been so argumentative and hadn't put her foot in her mouth, she may have been planning what to wear for a date this evening instead of deciding what movie she wanted to rent for another Friday night home alone. What a fool! Her grandmother had plopped a perfectly attractive, single black man into her lap and she had tossed him back. She had tossed back a model.

A model, Janelle thought as she shoved a cracker into her mouth and grumbled.

How many women would drop to their knees and grovel for such an opportunity? But it was she, Janelle Nicole

Howard, who had said "thanks but no thanks," or had he said it? She was so confused.

"If that frown got any lower, it'd hit the floor."

Janelle glanced up and saw the smiling face of Leila, one of her coworkers. The perky petite blonde flipped her hair over her shoulder and tucked a pencil behind her ear.

"What's up? What's with the sad face?"

Janelle shook her head. It was so hard to put her feelings and her uneasiness into words. She wasn't really in the mood to share her thoughts at that moment anyway.

"I was just thinking. That's all," she muttered.

"About what?" Leila persisted.

"Nothing," she said as she turned from the calendar and faced the computer screen again, hoping that Leila would take the hint.

"We'll it can't be 'nothing.' It's hard to think about absolutely nothing."

"Leila," Janelle whined and then grumbled. She shook her head and gave an exasperated laugh. "Look, I just—"

"Okay. Okay. Look, I wasn't trying to pester you, Janelle. I was just wondering if something was wrong and if you wanted to talk about it, but if you don't, that's fine." She stared down at her burgundy snakeskin flats and hid a smile. "I can always go back to Ted's desk and listen to him cry about how his wife is putting him through the wringer in divorce court. Or I can hear Mary's fifth recount of her root canal. I'm sure *they* won't mind sharing, and we all know how exciting those two can be."

Janelle couldn't help but laugh.

"So that's what you have to choose from? A twenty-seven-year-old depressed woman, a complaining divorcee, and a root canal?"

"Basically." Leila shrugged her shoulders. "And guess what? *You* won out."

Janelle shook her head and sighed. She gazed up at Leila

whose protruding pregnant tummy could be seen easily in her two-piece crimson wool suit. A month ago she had lost the swift gait that earned her the office nickname Road-runner and had slowed down to a steady and adorable wad-dle.

To Janelle, Leila's pregnancy and marriage were almost strange. Was it her imagination or had it all happened too quickly?

Leila had been like her less than two years ago. She had even been Janelle's occasional Friday night movie partner when neither of them had a date. Before seeing the movie, they would go shopping together and rant on and on about how they were young and sophisticated career women with goals and drive and had no time for relationships and wouldn't even consider marriage or children anytime soon. Janelle felt like Leila had deserted her, or at least she wasn't sure if Leila had just been patronizing her when she said (what seemed not too long ago) that she thought there was "more to life than a wedding ring and popping out babies." Now, in-stead of talking about her dreams of going back to school to get her Ph.D., or moving to India, Leila talked about the price of Pampers and her husband's new fitness gym. Janelle found it hard to open up to her now. What did they have in common?

"Just had a bad setup," Janelle began. "That's all."

Leila frowned. "Setup?"

"Yeah." Janelle sighed. She relented and decided to tell the entire story. "My grandmother trapped me into a blind date with this guy, a friend's grandson, and it didn't go well. But he was gorgeous, Leila, and polite." She tossed a pencil on her desk. "I guess it was my fault. I insulted him. He got pissed. He drove me home, which was a nice thing to do, but I ruined it again by asking him a question that came out wrong." She shook her head. "I guess I just don't know when to keep my mouth shut. But I was nervous . . . and angry.

Every time I tried to be nice and he got mad, I would start to remember how he beeped his horn at me—"

"He beeped his horn at you?"

Janelle shook her head and laughed softly. "It's an even longer story. You don't wanna know."

Leila pursed her lips, causing a thin white line to develop between them. She contemplated a bit before saying, "Well, to be honest it doesn't seem like you to insult a person for no reason. I'm sure he deserved it."

Janelle sighed. "I'm not so sure."

"Well"—Leila shrugged—"that's water under the bridge. I say let it go. Forget him completely." She leaned forward as much as her stomach would allow. "But speaking of setups. I know the perfect guy for you."

Janelle laughed and covered her face. "No. No. No more setups! Didn't I just tell you that I insulted a guy my grandmother thought was 'perfect for me'? Forget it, Leila. I don't perform well under pressure. The next guy someone tries to set me up with, I'll probably accidentally knock spaghetti into his lap, or something."

Leila shook her head and laughed. "Well, that would be pretty hard, considering he's a vegetarian."

"A *vegetarian?* Leila, you aren't trying to set me up with one of your husband's beach boy friends, are you?"

Leila pretended to be insulted. "No, I'm not setting you up with one of them. And just because they know how to surf doesn't mean they're beach boys!" She laughed. "Actually, he's a guy I know from college. Cedric Williams. He's single. He's smart. He's cute, not my taste exactly, but far be it for me to deny anyone else. He runs his own restaurant in Chicago." She rubbed her hand over her stomach to calm the baby's kicking. "I think he's a catch, Janelle."

Janelle sighed and frowned. "I don't know."

"Oh, come on, Janey. He's a good guy and you won't even give him a chance. You two might really hit it off."

"Leila, it's not him. Really. I just don't know why everyone is doing this? Trying to set me up with people. I'm not that bad. If everyone just left me alone—"

"No," Leila said as she fervently shook her head and waddled closer to her. "You aren't that bad, Janelle, but its just . . . you seem . . . you seem sad. Believe me, I know plenty of women who are a lot closer to thirty than you are who are single and active and happy, but they're rare. And you're not one of them. When we hung out together it seemed that you went out rarely—"

"So I like staying at home," she said with a shrug, facing the computer screen again to type. Her anger now piqued.

". . . And you haven't been in a relationship as long as I've known you, and that isn't a short period of time," Leila insisted.

Janelle's fingers paused over the keyboard, and she took a steadying breath.

"So now being unattached and independent is a bad thing?" she asked, wanting to clench her hands at her sides. She closed her eyes, shutting out the obvious stares from people in the cubicles around them. It seemed that their little conversation had become the focus of the entire office.

She shook her head. She had been crazy to confide in Leila. She should have known that she would only get lectured from Mrs. Martha Stewart. Not only lectured, but embarrassed.

"No. No. That's not what I'm saying," Leila said while holding up her hands as if she were in front of a line of policemen. "No, it isn't a bad thing usually, but it *is* a bad thing if being 'unattached' makes you unhappy, which is what I see happening with you. It's like you're stuck in a rut or something." She shrugged. "I see it. Obviously, you're grandmother sees it. We're only trying to help."

"Well, I don't *need* any help," Janelle said through clenched teeth. "I don't care what anyone else thinks—not you or my grandmother. I'm not a charity case. If I want a date, I'll sure as hell get one and I don't *want one!* Besides, who died and made you a relationship expert? So now being married and pregnant makes you an authority on life?"

Leila's pale face turned beet red. Her lower lip began to tremble. She sniffed loudly at first, and then puddles of tears began to flood from her round blue eyes.

She had done it again. Janelle instantly regretted the words once they leapt from her mouth.

"I'm sorry," Leila said between sobs. "I didn't mean to upset you! I was only trying to help!"

Janelle turned away momentarily to dig through her desk drawer for a box of tissues. She handed one to Leila who blew into it loudly, still crying as if someone had ran over her dog.

"No. I'm sorry, Leila," Janelle said standing up and leaning forward to clasp Leila into a hug, hoping to calm her down. She let the woman cry on her shoulder and through the tangled mass of blonde hair in front of her eyes, Janelle could see that they had the entire office's attention.

Leila leaned back, still wiping at her wet nose. Her tears subsided. She looked around and then stared back at Janelle.

"You know I cry all the time now?" Leila said as she smoothed down her tussled mass of hair. "I stub my toe on the edge of the bed. I cry. I finish off the last of our strawberry ice cream. I cry. I even cry when I miss my favorite soaps." She gave an awkward laugh before tossing her ball of tissue into a nearby trashcan. "This baby is doing horrible things to my hormones. She's turning me into a basket case."

"Leila," Janelle began slowly, "I won't promise you anything, but give me his number, okay? When I work up the nerve, I'll give him a call."

Leila shook her head. "You don't have to do that, Janelle.

I cry like a banshee and you go on a date even though you don't want to. That's not right, Janey."

"It's okay, Leila," she said with a smile. "I—I want to."

Janelle regretted that lie as she heard the doorbell ring one week later. She took a few calming breaths to gather herself and continued to put on her teardrop earrings. She called out to Sharon to answer the door.

"Why do I have to answer it?" Sharon said as she peeked her head into the doorway of Janelle's bedroom. "He's *your* date."

Jazz rose from the bed long enough to bark at Sharon angrily and then sat back down, letting her ears flop against the lavender comforter.

"Yes, he's *my* date but I'm still getting ready. When you aren't ready when your dates arrive, I let them in."

Janelle sighed and studied her image carefully while Sharon looked her up and down and sucked her teeth.

"Why do you insist on dressing like a school mom?"

Janelle patted down her black velvet cocktail dress and faced Sharon defensively.

"I am not dressed like a school mom. It's a first date . . . I want to look sophisticated, not trashy. Besides, Sharon, its thirty-eight degrees outside. How can I be daring when it is almost below freezing?"

"Well," she said with a raised eyebrow, "if you wore something hot, Janelle, the temperature outside wouldn't matter."

Janelle added a touch of blush to her cheeks and tried her best to ignore Sharon's words of wisdom.

"Thanks for the advice, roomie. Now could you go downstairs and answer the door so that he doesn't turn into a Popsicle while he's waiting outside for me?"

"Whatever," Sharon said with a shrug, lifting her chest as

she turned toward the stairwell. "Don't say I didn't warn you."

"Believe me, I won't," Janelle mumbled as she added the last finishing touch to her wardrobe. She had pressed out her mass of curls early that day with a hot iron so that her hair now hung to her waist. She tucked a small diamond clip into the swell of curl that hung over her eye and smiled. She turned her head to the left and then to the right, trying to convince herself that she looked fine and that there was no need to be nervous. But she still couldn't calm the beating of her heart or the shaking of her hands.

She stood there for what seemed an eternity until laughter erupted from downstairs. She could identify one voice to be that of her roommate, but the other was throaty and masculine. Well, at least he was getting along well with Sharon. Janelle frowned. Wait. Cedric getting along well with Sharon is not a good thing. With that, Janelle grabbed her purse and slid her feet into her high heels before rushing downstairs to meet her date.

The Chinese restaurant was fine with the exception that Cedric insisted that she try the uncooked tofu. She smiled when he offered her the gelatinous cube between chopsticks and even managed not to cringe as he placed it in her mouth and she began to chew. She swallowed it quickly and gulped down the rest of her soda, resolving to scrub her tongue with her toothbrush as soon as she arrived back home.

Cedric admitted with a smile that he didn't exactly own a restaurant in Chicago. Leila had "misinterpreted" him. Janelle wondered just how much about Cedric Leila had misinterpreted, for the person who sat before her seemed a lot different from the guy Leila had described.

He wasn't a blond beach boy by any means, but once Janelle saw the dated high-top fade, khakis, and penny loafers, she realized he wouldn't make the cover of *Ebony* either. But she figured that she shouldn't be so particular. She decided to look past the corduroy patches on the sleeves of his jacket and bitten-to-the-bone fingernails and give him a chance for that night at least.

"You know," Cedric said as he took a sip from his teacup. "Your roommate is really funny."

His dark gaze focused on Janelle as he leaned forward. She could almost feel the whiskers of his goatee brushing against her ear and she had to avert her face to keep their noses from hitting. She turned and pretended to be engrossed by the Chinese calligraphy on the wall so that she no longer had to feel his hot and slightly tart breath on her cheek.

"Yep," Janelle said, wiping at the corner of her mouth with her dinner napkin. "She's a funny girl."

"She asked me how I felt about threesomes."

Janelle coughed out the piece of shrimp she had in her mouth into her dinner napkin. She grabbed a glass of water and swallowed it.

"She did, did she?" she asked after regaining her breath.

"Yeah," he said with a devilish grin, making his brown eyes twinkle. "She said you guys do that sort of thing all the time. She asked me if I was interested in joining you."

"Oh, that Sharon," Janelle said with a forced laugh. "Such a funny girl."

His face fell and he leaned back slightly. He picked up his chopsticks and began to eat again. "Yeah, I—I figured that."

Janelle shook her head and decided the minute she returned home, she would kill her roommate.

"So I heard you and Leila know one another from college."

He looked up from his plate and nodded. "Yeah, we were

in the same art class. I was in Culinary Arts, she was in Sociology."

Janelle smiled. "So you two shared art brushes or something?"

"No, I wasn't actually in the class. I was the model."

Janelle stopped chewing. "Come again?" Not another one.

"I was the nude model. It was the class for sketching human forms. You got paid decent money for that stuff. Got free fruit from the bowl from the still life class before that." He laughed and nudged her shoulder, catching her off guard and making her slosh water up her nose.

She wiped her face and forced a smile. "Well, if Leila was just supposed to be sketching you and you were modeling, then how did you guys start talking?"

He gave an unapologetic grin and shrugged. "I guess she liked what she saw. Most of the girls there did. Had to fight them off with a stick." He paused to take another bite of tofu.

Janelle didn't argue with him, but she distinctly remembered Leila saying that he wasn't her type. *Oh, well,* Janelle thought, *let him live with his illusions.*

"Is that so?" she asked sarcastically.

"Yeah," he whispered. "Want to test the product for yourself? Like the commercial says, 'Satisfaction guaranteed.' "

When she stared at him blankly, not accepting his offer or even smiling, he feigned a laugh.

"Just kidding," he said while nudging her shoulder again.

Janelle smiled and looked down at her watch. "Would you look at the time? I have to be home by ten. I think we'd better finish up."

He frowned. "Why?"

She nodded her head as she gave a pleading glance to the waiter to bring the check.

"It's my dog," Janelle said. "She gets so antsy late at night,

and I know Sharon hasn't fed her or took her for her walk.
I—"

She stopped talking when she realized Cedric was no
longer paying attention to her. He frowned at the check in
front of him and pulled out his wallet. He began to flip
through the stack of bills, which was mostly composed of
ones, and gave a long sigh.

Janelle pursed her lips and placed her hand on top of the
leather casing.

"Its okay. I brought a credit card." She scanned her eyes
over the total. "I'll take care of the check but *you* handle the
tip."

He drove her home and she didn't remember ever being
so happy at the sight of her front door. She cursed Leila. She
cursed Sharon. She cursed her high heels as she limped uncomfortably up the steps with Cedric inches behind her. She
took a deep breath, pasted a smile to her face and turned
back to him.

"Well, thank you for the nice evening. It was great meeting you, Cedric."

"No, problem. I hope we can do it again sometime."

She continued to smile silently and waited for him to
walk back to his car.

"Well," she said awkwardly, "goodnight."

"Goodnight, Janelle."

She had hoped he was leaning toward her for a hug, but
when she felt his mouth touch hers, she figured she had been
wrong. She parted her lips in disgust and instantly felt his
tongue hitting her teeth and darting in and out her mouth
like an excited lizard. The couple suddenly became involved
in a tussle on the front steps that would have looked like hurried passion from a distance. She tried to pry her mouth
away but he held her firmly, grabbing at her dress through
the opening of her wool coat and sliding his hand up to her

breast. Her daily nightmare seemed to have materialized itself and she became overwhelmed by panic. She finally
managed to wrench herself from his grasp and when she did,
she pulled back her arm and punched him squarely in the
jaw.

"What was that for?" he cried while clasping his face.

"It was for trying to molest me on my own front porch!"

He narrowed his eyes and stood tall as he looked down at
her.

"What is it with you, huh? Your roommate is up front
about everything and you hide behind the goody-goody
crap! You want to go upstairs and do what we have to do,
fine! But I'm not going to get the mess knocked out of me
because you like it rough!"

Janelle's eyes narrowed. *"What?"*

"Ask your roommate," he spat.

Janelle placed her hands on her hips and gritted her teeth.
It felt as if her ears were on fire. "Get in your car and go
home, Cedric, before I call the police."

She didn't wait until his car pulled off before she opened
the front door, slammed it behind her, and tore off her coat.
Her eyes darted with fury from room to room, in search of
her roommate.

"Sharon," she screamed. "I want to talk to you!"

Chapter Five

Terrence peered into the skies and breathed in the fresh
autumn air. The maple, oak, and pine trees of Rock Creek

Park towered over him, but most of their leaves were now scattered on the park grounds. Only a few dangled carelessly from the overhead branches, dancing with each gust of wind. Sven walked a few feet in front of him, slobbering happily, tugging on his leash so that Terrence had to quicken his pace every now and then. The dog gave a few joyous barks and continued to trot, occasionally looking back at Terrence with his doggie grin as if saying, "We're free! We're free!" and Terrence had to agree with him. He felt as if he had been freed too.

He had watched Kara's flight depart BWI less than three hours ago, and as he viewed the spinning wheels rise from the runway and the plane's uplift, he breathed a sigh of relief. When she came into the bedroom that morning with a pout, saying that the agency had booked her some shows in Munich and she had to catch a flight that day, Terrence had to force himself not to smile. For almost a week, she treated him as if he was a cross between a barnyard stud and manservant who was at her beck and call twenty-four hours a day. She treated his dog as if it were some pest that should be permanently locked in a closet. He wasn't sure if Sven would try to rip her throat open while she slept.

This morning Terrence had been more than ready to have a break from Kara, but the very idea worried him. He had not seen her in over a month and yet she had only been with him less than seven days and he was already anticipating when she would leave again. The sex did not seem worth the frustration anymore. She sapped whatever emotional energy he had with her constant need for attention, and when he could no longer give her what she wanted physically because he was tired or drained of passion, she climbed on top of him and "did it herself." He had watched her bounce up and down as if she were on a pogo stick. She had grunted and moaned and he tried his best not to fall asleep or laugh out loud. Finally, she realized that Terrence just wasn't into it, climbed off of him and slammed the bathroom door closed behind her.

Terrence whistled and lifted the zipper of his suede jacket. For the first time in over a week, he had privacy. He had peace.

He took in another deep breath of fresh air but coughed this time. That wasn't bark and spruce he smelled. As the sound of the thudding radio sound system grew louder and the five teenage boys came into view between the trees, he knew instantly where the stench was coming from. They passed the roll around and laughed as each one took a puff, alternating it with a drink from the bottle wrapped tightly in a brown bag.

Terrence frowned, knowing not to let his gaze linger. Boys like that—ones he remembered vividly from his childhood neighborhood—only took staring as a sign of aggression or challenge. But his eyes kept darting back. One of those boys looked familiar. He could easily be one of the kids who had once attended the youth center where Terrence had worked a year ago. He hoped to God it wasn't.

One of them seemed to notice Terrence's glance in their direction. He stuck his hand into his jacket pocket, pulled it out slightly before sneering and showing the butt of a glock. Every muscle in Terrence's body tensed and he knew he had about three seconds reaction time before a bullet whizzed past his head. But when the boy felt as if his point was duly taken, he lowered the weapon back into his pocket. After that, he grinned.

Just then Sven barked, trying his best to pull his leash out of Terrence's grasp.

"Down, boy," Terrence ordered through gritted teeth. He then looked up to see what had grabbed Sven's attention. He recognized her instantly.

She walked toward him wearing earmuffs and gloves

while trailing behind a small dog that basked furiously at Sven. Her swelling curls were pulled into two pigtails at the back of her head and her fitted jeans revealed the contours of her hips and legs. She tugged at the edges of the hooded college sweatshirt she was wearing, its bright red shade standing out like a stop sign even at this distance.

"Little Red Riding Hood," he thought, for that was what she looked like. All she needed was the basket. She had just wandered into the big bad forest and was about to be eaten by five hungry wolves.

"I wouldn't go back there if I were you," he said as she drew closer.

She frowned slightly as if she didn't recognize him. Her face brightened after a few seconds.

"Oh, man! It is so strange running into you again. I was just—"

"I wouldn't go back there if I were you," he repeated again but this time with more warning in his tone.

She stopped and he saw fire ignite in her doelike brown eyes. She raised a hand to her hip.

"Well, hello. How are you doing? I'm doing fine. How about you? God!" She shook her head and paused to tug at her dog's leash. The beagle was engaged in a barking battle with Sven. He supposed the animals had picked up on their masters' hostile vibes and decided to start an argument of their own.

"Are you always like this, Terrence, or just on weekdays? And why shouldn't I go back there? I *always* take that trail."

He gritted his teeth. "Well, the trail isn't good today. There are a few shady characters that I'm sure would be happy to make your acquaintance, but I doubt you'll share the pleasure."

She raised her chin indignantly, pushing a strand of hair out of her eyes that had escaped from her rubber bands. "Thanks for the advice, but I know how to take care of myself. I nearly broke a man's jaw," she said proudly while puffing out her chest. "Now if you'll excuse me—"

Terrence found himself with his hand clasped firmly around her arm and Janelle looked up at him as if he had just escaped from a mental ward. An electric shock passed between them as his thumb brushed the silky skin of her wrist and he could tell from the way she gulped for air, she felt it too.

"What the hell are you doing?" she squeaked. "Have you lost your mind?"

She attempted to wrench out of his grasp but he wouldn't, or better put, couldn't release his hold.

"Pipe down," he said in a surprisingly calm voice. "Just walk with me and we'll both be fine. I don't want anything to happen to you, and I don't want anything to happen to me because I had to rescue you."

"Well, aren't you a gentleman?"

Janelle waited until his hold loosened before snatching her arm away. She angrily pointed her finger up at him.

"You're lucky my knuckles still hurt. I should beat the stuffing out of you for that one. Stop it, Jazz!" She picked her dog off the ground and shushed her before lowering her back to the concrete. "So may I ask, gentle sir, where the hell am I supposed to walk now?"

"Follow me," he said while turning left at a fork in the road, waiting until she followed suit.

They walked quietly down the path while their dogs growled at one another. He glanced over at her occasionally, seeing that she had her lips pursed tightly together and her nose in the air. She had to walk quickly to keep up with his long strides for he knew she wouldn't give him the advantage of taking the lead. Her ponytails flopped like cheerleaders' pom-poms behind her.

"So," he began while shoving one of his hands into a pocket, "whose jaw did you break?"

She looked up at him, smirked, and returned her focus to the trail in front of her. "It was almost broken, well, bruised actually. It was my date's and he asked for it."

"You don't have a very good dating track record, do you?"

She turned to him with eyes blazing and didn't answer.

"So why'd you hit him?" he persisted.

She shrugged. "It's a long story. Let's just say that he ended up with a punch in the mouth because my roommate led him to believe something about me that wasn't true. So my roommate is now looking for another place to live."

Terrence frowned, torn between worry about her and wondering what exactly her date had done to earn a thrashing, since she seemed to be elusive about the topic. He felt his grip tighten on the Sven's leash, imagining that it was her date's neck.

"Are you okay?" he asked. "I mean . . . car repairs and the loss of a roommate is a lot of unexpected expenses."

She narrowed her eyes. "Are you about to write me a check?"

"No, but—"

"Then what's it to you?"

He sighed. Her porcupine needles were sticking out again and he couldn't fathom why he cared. She seemed like the type who was quiet and reserved until she felt someone inquiring into the independence she coveted as if it were her last lifeline. She probably snapped at anyone who tried to help her, but there was something inexplicable about her that was driving him to pry. Maybe it was the fact that she seemed so quiet and withdrawn. Maybe it was her sad tone. Either way, there was a part of him that wanted to solve whatever problems she was having.

"Its no concern of mine. I was just trying to make conversation, that's all," he lied as he kicked at a pebble. "Hang a man just for trying to be social."

She studied him carefully. "Well, I *do* have enough money saved to cover this stuff, if that's what you were asking. I was just hoping that I wouldn't have to use it. I wanted to do something else with it."

"What else?"

She laughed and raised an eyebrow. "Well, aren't we nosey? I wanted to travel Europe. See the Louvre, the leaning tower of Pisa, or the temples of Athens. Then maybe I'd head over to Morocco and then Ghana . . . I don't know. I wasn't really sure of my travel plans but I knew I wanted to see the world. I guess I'll have to put that off for another few years."

She sadly looked at the trees around her and sighed.

"Well," Terrence said, "when you do, you should skip Europe. I head there four times a year, and let me tell you, its highly overrated. You aren't missing out on much."

"You've been to Europe that many times?" she asked with wonder in her voice. Her eyes widened as she grinned.

"Don't look so surprised," he answered with a chuckle. "It's a job requirement, not vacation. Janelle, I've been to a lot of places in the past year and none of them compare to here." He pointed down at the ground. "If anyone asks me what's my favorite place in the world, I say home. The streets are rarely cleaned, the traffic is horrible, the public education system sucks, but there's nothing that compares to the people, the food, and the Potomac. I love this city. No joke."

She laughed. "DC should hire you for tourist commercials."

He shrugged. "Maybe they should."

"Well, you can love it all you want, Terrence, but I still say it's spoken like a true traveler. At least you have a point of perspective to say that stuff. I've never left the area. All I know is here. But I know there has to be more." She sighed. "There has to be."

He gazed at her with unyielding focus.

"The grass is always greener," he muttered.

"Huh?"

"The grass is always greener on the other side for you, isn't it?"

She frowned. "I'm not understanding you."

He rolled his eyes heavenward. "You're always looking for a better game or a better deal but what you don't realize is that what you have now *is* the best. There's no better deal, Janelle. There's no better place. There are people in Paris who live next door to the Eiffel Tower who are unhappy and wishing themselves somewhere else, and so are people in Tokyo, Berlin, London, and Istanbul. They're no different than you."

He could tell he had touched on a key of truth and scratched at a nerve for her back straightened haughtily.

"Like I said," she muttered, "I don't know what you mean."

"Sure you don't."

They walked in silence again before she started to grumble with irritation. She glared down at the lumbering animal in front of him.

"Would you please tell your dog to stop harassing mine? He's been growling at her for the past fifteen minutes."

"Well, it takes two to tango, sweetheart. She's been doing quite a lot of growling herself. Besides, he only harasses the ones he likes," joked Terrence with a smile.

And so does his master, he thought wickedly.

It was as if he had expressed the thought aloud for she turned to him with a raised eyebrow.

"Could we stop for a minute? My legs are getting tired, and I think Jazz has to take a trunk break."

Terrence smiled. "A trunk break?"

"Yep, it's the ladylike way of saying 'peeing on a tree.' "

Terrence laughed.

They walked over to a park bench, and Janelle sat down

and released her beagle's leash. She shooed her dog in the direction of a nearby pine and rubbed her hands together, puffing into them before rubbing her nose. She tugged her hair out of her two ponytails and ran her fingers through the tangles in her curls.

"God, it's getting cold," she muttered.

Just as if Mother Nature had heard her cue, a light sprinkle of snow began to fall. Janelle stood up and smiled.

"It's snowing," she exclaimed. She looked up, opened her mouth to let the flakes fall on her tongue, and closed her eyes.

"You better be careful," he chided. "That snow's probably toxic."

"I don't care," she said with a giggle before sticking her tongue out again. "It won't kill me."

He stood there watching her as the snowflakes dappled her eyelashes and her hair, as she stood with her head leaning back and her body less than one foot away from him, looking almost angelic. He could see the rise and fall of her chest and the visible gusts of breath that leapt from her mouth into the cold air. He could smell the scent of her perfume and the musk of the trees and dry grass around them. He had been kissing another woman less than five hours ago but desire now welled up inside him and thundered through his chest, gut, and loins like a freight train. Before Terrence realized what he was doing, he'd crossed the small threshold between them and had lowered his mouth to her lips. He took her in his arms and held her there.

The kiss had taken her off guard so that she let out a small gasp of surprise as their lips met. At first she tensed against him for she found it hard to move. Her arms were firmly locked at her sides, immobilized in his embrace. He could sense her alarm.

Terrence loosened his grip and continued to kiss her. He instantly felt her lips softening and then parting slightly. He fisted his hands in her hair, letting the threads of silk run over his fingers. He coaxed her tongue forward with his own, wrenching out a moan from the back of his throat when it finally did. Their tongues danced. Her fingers clawed at his back through the heavy suede of his jacket, and his heart pounded. He could even hear the heavy thud in his ears and it felt as if his heart would burst through his rib cage. He closed his eyes, astonished by the fact that he was hardening with arousal. When he finally pulled away to regain his breath, he looked down into eyes that were coated with a glaze of hunger and need as thick as his own.

Her lips were swollen and her legs wobbled slightly. Janelle raised her fingers to her mouth, looked down, and turned.

"Jazz," she called weakly as she walked away from him. "Time to go, girl."

Two days later, Terrence lay awake in the bed of his hotel suite, staring into the ceiling lights. He had not called Kara to tell her that he was in town, nor did he have the urge to do so. He was content to sip his bottled water, listen to the soft murmur of the wide-screen television in the living room and think of Janelle.

A few hours earlier, after the fashion show and its party had ended, he had taken a walk around Times Square for a change of scenery. He gazed up at the buildings and decided that he liked it better when the streets were lined with girlie joints and blazing neon signs advertising XXX this or XX that. The streets seemed plastic to him now with their giant billboards—one of which sported his face—and endless franchises.

He could draw the same distinction between the women he had walked down the runway with that day and the one who was probably sleeping now in her rented townhouse in

DC. They lacked the grit, complication, and heart she had. Take away the thousand-dollar wardrobes, the extensions, the makeup, and the padding and they were all a fraction of the woman she was, inside and out.

He realized those were the thoughts of a man who was about to lose his heart to a woman and had no idea when he would get it back. He sighed and lifted a white sheet of paper from his night table, gazing at the numbers written in black ink.

Terrence had asked his grandmother for Janelle's home phone number before he'd left for New York. He had ignored the elderly woman's smug expression of pleasure as he sat at the kitchen table.

"What do you want to call her for?" she asked as she continued to peel her Idaho potatoes.

He shrugged and fiddled with the salt and pepper shakers. "I don't know. She just seems like she needs to get out more. Maybe I could introduce her to a few people . . . take her a few places."

"Is that so?" His grandmother raised an eyebrow. "You know of some nice men that she might want to meet, Tory?"

For the first time in his life, he glared at his grandmother. "I don't think it's a good idea to subject her to anymore of your matchmaking, Mother. Especially when it's with just about anyone. She has standards, and she's a grown woman. She can make romantic decisions for herself."

His grandmother wagged her finger at him and frowned.

"Just who, chile, do you think you talking smart to? You aren't too big for me to whip you. Remember that," she barked before turning her back to him and smiling with joy. She cleared her throat and pretended to be angry again. "I was asking about *your* friends, Terrence Kendrick Boyer. So if there were any wolves or duds in the pack, it would be your fault, now wouldn't it? Not your grandmother's." She threw the last of the potato peels into the trashcan and turned on the faucet. "Seems like to me, young man, you're being selfish. You want to have her socialize with a few people, but those few people seem to be just you and yourself. If you're interested in courting the girl, I wish you would just say it. Save yourself a lot of time and energy. Save me the sweat."

He leaned back, crossed his arms over his chest and sighed.

"Okay," he relented, "I *am* interested in . . . courting her, as you say. There, I said it."

She puckered her lips. "So does that mean you got that Kara girl out of your system?"

He shrugged. "I don't think Kara was ever *in* my system, Mother. Now can I have Janelle's number?"

His grandmother smiled triumphantly and tossed the potatoes into a Crock-Pot filled with water.

"Of course you can, baby! Just let me talk to her grandmother and I'll have it for you by the end of the day."

Even now, Terrence was still debating over whether or not he should call her. The number had sat on his night table for the past two days and he hadn't touched it. He had only looked at it.

Terrence sighed and found himself dialing the digits on his cell phone, listening to the rings on the other line for what seemed an eternity. Just as he was about to press the button to hang up, the ringing stopped and then the sound of the receiver banging against the floor erupted.

"Hello," she called groggily. "Hello?"

He cleared his throat. "Janelle?"

"Yes, this is she," she said in a voice laced with sleep. "Who's calling?"

"It's Terrence. I'm sorry I called so late."

There was a long pause and then he heard the sound of

the phone being dropped again. He could imagine her dragging the receiver from the floor and bringing it to her ear.

"Terrence. Oh, hi. I was, um, I was . . . how did you get my number?"

He frowned. "Is it a problem that I called you?"

"No. No. No problem. It's just . . . I wasn't expecting it."

"Well, I'm in New York," he said as he pulled a string, closing his window blinds and blocking out the lights of Manhattan. "So I wanted to hear a familiar voice. I decided to call you."

"You're calling me from New York?"

She sounded dumbfounded and for some reason that irritated him. While he had been thinking of her nonstop, unable to control the urge just to hear her voice, it seemed as if he hadn't crossed her mind.

He rubbed his forehead and sighed gruffly. "Well, maybe it was a bad idea—"

"No! No! It wasn't. Please. Stay. Stay on the line." She cleared her throat. "So how's New York?"

He slowly smiled. "Its fine. It's the usual."

"So why are you up there, anyway?"

"Uh, nothing really. I did a show today for Donna Karan and went to the afterparty. I have a photo shoot tomorrow for *Esquire,* and then I'm heading back home."

She laughed and he instantly felt the hairs on the back of his neck stand on end. His fingertips began to tingle.

"Oh, I just did a show today for Donna Karan and I have a photo shoot with *Esquire* tomorrow," she said in a deep voice, mimicking him. "You know, the usual." She laughed again. "You are so full of crap, Terrence. Don't play casual with me. I envy the hell out of you. Remember what you were telling me about the grass being greener? You can't tell me it isn't greener there."

He leaned his head back against the headboard and rubbed the palm of his hand over his chiseled stomach and chest. He could feel the ache knotting itself inside him again. If he could only keep her talking . . .

"Well, I can't say much about the grass because there isn't any right now, but if you're asking me whether or not I'd rather be home, the answer is yes."

Janelle grew silent and he listened to the sound of her phone being shifted to her other ear.

"Okay, Terrence. You're very big on asking questions and sharing your point of view on things, but can I ask you something? If you don't like to travel away from home and you're so blasé about your work, why do you model?"

"Good question." He sighed. "I guess because it pays a hell of a lot more than what I was paid as a counselor, and it takes a lot less out of me emotionally. Plus—and this may sound conceited—I have a nice face. I figure, I may as well use it to my advantage."

She laughed. "No, it doesn't sound conceited, oddly enough. Coming from you, at least. You used to be a counselor?"

He smiled and sat up. "Yeah. There's a youth center in Northwest where I worked six days a week. I handled peer groups, taught the kids basketball and took them on trips to the country. Some of them had never seen a horse or a cow before except in movies or TV. I was like that when I was young . . . sort of. If it weren't for Mother, I wouldn't know anything but the city. But urban life is kind of like looking at the world with just one eye open. You aren't seeing the whole thing."

"You're just a treasure trove of sayings, Terrence," she said with a laugh.

"Well, you know what they say. Never look a gift horse in the mouth."

"And if 'if's' and 'ands' were pots and pans the whole world would be a great kitchen," she chimed.

He smiled and leaned forward. "Janelle?"

"Yes, Terrence?"

"Do you . . . do you want to try to, uh, get together when I get back?"

The phone line went silent and she cleared her throat. "I don't know, Terrence."

He dug his fist into the mattress and bit his lower lip. "Are you seeing someone Janelle?"

"No, it isn't anything like that. It's just . . . it's just—"

"It doesn't have to be formal," he insisted. "We don't have to label it as a date. I know how you feel about that stuff. But I just want you to know, I like talking to you. I think you like talking to me, too. Maybe we could extend that to something a little more than . . . talking. Go out sometime."

"Terrence," she began shakily, "whatever happened in the park two days ago shouldn't have happened. I'm not ready for anything close to that right now. I like you very much. I think you're a great guy, but I hardly know you. Our grandmothers may think we're great for each other, but I'm not so sure. I have to get to know you more, okay? And there's stuff about me that's really . . . complicated. We can . . . go out but I—I want to take it slow."

His shoulders fell and he had to fight the urge to sigh. He clenched his fingers tightly before releasing them.

"No problem," he said. "I feel that way exactly."

"Good," she murmured softly.

Chapter Six

"Do you have an eight?"

"Go fish."

Terrence coughed while Janelle pulled a card from the deck.

"Do you have an ace?"

Janelle looked over the fan of playing cards in her hand and passed an ace to Terrence. She watched him neatly lay the two aces in one of the many stacks on the wooden table in front of him and compared them to her mere three stacks. Janelle sighed and ran her fingers through her hair. She was going to lose again.

They had been playing the game for at least an hour. Earlier that evening, she had rifled through her old stacks of board games in the closet but finally decided to pull out a deck of playing cards instead. After they exhausted rounds of spades and gin rummy, they settled on Go Fish. They tried their best not to bore each other, but a night of this type of "fun" had not been in the plans.

A trip to the movies had to be canceled due to the on-slaught of an unexpected snowstorm and because the flakes continued to fall at a thunderous pace both of them decided that Terrence should at least wait until the storm subsided before he tried to drive home. They agreed that a game of cards would be the best way to entertain one another, not to mention it provided a distraction from the obvious sense of awkwardness. Janelle felt like she was in high school again, trying her best to keep a boy from feeling up her shirt.

Janelle drummed her fingers on the arm of her chair and began to hum with the commercial on the television.

She hated being cooped up with Terrence like this even though they had been daily companions for the past month. She had attended football games with him and cheered as he did in the stands. Sometimes they rooted for the same team. Sometimes they didn't. She had wandered into the house parties of his friends, holding his hand and accepting a glass as he passed it to her. He dragged her around in front of his buddies like a treasured memento, and she smiled nervously, laughing at their jokes and blushing when they flirted with her. She had waited for his long-distance calls from places in

Europe and sometimes from places she had never heard of. Often the calls came at two or three o'clock in the morning, but she still took them, appreciating the fact that out of all of the people he could have phoned, he chose her.

But even with all this they had managed to dodge an air of intimacy. They held hands but rarely hugged. He hadn't kissed her since that day in the park and only focused his sweltering gazes on her once in a blue moon. It got to the point that she occasionally wondered if he was just keeping his distance as she had asked him to, or if he was no longer attracted to her. Janelle sighed mournfully. God, she hoped that wasn't the case.

All in all, their relationship seemed more like a brother-and-sisterly sort of thing, that is, until they were left alone in close quarters with one another, like they were now. With an empty and relatively quiet room and him a few inches away from her, it felt as if she could slice the sexual tension with a knife. It was that thick.

"Go fish," she said and he lowered his last group of cards to the table. "Want to play another round?"

"No, I think that's enough cards for one night."

He stretched his arms over his head and yawned. His milk-chocolate eyes flickered slightly, standing out like semi-precious stone against his caramel features.

Janelle turned away from him, not liking what the soft orange glow of the living room light did to Terrence's face and how it made her feel. She tore her gaze away from his lips and the dark peach fuzz around his mouth and began to gather all the cards into a single deck.

Terrence slowly rose from the table, tugging at the front of his jeans before walking over to the sofa. He flopped back against the cushions, grabbed the remote control, and began to flip channels.

"I think your cable is out. It's probably due to the storm."

"Oh, really?" she said as she walked over to a nearby

window and peered through the windowpane. "That's horrible."

Janelle furrowed her eyebrows and sighed. The snow continued to fall in heavy sheets and only the occasional car passed her window. The traction for some cars was so bad that they skidded and slammed into the curb. She pressed her forehead against the cold glass. Terrence could be here for hours and the torture she felt now would only be lengthened.

"What are you doing over there?" she heard him call from behind her.

She turned to him, shook her head, and smiled. "Nothing. I was just seeing if the storm had died down."

"In a hurry to get rid of me?"

She pulled the sleeves of her turtleneck over her knuckles and crossed her arms over her chest.

"No, but I figure you were in a hurry to leave. A man can only take but so many games of Go Fish before he's suicidal."

"Let me worry about that," he said with a grin as he patted the space beside him on the couch, urging her to sit down.

She eyed the spot cautiously and slowly walked over to the cream-colored sofa. She kicked off her shoes and quickly lowered herself to the cushion, pulling her knees to her chest and wrapping her arms around them. When he raised an eyebrow, silently questioning her protective pose, she tugged at the sleeve of his sweater playfully and smiled.

"I don't want to catch your cold," she joked.

"It seems to me you're worried about a lot more than my cold," he muttered dryly as he began to flip channels again.

Janelle bit her lower lip and tucked her hair behind her ear. She hated being like this. She wanted nothing more than to crawl over to him and have him wrap her in his arms like he had in the woods that day. Janelle would happily take any

sniffle or cough he passed on to her if only she could have
him kiss her and feel the pounding of his heart through her
hands again, but she was too scared. The constant night-
mares of being suffocated had subsided lately, but she had
no idea if her old sense of panic would be renewed. For the
first time in a long time, she had opened herself up to someone, but she didn't want to scare him away. If it meant keeping him at arm's length then she would have to do just that.

"Have you spoken to Steve lately?"

He turned to her and narrowed his eyes. He pulled the
sleeve of his sweater from her fingers and rested his arm beside him.

"Why do you ask?"

Janelle shrugged, wondering why asking about Steve had
sparked Terrence's anger. She hoped they hadn't fought.

"I don't know. I figure he was your best friend and you
talk to him at least once a week. I was just wondering. That's
all." She frowned. "So you haven't heard from him?"

Terrence finally settled on a channel and rubbed his jaw.

"I talked to him yesterday. Steve was telling me about a
bash he's having next week and he asked me if I was going.
He suggested I invite you, too."

She smiled. "That was sweet of him to consider me."

"He wasn't trying to be 'sweet,' Janelle. Man, it's good
both of us aren't naïve." Terrence rolled his eyes and sighed.
"He's been asking a lot of questions about you lately. He
wants to know stuff about your job, how I know you, and
where you live. He asked me just how involved I was with
you . . . if it was serious . . . if it was casual."

Janelle gazed down at her fingernails and held her breath.
"And what did you say to him?"

He turned to face her and glared. "I said I wasn't sure
what we were exactly but if he was really that interested, he
should go for it. I wouldn't hold a grudge and it's a free
country."

"That was . . . nice of you," she murmured.

"Wasn't it?"

She rested her cheek in her hand and fiddled with a loose piece of thread in the sofa. She felt an ache well in her chest and she fought the need to pinch herself as she blinked back her tears.

Stop acting stupid, Janelle, she thought as she sniffed loudly.

"Well, then it's good we're hanging out together, Tory. It seems you've expanded my dating opportunities. Maybe I'll improve my record."

"And maybe you'll repay the favor someday."

She bit her lower lip and tightly twisted the thread around her finger, watching a white line form and her fingertip swell with blood.

"Maybe I will."

The day of Steve's soirée, Terrence arrived late at her house. Janelle paced around her bedroom and stared down at her gold wristwatch worriedly, gnawing her lower lip. He was usually so punctual. She hoped he wasn't having car trouble, or, heaven forbid, had gotten into a car accident. All the layers of ice had yet to be cleared from every one of the city's streets and corners. Anything could have happened to him, but she didn't want to think about what that anything could be.

Janelle stopped to gaze in the mirror, patting the front of her dress, tucking away stray strands of hair into her straightened tresses that were pulled high into a genielike ponytail at the crown of her head. She tried to calm her frail nerves by focusing on her appearance. She had chosen the outfit carefully, hoping that he would like it. It was a lot more of a seductive ensemble than she would usually go for. Janelle had skipped her favorite color black and switched to a shade of purple; admiring the vibrancy it gave her. The dress was sleeveless and backless. The only thing that held it to her body was a silk string tied around her neck. The fabric emphasized her every curve and contour appreciatively, but it made her want to grab a robe and cover herself. She just wasn't used to showing so much flesh, but she fought the urge. Janelle finished off the outfit with a pair of four-inch heels that laced around her ankles and gave her the stance of a ballerina.

When the doorbell finally rang, she had to keep herself from dropping to her knees in thanks. She ran downstairs and swung open the front door and smiled.

He stood before her in an ankle-length wool coat, a revamped winter version of the trench coats worn by Dick Tracy. He rubbed his hands together even though they were covered with black leather gloves and stepped inside, brushing past her. Light flakes of snow sprinkled his collar, and Terrence wiped at the neat goatee he had started to sport lately before clearing his throat.

"You look handsome, Terrence," she said, her voice catching in the back of her throat.

She noticed how his eyes swelled at the sight of her, making her stomach clench, but he instantly steeled his gaze and looked down at his feet.

"You may want to wear something heavy over that. It's colder than usual and we wouldn't want you to freeze to death."

Her shoulders slumped. That's it? No, you look nice, too, Janelle, or I'm sorry I'm late? She fisted her hands on her hips and pursed her lips together after loudly closing the door behind him.

"Well, I would be wearing my coat but, when I figured out that you were going to be late, I took it off. Where were you, Terrence? You were supposed to be here thirty minutes ago."

He shrugged his shoulders. "Just lost track of time."

She lifted her chin and turned away from him. With that she stomped into the hallway and opened a closet. She pulled out something to wear and started to put it on while mumbling to herself. Terrence came up behind her, attempting to guide her arms into the sleeves of the coat but she recoiled away from him and frowned.

"I can do it myself," she growled, ignoring the electric shock she felt as his hands accidentally grazed over her bare back and shoulders. She pulled her hair out of the collar and muttered, "I'm ready," before swinging open the front door and heading into the wintry night.

They quietly stepped into Steve's condo, not speaking to one another and acting as if they hadn't arrived together. The drive to his place had been carried out in silence so she was happy to step into a domain full of people lost in conversation with the sounds of Jamiroquai and The Brand New Heavies swelling around her. A few of the partygoers looked familiar as they sipped their martinis and margaritas, but she still felt uncomfortable. Maybe it was the fact that her companion acted as if he didn't even notice she was standing beside him.

She saw Steve walking toward them. The towering, attractive male with his ebony skin and glistening white teeth greeted her with a bewildered smile. He was the complete opposite of Terrence and it often made her wonder just how those two had managed to become friends. Steve, unlike the man standing beside her, was far from reserved or word-choosy, but he always seemed to make a person feel at home with his warm laugh and happy-go-lucky nature. Surprisingly, he even managed to relax Janelle who was always nervous and uncomfortable.

Steve demonstrated his friendliness now as he enveloped

her in a bear hug. She gave out a gasp of surprise as she felt her feet rise from the floor and she was swung around in circles in the air. She squealed until he let her down, noticing how Terrence rolled his eyes and removed his coat, throwing it over his arm sullenly.

"Girl, you look good," Steve proclaimed in a deep voice before holding her at arm's length and staring at her with heat-filled eyes that made her blush. "Is all this for me, Tory?"

"I'm going to get a drink," Terrence muttered before walking toward the other side of the room.

Janelle's smile fell and she couldn't help letting her gaze follow him. She watched as he stopped on the way to the bar to talk to a beautiful woman in a red dress. The woman with the bob threw an arm around his shoulder as if she had known him for years, and Janelle closed her eyes.

Steve gave a knowing smile and placed his index finger below her chin. He turned her face to him and winked.

"Would you like me to show you around Steve's Joint, princess?" he asked.

She slowly nodded, taking his large hand in her own before forcing another smile.

"I would love to, Steve. Lead the way."

That entire night she only caught glimpses of Terrence as she peeked at him from the corner of her eye. She did it while she pretended to admire Steve's African artwork from tours of the continent and pretended to be enthralled by his architectural sketches hanging on his studio wall. Terrence hadn't looked at her at all, seeming to be at ease among his friends and basking in the attention of the many females who were more than happy to get to know Steve's runway model buddy better. Steve behaved like a gentleman, only allowing his hand to rest on Janelle's shoulder or the crook of her back. So Janelle made every effort to be kind and friendly, but also let him know by her body language that he should tread the waters carefully.

She hesitated for a bit as he walked into a darkened room. She paused in the doorway, flicking a switch and then realizing just what she had wandered into. Steve's bed sat on the opposite wall embossed with a black lacquer and gold trim. The lighting was dim. The ornamentation and sculptures were so "mack-daddyish" that it would make most women cringe. She gazed up at the painting of the naked woman crouching with her finger in her mouth over the headboard. If Janelle weren't so nervous and filled with alarm, she would have laughed. She heard the door shut behind her and her eyes widened.

"Don't worry," Steve muttered as he walked over to a chair in the corner. He swirled the champagne in his glass and took a gulp. "You can come in. I'm not in the habit of trying to seduce women who aren't interested in me."

She blinked and frowned, taking small steps into the room and pausing a few feet in front of him.

He smiled and sat down after pulling a chair up beside him.

"I brought you here, Janelle, to ask you a couple of things. I didn't want anyone running in and disturbing us. I'm sorry, there weren't many rooms to choose from."

When she looked at him as if she still didn't believe him, he shrugged.

"Okay, you can stand if it makes you feel more comfortable."

"I think I will," she muttered while crossing her arms over her chest.

He hadn't locked the door. If he tried anything funny she could always leave.

"Okay," Steve said with a raised eyebrow, "then we can begin. How do you feel about Terrence exactly?"

She furrowed her eyebrows. "What do you mean?"

"I mean like I said. How do you feel about him?"

She shrugged. "I don't know . . . he and I are friends, I guess."

Steve narrowed his eyes. "From the way you both behave you seem like a lot more than friends. Forgive a brother for being nosey, but . . . I would say you're a hell of a lot more. At least, Terrence seems to think so. He won't admit to it, but I've known that guy for a long time . . . since high school. I can read between the lines."

Janelle slowly smiled. "Why, Steve . . . are you about to ask me what my intentions are with your good buddy Terrence? You don't come off as the protective type."

"You could say that, I guess. He's showing a lot of patience toward you, Janelle, because he thinks he's holding out for something . . . something really important. But you know what? I'm not so sure he's right. He's dated his share of girls in his time who were more interested in games than they were interested in him. It would really hurt him if this same runaround were happening all over again. I hope it isn't. You seem like a nice girl." He let his gaze wander up her frame and licked his lips. "And you know how to use your gifts. Just don't use them against him."

She took in his words silently. Janelle shifted between anger at the idea that Terrence may have been discussing her in conversations with his friends, and fury that Steve would actually consider that she would do something so contemptible. But she softened, realizing that Steve was only a concerned friend who had insight into Terrence's heart and wanted to protect his affections.

"You don't have any worries, Steve. I can assure you that it is not my intention to give your friend the 'runaround.' I care about him very much. So much it hurts sometimes, and I would walk away before I let something like that happen."

She smiled. "I think there's more chances of him hurting me than me hurting him, anyway."

He beckoned her to sit down on his knee, making her frown. She motioned for him to stand instead and he did while rolling his eyes. She surprised them both by kissing him on the cheek, blushing the instant she did it.

"He's lucky to have a friend like you, Steve," she said.

Steve grinned. "I know he is. And he's lucky to have a girl like you. Now if you just stop teasing the man and let him have a little somethin' somethin' before the brother explodes."

"He told you that?" she exclaimed, pulling at his arm.

"Damn right he did! That's why he thinks you don't like him. He says you act like he's trying to rape you if he even gives you a hug! You know, that boy has been taking cold showers and ice baths for the past three weeks?"

She laughed with embarrassment. Just then the bedroom door opened.

Terrence called from the doorway. "Steve, are you in here? You're running out of vodka and gin. Derrick was wondering if he should make a run to the corner store but he was—" His voice trailed off.

Janelle's hand still rested on Steve's arm. A red imprint of her lipstick stood out on his cheek while Terrence stared.

Terrence's mouth gaped open momentarily before he closed it and clenched his teeth.

"Sorry. I didn't mean to disturb you. I'll come back later." He glared at Janelle. "When you're done."

She quickly looked over at the dark-skinned man with panic in her eyes. Steve sighed.

"Terrence," Steve called. "Slow down, man! You don't have to rush out. We weren't doing anything."

"Of course you weren't," Terrence spat as he stormed into the hallway. "So I guess that was just a mirage. I was seeing things, right? You look like you were starting *something*."

Janelle walked quickly to catch up with him, hoping that she could do it before he returned to the party filled with people and they had an audience.

"He's telling the truth, Terrence."

He turned to her with fury and stared at her with contempt. It was as if he had caught her and Steve in "the act" itself.

"And why the hell should I listen to you, huh, Janelle? Because you've been so truthful up until now? I touch your shoulder and you jump away, and I find you kissing him? You said you needed space. You said you weren't ready for *that* type of thing right now. But what you should have said is that you weren't ready for that type of thing with *me.*"

Steve crossed his arms over his chest and rolled his eyes. "Man, calm down. It was just a kiss on the cheek. You act like I had her laid across the bed with her legs up, or something! You're getting angry over nothing. Besides, if I remember correctly you told me go to ahead and give a try if I was really interested in her. So what if I did? What if I wanted to? You shouldn't say things knowin' damn well you don't mean it!"

Janelle turned to glare up at Steve who shrugged unapologetically.

"You can go to hell!" Terrence roared at his childhood friend and then returned his wrath to Janelle. "And you can go with him. Let him drive you home!"

Janelle watched Terrence walk away from her. She wanted to crawl into a hole as he pushed his way through the groups of people and caused quite a few of them to spill their drinks and drop their hors d'oeuvres to the floor. They glared after him as if he had lost his mind.

Steve sighed and rubbed her shoulders.

"Don't worry, princess. He'll calm down in a few days. I know him. I'll call him tomorrow and explain everything."

She nodded and stared down at herself. Janelle picked up

the hem of her dress and bit her lip. She had dolled herself up, all for Terrence, and yet she had spent the entire night without him and probably would have to from now on.

Chapter Seven

It had been one week, two days, seven hours, and five minutes since she had heard from Terrence. She couldn't concentrate at work and had turned at least three copies in late to the senior editor. She grew tired of pacing back and forth in her house, dialing into her voice mail over and over again to see if she had missed his call. When she grew tired of even that, she checked the telephone plug to see if it was still connected to the wall. Finally, Janelle dealt with the idea that he just did not want to talk to her. She grabbed her coat and purse and headed to her grandmother's house, hating to stay in her own home because it reminded her so much of him.

She now lay on her grandmother's couch, biting her nails and listening to her grandmother's hum as the older woman embroidered a throw pillow.

"I wish you wouldn't do that, Janey. You've been biting your nails since you were seven years old." She pulled the needle and thread through the white cotton and shook her head. "I should have put Tabasco sauce on them nails fifteen years ago like I said I would. You'd have nails like Cleopatra by now."

"I'm upset, Grandma," Janelle muttered. "I only bite my nails when I'm upset."

Mrs. Howard pursed her lips and looked at her granddaughter over the top of her bifocals. She sighed deeply before pushing the needle through again.

"Why are you upset, baby?"

Janelle threw up her hands and shook her head. "I just don't understand it. I thought I was doing everything right. I thought I was making the right moves and handling this thing very carefully. But in one night, I managed to screw it up, and I didn't even mean to. How could he think I could like Steve that way? Steve's just a . . . a . . . a friend. *His* friend!" She closed her eyes and breathed deeply. "I don't know, I guess it just wasn't meant to be."

"What wasn't meant to be, baby?"

"Terrence and I," Janelle said quietly.

Mrs. Howard sat back and fought the urge to smile. It seemed that she and Mrs. Boyer had stewed their magic love potion and caused quite a lot of fireworks. She frowned down at the daisy she was stitching and shook her head. But something had gone awry somewhere. Leave it to those two children to foul things up. She removed her glasses, wiped her eyes, placed them back and shrugged. Oh, well, she guessed she would just have to meddle again in order to fix this mess.

"Why do you think you two aren't meant to be?"

Janelle puffed her cheeks and blew out a gust of air. "Because every time we get together something goes wrong. It's like we're cursed. Maybe he's better off with someone else. Someone who understands him better and plucks the right chords in him."

'Let me tell you something, Janey," her grandmother began. "When your grandfather and I, rest his beautiful soul, first started courtin' one another down in North Carolina, we used to cuss and fuss all the time. I started to wonder, too, if he was meant for somebody else. It seemed that I was the only one who could manage to get him fired up over the littlest things and it hurt my feelings some kind of bad to see that he could be so nice to everybody else. With the other girls he could smile and work his charm, but for me, all he ever seemed to have was mean words. But then," she said as she threaded her needle again, "your grandmamma started to realize that the only reason why I could get him so fired up was because I was the only girl he wanted in . . . that way. I figure that I could pluck his bad chords but I could just as well pluck his good. That's the power that his love gave to me. And when I plucked his good chords, baby," she laughed, "he could sing like the harp of an angel."

She paused to point her finger at Janelle. "That's what you need to do, Janey. You need to get on that Terrence boy's good side. You know just as well as I that it can be done. You just got to try. Can't win him over moping around in my living room. That's for sure."

Janelle rolled her eyes. "Grandma, I'm not going to chase after him. I didn't do anything wrong."

"I'm not asking you to chase after him," her grandmother said, raising her voice. "I'm just asking you to set the record straight. Who cares who was wrong and who wasn't wrong? You like him. He likes you. It ain't any point wasting time because the both of you are acting silly."

Janelle sat quietly, contemplating her grandmother's words. She slowly smiled and rose from the couch. Janelle walked over to the older woman and kissed her on both cheeks before gathering her things and waving good-bye.

"I better leave."

Her grandmother frowned. "Where you going?"

Janelle winked before closing the apartment door behind her.

Terrence pattered around his apartment barefoot, wearing nothing more than a white undershirt and old college sweatpants. He scratched his face, feeling the briskly hairs of his five-o'clock shadow. He shoveled another spoonful of wheat cereal into his mouth before heading back over to the couch where Sven lazily "watched" a football game.

Terrence hadn't shaved in three days, but then again, he hadn't been to the gym in over a week, not having the energy. He frowned and pinched at his lean hips and torso and tried to pull at the skin over his granitelike stomach, grappling for imaginary love handles and an unappealing bulge. He shrugged, gave up searching for particles of fat and figured he was a little heavier. Unfortunately, his agent would not take such physical changes so lightly. The Palm Pilot–toting, headset-wearing woman would not be happy, but that mattered little to him now. He had already piqued her anger almost to the point of no return.

She had called less than an hour earlier, telling him that the people at *Top Tier* had phoned the agency to recruit Terrence for an ad campaign. He had sighed and quickly thought up an excuse, deciding that he was perfectly happy sulking in his apartment alone. He didn't feel like forcing a scowl and a smile for a photographer and having makeup artists tweeze his eyebrows. Terrence apologized, hacked up a series of coughs and told her that he had contracted a virus and would be out of commission for a week at least. She flustered for a few minutes and started to rant, telling him that he would think better to pack his things and get his butt on the first plane to New York.

"Sorry, I can't, Sophie," he said with a shrug. "Doctor's orders."

Terrence knew she had been a heartbeat away from screaming she would no longer be his agent. Sophie hated it when her clients walked past opportunities to schmooze with the big boys and hated it even more when they walked past opportunities offered by the likes of *Top Tier*. But instead of dropping him, she lectured him instead. He was still valuable to the agency, being one of the few black male models they had on their roster. According to her, he was "damn sight lucky black was 'in' this season." ·

"Fine." He rolled his eyes as she seethed into the phone's receiver. "You stay there in Washington and patch your cold with chicken soup and a hot water bottle, but let me tell you something, Terrence Boyer. Our agency does not waste its time on models that have no intention on succeeding in this business. Your face may be on our wall now, but it can quickly be replaced by someone else's three months later! Ask the men *you* replaced! Do you think you're special? I could find a hundred people who look like you . . . better than you!"

"Then get one," he said blandly before hanging up on her.

He smiled to himself now, imagining her hurling her cappuccino against the wall when she realized he wasn't afraid of her or the agency, or of the possibility of screwing up his modeling career.

The doorbell rang. Terrence frowned, wondering who it could be since he wasn't expecting anyone.

He looked over Sven and pointed toward the bedroom. "You know the drill, buddy."

Sven grumbled and gazed up at his master from the couch's cushion.

"Nope. When you learn not to growl at company, I'll let you stay in the living room. Go on," he ordered sternly.

Sven barked before pattering to his master's bedroom. The door was shut firmly behind him.

The doorbell rang again but this time it was a series of rings as if someone was holding their finger down on the button. He frowned and walked over to the peephole, peering through it into the hallway. When he saw who it was, he let out a grave sigh and slowly swung the door open.

Janelle leaned back slightly, trying her best to balance the weight of the grocery bag and the bouquet of flowers in her hands. He noticed how she swallowed deeply and forced a smile.

"Hi," she said in a shaky voice. "I was just in the neighborhood so I . . . I decided to pay you a visit."

He didn't respond, but merely leaned against the doorframe and stared at her quietly. She pursed her lips before awkwardly shoving the bouquet of orchids at him.

"These are for you."

Terrence narrowed his eyes and frowned down at the flowers wrapped in clear cellophane before taking them. He wanted to smile in surprise but fought the urge and raised an eyebrow instead. They were deep-purple and white orchids with freckles near the slivers of yellow at each center. They seemed soft, delicate, exotic, and beautiful. They reminded him of her.

He swallowed, gritted his teeth, and held the flowers in his hands as if the bouquet were a roll of newspaper he had just dragged off the street. He thumped the orchids against his side and pretended not to notice as a few petals fell to the floor.

"No one's ever brought me flowers," he finally muttered. "But then again no one's ever tried to kill my doorbell."

She laughed as she forced her way past him into the foyer, deciding to no longer wait for him to invite her inside his home.

"Well, there's a first time for everything, Terrence," she muttered.

He closed the door behind her and raised an eyebrow when she handed the grocery bag to him. She walked in a wide circle around the living room and headed over to the framed photographs on his bookshelf.

"You know," she began, "I've known you for a while now and I've never seen the inside of your apartment. That's so weird. I thought you were hiding it from me because it was dirty or something." She looked around and slowly nodded her head. "But it's not dirty at all. Much neater than I thought it would be. You sure you don't have a cleaning lady?" she asked with a smile.

He slowly walked over to her with his hands firmly clasped behind his back. Terrence would never tell her that he hadn't invited her to his apartment because the idea of having Janelle inside his home, inside his domain, had been too much of a temptation for his weakened senses. He couldn't uphold his resolve to maintain his distance from her here. He stood behind her, while her eyes scanned over each picture. The enticing scent of her perfume overwhelmed him.

Janelle hummed to herself and stopped at a photograph of Kara. She lifted the frame from the bookshelf and narrowed her eyes.

"She's beautiful, Terrence. Is she your sister?"

"No, she's not my sister."

Janelle turned to find him standing inches away from her. She jumped back in surprise and almost knocked down the photographs. Her eyes widened as he steadied her. Terrence rolled his eyes, took the photograph from out of her hands and placed it back on the shelf.

"She looks like she could be your sister," she said softly. "I mean . . . she's a little . . . a little lighter than you, but the facial features are about the same."

"Well, she's not."

He walked away and turned down the television.

"Look, Janelle, you and I know you didn't come over to my apartment to look at pictures and guess which one's my sister. Why are you here? What do you want?"

"You aren't going to put those in water?" she said, pointing down at the flowers he still held in his hand.

When he didn't answer her, she walked around him,

hoisted her grocery bag onto her hip and took it into the kitchen. She began to open cabinets, taking down pans, plates and glasses.

"You have a choice between veal Parmesan or honey-glazed chicken. I brought both because I wasn't sure which you'd prefer."

"I've already eaten," he muttered.

"I brought red wine and white wine, too," she continued, pretending not to hear him. "I don't know which goes better with which meal. You know I'm not much of a drinker."

"Look, I don't want you to make me dinner! Keep the veal. Keep the chicken. Keep the wine. Put it back in the bag and take it home."

She stopped and closed her eyes. "Terrence, why are you acting like this? Let me finish this. Let me cook this stuff and put it on a plate and set it on the table. I've practiced at least a dozen times what I want to say to you and the only way I imagined doing it is over a meal. If I don't have the food, I'm going to mess up! If I mess up, I'm going to get frustrated! If I get frustrated, I'll just say something I'll regret!" She waved around the vacuumed pack of veal. "Jesus, you don't have to eat it! Just let me cook it!"

He slowly shook his head, wanting to laugh. Only Janelle would say something as crazy as that.

He ended his protests and she sighed. She opened the freezer, quickly pulling out two trays of ice. He raised his hand and opened his mouth to stop her, but the water splashed onto her face and the front of her shirt and wool skirt before he could. He rolled his eyes and sighed gruffly as a puddle collected around her feet.

"Move back," he ordered roughly, grabbing her wrist and dragging her behind him so that he could clean up the spill. Terrence opened one of the cabinets and retrieved a paper towel roll. Without looking, he tossed a few at her over his shoulder so that she could dry her face at least and began to drop quite a few more to the floor. He wiped at the puddle with his foot and threw the soaking wet paper towels into the trash.

"I'm sorry," she said quietly.

"Yeah, I know," he muttered. "You're sorry about spilling the ice trays that I just filled fifteen minutes ago all over my kitchen floor. You're sorry for busting into my apartment, picking up *my* things and going through *my* cabinets as if you owned the place. You're sorry for shacking up with my former best friend and giving me some rigamarole about how you wanted to move slow." He turned to her coldly, holding up his hands. "You know what, Janelle? You can save your sorrys. You're only wasting them."

He watched her as she clasped the paper towels in her hands. Beads of water clung to the front of her hair and dripped down her face. He tried not to notice the white lace and outline of her bra through her wet turtleneck and how the nipples stood out in sharp contrast to the fabric and rest of her skin. She watched him silently.

"We didn't do anything," Janelle murmured softly. "I can repeat it a thousand times, Terrence, but it won't mean anything if you're bent on not believing me. He wanted to talk to me about you to ask me about how I felt about you. Even he knew I came to that party to be with you. Not him. If you can't see that by now, Terrence—" She flapped her arms helplessly. "Then I don't know what else to do."

He stood there silently and watched her turn away from him.

"What did you tell him?" he blurted out.

Janelle returned her gaze to him. She frowned in confusion.

"Huh?"

"When he asked you how you felt about me. What did you tell him?"

She gave a hesitant smile. "I said I care about you so much . . . sometimes it hurts. It sounds corny but it's true."

He considered her words carefully before slowly walking over to her and cupping her face in his hands. He wasn't sure what he had expected but he hadn't anticipated her gaze to be so focused, so intense. He let his eyes trail over her features, from the eyelashes that were now caked together with pearls of water to the freckles that dotted her button nose to the swell of the full lips that whispered his name. Before he lowered his mouth to hers, Terrence concluded that he had never seen a face more beautiful on any magazine cover or runway.

Janelle did not waver from his passion or flinch from his touch. His kisses were hesitant and tentative, and his arms and hands seemed as if they had no idea where to go, not knowing whether she would soon erect a wall between them again and push him away. But she let her fingers dutifully clasp at his neck and head while the others snaked up his back. She urged his mouth open with her own and teased him with the pressing of her wet chest against his T-shirt, dampening it with each caress. He let out a throaty laugh of surprise and allowed her to suckle his tongue and nip at his lower lip before he returned the gesture. He moaned her name against her lips.

Terrence felt her hands inching his shirt up his stomach. He felt her fingernails rake over the dark hairs around his navel as she tugged at the drawstring of his sweat pants. He grunted with pleasure and for the first time realized that there would be no timidity from her. Her eyes were glazed over with the same need and hunger that had been there in the park more than a month ago but she seemed to have no intention of running away from it this time, and he could enjoy her and her body as much as he wanted.

He smiled wickedly and helped her pull his T-shirt over his head before tossing it to the floor. They did an ardent dance in the center of the kitchen before he turned her around, guiding her back until they slammed against the coldness of the refrigerator door. She slipped slightly on the last traces of the spilled water and let out an astonished laugh but he caught her at the hips and pressed himself against her, parting her legs with one of his own. The refrigerator door steadied her from behind but she clasped her hands at his back and kissed him forcefully.

Terrence was torn between two urges. He wanted to mesh his body with her until each arm and leg touched, until it could not be determined where one ended and the other began. But he had to remove her clothes. That lust-filled fantasy had to be gratified first. He tore his mouth away from her and she let out a passionate grumble.

"Why'd you stop?" she asked irritably as he tugged the hem of her shirt out of the wool skirt.

After he finally managed to pull the wet cloth over her head, he pulled down the straps of her bra and lowered the garment to her waist. He admired the sight before him by running his thumb over the dark, hardened nipples and surrounding goose bumps, letting each breast swell in his hands, making her sigh at his touch. Terrence slowly dropped to his knees and gazed up at her. She smiled down at him angelically and leaned forward. She let her lips trace over his forehead and eyes.

"What are you doing, baby?" she murmured against his lips and laughed softly. "Get off the floor and kiss me again."

He ignored her and pressed her back slightly so that her breast and his mouth met. He circled his tongue around one of her nipples and began to suckle.

She cried out in delight and he pulled his mouth away, letting his hand travel up the junction of her thighs. There was a mixed texture that his fingertips experienced. First he felt the nylon of her thigh-high stockings, the lace of her underwear and then the scratchiness of her wool skirt. His fingertips trailed past these regions and nestled in the silkiness of the hair between her thighs. They finally delved into the wetness that slicked the center and began to massage it until another moan erupted from her lips. Her pelvis met the rhythmic thrust of his fingers, and Terrence could not help but delve deeper into her. All the while he felt his arousal hardening but he held his lust in check and continued to give her pleasure instead, feeling beads of sweat form near his temples.

"Terrence," she called breathlessly down to him. "Terrence. Please stop."

He slowly pulled his hand away and rose from his knees, meeting her drowsy gaze.

She brought her lips to him while he felt her hand urgently tugging past the drawstring of his pants and at the waistband of his underwear. She tugged again and he grabbed her wrist, pushing it away, feeling his heart thud like a snare drum in his chest. With a series of artful moves, he pulled down his pants and boxers and dragged her own undergarments completely off. He steadied her against the refrigerator door as she snaked her legs around his waist, and he thrust himself into the damp, warm place where his fingers had been minutes earlier. She cried out in shock and he gasped for air as his head nestled in the crook of her shoulder. Their bodies joined into a steady rhythm with each following thrust and they breathed air into one another's mouths as they continued to kiss hungrily, clinging to one another as if the ground would fall from under them. The tremors raked her body first, and she dug her nails into his back and shouted his name. His soon followed and he shouted hers. When the spasms passed they crashed to the floor, sapped of energy. He let her shudder on top of him and sighed gruffly, feeling as if he could stay that way forever.

Chapter Eight

Janelle awoke contentedly from a peaceful sleep. The glare of morning sunlight streaming through her bedroom window greeted her. The sound of Terrence's tempered snores reverberated in her ears and so did the even louder snores of their two dogs that slept in a piled heap in the bedroom doorway. She nuzzled closer to him and didn't mind how his arm draped heavily onto her side. He mumbled softly as she trailed her fingertips over his forearm, and she admired the way the fine blond hairs stood out against the light of dawn, like acres of gold. She smiled and raised an inquisitive eyebrow. Where in the world did he get blond arm hair?

Janelle sighed and crawled from under him, feeling the cold air instantly against her naked body as she pulled back the covers and let her feet fall to the floor. Terrence twisted and rolled to the other side of the bed, sinking further beneath the heavy quilts and grumbling in his sleep. She smiled over at him and shook her head before grabbing her robe and tugging it on. Janelle looked around her room and gazed at the surrounding mess. There were clothes everywhere and doggie toys in every corner. Frames that had tumbled from the wall during their lovemaking last night lay behind her bed and shattered glass had spilled onto the floor. She sighed and decided to walk to the kitchen to retrieve a broom and dustpan.

Janelle shoved her feet into baby-blue bedroom slippers and tried to climb over Sven and Jazz without disturbing them. But the second she drew close to them, Sven lifted his head and began to pant. Jazz opened drowsy eyes and barked up at her.

"Alrighty, then. So much for not waking you," she whispered. "You guys hungry?"

When Sven's tongue dropped lower to the floor, Janelle laughed.

"Go on. Momma's going to get you breakfast," she said as she shooed them into the hallway and they pattered down to the first floor. She closed the bedroom door behind her and twisted her unruly hair into a bun at the crown of her head. She hummed happily to herself. Janelle opened her cabinets and pulled out two dog watering bowls. She poured Kibbles and Bits into them and then rubbed each dog playfully on their respective chins.

Just then, the phone rang. She rushed over to the receiver on the kitchen wall and poured herself a glass of orange juice as she picked it up.

"Hello?" she said into the cordless before sipping from her glass.

"Hello, Janelle."

Her eyes widened. She choked on the juice in her mouth and coughed, holding her chest.

"Uh, hi, Mrs. Boyer. How are you?"

The older woman gave a rumbling laugh. "I'm doing fine, baby. Didn't mean to surprise you. I was just looking for my grandson. I tried calling his house for the past three days but he hasn't been home. I figure he could be on one of his modeling trips but I thought I might try your house first."

"Oh, okay. So, um, you want to talk to Terrence?"

Mrs. Boyer grew silent. "If that's okay."

"Definitely. I'm sure it's okay . . . it's just that he's asleep."

"Still asleep in bed on a Saturday at eleven o'clock? So my baby is just slumbering the day away. You haven't been wearing him out, have you, Janelle?"

Janelle's eyes widened and she lowered her glass to the counter, not quite sure exactly what his grandmother was asking or suggesting.

She forced a laugh and twisted her finger in a loose strand of hair.

"He had a long night I guess."

Mrs. Boyer laughed. "I bet he did. Would you tell him to give Mother a call when he wakes up?"

"Of course, I will."

"Good-bye, honey. You have a nice day now."

"You, too. Good-bye, Mrs. Boyer."

After hanging up, Janelle bit down on the rubber antenna of the cordless and smiled. She gazed down at the two dogs whose faces were lost in their respective doggie bowls and shook her head.

"I think grandma thinks your mommy and daddy are being bad, kiddies," she muttered. But then Janelle thought back to the night before when she throbbed and moaned in Terrence's arms and shrugged. "Trouble is, she's right."

With that, she picked up the broom in the corner and the dustpan and quietly trudged back upstairs.

When she opened the bedroom door, she found Terrence wide-awake, leaning up against the headboard watching midday cartoons. The quilts were kicked down around his ankles and only a thin white sheet lay over his bare chest. When he saw her, he smiled and raised himself to his elbows.

"I was wondering where everybody had gone."

She grinned and walked over to the edge of the bed.

"Well, the two canines are downstairs eating breakfast. I decided to do a little cleaning. This place looks like a tornado hit it."

He frowned. "And where's my breakfast?"

"In the refrigerator and cabinet, waiting to be made by none other than you, sweetheart."

Terrence rolled his eyes and gave out a playful sigh. He puffed the pillows behind his head and gazed up at her. "So I guess the honeymoon's over?"

"It's been a few weeks, so I guess you could say that." She laughed. "Your grandmother called."

"For me?"

Janelle began to sweep up the pieces of glass behind the bed and smacked Terrence's hand away as he tugged at the belt of her robe.

"Yes, for you. I had to tell her you were asleep. She wanted to know why you were still in bed and if I was 'wearing you out'?"

He grinned. "So the jig is up?"

"I guess you could say that, too." She sat down beside him on the bed and stared out the window in front of her. "Part of me really doesn't care what they think. My grandmother had come to terms with the fact that I'm not a virgin years ago, but I don't know about letting two well-meaning but meddling old women get the satisfaction of knowing their meddling worked. It's destructive."

He shrugged and rubbed her back. "Well, we haven't walked down the aisle, Janelle."

She narrowed her eyes at him and raised her chin. "But we're sleeping with one another on a daily basis."

Terrence smiled and chuckled. "Okay. I'll give you that one, though I don't think that's exactly what they had in mind. But technically," he muttered as he fiddled with her robe again, "we haven't had our daily supplement today anyway."

She laughed as he tossed her back onto the mattress and towered over her. He tugged at the knot in her belt and cursed under his breath when it wouldn't budge, making her laugh again.

"It's only 11:30, Terrence. We have the whole day and besides, don't you think I should get the glass off the floor. You wouldn't want to cut yourself, would you?"

"What difference does it make? We're just going to knock more pictures down anyway."

"Oh, I see. *You* get to have the nice, neat apartment while I live in a pigsty. Is that it?"

He finally managed to open her robe and threw the terry cloth aside. He skimmed his palms under her hips while smiling triumphantly. Terrence parted her legs and situated himself between them and her eyes widened as she gazed at his already fully erect manhood. She blinked and swallowed. Was he kidding?

"We haven't even brushed our teeth yet!" Janelle exclaimed.

Terrence sighed, thought a minute and then held up his index finger. She frowned up at him as he leaned over to the night table and retrieved two packets of peppermints. He placed one on his tongue and stuck the other in her mouth before giving her the thumbs up sign.

Oh, no he didn't! Janelle erupted into laughter and she grabbed her stomach just as he leaned down and kissed her, stripping her of all her senses. She was lost in a daze as Terrence lifted her pelvis so that it met his own. He teased her body with the sound of cartoons playing in the background and thrust himself into her, catching her off guard and making all laughter instantly die on her lips. She quickly joined his erotic rhythm and reveled in each plunge. All thoughts except for the pulsating urges inside her filled her brain.

The two men walked onto the indoor basketball court amid the sounds of grunting and the thuds of bouncing basketballs. Terrence pulled his sweatshirt over his head and looked around him. One end of the court seemed vacant for the most part with the exception of a teenage boy who tried his best to slam-dunk a ball, but landed sprawled out on the floor instead. Terrence bit back a smile and began to stretch, extending his arms over his head and flexing his legs. An instant later he felt the snap of a towel against his back. He looked over to find Steve smiling at him.

"Man, stop stretching and play some ball. I'd like to do this sometime today."

Terrence slowly picked up the basketball and dribbled it. He spun the basketball tip of his finger and grinned.

"Steve, we got all the time in the world. Why are you in such a hurry to get a beat down?"

"Please, Tory. Save talking trash for the victors, alright? Don't make me have to school you, boy."

Terrence laughed. "Oh, you're going to school me?"

"If I have to." Steve grinned. "And you better be taking notes."

The two men had decided to reconcile but without apologies. Terrence hadn't spoken to Steve since the night of the party and only started speaking to him again because Janelle insisted that he do so. Neither of them wanted their reunion to contain an ounce of mushiness, so instead of meeting at Terrence's apartment or Steve's condo or even a restaurant to talk things out, they agreed to meet at the local gym's basketball court.

Yes, Terrence truly believed that nothing had happened between Janelle and his best friend that night of the party, but he found it hard to admit that he was wrong, especially to someone like Steve. Terrence knew he would probably have to hear Steve's laughing account of Terrence's fury over a female—of all things—for the next twenty years. He would grant him no mercy.

Their tennis shoes squeaked loudly on the sparkling wooden floors and they pivoted about one another, each battling for the ball. Sweat dripped into their eyes and perspiration collected under their arms and on their backs. Steve raced toward the basket but slipped and crashed to the ground. Terrence took the opportunity to capture the ball and make a three-point shot. He smiled smugly and let the ball bounce to a far-off corner. He reached down, offered his hand to his friend, and pulled Steve back to his feet.

"Sixty-four to forty." Steve muttered as he walked toward

the wall to retrieve the basketball. "That's a new record. You're lucky she helped your game, man."

"What trash are you talking now?" Terrence smiled in confusion. "She? She who?"

"She who? Listen to this guy. 'She who'?" Steve rolled his eyes and grinned. He hurled the ball back at Terrence, crouched and rested his hands on his knees. "Don't act like you don't know, Tory. I'm talking about she with a capital S. The love of your life . . . your Nubian queen . . . the only woman you ever let answer your phone."

Terrence stopped dribbling and lost his smile. He held the basketball against his hip and shook his head.

"Don't play like that, Steve."

"Don't play like what?"

"Don't make fun of that. Don't make fun of her."

Steve shook his head and smiled. "I'm not making fun of her, Tory. I'm making fun of you."

"Why me?"

Steve shrugged. "Because its easy to make fun of you. You've been glowing like you got a piece of uranium in your pocket, brotha." He wagged his finger at him and laughed. "You slippin', man. You slippin'."

Steve shook his head and slowly smiled. "I'm not slippin'."

"Yeah, right. Sure you aren't?"

"I'm not slippin, Steve!" exclaimed Terrence as he dribbled. "Look, stop running your mouth and save what little face you got left. You're just trying to distract me. That's all."

Steve shrugged and grabbed the basketball away from Terrence. He winked before attempting a shot, watching as the ball circled around the rim and finally went through the basket.

"Hey, believe what you want, brotha . . . but I know what's up."

Terrence rolled his eyes. "Okay, tell me what's up."

"You're gonna ask her to move in with you, aren't you?"

When Terrence did not answer him, Steve laughed. "I knew you were, man. I knew it."

"Okay, okay. But think about it. No, think about it, Steve. It's a practical move. Renting that house all by herself is too much for her on her salary. If we moved in together, she could save money. I could save money. And we could share utilities and—"

"Yeah," Steve said while rolling his eyes. "I'm sure you're asking her to move in with you because of financial reasons. Right. Keep believing that, Terrence. Man, if you start reasoning things out like that, next thing you know you'll be asking her to marry you. You'll say you're doing it so you can file taxes together."

Steve laughed and turned to his friend. When Terrence stared at him blankly, he frowned.

"Tory, I was kidding."

Terrence forced a laugh and walked over to the benches to get a towel. "I know you were kidding, man. I know you were kidding."

Steve narrowed his eyes at Terrence's back, jogged over to him, and turned him around so that he could see his face. Terrence grumbled and shrugged Steve's hand away, making Steve frown more and slowly shake his head.

"You weren't . . . you wouldn't—"

"I wouldn't what?"

Steve let out a shocked laugh. "Oh, crap. You *are* going to ask her."

"I don't know what you're talking about," Terrence mumbled.

"What is this? The third month you've known her? You're going to ask her to marry you this soon? You don't want to give it a year or two at least, Tory? Living with her is bad enough, but this? Man, this is blowing me!"

Terrence threw his towel around his neck and stared at the floor.

"I didn't say a damn thing about asking her to marry me! Stop putting words in my mouth," he argued. "Besides, even if I *did* ask . . . which I'm not saying that I am, but if I did . . . the wedding wouldn't have to be right away. We could have a long engagement. I'm comfortable with waiting a few years. I know how to give a woman space."

"Tory, you're talking about it like you're seriously going to do this. You don't think asking her to marry you this soon is gonna scare her off?"

"Not everyone has your fear of commitment or wants to play the field."

Steve sighed deeply and rubbed his hands over his glistening bald head.

"This has nothing to do with fear of commitment, Tory. There's nothing to commit to! You're having a good time. It's just a good time with a nice girl. Don't let it get to your head. I swear you get whipped faster than any other man I know. Good sex, good time, move on. Repeat it with me. Good sex, good time, move on."

Terrence closed his eyes, took a deep breath and shook his head.

"I understand what you're saying, Steve, and I appreciate the advice. But you don't think I realize how crazy I sound when I say I want to move in with her and ask her to marry me? You don't think I hear myself?" He pointed at his ear. "But I gotta do it, man. I *have* to do it. If she says no, that's fine. But I have to do it. When you meet a woman that you love the way I love her, then maybe we can talk. Until then, mind your business."

Steve sighed again and slowly shook his head. He stood silently, letting the ball thud as he bounced it beside him.

"My Uncle Clyde," he began, "works for a jeweler. He knows a lot about rings and diamonds and stuff along those lines so he could give you advice on what to choose. Maybe he could talk his boss into giving you a good deal on an engagement ring too. I'll give him a call for you."

Terrence slowly smiled and playfully punched his friend in the shoulder.

"I appreciate that, man. I appreciate it a lot."

Chapter Nine

Janelle watched Terrence close the front door behind him and frowned. All day he had been behaving strangely, hopping around like his feet were on fire or like something was burning a hole in his pocket. She had to clasp his face in her hands at some point and urge him to calm down. She just couldn't take it anymore. But Terrence smiled and assured her everything was fine. He said that he always got a little jittery or "pretipsy" on New Year's Eve. The day's festivities got to him now like Christmas did when he was a kid.

Satisfied with his explanation, Janelle slowly smiled and walked over to the dresser mirror to apply her makeup. But Terrence walked up behind her and simply stared at her reflection, absently rubbing her shoulders.

"Terrence," she said through gritted teeth after her mascara wand bobbed into her eye a second time. "Honey, if you keep rubbing my shoulders, I'm going to blind myself."

He cringed. "I'm sorry, baby."

"No, no. It's okay. It's a useless eye anyway." She grinned up at him and kissed his cheek. "Hey, could you go out to buy me some black panty hose? I forgot to get them on the way here. All the ones I have are white."

The ploy to get him out of her hair for at least a half an hour had worked—to her surprise. He had actually gone out to buy her stockings and without a protest. Janelle frowned, wondering if she had asked him to get her tampons, would he have done that, too? If he did, she would definitely know something was wrong with him. Terrence wouldn't walk to a store counter to purchase a box of tampons even if he were threatened to do so at gunpoint.

Janelle sighed deeply as she now stood in the quiet of his living room in her robe while brushing her hair and trying her best to tame her wild curls with the help of leave-in conditioner. She had decided not to straighten it for the New Year's Eve party because Terrence insisted that her hair was much prettier au naturel. He would often run his fingers through it as they drove or sat on the couch watching television, even while they lay awake together in bed. It was ironic how something that had been such an annoyance for Janelle throughout most of her life fascinated him.

She glanced over at Sven and Jazz who were sleeping on the couch. It was a pastime they seemed to enjoy a lot lately. She walked into the kitchen and opened up the refrigerator, pulling out a carton of milk, a chilled banana, and a basket of strawberries. She smiled as she placed each fruit into the blender along with a cup of milk, preparing to make Terrence his favorite shake so it would be ready for him when he got back.

We're a good little wifey, aren't we? a cynical voice in her head murmured.

Janelle jumped away from the blender as if it had shocked her.

You wear your hair the way he wants you to wear it, the voice continued. *You make him milkshakes. You even let him pick out the dress you're wearing tonight! Who do you think you are, Donna Reed?*

She took a deep breath, closed her eyes and gritted her

teeth, drowning out the nagging voice with the grating of the blender.

She poured the pink mixture into a glass and looked down into it, staring at the strawberry seeds and chunks. She shoved the glass into the refrigerator, deciding that she had made the drink for Terrence simply to repay him for buying her stockings, nothing more.

Her fingers started to tingle with a familiar itch and her mind raced. She needed to write something and she needed to do it quickly. Janelle went over to the duffel bag and pulled out one of her notebooks. Her pen was poised in her hand as she flipped the pages until she arrived to the last entry. Her eyes widened.

It was dated November sixteenth. She had not written in her notebook in over a month!

Janelle slowly slumped onto the couch and cradled the notebook in her lap, making Sven grumble.

Where did the time go? Where had her mind been for the last forty days? Janelle shook her head. She knew where it had been. It was smothered under the mattress, pushed into a dim, dusty corner while she "played house" with Terrence for over a month.

When was the last time she'd turned in a copy to her editor on time? Hadn't she planned to submit a finished work to a publisher weeks ago? How did she plan to ever get her work out there if she lay in bed with her lips locked with his all day?

She frowned and tapped her pen against her notebook. But it didn't seem like Terrence had suffered any loss of concentration. He still left at least once a week on a modeling assignment, always kissing her breathless as he walked out the door and promising her that he'd be back. She'd squirm around and sulk for two days or so until he arrived back at his apartment. That same night, she would lay with a dreamy smile on her face after they made love and cuddle closer to Terrence, wondering how she had managed day-to-day life without him.

Like I said, the voice muttered again, *Donna Reed. No, scratch that. You're* worse *than Donna Reed.*

The doorbell rang and Janelle's frown intensified. She didn't think Terrence was expecting anyone tonight, especially an hour before they were supposed to·be at the party. Suddenly, she caught sight of the keys sitting on the edge of the coffee table out of the corner of her eye. She shook her head and smiled. Terrence had forgotten his house keys again.

"I'm coming," she called as she walked over to the door in her socks and robe. Sven followed behind her.

"So you locked yourself out, huh?" she asked with a grin while swinging open the door, not bothering to look through the peephole. "It's lucky I'm here to let you in or you'd be—"

Her words trailed off as she gazed at the woman standing before her. Sven began to growl. Jazz joined him.

"What is wrong with you two?" Janelle said as she frowned down at them. "Stop it!"

She seemed less like a woman and more like a gazelle as she walked—or better put, strutted—into Terrence's apartment. Her auburn hair was piled high atop her head and her silver heels clicked against the floor of the foyer, adding height to the woman who already towered nearly half a foot over Janelle. She glanced down at her with smoky honey-colored eyes as if Janelle were a hired maid whose job it was to answer doors. The beautiful woman peeled open her mohair coat, revealing a metallic dress with high slits at each side.

"Where's Tory?" she asked as she narrowed her eyes at the angry bulldog and looked around the living room.

He's not here," Janelle murmured, bewildered.

"Well, when will he be back?"

"Um, who are you?"

"I'm his girlfriend. Now his former girlfriend now that

I'm soon to be married," she said blandly. She let her gaze wander from Janelle's terry cloth robe to her white socks. "Unfortunately, for him."

Janelle's mouth dropped open. Who the hell was this female, and why was she talking trash? Terrence had never mentioned any woman, let alone a girlfriend, in the past three months she had known him. Clearly, this person was deranged.

Janelle opened her mouth to tell the woman off, but stopped and slowly turned to the bookshelf. The woman's image stared back at her from amongst the framed photographs. She slowly swallowed.

"Like I said," Janelle muttered, overwhelmed by a sense of nausea, "he's not here."

The woman peered down at her and twisted her mouth into a smirk.

"Oh, dear. It seems Tory's been a very bad boy." She raised an eyebrow. "You're not just a one-night-guest at *la casa de Terrence,* are you?"

Janelle balled her fists and gritted her teeth.

"Don't get angry, pet. I could spot the saddle burns Tory gave you at twenty meters. Not to mention the walk. I could trade stories with you if it weren't for the limo waiting for me downstairs."

Janelle gazed at her, torn between shock and fury. How could such a gorgeous woman be so blunt and crude? How could Terrence have possibly been attracted to a woman like her and then a woman like Janelle?

Easy, she thought angrily. Terrence hadn't been thinking with the head on his shoulders.

"I think you'd better leave," Janelle said as she walked over to the front door, unlocked it, and swung it open. "I'll tell him you tried to get in touch with him, Ms. . . ."

"Djibutar," the tall woman said with a smile as she strolled into the building's hallway. "Kara Djibutar. Oh, and could you also tell him to pick up his things from my loft? I would send them through the post but I'm moving to France in two days. Tell him Carmen will be there though. I'm leasing the loft to her."

"Fine," Janelle muttered as she slammed the door behind her.

She grabbed her forehead, feeling as if her head were on fire.

So what are you gonna do now? the cynical voice murmured in her head.

She pushed her hair out of her face and walked back into the bedroom to continue to prepare for the party.

Terrence gazed at Janelle over the rim of his champagne glass and frowned. A few of the partygoers had pulled him into a conversation, but he now gave them little of his attention, feeling a little uneasy. He had been laughing with the group seconds earlier and absently placed his hand on Janelle's shoulder. Terrence had not thought about the affectionate gesture as he did it, being so accustomed to making sure she was standing by his side. He hadn't meant to come off as possessive or "touchy-feely." But he couldn't convince himself that he had imagined it. She *had* shrugged his hand away.

Terrence let his gaze follow her as she strolled away from him to the other side of the ballroom, over to the towering windows. She pulled back one of the red velvet curtains and peered at the traffic and people below, in front of the hotel. She leaned back and gazed up at the full moon, letting her curls cascade past her shoulder blades and sweep the low back of her dress. Janelle wrapped her arms around herself and pressed her forehead against the cold glass, staring into the twinkling lights. He could tell from her posture that she was lost in thought and looked as if she wanted nothing more than to be alone. But it was the coldness that radiated from her that made him quietly walk over to her, to press his chin against her cheek and wrap his arms around her. The instant he did, catching her off guard, he could feel her body stiffen.

"What's wrong?" he asked, his voice filled with concern.

He gazed at their reflections in the window. Terrence noticed how she rolled her eyes and sighed.

"Nothing's wrong," Janelle muttered as she pulled away. "I just have to get to the ladies' room. I'll be back."

Terrence shoved his hands into his pockets and shook his head as she eased her way through the throng of couples on the crowded dance floor. He hadn't remembered them arguing over anything before they left for the New Year's Eve party. So why was she behaving so strangely?

He fingered the small gold satin box in the pocket of his pants and furrowed his eyebrows. She wasn't going to make this easy for him, was she? He had already stretched his nerves until they vibrated like rubber bands because he was anticipating the coming of midnight, waiting for the moment to ask her. It was hard working up the nerve to propose to someone under hostile circumstances.

How can I ask her to marry me if she's pissed off? he wondered. He turned back to the window and fingered the box again. He wanted nothing more than to open it and look at the engagement ring though it would be the fifth time that day that he stared at the jewel. But it seemed to be his only form of reassurance right now.

Steve had not lied. Uncle Clyde was a volume of information on precious stones, but even more surprising was how the old man managed to connect a type of jewel or jewelry to a type of woman. After assuring his boss that he would handle this sale personally, he asked Terrence not only what engagement ring he intended to buy for his lady love, but also questions about the woman herself. Terrence had frowned as he gave tidbits of information on Janelle, wondering what the perfume she wore and her favorite flower had to do with purchasing an engagement ring. He waited impatiently while the small, stoutly man shuffled to the back of the store, claiming that he had the perfect ring for her. When he laid the gold box on the glass counter and slowly opened the lid, Terrence began to nod. He was right. It was the perfect ring for Janelle.

Uncle Clyde had chosen an antique piece: a diamond-cut amethyst surrounded by pearls and etched gold. The instant Terrence saw it, he imagined how it would look against the red hue of Janelle's hand and he smiled. It would look beautiful.

Rubbing the ring box must have made her materialize. She now walked toward him carrying two party hats decorated with glitter and the numbers 2001, along with two noisemakers. The band began a slow song and even more couples crowded the floor. Janelle placed one hat on her head, tugged it down over her hair, and gave an awkward smile.

"They should start the countdown in ten minutes," she said while pointing down at her wristwatch. "I know it doesn't match the suit exactly, but I thought you might want one."

As she handed him the party hat, Terrence gently clasped a hand around her wrist. He pulled her to the dance floor and draped her arm over his shoulder, making her laugh. They fell into rhythm with the song and Terrence drew her close, ignoring the way her body tensed against him.

He leaned over and whispered in her ear.

"Do I have to wait until midnight to kiss you?"

Janelle leaned back and closed her eyes tightly. Rising to her toes, she placed an awkward kiss on his cheek.

"I think the rule says that official kisses have to be saved until New Year's Day so that will have to do," she joked.

Terrence chuckled. He let his gaze drift over her, admiring the glow of her shoulder and neck under the lights of the chandelier. He let his hand drift down the ridge of her back and his pinky casually skimmed the top of her behind. His eyelids lowered and he dipped his head, touched his lips to her ear. Instantly, Janelle raised her arms between them and pressed her hands firmly against his chest.

"Not here, Terrence," she said through gritted teeth.

"What? What's wrong?"

"Nothing's wrong," she mumbled as she twisted out of his arms. "Just because I wouldn't let you feel me up on a dance floor filled with two hundred people something has to be wrong?"

She pushed her fingers through her hair and bit her lower lip.

"I need some air," she proclaimed, swishing away from him again.

He watched her receding back for the third time that night and stood on the dance floor fuming, wanting to punch his fist through a wall. Part of him calmly whispered that he should take a few deep breaths before he followed her, but the thumping of his heart quieted that calm voice quickly. He stormed behind her into a deserted hallway, catching up with Janelle as she stepped onto a vacant terrace. She paced back and forth with her arms wrapped around her shoulders, providing little warmth against the cold wind. She finally looked up at him, rolled her eyes and fisted her hand against her hips.

"I said I needed air. I guess I should have just told you to leave me the hell alone."

He narrowed his eyes at her.

"What the hell is wrong with you?" he asked icily. "You don't want me to touch you. You don't want me to kiss you. Now you don't want to be in the same room with me. Is it just me or have you been acting like . . . like a bitch since we got here! Before we got here!"

"Don't you dare call me that, Terrence!" Janelle jabbed her finger at him with eyes flashing. "I'm not a bitch! I'm not a female dog! If anybody's the dog here, Terrence Boyer, it's you! Okay? It's you! So don't start with the name calling!"

"When have I been a dog, Janelle? I've treated you with total respect! I've devoted myself totally to this . . . this . . . what we have . . . together! I was even going to ask you to—"

"You had a visitor today," she interrupted while crossing her arms over her chest. "A woman named Kara Deji-something came by who claimed to be your girlfriend. She told me to tell you that you can pick your things up from her loft, because she won't be able to send it through the *post*. She's moving to France."

Terrence felt the blood drain from his head.

"Kara came by my apartment today?"

"That's all you have to say, Terrence? 'Kara came by my apartment today?' " Janelle balled her fists at her sides. "That's all you have to say?"

"What more do you want me to say?" Terrence yelled, feeling nauseous.

"I want an explanation, damnit! I want you to tell me who the hell she is, and why hadn't mentioned her yesterday, or the day before that, or the day before that!"

When he stared at her blankly, Janelle gritted her teeth.

"Oh, you thought you were real cute playing stupid when I asked about the woman in the picture a month ago, didn't you? 'She's not my sister, Janelle.' No, she's your damn girlfriend!"

"She's not my girlfriend, baby. We haven't even spoken in over two months."

"Well, she didn't seem to think that!"

"I don't give a damn what she thinks," he roared, feeling his temple pound. "Look, I didn't mention her because she didn't matter. She doesn't matter now, either. I don't know why she came to the apartment today, Janelle. I'm sorry if me not mentioning her hurt you, I just . . . I just . . ."

He sighed as Janelle slowly shook her head.

"I don't believe you, Terrence. I can't believe you. Why should I believe you now when you've obviously not been upfront about everything?" She swallowed. "I feel like I put a lot of my trust in you! If you just wanted something casual, then you should have told me. Then I could have been given the choice to walk away before I got involved. But I wasn't given that choice."

She shoved past him, through the glass doors and into the hallway.

"Don't call me, Terrence. Leave me the hell alone," she yelled over her shoulder.

He listened to the sound of her heels clicking against the floor of the hallway and then the swinging open of the ball-room doors.

The party had reached its pitch. The crowd yelled out the last few numbers of the countdown and he could hear them cheering as he leaned against the railing. Terrence pulled the gold box out of his pocket and opened it, running his finger over the ring. At that moment he wanted nothing more than to toss it into the darkness and let it fall to the ground below.

But Terrence balled up his fists and straightened his shoulders. He quickly strode through the door of the terrace and walked toward the ballroom.

It would be hard to find her. Confetti fell from the ceiling and people danced drunkenly to the thriving music, bump-ing into one another as if it were the best thing in the world. Terrance scanned his eyes through the crowd and noticed her walking to the front door, her hair standing out like a beacon in the pandemonium.

He pushed his way toward her, feeling as if something

important were slipping through his fingers as the distance between them widened. He swallowed and called out her name, though she didn't turn around. He wasn't sure if she had recognized his voice and decided to run faster or if she could not hear him over the clamor of the ballroom.

He gave one more shove to the people in front of him and burst toward her. He ran and caught up with Janelle just as she reached the marble staircase.

Not taking a chance this time, he did not call out her name. He grabbed her arm and twisted her around as she tried her best to yank her arm away.

"Terrence," she yelled. "Damnit, what part of 'leave me alone' did you not understand? Tell me so I won't confuse you again this time!"

He kept an iron grip on her arm while he dug in his pocket. He pulled out the gold box and shoved it at Janelle.

"You wanted to know if I was casual about this . . . about you? Open it!"

Janelle turned to a couple walking past them down the staircase.

"Excuse me, could you notify security that a deranged man is harassing me? Tell them to bring handcuffs and clubs."

The couple laughed and continued down the stairs.

"Janelle, please open it," he muttered. "At least see what's inside."

"You open it! If it's for me, I don't want it!"

"Fine," he murmured.

He showed the ring to her and she stopped her tussling. Her mouth dropped open slightly before clamping shut.

"Is this supposed to be a joke?" she asked softly.

He smiled. "Does it look like one?"

"Don't do this, Terrence," she said through gritted teeth. "If you do this to me again I swear . . ."

Terrence dropped to one knee, ignoring the people who

stared at them and the dust that collected on his one thousand dollar suit.

"Will you marry me, Janelle Howard?"

She bit down on her lip and gazed at him blankly.

Epilogue

Terrence woke up alone in his bed to the ringing of a phone and with the window blinds firmly closed. He leaned over and felt around in the darkness for the receiver. He finally found it, brought it to his ear, and yawned.

"Still asleep are you?" his grandmother asked over the crackling line. "Sleeping the day away."

"Good morning," Terrence murmured while scratching his stomach.

"Good afternoon is more like it," she declared indignantly.

Terrence glanced at the clock on the night table. It read 10:15 A.M. But she was his grandmother and that naturally made her infallible, so he did not dare correct her.

"How are the casinos in Delaware, Mother?" he asked.

"Oh, fine. Fine enough. I like the food more, but Annie's partial to the slot machines. She sits there all day clinkity-clinking away."

Terrence smiled.

"By the way, we were going to one of the restaurants, and Annie and I saw one of the nicest gentlemen at a far-off table. He was handsome, looked around thirty years old. We of course decided to keep him company and got to talkin'. He's single, employed, and absolutely perfect for your sister, Olivia."

"Mother—" he began in a warning voice.

"Really, Terrence. He's a nice man and I'm sure we'd do it better with Olivia than we did with you and Janey. It's just that you two were so ornery. Her grandmother and I tried our best but you two just—"

"Mother, let's not talk about that now, okay?"

His grandmother grew quiet and Terrence rolled his eyes.

"I didn't mean to upset you, Terrence."

"You didn't upset me, Mother."

"I love you, baby."

"I love you, too."

The older woman hung up the phone and Terrence slowly did the same. He climbed out of the bed into the coldness of the room and stretched. He headed into the hallway and walked to the end of the corridor and swung open a door. The bright light from the window momentarily blinded him.

"Look, your daddy's just in time, sweety," Janelle cooed with a smile. "He can give mommy a break and burp you."

Terrence gazed down at their infant son and grinned. Damon, their son, was the only other male Terrence would willingly share his wife's attention with.

Terrence watched Janelle gently pull her breast from their son's mouth while he threw a baby towel over his muscled shoulder.

"Did he wake up early again?" he asked as she handed the bundle, with the same springy curls as his mother, to Terrence.

"Yes, he did and when I heard the phone ring I was about to jump out of a window. There's no way I can nurse and talk on the phone at the same time. I decided that if you didn't wake up soon, I would smother you in your sleep," she joked as she kissed him on the cheek, buttoning her nightshirt back up.

"Did you hear that, Damon? Your mommy said she was going to smother me?"

"I sure did," Janelle grinned. "Who called?"

"My grandmother."

"Oh? Is she winning big in Delaware?"

Terrence raised an eyebrow. "It depends on what you would call 'winning big.' As far as she's concerned she's won the lottery. She's found a husband for Olivia."

Janelle laughed and shook her head, watching as Terrence gently patted the infant's back.

"You'd think they'd learn their lesson about meddling, wouldn't they?"

Terrence gazed around at the warm glow of the pale blue nursery, glanced at the baby who huddled against his shoulder and smiled down at his wife.

"Yeah," he muttered, "all they do is cause trouble."

He leaned his head down and planted a tender kiss on Janelle's lips.

The Perfect Story

Kendy Ward

This story is dedicated to my parents, Kenneth and Trudy, for their love, support, and financing! Without you, college would have been the impossible dream. I also dedicate this to the Class of 2001.

Prologue

After four years of grueling courses, hostile professors, asinine roommates, and a lot of growing up I, Sierra Simone Allen, have finally arrived. I guess some folks, namely grown folks, would call me naïve for thinking that at twenty-two years old I have "arrived," but I beg to differ. I have been in school most of my life. My parents enrolled me in kindergarten at age two. Just think, I've been in an educational institution since I was two years old. I have spent twenty years of my life in school. Isn't that a scary thought? What were my parents thinking? You know, that's why I am the way I am. I strongly oppose the confines, rules, and regulations of formal education. I believe that knowledge is not only attainable through schooling, but through everyday living. A Ph.D. doesn't make you smart. That piece of paper doesn't mean shit if you can't apply it to real life. I've seen people I graduated from high school with who were super smart, now sitting at home with no job, getting fat, eating up their parents' food. Then there are others who have never set foot on a college campus and have some of the most brilliant minds I have ever seen. Just goes to show that it's what you do with what you have that counts.

But, anyway, now finally I'm done. That has to mean something. Don't tell me I went to school all these years and it doesn't mean anything. Please don't tell me that I'm going to have to pay my dues. Twenty years in school, that's enough dues already. Thank you very much. Please don't tell me that it's true. That I'm going to have to go back to school to get a master's degree before I can even think about arriving. I wouldn't be able to take that. Even though I know that "they" are probably right. A master's would be an added plus—for other people, but not for me. You see I've been blessed with this characteristic that helps me to succeed regardless of popular opinion. Well, I don't know if it's really a blessing. Sometimes I think that it's a curse. Some people may call it cockiness, others may say I'm arrogant, or conceited, or, worse yet, a bitch, but I'm not. Really I am not any of those things. What I am is confident. With that I don't need a master's degree in banking and finance, because I have a dream to succeed by any means necessary. End of discussion.

Despite all my talk I am a bit apprehensive about this whole independence thing. I mean, all my life I've depended on my mother and father, and now all of that is supposed to stop. That's going to take some getting used to. When I need a couple Blue Marlins (equivalent to Benjamins), I'm not going to be able to say, "Daddy, I need." Scary isn't it? It really is a different world out there. Outside the cocoon of my parents' home it's a dog-eat-dog world. Nobody's going to care who the hell I am. To them I am the competition, and all is fair in love and war. Another thing is that I've never not been in school. You know, my life has revolved around a classroom schedule for the past twenty years. A nine-to-five is something foreign to me. I won't be able to have summer vacations any more. Being grown up is not all it's cracked up to be. When I was younger I couldn't wait to be right where I am right now. Now that I'm here, I'm holding on to my mama's apron strings as tightly as I can.

It's scary. I'm not even going to front and try to convince myself that I'm not scared. Today is the beginning of the rest of my life. Only I can determine my destiny. When I walk across that stage and shake the dean's hand there will be no turning back. The funny thing is, even though I'm scared and I don't know where life is going to lead me, I wouldn't turn back for all the money in the world. Finally, it is time to prove myself. It's time to let my star shine.

I sat in the pew at Bahamas Fellowship Church as low as I could without making it obvious that I was trying desperately not to be seen. In case I didn't mention it before, I am the notorious preacher's kid. I know that you've heard about us before. Our reputations precede us, and, sad to say, it is not a good reputation, either. I never did fit the stereotype. I was always a little angel. In elementary school I never got into any trouble. Not even for talking in class and I love to talk. It was easy to be good because being bad wasn't worth the energy, and I really was afraid of my father having to beat me.

All my angel-like qualities disappeared the day I met Chicago Johnson. It was the first day of junior high school, and I was not in the best of moods because my uniform skirt was a tad bit too long for my liking. I knew that I was going to get teased for wearing a skirt that was so long it looked like it was made for someone else. My brother, Savaughn, didn't make matters any better. He asked me where I was going in my nun getup, and teased me all the way to school. Needless to say, I didn't want to go to school in the skirt, but my mother insisted. She said that I was the preacher's daughter and shouldn't be wearing minis. I didn't want a mini. I just didn't want to wear something that looked like a wedding gown. I got to school and, sure enough, I got teased. I'd never been teased before. I didn't know what to do. I'd always kept to myself. Nobody ever bothered me. I was at a new school, though. I guess the rules had changed. I hadn't done anything to these kids, but there they were calling me names. I was hurt. I wanted to cry, but I would be damned if I cried in front of them. The only other thing left to do was to fight back, but I didn't know how to do that. So I took a script straight out of the Bible and turned the other cheek. I walked away. I didn't feel any better. In fact, I felt worse. I felt like such a coward. Now I was going to be the girl that the kids knew they could pick on. I sat alone under a tree at lunchtime, hoping that my brother would see me, and have pity on me and invite me to eat with his friends. I had no such luck. My brother was nowhere to be found. Enter Chicago.

"Hey," he said as he took a seat. He didn't even ask if I minded.

"Hey," I said back. I looked at him questioningly. He just stared back at me with his huge brown eyes. He was a cutie, I concluded. What I couldn't figure out was why he was sitting beside me.

"I don't think you handled yourself right today," he said, taking a bite out of his sandwich. I looked at him blankly.

"Excuse me?" I said.

"You let those assholes make fun of you, and you fucking walked away. What the hell was that all about?" I couldn't believe my ears. My eyes bugged way out of my head. He had cursed. I had never heard anyone my age curse before.

"You said a bad word," I whispered to him.

"You call *those* bad words? I could've said a lot worse. Trust me. Seriously, though, I don't like them teasing you. Tomorrow you ga hafta say somet'ing to them."

"Something like what?" I asked curiously.

"Tell them their mama's so dumb she thought a quarterback was a refund." It was funny. It was quick. It would definitely embarrass.

"That could work," I said.

"Of course, it'll work. I'm no amateur. Stick with Chicago and you'll make it outta here just alright," he said as he stood.

"Chicago?" I questioned. What kind of name was Chicago? It was a city, not somebody's name. "I know your mother didn't name you Chicago." I laughed.

"Hey, it ain' even no joke so don't be laughing. It's a long story that I'm tired of telling. What's your name?"

"Sierra."

"See ya tomorrow, Sierra," Chicago said and left. The following day I did exactly what Chicago told me to do. I told one of the girls something about her mama, and she punched me in the mouth. I was tired of turning my cheek so I decked her back. That was the first time I ever got suspended from anything.

That's how I met Chi, and I haven't been the same since. In fact, Chi is the reason I'm ducking down in church right now. I know that without a doubt I'm going to be called on to partake in the service in some form or fashion, and I really don't want to. Last night Chicago told me that we were going out to celebrate my graduation, and told me to meet him at the Zoo. Chi never asks anything. Being the only child he is accustomed to getting his own way all the time. I conceded because after twenty years I felt that I had the right to celebrate all I wanted. It didn't matter that I went out every night that week. It didn't matter that I maxed out my father's credit cards on new outfits for all the parties I had to attend. It didn't even matter that I had to be in church bright and early the next morning. So we went. We never got home until five in the morning because Chi got into a fight with one of his ex-girlfriends' new boyfriends. The police came and Chi was taken down to the station. Then he started a fight with one of the arresting officers. Chi's behavior was due to the fact that he drank a bottle of Moët and half a bottle of Alizé. I was no better. I drank a half a bottle of Moët myself and almost left with some strange man. I promised myself that I would never ever ever go out with Chicago again. Of course, that was a vain threat. Next weekend we would be at it again. But because of Chi I had a hangover. If he hadn't have called me, I would have been at home in my bed with a good book. Right then the last thing I felt like doing was reading the scripture lesson, but, of course, the Lord works in mysterious ways. So my father, the Rev. Dr. Barry Allen, just had to call on me to read the scripture lesson. Of course, the scripture had to be the one about your body being the temple of the Lord and you aren't supposed to defile His temple by putting stuff in it that doesn't belong there. That would include alcohol and I was feeling really guilty. I looked over at Chi who was sitting beside my brother. They weren't even listening. Savaughn was writing something on the weekly bulletin. Probably his name because the only person he thinks about is himself. As for Chi, the boy was asleep and the service wasn't halfway over yet. My father is extremely long-winded. Most likely we would be in there for at least another hour and a half, and it was 12:15 already.

Chi and I are opposites in every sense of the word. He's athletically inclined. I'm academically inclined. He's lackadaisical. I take everything seriously. He's careless. I'm responsible. Chicago is wild. I am calm. You get the picture. Regardless of our differences, or maybe because of our differences, we've been able to sustain a friendship for so long. Through it all, we've been there for each other, and no matter what happens, we'll continue to be down for each other. He's my best friend, and a lot of people can't understand that. They always assume that we are a couple. When we tell them that we're friends, they um-hmm and say that they know what kind of friends we're talking about. Men and women can be friends. It's when you throw in love, sometimes sex, into the equation that things get difficult. With most men and women they set out with the intent and purpose to get with that person. They aren't looking for a friend.

Maybe if we would all slow down a bit and get to know one another before the baby is born, we wouldn't be just finding out that the baby's daddy is no good. You would've known that from jump and he wouldn't have been the baby's father. Point taken?

The thing that has our friendship cemented is the fact that Chi accepted me for who I was. He never has tried to change me. My parents want me to be a carbon copy of them. My brother thinks that I should be a little more submissive. He says that I have too much to say. Society wants me to maintain my place as woman, which means to sit down and shut up. Chi said to me, "We aren't anything alike, but I like you. We can learn from each other." And that's exactly what we've been doing since the first day of junior high school. The funny thing is that I have changed. Chi has been a major influence in my life. When we first met I was this shy, quiet, goody-two-shoes daddy's girl. Now I am as far from that description as possible. Some of him rubbed off on me and some of me rubbed off on him. Sure I changed, but that wasn't his objective. He has made me a better, stronger, more confident person. I recognize that, and I thank him every chance I get for being my friend. So what, he's a man. Everyone has their faults, but we are friends. That's proof that this is not some unattainable thing. It is possible for a man and woman to be friends. Besides, whether he is male or female, it is Chi the person, that's got my back, and not his sex.

Chicago and I walked into Renaissance Café on Sunday night knowing that it would be a while before we could again party like we did the week before. You couldn't be staying out all hours of the morning when you had a nine-to-five. We both walked over to the bar in a melancholy mood. It was indeed a depressing thought. My life would soon start to revolve around my job. Then, before I knew it, I would have no life. I would be like all those people who I had often pitied because they had to stay home on Thursday, Friday, or

Saturday nights. The bartender offered us drinks, and I had to decline.

"So this is what it's like," Chi said as he took a sip of his gin and coconut water.

"What?" I asked, sipping water.

"Being all grown up. I remember you couldn't wait to have 'the job.' Well, you got the job, kid. What you gonna do now?"

"Get up tomorrow morning and go to work," I said. Chicago laughed.

"Scared?"

"Naw," I said it like it was impossible for me to be afraid of anything. Chi knew me better than that. He chuckled. "Maybe a little," I confessed.

"You've got nothing to be afraid of. You're going to go in there and be the best employee that Bahamas First National Bank has ever had. 'Sides, they know what you're capable of. You've only been working there since the summer after we graduated from high school. They know that you can get the job done. If they didn't believe that they wouldn't have hired you."

"Well, you know that it was my cousin who initially got me the hookup at National. It wasn't because of my brains."

"Regardless of how you got put on with National, they kept you. They didn't have to ask you to come back the next summer, and the next, and the next. You're going to be alright."

"If you say so." I shrugged.

"You know I'm right. I'm always right. Now let's go show these fools how to wind down," Chicago said, pulling me onto the dance floor.

Sometimes my brother knows how to get on my last damn nerve. I think that he thinks that because he's older that gives him the right to tell me what to do. Besides he's only two years my senior. What more could he have possibly learned during the two years he was here prior to my arrival? How to go to the bathroom? How to talk? Who gives him the authority to dictate to me how to live my life? The boy is so presumptuous.

"All I'm saying is that I'd think about moving out if I were you," Savaughn said in that tone of voice that comes out as, "I'm older than you, so you better listen to me".

"Savaughn, I hear you, but I can't stay here. Come on, for four years I've been on my own. I came and went as I pleased. My belongings weren't confined to a twelve-foot by fourteen-foot room. I had my own apartment. They want me to come back here and they expect me to abide by the same rules I did when I was eighteen. I'm a twenty-two-year-old woman now. I don't think I should have to have a curfew," I said. Savaughn ran his hand over his face. He knew that he wasn't getting anywhere with me. When I made up my mind about something, that was it. There was no changing my mind. And I had decided a long time before I told my parents that I was not, under any circumstances, moving back home. I wanted to be independent in every sense of the word. I wanted to prove, not only to them, but also to myself, that I could make it on my own.

"Sierra," Savaughn said obviously frustrated. "You're not going to have daddy to go running to when you can't pay your phone bill or electricity bill or cable bill."

"I've no intentions of calling daddy for anything," I said defensively.

"Come off it, Sierra. You can't live by yourself."

"I did it for four years."

"Please, girl, you lived on campus. You didn't have bills to pay."

"Whatever, Savaughn," I snapped.

"Whatever, ey? You know that I'm right. You're not responsible enough."

"I'm not responsible? You're telling me that I'm irresponsible?" Nobody had ever called me irresponsible. Savaughn might as well have cursed me out. Irresponsible was a very bad word to me.

"I didn't say that. I said that you weren't responsible enough."

"Same difference, Savaughn. I don't believe you. You know what it is? Mr. Big Time Accountant is still a mama's boy. Just because you wanted to be here doesn't mean that I should want to be here, too."

"You are way off, Sierra. Sierra, just last week you and your boy, Chicago, were at the police station."

"What does that have to do with anything?" I asked.

"That has everything to do with everything. You two prance around town, spending money like it's water. You go to every party that's thrown. The bouncers at all the clubs on the island know you by name. You can't even cook, Sierra."

"I'll learn. Look, Savaughn, thank you for your concern, but you can tell mummy and daddy that my mind is made up. Come tomorrow I'm moving out," I said as I turned to leave. Savaughn just sucked his teeth, exhaled and said more to himself than to me,

"You have a lot of growing up to do, Sierra."

Chapter One

"Sierra, are you coming to church on Sunday?" my mother asked.

"No, I won't be able to make it. I've . . ." Before I could finish my sentence she began with her sermon.

"Sierra, I don't believe you are going to miss church again. You've only been once this month. You need to come to church more often. How does it look to your father's congregation if he can't even get his own daughter to come to church? The Bible says that we should not forget the assembling together of ourselves."

"Yes, I know," I managed to get in.

"By the way when are you moving from Nassau East? I don't like that area at all. There have been a lot of robberies reported in that area, and a few rapes, too. It's not safe out there. Why don't you move back in with us?"

"I like it where I live. Mummy, I'm not moving."

"Sierra, you really should reconsider."

"I'm not going to reconsider," I said firmly.

"Oh, Sierra, Sierra, why can't you be more like your brother?" The wrong set of words left my mother's mouth. One thing I hated was being compared to my brother, or anyone for that matter.

"I can't be like my brother because I am not my brother," I said, trying to maintain my temper. "I am an original, one of a kind. What you see is what you get, and if you don't like that that's your problem not mine."

"Sierra, there's no need to get upset."

"I have to get upset. You're always comparing me to someone else. I can only be me. You're asking me for perfection, and I'm not perfect. None of us are perfect. If you stopped trying to make me someone I'm not, you'd be able to see that I'm just all right the way I am."

Perfection. My dictionary defines this noun as faultlessness, flawlessness. For the majority of my life this word has haunted me. I thought that once I got my BA it would go away, but it didn't. Then I figured that once I was making $70,000 it would go away, but it didn't. So then I said to myself maybe when I started driving an expensive car it would go away, but it didn't. I have everything that a person could need or want, yet that word still haunts me.

I've always been what everyone has expected me to be. I was a model child. I made perfect grades. I didn't curse or drink or have sex or smoke. Still something was wrong with me. I wore the right clothes, spoke the right words, but perfection still eluded me. My parents expected so much of me. They didn't want me to make A's. They wanted me to make A+'s. I couldn't come in second place in a race. It had to be first. Second best was never good enough. I always had to be the best at whatever I did, and I *was* the best. Anything that I tried I excelled in. I didn't even have to put any effort into it. I was just smart or fast or strong or whatever it was that I had to be. I have more trophies and awards than I can count. The country has recognized me more times than I can remember. In five years I've excelled to a Senior Offshore Banker. I make a whole bunch of money, more than I can spend. I live in a nice house in one of the nicer parts of the island. I drive an SUV. I have dinner with lawyers, doctors, and politicians. I am the best of the best, but still I haven't quite reached that plateau, at least not in my parents' eyes.

To them I'll never be smart enough or fast enough or successful enough. There will always be someone that they can compare me to. Someone who makes more money than I do. Someone that has more connections. Someone that's married. Some folks have kids that are crackheads. Others have children that are alcoholics, murderers, or rapists. My parents have been blessed with a child that is an overachiever, but all they can do is complain. Nothing I've ever done has pleased them. When I decided to go to business school, they wanted me to go to law school, to find a husband. I would never please them, so I stopped trying. That doesn't mean that I don't want to, though. I would have given anything to hear my parents say that they were proud of me, but I don't think that day will ever come.

I was sitting at my desk, trying to figure out exactly how I was going to convince the Chief Executive Officer of Renaissance Holdings that she should do business with National. I had to convince them that they should really invest some of their dollars. True, they had called us, but then they got cold feet. Stopped calling. Stopped talking. We needed Renaissance. Renaissance was a multimillion-dollar company that is Bahamian owned. If we got Renaissance to bank with National that would be such a boast for us. National is the only Bahamian-owned and -operated bank in the Bahamas. We've managed to compete with the bigwigs over the years, but we needed a client like Renaissance to take us over the top, give us some sustaining power. How was I going to get an appointment with the CEO, Laken Knight?

"Sierra?" Billy Rolle said, interrupting my plans to steal Renaissance from Royal. Billy was one of the first people I met when I started on with National. He was a business banker. I was, too, back in the day. He kind of took me under his wing, and showed me the ropes.

"Yeah, Billy," I said, giving him my full attention.

"You heard? Your boss, Mr. Vaughn, called a meeting for four o'clock."

"What!" I exclaimed. "He can't do that. He's never had

an hour meeting before. It'll be at least six o'clock before we get out of here, and I've got a flight to catch." I wanted to throw something. Mr. Vaughn was the Director of Offshore Banking for National. We were responsible for luring in million-dollar accounts. You had to have a minimum of one million to open an offshore account with National. Vaughn had a very bad habit of calling meetings without any notice. I didn't like him very much. I don't want to say "hate" because it's such a strong word, but my feelings for him ran pretty closely along those lines.

"I know exactly what you're saying, Sierra. Roberts is the same way. I have to pick up my kids from my mother's house. He never considers what an inconvenience he can put people in. Anyway, I'll see you later."

"Okay."

"Ciao."

If you asked me, I wouldn't be able to tell you one word Mr. Vaughn was saying. For the life of me, I couldn't understand the man. A meeting on a Friday at four o'clock, one hour before it was time to go home! My mind had been in Freeport since lunchtime. It was just waiting for my body to join it, and this man was delaying that event. I had a plane to catch in two hours. I knew that I was cutting it pretty close when I booked the flight, but it wasn't impossible. Now Mr. Man here wants to go on and on forever about God only knows what.

I hadn't been to Freeport in ages. It's our country's second city, but it pales in comparison to Nassau. Nassau has all the hustle and bustle, excitement, and pace of a city, while somehow managing to maintain the tranquility and serenity of an island. Driving down Bay Street in downtown Nassau is like walking down any street in Manhattan. When I want to get away I don't have to hop on a plane. All I have to do is walk across the street from my house and there's a beach.

Freeport is boring. There is nothing to do and nowhere to

go. I've been there enough times to draw that conclusion. You have to drive forever just to get to the beach. I'm not knocking Freeport. It's all right if you like that deserted atmosphere.

So why am I going to Freeport if I detest it so much? Well, my friend Krystal is tying the knot. She asked me to toast her at the wedding. There was no way I was going to say no. We go back to kindergarten. So I'll have to endure the city for a weekend. Maybe it'll be exciting. Who knows? We may have some of "The Best Man" action going on. But if old boy didn't hurry up I wouldn't be going anywhere.

"Sierra," I heard Mr. Vaughn saying. I wanted to yell "What?!" at him, but all I said was, "Yes, Mr. Vaughn."

"How's it going?" I was clueless. What in the world was this man talking about. I looked over at my home girl, Jessica, who was sitting next to me. She quickly scribbled INK on her notepad. *What about Ink?* I thought. I decided to tell him everything that was going on with Ink Corp., which actually was a publishing company. They published newspapers and magazines. Local ones, of course. I tried to focus on my work and away from the wedding and my flight.

"Well," I began. This man knew that he made me nervous. It was just the way he looked at me with those dark, beady eyes. He looked kind of like the Penguin in *Batman*. He was not a beautiful man, and I didn't trust him one bit. "On Wednesday I went down there and spoke with Keith Knowles. Unfortunately, they weren't interested in investing. Mr. Knowles was hinting that they might need another loan. They're considering expanding to the Family Islands. That's not confirmed, though."

"Damnit!" Mr. Vaughn said, slamming the desk with his open palm. Money was always first and foremost in his mind. I knew we worked at a bank, but come on.

"Well, get on the ball with Renaissance. Have you got an appointment with Knight yet?" Mr. Vaughn asked.

"Not yet." I said, wanting to roll my eyes.

"Keep on it." He barked before moving on to someone else. He then proceeded to ask all nine of my colleagues what was going on with their most profitable accounts. That took another half hour. Then finally it was time to leave. I looked at my watch as I stood up to leave. My flight left at seven. I could make it, I told myself.

Of course when you're in a rush there's always something or someone to hold you back. Just as I was about to walk out of the door of the conference room, Mr. Vaughn called my name. I let out a frustrated sigh and turned to face him.

"Yes, sir. What can I do for you, Mr. Vaughn?" I asked with a fake look of interest.

"You look especially lovely this afternoon," he said, walking around the table toward me. I took a few steps back. Mr. Vaughn was known for his womanizing ways, and he had made it crystal clear from my first day at National that he was interested in me. I don't know about other folks, but old and wrinkled is not attractive to me. Short and old is not attractive to me. Old and old is not attractive to me.

"Have you reconsidered my proposition?" he asked. I looked at the fool like he was mad. In the five years that I'd been working for National my answer to his proposition had always been the same: *No!* Which of those two letters didn't he understand? If he was anybody else besides my boss I would have told him exactly what he could do with his proposition, but he was my boss, so I had to be nice.

"Well, Mr. Vaughn, as I explained to you before I don't mix my personal life with my professional life. I like to keep my personal and professional lives very separate," I lied.

"That's understandable, but I think you're only using that as an excuse, Sierra." Damn right I was using it as an excuse. I couldn't very well tell him that he's an old fart and there was no way on God's green earth that I would ever go out with his old ass. He continued, "You'll see things my way someday." He then walked past me and out the door.

I relaxed as I cruised down Eastwest Highway and put in my *Destiny's Child* CD. It had been a while since I partied. A long while. Sometimes it was hard to believe that, once upon a time, my weekends were filled with parties and clubbing. From Thursday to Sunday there were events to be attended. Now my weekends consisted of overtime and housework. Sure 'nough I had become what I had dreaded the most—a homebody. I guess this was all in the process of maturing. Partying didn't mean as much to me now. Other things held precedence in my life. First and foremost was my job. I wanted to climb the corporate ladder as quickly as possible. Some folks would say that I could climb it a whole lot faster if I got with Mr. Vaughn, but I'm sorry. I'd never go that route.

I'd moved past that partying stage in my life. It was really taking a toll on me. Night after night, dancing and dancing. That was more of a workout than any of those Tae-Bo tapes. Besides, my partying partner had traded in his dancing shoes for a wedding band. Yup, that's right. The president of the Playa's Club turned in his membership card. Chicago has three years of marriage under his belt. He has been a really busy man.

I've been fortunate enough to witness Chi's evolution. I must say love is indeed a beautiful thing. The very first time they laid eyes on each other I knew that it was something special. Chi agrees with me, too. He says that the first time he met Ashley he knew that his days as a single man were numbered. I had never been one of the supporters of that love at first sight bit, but Chi and Ashley made me a believer.

Chicago was always a ladies' man, and I thought that he would always be a ladies' man. He was the brother whose little black book had about five hundred telephone numbers in it. We couldn't go anyplace without him seeing some sister he had dated. One time we walked into the dentist's office, and he'd dated every patient in the waiting room—young, old, or indifferent. So I, at first, thought that this was a fluke, but then I noticed that sparkle in his eyes whenever he talked about Ashley. I noticed the way he didn't make a move without telling her where he was going. There was a definite change. He started talking about the future. The future had been a foreign land to us before. When we said the future we may have been talking about a year down the road. All of a sudden that started to mean ten years down the road. He was talking about owning a house with a white picket fence and a dog. He tried desperately to get hired by the best law firm on the island. He was making sure that he had something to offer Ashley when he asked her to leave her parents.

I have to commend that. I know that some may say that a new husband and wife are supposed to build together, but I don't know if I totally agree with that. When a man asks a woman to marry him, what he is saying is I want to be your protector, I want to be your provider, and I am going to give you everything your parents gave you and more. I'm not supposed to be leaving a house where I have to one where I don't have. Of course, I believe that part in the wedding vows about for better or worse, but I don't think that means that I should step into worse. Chi was making sure that he could tell Ashley's parents that he had job, a house, a car, and, most importantly, stability. That's what any parent would like to hear. Not we're living in a one-bedroom efficiency apartment with no electricity or telephone, and we are going to have to catch the bus because we don't have a car. Oh yeah, and I forgot I don't have any money in the bank. My credit is bad, and I am a bum. Sounds like fiction. Believe me it's as real as it gets.

Anyway, Chi is a married man now and married men don't go traipsing about the island club-hopping. Chi doesn't do much of anything now. The brother doesn't even call like he used to. We talk maybe once a month. It's amazing how it's not Chi or Ashley anymore. It's we, them, or they. I am a lonely soul. I don't even have a best friend. Woe is me.

Amazingly, traffic to the airport was not as bad as it usually is on a Friday. I switched from Destiny's Child to my Whitney Houston's *The Greatest Hits* CD and continued on my merry way. The devil must have been busy that day because just as I was rounding the Harold Road roundabout some idiot decided that he was in more of a rush than anybody else and ignored the GIVE WAY sign at the end of the Sir Milo Butler Highway. A black Lexus slammed into the side of my beautiful Ford Explorer. I was mad. I was beyond mad. I was furious. Not only was I going to miss my flight, but my baby got hit, too.

I slowly counted to ten before I got out of my car. This technique usually would calm me down, but right then it failed me miserably. I was ready to draw blood. What kind of idiot was I dealing with here? The driver of the Lexus was still in his vehicle. If he knew what was good for him he'd stay in his car. I gasped as I surveyed the passenger's door on the driver's side. Mashed right up. It looked like an F-450 ran into the side of my car instead of a little itsy, bitsy sports car. I heard the Lexus's car door open. I spun around good and ready for a fight.

"What the hell is your problem? Can't you read? That sign says 'give way' not run into on coming traffic. Asshole."

"Well, if you weren't speeding like a bat out of hell maybe I wouldn't have hit you. One minute you were all the way down there the next you're flying in front of me," he said. More with his hands than with his mouth.

"Well, excuse me. I thought that I had the right of way," I yelled.

"I thought the speed limit was forty-five mph," he yelled. I glared at him. I wanted to throw something at his arrogant ass. I could tell that he was one of *those* brothers. You know the ones. The ones that were so full of themselves they couldn't see pass their own bullshit.

"Well, don't just stand there. Call the police," I snapped. I watched him as he walked over to the car to get his cell. I gave him a quick once over. He had the nerve to be ugly and have an attitude. Mr. Lexus was about six-foot-two. Looked like Gold's Gym saw a lot of him. His jet-black hair was cut nicely, close to the scalp. He sported a goatee. Had eyes and skin the color of caramel. His lips had my imagination running wild. And he had big feet, too. So I lied. Mr. Lexus appeared to be the complete package—what fantasies were made of. But as I listened to him on the phone all pleasant thoughts vanished as a scowl appeared on my face.

"Yeah, I ran into some speeding idiot. Of course, it's a woman." He then had the audacity to start laughing. Chauvinist! "Imma be late aight. Peace."

"I hope that was the police you were talking to," I said. He rolled his eyes at me, and didn't bother to answer me. After a half hour of waiting, the police finally showed up. If it was more serious we would've been dead by then. We went through the procedures, and, finally, I was able to escape that man's annoying presence.

"You'll be hearing from my insurance company"—I looked at the card he'd given me—"Mr. Quant." Finally this incident was all over.

"I'll see you in court," he said.

"Court?!" I asked stunned. "A blind man could see that this was all your fault." I said through gritted teeth. How could one person be so damn aggravating?

"A judge will decide that. I'll see you in court"—he mimicked my actions moments before—"Ms. Allen." I couldn't believe this man. Court? If that's what he wanted, that's what he was going to get. I wondered if Chi would represent me. If I never saw Mr. Adrian Quant again in my life, it would be too soon. "Caught Out There" by Kelis came on the radio. How appropriate.

Now how and when was I going to get to Freeport? I really, really didn't like that man.

Chapter Two

"Hey, Adrian. What's up?"

"Everything cool. What have you been up to, Playa?"

"Just chillin'. You know how it is. We missed you at the gym last weekend."

"I was in Abaco. Business. I hear ya'll let Ken and his boys dog ya'll." Adrian laughed.

"Now who told you that lie? It wasn't even like that. They only beat us by two points off some pray shot from Shortie."

"Ya'll let Shortie hit the winning shot? That boy has never hit a shot in all the years we've been playing against Ken and them. That's bad. I guess our winning streak has come to an end."

"We'll regain our title next week. What you have up for the weekend?"

"Nothing at all, but work."

"Come on, Adrian. You know what they say about all work and no play."

"Korey, you know I have that interview with National tomorrow. I have to be on point, dog."

"That's right. I forgot all about that. Kind of snuck up on me. So you really gonna leave Royal?"

"Don't even go there, man. You know that I want advancement in my career. I can't do that at Royal. The powers that be are too loyal to the old staff. I'd be stuck in the same damn position for years. I've got to move on."

"I'm not like you, Adrian. I'm satisfied with my job, my house, my wife, and my two-point-five kids. I don't need to be the president, drive a Lexus, and have a model on my arm."

"Stop lying, Korey. Didn't Vivian model for a while?" Adrian joked.

"Adrian . . ."

"I'm joking, Korey. I understand where you're coming from. Hopefully, I'll be able to snag this job."

"You know you're gonna get it. You've never failed at anything, ever. So what happened to Vaughn?"

"Nothing. Old man Garret died and Vaughn is getting his position. That leaves Vaughn's position open for me."

"You'll get it. What about that chick that you took to court? Didn't you say that she worked there?"

"What about her?" Adrian asked.

"Come on. You said it, not me. I haven't even seen her. If she looks good, she looks good."

"And?"

"And I know how it goes with you and pretty women."

"It won't even be like that. She has zero tolerance for me. 'Side she's a straight-up bitch. Pretty, but bitchy."

"You admitted it, though. She is beautiful."

"So, I don't have get with every pretty woman I meet."

"This one you will, though. I've got that feeling. I'd put money on it."

"Whatever, Korey."

"Yeah, whatever. So you still ain't going to come with me to the club tonight?"

"Nope."

"Bye, then."

"Peace."

* * *

I really can't explain how I get myself into these situations. So there I was in KFC minding my own damn business when I felt a tap on my shoulder. I turned around to see Mikayla Cunningham. I hadn't seen her since we graduated from high school. I was ecstatic to see her. She was usually a third wheel during Chi's and my adventures. We could tell you some stories. The crazy stuff we did, sometimes I wonder what was going through our heads. Like the time we stole Mikayla's brother's pit bull and held it for ransom. A pit bull? You couldn't get me to go within a hundred feet of one of those animals now.

Mikayla and I started talking like a day hadn't passed since the last time we saw each other. You know how we women do it. We can talk for hours nonstop, and that's exactly what we did. When I got to KFC it was ten minutes after six. I left the place at 8:47. We exchanged numbers. Mikayla gave me a call the next day and invited me to a party her brother was throwing. A party, free food, and drinks. You know me. I said I would be there.

Got to the party. Got out of my car. Got into the house. Started to mingle. Who do I see? Shane Lloyd. What's the big deal? Let me explain something to you about Mr. Shane Lloyd. I met Shane at a basketball game in high school. He was playing for the St. Thomas Blue Waves, our high school's rival. The brother was beautiful. He reminded me of Shemar Moore. I never thought in a million years that he would talk to someone like me. I was still shy and selfconscious. Not what Mr. Popularity would want in a girlfriend. I was more than surprised when Chi called me up that weekend and asked me if it was okay if he gave his boy Shane my number. I almost died. Shane and I went out and I fell in love with him. This was my first real boyfriend. I loved everything about Shane. My world revolved around Shane. Every word that came out of my mouth was Shane. I wanted to have hundreds of Shane Juniors running around the place.

Then our relationship met its demise. I was at home chilling, again minding my own business, when Chi called and asked if I wanted to grab something to eat. I was game. Shane lived two minutes from my house, so Chi suggested that we go and get him. Got to his house and met him laid-up with some ho. I couldn't believe my eyes. He was cheating on me. I got mad. I don't think you understand, I got really, really mad. Let me tell you how mad I got. I kinda, not on purpose or anything, but I kinda went home, got a bat, and broke every window on his brand new Honda Civic. Then I proceeded to smash the hood with a large rock. I flattened the tires, and spray painted the car. That's what I did. No, it didn't get me my man back, but it made me feel a whole lot better about getting played. So, needless to say, I hate Shane Lloyd. Even after ten years I still hated him. Well, "hate" is a strong word. I disliked him a whole lot.

I see Shane and guess who he's with? You know it—Hoisha. Her name is Tanya Lloyd. Yeah, they got hitched. Guess it was a match made in heaven. I couldn't even console myself with the fact that he had let himself go, because he hadn't. He still looked like Shemar, maybe even better. Shane's one-time Afro had been replaced by a close-cut do. His honey-glazed skin was still baby smooth, and I still wanted to stroke its softness. He had eyes like onyx and a personality that was just as hard. Yeah, Shane still had what it took to make me dizzy.

So he walked over to me and had the balls to converse with me. I guess he thought that I was over that whole little incident. I wasn't, though. I invested four years of my life in him, and look at the return I got. He introduced me to his wife, and suggested that we get together some time. What the hell for? So we could reminisce about how much of an asshole he is? I didn't have anything to say to him. Dog!

They were acting like the most disgustingly happy couple I'd ever witnessed. I wanted to throw up. He went on and on about his job. He was some kind of doctor. If I was dying and he was the last doctor on Earth I wouldn't see him. Then he babbled on about their new home in Skyline Estates. Of course, she had to throw that big-ass engagement ring and sparkling, platinum wedding band in my face about a hundred times. I wanted to slap her. I couldn't believe it. I thought that she had to be the luckiest woman on the face of the planet. She had a beautiful, educated, rich, loving black man worshipping the ground she walked on. I was jealous. Why couldn't it have been me? Not necessarily with Shane, but with my Prince Charming. How did she do it? Oh, yeah, by stealing my man. As they say—what goes around comes around, and she got plenty of what came around.

I couldn't take them any more so I excused myself to the bathroom. While I was in the little girl's room I heard a bit of gossip, just a little bit. Mr. Lloyd had a malpractice suit coming up. It looked like he was going to lose. I also heard that, for entertainment purposes only, he beat the crap out of his wife. To top it all off, he seemed to have a problem with monogamy, but I knew that. Boy, was I glad he cheated on me, because if he ever came out of his skin, lost his damn mind, and tried to hit me he would be a dead man. I'm not just saying that either. I would kill him. I wouldn't even think twice about it. I have no tolerance at all for abuse.

So that situation didn't turn out all too bad, but I couldn't find an excuse to decline an offer to dinner from them. So I had dinner with them the next month at their soon-to-be repossessed home. Isn't life a beautiful thing?

Some people might say that I'm nosey, but I'm not. Really, I'm not. Nosiness is not what had me peeking through my office blinds. It was just that the new director of offshore banking was supposed to start soon. They kept everything so hush-hush. I hadn't even known when they held the interviews. They were having a big press conference that afternoon, and then some kind of reception to welcome him or her. They didn't do all of that for me when I started at National. I figured that this guy must really be good. They were pulling out all the stops for him. The CEO himself, who I'd only seen a handful of times since I'd been working at National, was out and about. They probably stole this guy from some other bank. They probably thought he was a whiz kid. He must be like twenty-four, fresh out of college, made a 4.0 GPA, speaks about four or five languages, and has parents with a lot of clout. He must be perfect. He must be Adrian Quant. That couldn't possibly be right. I refused to believe it. If I was not mistaken, I could almost swear that I saw Adrian "The Jerk" Quant walking around being introduced to people by Mr. Larimore, the CEO, and the bank's president, Mr. Graham. That couldn't be right, though. Could it?

They were walking right past my window. I was sure to get a perfect peek at The Jerk look-alike. My eyes were not deceiving me. This had to be some kind of sick, deranged joke, an awful prank. Fate's idea of payback for some wrongdoings of mine. Who in the world would hire this arrogant son of a bitch? But, of course, that would fit right into to everything else. The overachiever who worked so damned hard to get where he wanted to be by stepping on everyone else along the way. I bet you he had some kind of ten-year plan that he just had to complete. He wanted to climb the corporate ladder. Shit, why couldn't he climb it somewhere else?

They stopped directly in front of my door. I prepared myself for their entrance, but when I didn't hear a knock I placed my ear against the door and proceeded to eavesdrop. Not only did he look like the Asshole, he sounded like him too. I thought for a moment, but I knew that no amount of prayer would make Adrian Quant drop off the face of the planet.

Finally, the knock came. I opened the door to a grinning Mr. Graham and a cheesing Mr. Larimore. You could have sworn that they had merged with Barclays or something.

"Good afternoon, Ms. Allen," Mr. Graham said extending his hand. I shook it and returned his pleasantry. I then greeted Mr. Larimore and didn't even bother to look in Adrian's direction. That took a lot of willpower because he did look good in that Armani suit.

"I'd like you to meet our new Director of Offshore Banking, Adrian Quant," Mr. Graham said. "Adrian, this is Sierra Allen. She's a senior offshore banker with us."

"So this is the man I've been hearing so much about," I said sarcastically, knowing good and well that nobody had said anything about anyone. I was being faker than fake, and I hated fake people. "It's a pleasure to finally have this position secured, Mr. Quant." I extended my hand to him.

"It's a pleasure to be here. I feel humbled that Mr. Graham and Mr. Larimore would feel that I'm the right man for the job," he responded smoothly. Lies, all lies. I bet that he knew he had the job from the first question. Confident motherfucker.

"Ms. Allen is currently working on bringing in a major client. I'm sure you've heard of Renaissance Holdings," Mr. Larimore was saying. I was shocked. I didn't know that the Big Willies kept tabs on what we little fish were doing.

"Of course, who hasn't?" Adrian responded, flashing his toothpaste-white smile. I never noticed before but he had a perfect smile and beautiful teeth. I like a man with nice teeth. I stopped my thoughts dead in their tracks. Even though there was no direct connotation between Adrian and myself in that thought. I knew where it was headed, and I wasn't about to take it there. No way. No how. Fine (and this man was beautiful. The things I could do to him.) or not he was *off limits*.

"Is that okay with you?" Mr. Graham asked, interrupting my thoughts.

"I'm sorry, Mr. Graham. Could you repeat that please?" I said. Somehow my thoughts had wandered off somewhere in the direction of Adrian Quant.

"What he was saying," Adrian answered with a smirk, "is that he and Mr. Larimore have a meeting now. We wanted to know if you would mind showing me the rest of National?" They had to be kidding, but the looks on their faces and the smile on Adrian's face told me that they weren't. I couldn't tell the CEO "Hell no." I cut my eyes at Adrian and then turned my one hundred-watt smile on.

"Of course not. It would be my pleasure," I lied. It would be pure torture. While they said their good-byes my phone rang. It was Chicago.

"Allen," I said.

"Hey," He said.

"Hey," I sighed.

"What happened?" he asked. "Adrian Quant is the new director."

"How did you know that?" My eyes almost fell on the floor.

"I've got my sources." He laughed. "So have you seen him yet?"

"Yes."

"Really? Did you behave yourself?"

"I am."

"Oh, so he's nearby?"

"Very." Chi laughed some more. I knew he was getting a kick out of this. "So I'll call you later."

"Sure. I want to hear everything."

"Of course."

I hung up the phone and looked up to see Adrian staring at me. My first impulse was to look away, but I didn't want him to know that he intimidated me to some extent.

"Why are you staring at me?" I asked and of its own accord my voice dropped an octave. You know how we do it. That so-called sexy voice.

"I can't stare?" he asked with a raised eyebrow. He was almost whispering.

"Look, but don't touch," I warned. This was bordering on flirtation. I was walking on dangerous ground. I was supposed to hate him.

"It's like that?" he asked.

"Like that," I confirmed.

"Gotcha. Why don't you show me the rest of this joint?"

"Okay," I said and we left my office.

I wasn't in the house five minutes before the phone started to ring. I knew that it was Chicago. I hadn't called him like I had promised.

"Yes, Chi," I said when I answered the phone.

"You didn't call me back."

'I know. I was busy."

"So spill it."

"Let's talk about you. What's going on in your life, Chicago?"

"Ashley is fine. My job is fine. I'm fine. Let's face it—being married is boring. You have the exciting life."

"Well, I had to give him the rundown of the place. I was forced to spend two hours with the man, not including lunch. He's one of those bougie, stuck-up types. He had the nerve to joke about our court incident."

"You have to admit, Sierra, it was funny. After he heard my presentation of the case he was quick to settle out of court."

"That shit was not funny. First, he hit my Explorer, and

then he took two years to get to court. He missed two dates. After all of that he decided to settle out of court. Fucking Asshole."

"Yeah, whatever. That doesn't have shit to do with your working together."

"It has a lot to do with it. I can't stand his ass and he can't stand mine."

"Really?" Chi asked like he knew something I didn't know.

"Really. I'm too loud, bold, confident, and independent for him. He thinks that a woman has one purpose—to serve a man's needs."

"You don't even know him."

"No, not him, but I do know his type."

"His type, huh?"

"Yes, and his type doesn't like my type."

"You know that's a lie. I saw him looking at you."

"He's intrigued. I'll give you that, but that's about all."

"He wants you." Chi said matter-of-factly. "And you want him, too. That's why you're buggin'. Nobody's ever had this effect on you, and, no matter how hard you try, you can't make those feelings go away. You can't control them, and for a person who's used to always being in control, this is fucking with you. So you're fighting it. But, Sierra, you can't control it."

"What's *it?*" I snapped. "It? Lust? Or do I dare say it? Love?"

"Not love, Sierra, but the possibility of love."

"Fuck you, Chicago," I yelled. He was too close for comfort.

"You'll see, Sierra. Watch and you will see."

I had my candles laid out around my bathtub. The week had been hectic. Adrian Quant had a lot do with that. He'd only been there a week and he was working us hard already. Not that I mind hard work, but just because it was Adrian delegating, I was getting stressed. He was the most aggravating, arrogant person I had ever met. During our "tour" he went on and on about how he had an MBA from Harvard and he worked at the number one bank in the country, about how perfect his life was. He pissed me right off. So what? Everything in his life goes exactly the way he planned it. So friggin' what! I couldn't stand him. He went on and on about his "vision" for National, and in our first staff meeting he had the gumption to criticize my work. I wanted to throw something at him. He really got on my nerves, but I couldn't lie, especially to myself. He was one beautiful man and I was digging him like a grave.

Chapter Three

The clock on the wall facing Adrian said 5:45. Adrian could hardly believe the time. The last time he had looked at the clock it had said 2:29. Almost three hours had elapsed, and he hadn't even noticed. Adrian ran his hand over his head and let out a deep breath. National's Offshore Banking Center had a lot of problems. That was evident from Adrian's first day on the job. Offshore banking was almost nonexistent. There were almost no foreign investments, mainly because of the G7 putting the Bahamas on a money-laundering blacklist. The Offshore Banking Center of National was struggling, to say the least. Adrian was determined to change all of that, though. If that meant working sixty hours a week, then so be it.

Tonight, though, he had to go. He was supposed to meet Toney and Korey for drinks at Club 601 at six. Then he had a date at eight. As he got into his car he shook his head, disgusted with his boys. They were acting like a wife, complaining that they never spent any quality time together. They both knew how he was about his job, especially when things were so unstable. Adrian pulled up at the Club at exactly six. He met Korey waiting inside but Toney was nowhere to be found.

"Watcha sayin' dog. Can't see ya." Korey said as he embraced Adrian in a manly hug. They went way back. As far back as preschool.

"You know how it be," Adrian said, taking a seat. He looked around the Club. The crowd was filled with older folks, twenty-five and over. This was where the grown folks came to party, as they said on 100 Jamz, the number one blazing station in the nation.

"So where's that fool, Toney?"

"You know his ass is always late." Korey laughed. It was true. Toney would be late for his own funeral.

"Well, I'm not waiting on him to get my drink on. 'Sides, I've got a date." Adrian said, trying to get the bartender's attention.

"A date?" Korey questioned, raising his thick eyebrow. Everything on Korey's six-foot-five-inch frame was thick from his lips to his muscles. He was handsome if you liked the Shaquille O'neal type.

"Yup." Adrian said, downing a shot of Hennessey.

"With who?" Korey said, firing another question at Adrian. He had always been the nosy one, interfering in everyone's business, and still managing to take care of his own.

"Someone from my job."

"You don't waste time do you?"

"She's cute, educated, and funny. Wouldn't you have asked her out?"

"Ask who out?" Toney asked as he walked in on the conversation.

"Some chick from his job," Korey supplied.

"Is she fine?" Toney asked Korey as if Adrian wasn't there.

"This is Adrian we're talking about. You know that she looks good."

"Okay can we talk about something else now?" Adrian cut in. Korey and Toney shrugged their shoulders as if to say, "what else is there to talk about?"

"So, Mr. Johnson, how's the job?" Korey asked Toney in his most professional voice. Adrian had to crack up. That's why he loved these guys. They were two comedians.

"Well, Mr. Campbell, we recently acquired two more contracts. One for a shopping mall out west and the other for an office building," Korey said with an English accent. Korey owned a contracting company. A lot of the newer buildings around town were his handiwork. "And you, Mr. Campbell? How is your job?"

"Nothing as big as what you and Mr. Quant have on your plates, but things are fine." Toney was the VP of Marketing for Renaissance Holdings. As Adrian laughed with his boys, he couldn't help but think of his humble beginnings.

Dumping Ground Corner. Bain Town. The ghetto of ghettos. Adrian's father was a coke-sniffing alcoholic who beat his wife for the hell of it. His mother had to support them all, his father, his three sisters, and him on her maid's salary from Crystal Palace. Nine people had to cram into a tiny three-room clapboard house. His sisters, who were teenage mothers, had babies whose fathers were no better off than their own. A lot of folks wouldn't believe that the Lexus-driving, Armani suit–wearing, Queen's English–speaking Adrian Quant could relate to Beenie Seagal and Eve's "Remember Them Days." He knew about running an extension cord from the neighbor's house to get electricity. He was a sugar-water baby. He knew what it was to wear one pair of shoes for an entire year or none at all. Toting water from the community water pump to take a bath. Did that. Mayonnaise sandwiches for lunch. Did that, too.

They were poor, dirt poor, but unlike his sisters, Adrian was determined to rise above the poverty-ridden, crime-infested, violent community he grew up in. He worked three jobs to get through two years at the College of the Bahamas. He graduated valedictorian and managed to get a full scholarship to NYU. He worked his ass off for two years of his undergraduate studies at NYU, and it paid off because Harvard Business School offered him a scholarship. After that it was back to Nassau to give back, and give back he did.

His father died while he was at NYU. One of his sisters moved to Freeport and became a domestic caregiver, aka housewife. Another was married and a teacher. The other, he didn't know where she was. He bought his mother a house, got her a maid, and insisted that she didn't lift a finger. He had accomplished a lot, but Adrian knew that he had still a lot more to accomplish.

"Hello!" Korey yelled in Adrian's face.

"Man, why are you yelling?" Adrian asked.

"I've been trying to get your attention for the last ten minutes." Adrian rolled his eyes at Korey's exaggeration.

"I was thinking."

"I hope it wasn't about work," Toney piped up. "You're a workaholic and the sooner you realize it, the sooner you can get help," Toney said, trying not to laugh.

"Whatever," Adrian said.

"Hey, Adrian, do you know that honey over there?" Korey asked, looking behind Toney at someone. "She's been staring at you for a bit."

"She's fine," Toney said staring at her. "You better introduce me to her." Adrian looked around to see who they were tripping over. A frown creased his lips. Five feet eight inches, cinnamon-toasted legs that went on forever, round hips, flat stomach, just the right size breasts, a neck that yelled to be kissed, shoulder length auburn hair, big brown eyes, and full, kissable lips. Sure, he knew her.

"She works at my job," Adrian said finally. Sierra Allen was a beauty. There was no way around that fact, but she was into playing games. One minute she hated him. The next she was flirting with him. The next she was shooting him down. He didn't have time for bullshit like that. But, damn, staying away from her had to be the most challenging thing on the job.

"That's the chick you're going out with tonight?" Toney asked wide-eyed. Adrian always got the pretty women.

"Naw, that's Sierra Allen."

"The maniac driver?" Korey asked.

"Sure is."

"Dog, you never said that she was that fine," Korey said.

"So she's fine," Adrian said with a shrug like Sierra's beauty didn't leave him in awe the first time he saw her, much like the way it had Korey and Toney then.

"Adrian, we're going over there and you're going to intro-duce me to her," Toney said. Adrian shrugged and they headed toward Sierra.

"Hey, Sierra, I didn't think that I'd see you here. I thought you were more of the Renaissance type."

"Looks can be deceiving, Mr. Quant," Sierra said before taking a sip of her drink. There, she was doing it again, flirt-ing. She had to know how sexy she looked with her eye-lashes downcast like that. They stared at each for a while, but the exchange was interrupted when Korey and Toney began to clear their throats.

"My bad," Adrian said. "Sierra, these are two of my best friends, Korey Campbell and Toney Johnson."

"It's a pleasure to meet you both. Don't you work at Renaissance?" Sierra asked Toney.

"Yes, I'm in their marketing department."

"I thought I saw you there. Hopefully, we'll be doing business with you pretty soon."

"Really?" Toney said.

"Yeah."

"Can I buy you another drink?" Toney asked, going into mack mood.

"Why not? My friend doesn't look like he's . . ." Sierra's words trailed off when Jessica Albury approached them.

"Hi, Jay," Sierra said.

"Sierra, girl what's going on? I saw Chi outside. He's talking as usual."

"What you doing here?"

"I came to meet Adrian," Jessica said wrapping her arms around Adrian.

"Oh," was all Sierra could manage to say. Adrian thought he saw a flicker of jealousy in her eyes but decided to chalk it up to the dim lighting.

"Yeah, we're going to Graycliff for dinner and then to the Poet's Lounge," Adrian put in.

"Okay. I hope you guys have fun," Sierra said.

"I'm sure we will," Adrian said and winked at Sierra before he and Jessica walked off.

I couldn't help it, although, I did try. Frown lines creased my forehead and there was a definite pout on my lips. This was totally unacceptable, and I refused, absolutely refused, to do it. Working one-on-one with Adrian was out of the question.

During his tenure thus far at National he had proved to everyone that he had what it took to propel this division to heights it had never seen. I had to begrudgingly give him his props. He may have been an arrogant, stuck-up asshole, but he got the job done. In four weeks he routed out all the problem areas and established teams to work on correcting each problem and that problem solely. Before, I would have had two and three jobs to do at once. That's why it took so long to get anything done. I liked working for Adrian. Working *with* him was a whole other ball game.

"Come on, Sierra," Adrian said to me as I looked at him skeptically. "It's not that bad. You're acting like I'm a serial killer or something." I just stared at him through squinted eyes. "If I didn't know better, I'd think you were afraid of me." Jackpot! I was afraid of him. I knew it. Knew it the moment I laid eyes on him. He made me vulnerable, susceptible. That scared the hell out of me. I could lose myself in this man if I let myself. So I tried to hate him. Tried with all my might, but I couldn't. How could I when he is everything that I've always wanted? No, I couldn't. This definitely was a bad idea. Working with Adrian alone until all hours of the night. I'd probably rape him, or worse, fall. Oh, no, I couldn't let that happen.

"Adrian, isn't there someone else? I'm pretty swamped right now," I lied, trying to get out of this predicament.

"I want you," Adrian said. Innuendo? My eyes almost fell out of my head. He chuckled. He knew.

"I mean," he corrected, "that you've showed me that you know OBC better than anyone else. I feel that you could offer me the most assistance. It's as simple as that."

"Simple for you," I mumbled. He was right, though. I did know my job. Oh well, my answer still was no.

"What about Jessica?" I asked slyly. Adrian shot me a look and it was my turn to chuckle. I knew that Jay wasn't talking to him because he hit it and then quit it.

"Sierra, will you be reasonable?" he asked, obviously frustrated with me. "Stop beating around the bush and tell me what's really bothering you." I looked at him hard. I didn't care too much for his tone of voice. Should I have just laid all my cards on the table? Whether it was right or wrong that's what I did.

"You know just as I know that us working together is not a good idea," I said, standing and walking around my desk to face him. "You, Mr. Quant, want me, and I'm not giving you an opportunity to add me to your list."

"My list?" Adrian laughed. "What makes you think that I want to put you on my so-called list?" He asked me with a raised eyebrow. "I think you've got that twisted, Ms. Allen." Adrian stood an inch away from me. I refused to let him get to me, but it was too late. My heartbeat had already run away and my knees threatened to give way. "I'll see you in my office tomorrow at nine A.M., bright and early." He turned around and walked off. Fuck. I cursed myself. He had kept his cool and I was the one left hot and bothered. Fuck! Fuck! Fuck!

"Pulling rank now?" I yelled at his back.

"Yup." I heard him laugh. "And I don't have a list."

I don't understand men. I don't pretend to, either. I've known Chicago since I was fourteen years old. That's over ten years and I still can't figure him out. My brother I've known all my life. Understanding him seems to be a lost cause. This particular man, though, takes the cake. He's like a jigsaw puzzle, and I can't get the pieces to fit.

I looked up at Adrian's clock. It was 6:24. After going through dormant offshore accounts all week and still having a long way to go, I wanted nothing more than to go home so my weekend could begin. But it looked like Adrian wanted to put in at least another hour.

"Ready to go?" he asked. I hadn't realized that he'd been watching me. He did that a lot—watched me when I wasn't looking.

"Whenever you're ready." I said.

"Liar," he smiled. "How about this? Let me take you out to dinner. Then we can hit up 601. I saw you the other night getting your boogie on," he said, standing to imitate my dancing. I had to laugh. Adrian could be a real clown when he wanted to be. I was hesitant to accept his offer, and he sensed it. He said, "You need to unwind. I know you're just going to go home and get on your computer and do more work because Chicago isn't here this weekend to take your mind off work." I was surprised. I wondered how he knew that Chicago was away, but then I remembered that my best friend has a big mouth so he probably told Adrian.

"Let this be my way of apologizing for working you so hard this week." I really wanted to leave, and having dinner with Adrian wasn't the worst thing I could be doing. I had fun with him. So dinner with him could only be entertaining.

"Let's go," I said, standing.

We pulled up at Café Junkanoo. This was my most favorite restaurant on the island. I was surprised when Adrian said that it was also his favorite. I shouldn't have been, though. Over the weeks I had learned that we had a lot in common. We both had Jagged Edge's "Let's Get Married" the reception remix on repeat in our rides. Eric Jerome Dickey's *Cheaters* was high on our list of favorite books. Fish, any kind, was our favorite dish. And I finally found someone that incorporated "shit" into their vocabulary more than I did. The shocker for me was our birthdays: June twenty-sixth. Exactly two years apart to the minute. Isn't that spooky?

It took us forever to be seated. Not because the place was crowded, but because Adrian seemed to know everyone there. Finally, we took our seats and ordered. After our appetizers and drinks were served I decided to break the silence that suddenly loomed over us. For some reason Adrian seemed a bit apprehensive or maybe a bit gun-shy. It was so unlike his regular personality. It made him a little vulnerable, a little more human, and a little less perfect.

"So, Mr. Quant," I began. "Tell me about yourself. And I don't want to hear about where you've been to school and what companies you've worked for. I want to know about you, the man, not the image."

"What is there to tell?" he asked. His confidence had slipped away, and I got a glimpse of the real man, faults and all. Something had happened to him between leaving the car and being seated. There was a look of pain in his champion-colored eyes. I wanted desperately to reach out and touch him. Sooth his troubled mind.

"What is it?" I asked. "Don't even think of telling me nothing 'cause I can see that something isn't right." He looked at me for a while. It seemed like an eternity that we sat there with our gazes locked on each other. A tug of war went on inside his head while I prayed that he trusted me enough to confide in me. I wanted to help him, if I could. Finally, he sighed and then spoke.

"Do you see that lady over there?" I looked out the window that faced our table, and saw a grimy looking woman with thick, matted hair that reached her waist. The dirt was so caked on her it was impossible to tell her coloring. She was a sorry sight, and I felt sorry for her. She let a drug control her mind and destroy her life.

"Yeah," I said.

"Right. She asked me for some change and I didn't recognize her." Adrian said. I didn't understand what he was talking about.

"Are you supposed to recognize her? Who is she?"

"That's my sister, Sierra. My sister. All my education, all my success, money, everything, and I couldn't help her. Look at her." Adrian was close to tears. I reached across the table and took his hands in mine.

"Adrian, you can't help her if she doesn't want to be helped."

"I didn't try hard enough, Sierra. After a while I started to pretend that she didn't exist, but she does."

"Adrian, this isn't about your sister, is it? This is about a past you want to disappear. You've been running from it for so long. You don't realize that running won't change it." Of course, I knew where Adrian grew up. The island is twenty-one miles by seven miles. I could find out anything about anyone if I wanted to. I had figured out a long time ago that all of the accolades Adrian had acquired were an effort to erase what he came from. His sister reminded him of a chapter in his life that he wished went unread.

"Maybe you should stop running and accept it. Because of it you are the man you are, and you should be proud of that."

"Maybe I should. Maybe I can't." Adrian paused and looked at me. "Have you stopped running, Sierra?"

"No, but I want to."

"I want to, too."

I had been running from my parents' lofty expectations of me for so long I didn't think I could stop. I was running from perfection. That's what they wanted me to be. For them that meant getting a degree in being a lady, marrying rich— preferably a politician—having two-point-five children, and eventually becoming the First Lady. All of which I didn't want. I am nothing my parents wanted me to be. Not because I couldn't be, but because I didn't want to be. Because I didn't want what they wanted for me. I always felt like the black sheep of the family. My brother lived up to everyone's expectations. He graduated from Stanford summa cum laude. He worked for an accountant firm for two years before he became an associate, and after six years he was a partner. He married Ms. Bahamas and they have two handsome sons. Could he be any more perfect? He is my parents' pride and joy. Me? I don't think I've ever made them proud. I keep telling myself that it doesn't matter. If they can't accept me for me then I don't need their acceptance. Running from the truth. The truth is that I want them to be proud of me and my imperfection.

At that moment, as we sat with our hands intertwined, a

bond was created. I felt it right then, and I knew that I was embarking on foreign ground. Despite my initial hesitance I enjoyed dinner with Adrian. I think I enjoyed it too much, because after Adrian was long gone his image still filled my head, his scent lingered in my space, and his touch (yes, that does say touch. It's not a typo.) still assaulted my body. What happened? What didn't happen? It wasn't me. I don't know what happened. One minute I was minding my business. The next I was minding his.

So Adrian drove me back to National where I'd left my car. Then he followed me to my place to make sure I got home safely, or so he claimed. Of course, when we got to my house, he had to walk me to my door, and this is where I started to trip.

"Did you have a good time?" he asked, seeming uncertain of my answer.

"Of course, I did. If I didn't, you would've known. I had fun," I assured him, and I had. I was thinking that we could do this more often.

"It's just that after all that stuff I laid on you at dinner . . ."

"I'm glad that you felt that you could talk to me," I said, taking his hand in mine. First mistake. "Anytime you need an ear you can borrow mine. Okay?" He smiled that smile at me.

"I knew that you'd be someone that I could trust. I don't have many people like that in my life," Adrian said. His eyes slowly caressed my face and I gazed into their depths. Second mistake. He instantly entranced me. His hands followed the trail his eyes had traveled. And my head, of its own accord, turned and my lips kissed his palm. I saw his head descending toward mine. I heard the warning signals that went off, and I ignored them. I let him kiss me and I kissed him back. At first he tested the water. His soft lips gently touched mine. My eyes drifted close. He deepened the kiss, and what happened after that I can't recall.

Adrian left. Drove off into the night. Went home, I suppose. Okay. Okay. I do remember. How could I forget? I am so ashamed. Here's what happened. My fingers loosely stroked his wavy hair as our tongues fought a duel that's as old as time. I wanted him. That was a first for me. I wanted him touching me, kissing me, in me, and I wanted to touch him, kiss him, and whatever else my imagination led me to do. I felt Adrian's rough hands on my blouse, loosening the buttons, one by one. Then his hand was inside my shirt, caressing the sides of my breast. I never let anyone make me feel this good, and I couldn't stop the moan that floated from my lips. I gave as good as I got, and I had Adrian's shirt out of his pants and was running my hands over his chest. When I felt his tensed muscles under my hands I gasped. His body was one that fantasies were made of. From the moment Adrian's lips had first touched mine all my senses had left me. I was operating on pure lust, and that was something that I didn't want to happen. That, I had never let happen before, but for some reason unknown to me, I couldn't stop him. My head wanted me to. My mind was telling me to tell him to stop, but when Adrian's kisses descended my neck and his hand found its way to stroke my inner thigh all reasoning left. I had to have him, and I knew that I probably would have done something that I would have deeply regretted if my nosey-ass neighbor hadn't turned on her porch light. She did, though, and as the lights illuminated the street, the dogs started to bark, and I was brought abruptly back to reality.

"I think you should go now," I said to Adrian as I pushed him away from me. I didn't want him to want me just for sex. I wanted something much deeper from Adrian. The problem was I wasn't sure that he could give me what I wanted.

"Yeah, I guess you're right. Goodnight," he said as he turned to leave without a backwards glance. I knew right then that kissing Adrian (if we can call it just that) was a huge mistake. The second-guessing myself had already begun.

* * *

I spent all weekend trying to figure out how Adrian would act on Monday morning. How would I act when I saw him? Well, Adrian's reaction was not what I expected in my wildest imagination. I came to work on Monday a bit early. I figured that Adrian and I needed to talk about whatever had happened between us, but I discovered that he wasn't talking to me anymore. I went to his office, but he wasn't there. So I waited for an hour, but he never showed. I went back to my office to do what I was being paid to do. When Adrian finally made it in to work he walked straight past me without even looking at me. He just ignored. That hurt. It hurt a lot, and I couldn't understand why it hurt so much, because we had nothing—no strings, no commitment, nothing. We shared one kiss. That's all. So why was he tripping? Okay, maybe it was a little more than one kiss, but he tripped out. His secretary called me and told me that Adrian had some other matters to attend to and we wouldn't be working together anymore. I didn't have the nerve to confront him. I was afraid. What could possibly be worse than him blowing me off? Shit, he'd already done that, but there was something worse, far worse—his telling me that he doesn't feel the same as I do. So I did what we women always do. Something that I had never done before. I cried. I cried over a man. A man that wasn't even my man. I cried like I hadn't cried in years. I cried about what could have been, what should have been, what wouldn't be.

Adrian lay awake in bed, vainly attempting to piece together a puzzle. One that had only two pieces, him and Sierra. Okay, so at first he thought that she was a bitch. Sierra was loud, bold, and aggressive. She didn't give a damn about anyone or anything. Those were definitely bitch ingredients. They were total opposites. He knew that. They came from two different parts of town. Sierra Allen was the daughter of the renowned Rev. Dr. Barry Allen. She went to private schools all her life, and she got that Explorer he crashed into for a graduation gift. He got an address book from his sister as a graduation gift.

It seemed to him as if the past molded them into the exact opposite of what was expected of them. Sierra was a far cry from the doctor's wife she was supposed to be. Sierra Allen was groomed to be somebody's wife, and not the independent, working girl she had become.

Everything Sierra was supposed to be is what he thought he had wanted. So why was it that she captured his heart? He liked her. He genuinely liked her, and that had nothing to do with his attraction to her. Besides Toney and Korey, she had become his most favorite person to be around. Problem was that being around her evoked fantasies of him making her shout his name. Yeah, so what? He wanted her like he had wanted so many other women. So why couldn't he hit it and quit it? That was the million-dollar question. It was a given that if he hadn't have cut Sierra off, she would be lying beside him right then instead of Vanessa.

He and Vanessa had nothing in common besides sex, and that could have been better. Why did he push Sierra away? A myriad of questions clouded Adrian's brain. Why? Because from Friday night to Monday morning he thought of nothing besides her. Nothing, not even his job, had ever monopolized his thoughts like that. Sierra Allen was turning out to be the real deal, the genuine article, his destiny.

But falling in love was not a part of his plans. At least not at that stage in his career. He had too much more to accomplish. He believed that you fell in love and got married. That's where a relationship with Sierra could only lead. He was certain of that. He had already felt himself tripping. A marriage took time, devotion, and sacrifice. None of which he could give then. So he had to do it. He had put the distance between them. He stopped talking to her. He stopped working with her, but he couldn't stop thinking about her.

I lied! Okay. I lied. No matter how hard I tried, I couldn't forget him. I couldn't stop thinking about him. I couldn't stop hoping. Even after he gave me the cold shoulder. One minute we were buddy-buddy. The next he wasn't speaking to me. He wasn't speaking to me! The audacity of that man! Still, I longed to hear his voice. I felt powerless. Just like Chi said I would.

I had just come back from having lunch with Chicago. His fourth wedding aniversary was approaching and he wanted some ideas for a gift for his wife. We talked about everything except gifts. It was just like old times when we used to cut classes and sit at home drinking and talking shit all afternoon. For the first time in a long time I didn't have Adrian on the brain. That is, until I got back to the office.

I was on the elevator, jamming to Janet Jackson's new tune. I had barely noticed someone was in the elevator with me (I was too busy daydreaming about you know who), that is until she spoke.

"Excuse me," she said. Flawless. She looked like she just stepped off the pages of *Ebony*.

"Yes?"

"Can you tell me what floor Adrian Quant is on? I thought it was seven, but now I'm not so sure." Curiosity was killing this cat. Why did she want to see Adrian? I knew that she wasn't a client. I faked cordialness and offered to show her to Adrian's office. It wasn't that difficult to find, seeing that it was the first thing you saw when you got off the elevator on the seventh floor. I just wanted to see what this visit from Tyra Banks was all about. I knocked on Adrian's door, which was ajar. I could see him pacing the floor with his headset on. He was deeply engrossed in a conversation. I walked into his office along with Cindy Crawford. It was like he didn't even notice me. He quickly finished up his conversation and practically ran to Rashumba.

"Hey, babe," he said, and they kissed.

"Hi, Sweetums," she said. Sweetums? What the hell was that? I wanted to slap that stupid smile off his stupid face. I cleared my throat loudly.

"Oh, Adrian, Ms. . . . I didn't catch your name," Rebecca said to me.

"I didn't throw it," I smiled. "It's Allen. Sierra Allen," I supplied.

"Ms. Allen was kind enough to show me to your office."

"Thank you, Ms. Allen," Adrian said. We had long ago ceased addressing each other by our first names.

"No trouble at all, Mr. Quant," I said not even trying to leave.

"Is there something else, Ms. Allen?" He said looking at me sternly. I guess he was trying to intimidate me. It wasn't going to work. I was fed up. I was tired of pretending like shit hadn't happened between us. The fact that he wasn't speaking to me proved that something did happen.

"I would like to speak to you in private whenever you have a moment," I said.

"Okay, when I get back from lunch I'll give you a buzz," he said, picking up his jacket.

"I'll be waiting," I said. "See ya, Tyra," I said. I couldn't help that one.

Adrian took his sweet time getting back from his lunch. When he did finally barge into my office without even knocking I was on a phone call with Chi. He was prepping me for this conversation. Chi believed that he knew everything about everything.

"Yeah," Adrian said after I hung up. "I hope this is about business," he said in an agitated voice. I cleared my throat.

"Actually, it isn't," I said. " You can have a seat."

"I'd prefer to stand."

"Suit yourself," I said and just stared at him for a bit. I wondered, *How did I fall for this stupid, arrogant, beautiful, intelligent man.* I knew that my silence and thoughtful staring was making him nervous.

"What is it, Sierra?" he snapped.

"Oh, so we're back to first names, Mr. Quant?" He sucked his teeth in annoyance.

"Sierra, I don't have time for games."

"Really? You could have fooled me. I thought you loved to play games, Mr. Playa." Adrian sighed loudly and turned to leave. I was acting a bit juvenile so I rescinded, and got to the point.

"I'm sorry, Adrian," I said and he turned back around. "It's just that I . . . you have me confused." He raised his eyebrows at me. "Don't play stupid, Adrian. Friday night you were all over me. Monday morning you were treating me like I have the plague. There was something going on between us."

"Something like what?" Adrian asked, throwing his hands into the air.

"We connected on some other level."

"Don't mistake lust for something more." Okay. That hit me like a ton of bricks. "What do you want me to say, Sierra? I want you? Yes, I want you. I want to fuck your brains out. Is that what you want to hear 'cause that's what I want to do. It was nothing, Sierra, nothing. You look good, I'm attracted to you, and I lost it. Be assured that it will never happen again." I turned away from Adrian so he wouldn't see the unshed tears in my eyes. Crying over the same man twice. I was disgusted with myself, but I couldn't help hoping, believing that he was lying to me. That he felt what I felt, too.

"Adrian, you're not a very good liar," I said with my back to him. I spun around to face him with some renewed strength. I wasn't letting him get away that easily. I came this far. I might as well go all the way. "If what you say is true, what was dinner all about? You told me things I'm sure you've never told anyone. You trusted me, and I know that your trust is not easily earned. As we sat at that table I felt something that I've never felt for anyone before, and I know that you felt it, too, Adrian. You said that you want to stop running, but I think that was a lie, too, 'cause you sure as hell are running from me." A pained expression was on Adrian's face. I knew that many conflicting thoughts scattered his brain.

"Sierra," Adrian said as he walked toward me and I held my breath, hoping that his response would be what I wanted to hear. "It is not that easy," he said as his expression changed, and his eyes held an adoration that no one had ever bestowed on me before. His hand caressed my cheek. "I could fall in love with you, Sierra, and that's not what I want," he said softly. His admission hurt to some extent. Why wasn't I good enough for him to fall in love with? As if reading my thoughts, Adrian continued, "This isn't about you. This has nothing to do with you. This is about my carefully planned life and me. You're not a part of that plan. At least, not yet." I reached up and took Adrian's face in my hands. I looked into his eyes, and tried to make him understand that this could work. I gently kissed his lips and then said, "Sometimes, plans change."

"I think mine just did," he said before kissing me back with all the pent-up passion of the weeks that he had ignored me. When our lips parted I felt light-headed. I knew then that we were about to embark on a fantastic voyage.

Chapter Four

The dark, ominous sky was a reflection of my mood. The wind whistled as the lightning streaked the evening sky. Thunder clashed, and I sank down into my comforter to let its warmth engulf me. I looked out the window as the rain came down in torrents. It had not been a good day. When I woke up that morning I was greeted by a pounding headache. I got to work to find that somehow the system had crashed and all my work that I had spent doing that week had been in vain because it had been lost and I would have to do it again. The icing on this foreboding cake was a call from my mother. I spoke to my mother once every two weeks. What possessed her to call me on a Wednesday is anyone's guess. She, of course, had to ramble on about my marital status and she went on for twenty minutes about redecorating my house. She hadn't liked it the first time she came to visit and she still didn't like it. Then the topic shifted to Adrian.

"So your brother tells me you're dating someone from your job," she said casually.

"Yeah, I want you guys to meet him sometime," I said. I really didn't want my parents to meet Adrian, but Adrian wanted to meet them.

"What your brother says is true?"

"What did he say?"

"He said that you're in love with this Adrian person." I hadn't even dissected my feelings for Adrian. I definitely was not going to discuss them with my mother. In the weeks that Adrian and I had been together I had come to care about him a lot, but that was obvious from the onset of our relationship. I didn't know what it was that we had, but I did know that it was a good thing. Did I love, Adrian? Yeah, I loved him. Was I in love with Adrian? Couldn't really answer myself, but I knew that I was headed there. I had tripped, stumbled, and I was about to fall. If I hadn't already.

"Well, he's entitled to his opinion," I said. I never knew that my brother was the perceptive type.

"Is this the Adrian Quant that ran for Member of Parliament for Fox Hill?" she asked.

"No, that was Michael Quant," I said.

"Adrian's brother?" she queried.

"No relation."

"Oh, Adrian Quant, Adrian Quant," my mother repeated and I knew that she was trying to figure out where he fit in on the who's who of the island ladder.

"Adrian Quant!" she exclaimed. "His father's name is Dylan Quant and he was accused of that stabbing on Arawak Cay about fifteen years ago. Bain Town, that's where they lived. His mother was a maid. One of his sisters is a crack addict, and the others were both teenage mothers.

"Oh god, Sierra, you sure know how to pick them. What does this say to people about your character and judgment? You can't possibly be serious about this Quant boy."

"Why not?" I asked calmly. I surprised myself.

"Because he's nothing. He's a nobody, Sierra. Come on, you don't get involved with his type. Who knows what skeletons he has hiding in his closet."

"What Adrian's father did fifteen years ago has nothing to do with Adrian," I said. My anger was rising like lava from a volcano.

"Don't you dare raise your voice to me, young lady. If you knew what was best for you, you would sever all ties with this man."

"I'm not going to do that. I love Adrian and if you can't accept that, then that's on you. You know what? All my life I've tried to please you and daddy, but it seems like nothing

I do will ever please you. I'm tired of trying. Until you can accept my relationship with Adrian, don't come to my house anymore. Bye."

"I'm sorry you feel this way, Sierra. You're making a big mistake."

"Yeah, well, let me make my mistakes. Bye," I repeated and hung up the phone. I couldn't help the tears that streamed down my face. Nothing I ever did was right. Nothing, not even choosing the right boyfriend. It hurt. It really, really hurt.

I picked up the phone to call Adrian, but then I remembered that he was off the island for the rest of the week. The thought of not having him here to wrap his arms around me made me cry even harder. I sobbed and rolled over.

I woke up and didn't even remember when I fell asleep. It was still raining, my head was still hurting and I was still in an awful mood. The doorbell rang and I really didn't feel like getting up. I had no intentions of getting up, but something in the back of my mind told me to answer the door.

"Sierra!" I heard Adrian's voice yell from the other side of the door. I swung the door open and ran into his arms. I held him so tight. I didn't want to let him go.

"What's the matter, babe?" he asked as he stroked my hair.

"Nothing," I lied. How could I tell him that my mother didn't like him? "I just missed you," I said as I took him by the hand and led him into the house.

"Maybe I should go away more often if I'll get that kind of response."

"Don't you dare," I said. "I wouldn't be able to bear it." I turned around to face him so he could give me the kiss I desperately longed for. The kiss was needy and I knew he sensed that. I didn't want our lips to part and the kiss went on forever.

When I finally let him go he asked me again, "Are you sure everything's alright?"

"Yeah. So how come you're back so early?" I asked, changing the subject.

"Needed to see you," was all that he said.

"So you cut everything short so you could come home to me?" I asked, skeptically.

"No, actually, I sped everything up so I could come home early." He laughed. "I know they hate me now. I had those folks in meetings until all hours of the night. What's for dinner?" Adrian asked, making his way to the kitchen.

"Well, I had steamed grouper, but I didn't expect you, so it's gone." I was teasing Adrian. I knew that steamed grouper was his favorite.

"You're joking right?" Adrian said. "You didn't really eat it all. I can't tell you the last time I had steamed grouper. Sierra, girl, don't play with me," Adrian warned and I laughed.

"Well, maybe I have a little bit left," I said.

"Maybe? You'd better."

After Adrian had eaten and we got caught up on what had transpired in each other's absence we made our way to my bedroom. My bedroom was my favorite room in my house because my bed is the most comfortable bed you'll ever lay on. Adrian also had great affinity for my bedroom. As soon as he got into the room he noticed all the chocolate wrappers, a telltale sign that something was not right with me. Adrian looked at me and I turned away from him. I couldn't tell him.

"Sierra, look at me," he said in his no-nonsense voice.

"Yeah," I said as I started putting the wrappers into the garbage. I then got into the bed. Adrian stood, running his hand over his head.

"I hate when you get like this," he said. "I don't like secrets. I asked you if something was wrong and you said no. I know you and I know you well enough to know that Snickers and Milky Way mean something is wrong. Talk to me," he said as he got in the bed beside me. I really wanted to talk to him. He was a good listener and I didn't like secrets either.

"I talked to my mother today," I said softly. "And nothing's changed. It's the same old same old."

"You mean about her not accepting the decisions you've made in your life?" he asked as he settled me against his muscular body.

"Yeah," I said as I rested my head against his shoulder. "But this time the decision she's ridiculed is you."

"Hmm," Adrian said thoughtfully. "I'm not good enough for the good reverend's daughter."

"Of course, you are," I assured him. "It doesn't matter what she thinks. It's all about what I think."

"But you do want her to be proud of you and accept you, and if that means dumping me, you'd do it."

"Adrian, you should know me better than that. I do have a backbone, you know." I said it angrily, but I couldn't blame him for his insecurity. I had gone too many lengths to please my parents before.

"Whatever you say, Sierra," I could feel Adrian's heart pounding. He was upset, and with just cause. We were both silent for a while.

"I told her that I love you," I said quietly. I did. The moment those words left my mouth I knew that it was the truth. I loved Adrian in a way I had never imagined possible. It was a strange thing. I needed him, and that was strange because I had never needed anyone before in my life.

"You said what?" Adrian grinned from ear to ear. "I bet you had her panties in a knot." He laughed.

"Sure 'nough did. I also told her that she mustn't call me until she can come to accept you."

"You think you made the right decision?" he asked. I nodded my head.

"Of course, I did. I'm tired of having to prove myself."

We lay enjoying the silence of each other's company for a while before Adrian said, "Say it again."

"Say what again?" I asked with a smile.

"Say that you love me." I looked up into Adrian's handsome face, and a shiver ran through my body. I loved him. The fact gripped ahold of me and made me smile again. This is what I wanted. To fall in love. It overwhelmed me.

"I love you, Adrian Quant."

Adrian's lips captured mine in a kiss that stirred my soul. I parted my lips to allow his tongue entrance. He let his tongue play and dance and tease me until I clung to him anxious for some more of his attention. It was his turn to look into my eyes and as he viewed the depths of my soul I became entranced by him. I was locked under his spell of enchanting seduction. I couldn't bear his eyes boring into me. So I closed them.

Then I felt featherlight kisses on my forehead, my eyelids, my cheeks, my nose, before descending to my neck. I just lay there and let Adrian work his magic. He gently lifted my T-shirt over my head and was surprised to discover that I wore no bra. Adrian quickly straddled me and took off his own shirt before taking one breast in his mouth while he tenderly massaged the other one. I moaned Adrian's name over and over again. It had to be a sin for him to make me feel this good. My hands stroked his solid back as I gasped in pleasure when he finally gave my other breast some concentration. His hands roamed about my body, exploring, teasing, and pleasuring. Each touch singed and I thought I would combust at any moment. My heart pounded and my blood soared through my veins. How could he do this to me? I wondered about this, but my thoughts came to an abrupt halt when I felt Adrian's fingers on my panties, tugging at them. Before I realized it, they were gone, and his mouth moved down my stomach, making a path to my center with a trail of kisses. His lips brushed over me there, and my breath lodged in my throat. I had never, ever, ever, ever gone this far with any man before in all my twenty-seven years. Not even Shane. When his tongue plunged inside me, seeking his treasure, I thought that I would die. I couldn't help it, didn't want to stop the scream that ran away from my lips. I barely recognized my own voice as sounds of ecstasy filled my bedroom. I lay spent, thinking that was it. Adrian had other plans, though. He brought his lips back to mine, a centimeter away from me, but he didn't kiss me. He looked into my eyes, and held my gaze as he placed my trembling hands on the button of his Polo jeans. I undid the button and pulled his zipper down slowly, all the while my eyes never wavering from his. My hand found its way inside his boxers and I timidly stroked his manhood. Adrian gritted his teeth as his eyes closed. I could barely hear my name whispered on his lips. Suddenly, he removed my hand and was out of his pants so fast I thought I imagined that he'd been wearing a pair. I lay perfectly still, nervous as hell. I didn't know what to do or what I was supposed to do. A lot of doubts started to cloud my mind while I waited for him to protect us. Adrian eased back on top of me, and I know that he noticed the look of indecision in my eyes.

"Sierra, I'm not going to do anything that you don't want me to do?" he said as he shifted his weight onto his elbows. I looked away from him. "Sierra," he prompted. I couldn't do it. I couldn't sleep with Adrian. Okay, I just couldn't. Not when I didn't know how he felt. I had just told the man that I loved him and he had said nothing. I wanted him to love me. Not like a little bit. Not care a whole lot. Love. I wanted him to love me. Suppose I did this, and then he dumped me. Suppose he realized that I wasn't his Cinderella. No, I couldn't give Adrian my virginity. Not now at least. Not until I knew that he loved me.

"I'm so sorry, Adrian." Adrian exhaled and rolled off of me. He wrapped the comforter around us and I snuggled up against his body.

"Talk to me, Sierra. One minute you were ready to do this. I know you were. The next you're pushing me away."

"It's not you, Adrian. It's just that I'm not into the sex thing like that," I said vaguely. I didn't want to tell him that I was a twenty-seven-year-old virgin.

"You mean that you've been abstaining," he said trying to figure me out.

"Kinda."

"Kinda?" he repeated.

"Well, actually to abstain from something you would have to have done it before." Adrian looked at me quizzically. Doubt clouded his face.

"Sierra, are you telling me that you're a virgin?" he asked and had the audacity to be laughing.

"It's not funny, Adrian."

"Sierra 'Hot like fire' Allen is a virgin? Could have fooled me. With your worldly ways I thought you would have some experience."

"You know better than to judge a book by its cover," I reprimanded.

"I didn't know that you folks still existed," Adrian joked. I elbowed him.

"I'm sorry," he said sobering.

"You're not upset?" I asked carefully.

"No, why should I be?" he asked. I shrugged. It had been my experience that men needed sex and when they didn't get it they went elsewhere. "The ball is now in your court, Sierra. I won't pressure you in any way. You're going to have to let me know when you're ready. And believe me you're going to be ready real soon." He grinned. Arrogant motherfucker. I laughed, closed my eyes and let Adrian hold me.

So there, that's my big secret. I'm a virgin. It's not as bad as it sounds. There is absolutely nothing wrong with being a twenty-seven-year-old virgin. At least, that's what I tell myself, but every time I utter that word to some guy he runs like

I've got the plague. That's what drove old boy, Shane, away and that's what drove every other man away. It's just that I've never loved someone enough to give them that part of me. I'm not saying that I've never been in love, 'cause I have been. What I'm saying is that I've never trusted anyone enough to give him the most precious gift I have to offer. Adrian knew how I felt, and amazingly he understood. He didn't try to pressure me or give me ultimatums. So then the script was flipped and I wanted him. Problem was, I didn't know how to go about getting him where I wanted him, if you know what I mean. I had no expertise in the area, and Adrian had thrown the ball into my court. I called a time-out but was ready resume the game. I just didn't know which play to execute.

Love is a four letter word that encompasses so much. No definition is adequate enough to explain the depths of a person's feelings for another. It can't be measured. It can't be counted. It can't be seen or heard or even touched, but it is manifested through another's actions toward you, and your reaction to them. Love is what makes you willing to put your life on the line for someone else. Love is what makes you unable to live without someone. Love is what makes you hurt way down deep when you've been done wrong. Despite it all, the ups as well as the downs, love is a beautiful thing. Love is what Adrian felt for Sierra.

He never imagined that he would fall for her. She was nothing like the dream girl he had conjured up in his head. Because of Sierra he had learned that you can't put limitations on love. Just because you want a five-foot-two, one-hundred-five-pound package and you don't see it on the shelf that doesn't mean the five-foot-eight, one-twenty-five-pound package doesn't have what you want. Love doesn't have a big ass and tight tits. That's superficial, and he had been basing all his ventures on superficiality. Love is real. Love is going to take time off from work to take care of you when you're sick. Love will stick up to the parents when they put you down. Love will be there through the thick and thin.

Sierra had showed him the potential love has. In all his twenty-nine years, Adrian had never been in love and had never been loved. It was all new to him and it was a bit over-whelming. The realization threw him for a while. Didn't know what it was. He didn't know what he was supposed to do. He knew what he wanted to do. He wanted to spend for-ever with her, maybe even longer if that was possible. Adrian was scared, and he was man enough to admit that. He didn't want to get hurt, and his instincts told him to run. But he wanted this more than he was afraid of it. Where did they go from there? Adrian didn't know, but definitely he was going to take this ride with Sierra.

Just as Adrian got to his office's door on Monday morn-ing the phone rang. It had been a rough weekend for him. Sierra was away on business and wasn't scheduled to be back until Friday. Now it was his turn to miss her.

"Quant," Adrian said into the receiver.

"Adrian, this is Vaughn. We've been put back on the blacklist." Adrian cursed under his breath. The country had worked so hard to bring their offshore banking industry up to the standard the G7 had set for them.

"The positive is that so have all the other Caribbean coun-tries. They're strong-arming us, Adrian. This is our liveli-hood they're messing with. All the heads of state have called an emergency summit in Barbados with all the banking peo-ple. The Bank of the Bahamas president is in the U.S. right now meeting with the banking industry's big-willies there, trying to find out what 'violations' have occurred. He called and asked that we go down there to represent the Bahamas. I would go myself, but the acquisition of New Providence Bank and Trust is being finalized this week. I need you and Sierra down there tomorrow."

"That's no problem, but Sierra is in Abaco."

"I already called her. She's flying out tomorrow."

"Okay, I'll be ready to leave whenever then," Adrian said pleased. He was going to get to see Sierra.

Adrian arrived in Barbados that night, and was in his hotel room by 12:45. Sleep eluded him that night as illusions of Sierra haunted him. Before his eyes closed he had made up his mind about what he would do. Even though his mind was made up, it would be a while before he could reveal his plans to Sierra. Until then he would come up with the perfect seduction for Sierra.

When Adrian woke the next morning he felt rejuvenated. It was the best he had slept in a while. He had a brunch meeting at 10:00, and the rest of his day was free to plan the perfect night for Sierra. He wanted her to not only hear the words, but feel them in his touch, see them in his actions, and believe them because of his loving.

I was sure 'nough pissed off when Mr. Vaughn called me to tell me that I had to detour to Barbados. I hadn't seen Adrian in over week. Mosquitoes had bitten me from head to toe. I had a permanent headache, and I felt like I was getting the flu. I didn't want to be in Barbados. I wanted to be home in my bed snuggled against Adrian's chest, and not in no damn Barbados attending damn meetings from sunup to sundown. I finally got to Barbados on Tuesday night. Flying on Bahamasair from Marsh Harbor there was an eight-hour delay. So instead of being there by that morning I arrived there that night. Of course, when I got to the front desk at the hotel there was some confusion and they had no idea what room I was in. After twenty minutes I was finally given a key. I was beyond pissed. After I took a shower the first thing I planned to do was call Adrian to vent. I had had a terrible, no good, very bad day.

You can imagine my shock when I opened the door to my room and was greeted by soft music playing. It was Babyface, my all-time favorite artist. If I was a sensible person I would have turned back around and went right back to the front desk. Since I have no kind of sense and am nosey I proceeded into the room. I walked a few steps into the suite and stepped on something. I looked down to see a trail of red and white rose petals. I continued on my trek cautiously. The room was candlelit. I sniffed the air. Jasmine was my favorite scent. I thought for sure that Adrian would pop up, but to my disappointment the room was empty. I peeked into the bathroom and saw that the tub was full of water and bubbles. I had flashbacks of that movie *What Lies Beneath* with Harrison Ford. So I looked around the room again, trying to wish Adrian into existence. I strolled over to the balcony and for the first time I noticed that there was table out there set for two. Curiosity made me go outside. The cool Caribbean breeze hit my face and I inhaled. It felt good.

"Good evening, Ms. Allen," I heard a voice whisper into my ear. A smile spread across my face. I turned to face Adrian. I had found my knight in shining armor, my Prince Charming.

"What are you doing here? I called you and they said you weren't in today. I called you at home too, but . . ."

"Sierra, shhh," Adrian said before his soft lips touched mine. His kiss was short, tame. I hadn't seen him in nine days. I didn't want a stage kiss. He laughed at the expression on my face.

"There is no need to rush," he said.

"I'm not rushing. I just want to be kissed properly," I said.

"Properly, huh?" he asked with a mischievous grin. Adrian

caught me off guard. He came at me hard, fast, and strong, taking my breath away. As our tongues battled I felt in his kiss a difference, a promise that tonight would be the night.

"Come," Adrian said, leading me inside. Adrian started to unbutton my blouse.

"What are you doing?" I asked.

"I'm undressing you," Adrian said boldly and proceeded with the rest of my clothes. Before I knew it I was in my underwear. Adrian just stood and stared at me as if it was his first time seeing me. He shook his head and said, "Go and take a bath before we don't make it through dinner."

While in the bathroom I had opportunity to think about this. To some this may not seem like an issue, but for me this was a big, huge deal. Adrian was telling me that he was ready to make love to me. I was ready—more than ready—but then my old friend, insecurity, crept up on me. Suppose this was some game he was running. Suppose after he got what he wanted he split. Suppose I was tripping, and I was. I knew that Adrian was for real. He loved me. I was as certain of that as I was of my own name.

When I walked out of the bathroom, Adrian was standing there in a suit. My favorite suit, too. It was a navy-blue, pin-striped, single-breasted Armani. Adrian looked beautiful in it.

"Why are you so attentive tonight?" I asked.

"I just want to make you happy, Sierra. Can you let me do that? Let me take care of you. Every day you go out there, taking on the whole world like you're invincible. You're the most independent woman I know. Sometimes I feel like you don't need me for anything," Adrian said running his knuckles over my cheek.

"Just because I don't act like I'm helpless doesn't mean that I don't need you. I need you more than the air I breathe. You are the single most important thing in my life. I love you," I said looking into Adrian's intense eyes. I saw in them something I had never seen before. They seemed to glow with a hunger that made me shiver despite it not being cold. Adrian took me by the hand, and instead of going to the balcony for dinner we headed to the bedroom. My heart pounded in my chest. I could have sworn that Adrian heard it. Just as we entered, the CD changed and LSG's *Your Body* flowed out of the speakers. Talk about mood music. I sat on the edge of the bed and tentatively watched Adrian undress.

"Aren't you going to help me out?" I didn't bother to answer. He knew that I was nervous and he was teasing me. I thought he was beautiful in his suit but he's even more beautiful without. Honey-dipped chest and abs stared back at me. I bit my bottom lip. Damn! This man looked good. I couldn't sit still any more. I walked over to Adrian, and pulled him toward me. My hands found the waistband of his boxers and my eyes met his.

"I'm ready," was all I had to say. He led me to the bed where he undressed me for the second time that night. He motioned for me to get into the bed and I obeyed. He stood before me in all his manly magnificence. I gasped at the size of him and became a little apprehensive. Where the hell did he think he was going with that thing? Adrian grinned at my expression. Adrian then joined me on the bed. He kissed me with a tenderness that I had not felt before. His eyes roamed my face, caressed my body.

"I love you," he whispered before he laid me down against the pillows and found my lips again. My hands were all over Adrian and his were all over me. Our caresses were urgent, demanding, burning. Our labored breathing echoed in the room as the foreplay went on. Just when I thought I could take no more of Adrian's sweet torture, he parted my legs with his knees and readied himself to enter me. Soon I felt him inside me. My eyes widened in astonishment. I gasped in pain as he deepened his penetration. Adrian stilled himself for a while, letting me adjust to having him inside me.

Then he started to thrust in and then out, slowly at first. He was a gentle, considerate lover. Even though I was inexperienced I knew that much. I soon found his rhythm and arched toward him. I wanted this. I needed this. My eagerness forced him to go a little faster. I felt myself losing myself in this man. With each of his thrusts he propelled me onto a new horizon, a place I had never been before, and for the first time in my life I knew what it was like to be loved, totally and completely loved by a man. And I mean that in a carnal way.

Adrian and I lay in bed, our limbs intertwined. I listened to his steady breathing as he slept. He looked so peaceful. I couldn't help but touch him. I loved him and he loved me. That was a phenomenon to me. It was all too new to me. I couldn't understand. Couldn't explain it. It was real, though. I knew that. Adrian's love was real. I still doubted it, though. I doubted its longevity. I wanted to be with him for the rest of my life, but happy endings weren't reality. Real life love stories did not begin with "Once upon a time," and they sure didn't end with "Happily ever after." This was too perfect, our love. I was just waiting for something to happen. For that part of love that everyone said hurt to creep up on me. Until then, I would enjoy what we had, every single minute of it.

Chapter Five

Half past seven. That was the time. Sierra was well over an hour late. She was supposed to meet Adrian at Café Johnny Canoe for dinner. Adrian let out an impatient sigh as he got up to leave. She had called about a half an hour before and said that she was held up at the beauty salon, but would be there soon. Adrian knew that would not be the case because Sierra went into the salon and didn't know how to come out. Just as Adrian got into his car his cell rang.

"Quant," he said, as agitation was evident in his voice. Caller ID had revealed who it was on the other end—Sierra.

"Adrian, are you still at the restaurant?" Sierra's question came out all in a rush.

"In the parking lot."

"Can you come and get me? My tire blew out right down the road from you. I'm standing right opposite the golf course. Right by Goodman's Bay."

"Your tire blew out? Why didn't you call me sooner? I hope you're not standing out there all by yourself," Adrian said concerned.

"I didn't call you because I thought I could change the tire by myself. Come to find out, my spare's got a flat, too. So that's why it took so long for me to call you, and, no, I'm not by myself. I was giving my friend a ride to her place right around the corner from the Café."

"OK, Sierra, I'll be there in a minute," Adrian said before he hung up. As he drove the five minutes it would take him to get to Sierra he shook his head. It was just like Sierra to play superwoman. Change the tire. Like Sierra knew how to change a tire. He'd bet she couldn't even find the jack. Adrian got a visual of Sierra changing a tire and started to laugh. He stopped his car when he spotted her red Explorer, and all traces of laughter left him when he saw who Sierra's friend was. His mouth went dry and the palpitations began. Mikayla Cunningham was the one woman he was afraid of, and Adrian had no problem admitting that. He and Mikayla had dated for about six months when he was at the College of the Bahamas. She was the complete opposite of Sierra. Very clinging and needy. She had to be around him twenty-four-seven. Adrian had felt suffocated and had dumped her.

She had become obsessed with Adrian after that and stalked him for a bit. She used the fact that Adrian was never quite able to say no to her when it came to sex to her advantage. Adrian knew, though, that good sex was not worth all the drama that Mikayla was capable of causing. The last straw for Adrian was when Mikayla had taken him to South Ocean Resorts for the weekend, seduced him, and asked him to marry her. When he had refused, she put a gun to his head and threatened to kill him. That was it for Adrian. He had a restraining order put on her and hadn't seen her since.

"Adrian!" Mikayla exclaimed as she ran into his arms. "I always knew that you were my knight in shining armor," Mikayla said. Adrian rolled his eyes. "My friend's tire blew out. Can you help us?" she said in a low voice as her hands wandered over Adrian's chest. Sierra stood back watching in disbelief. She couldn't believe that Adrian was just going to stand there and let Mikayla fondle him in front of her. It was obvious that they had a past, but he was hers now.

"Yeah, I know," Adrian said as he removed Mikayla's hands and walked toward Sierra. "Sierra called me to come and get her." Adrian took Sierra in his arms and soundly kissed her. He examined her thoroughly to make sure she was as he had left her that morning. "Did you call a tow truck?" he asked her.

"Yeah, they should be here soon. So I see that you two know each other," Sierra said to Mikayla and Adrian.

"Yeah, we went to COB together," Adrian said.

"It was little more than that, Adrian," Mikayla cooed and Sierra wanted to slap her.

"Really?" Sierra said.

"Adrian was my beau," Mikayla said and had the nerve to blush.

"Well, isn't it a small world. Adrian's my beau now," Sierra said in a mocking tone. Mikayla's response went unheard because the tow truck pulled up.

When Adrian got Sierra home he exploded with laughter.

"I didn't know that you could be so catty," Adrian said as he pulled Sierra onto his lap.

"I didn't mean to be. It just came out of nowhere."

"I want to get better acquainted with that side of you," Adrian said nuzzling Sierra's neck. She laughed, but then grew serious.

"I don't know what it is but I don't like the vibes I'm getting from Mikayla around you. What's the skinny on you two, anyway?" she asked. Adrian told Sierra the whole story and when he was done Sierra said, "I don't trust her around you."

"Don't stress it, Sierra. There's nothing there."

"She scares me."

"Me, too." Adrian said. "She tried to kill me."

I looked over at Chi. He was on the treadmill beside me. He was running like he was trying to complete the one hundred meters against Michael Johnson or somebody. I, on the other hand, was walking. We had just completed a Tae-Bo class and I was exhausted, to say the least. Chicago had a stream of energy that never seemed to stop flowing. After an hour on that damn treadmill Chi finally decided that we should call it quits. Chi worked me hard. He had to because Sierra Allen is one lazy person. I don't enjoy exercising, at least the kind that Chi always had me doing. I would much rather play a game of basketball or softball or something of that nature. Aerobics and running were not my cup of tea.

Chi and I walked to the locker rooms to get our gym bags. We planned on heading downstairs to the café to get a bite to eat. I know. I know. What good was the exercising if we just ate foolishness afterward? Oh well, a girl had to eat. We made our way to the cafe and I noticed all the stares directed Chi's way. I had to admit that he did look good in his basketball shorts and muscle shirt. You know the ones that show the cuts in the arms. He had a nice body going on there and he worked hard to keep it fit. Ashley was a lucky woman. Not as lucky as I was, of course. Chi couldn't shine a light to Adrian. Adrian was a god. Had to be with a body like his.

"So how's the pregnancy coming?" I asked once we were seated and had started on our dinner.

"First trimester was pure torture. Sierra, when you and Adrian decide to have little ones, please don't go asking him to find you mango ice cream at two o'clock in the morning." I had to laugh at that one. I also couldn't let Chi's remark go unanswered.

"What makes you think that Adrian and I will get all the way to having kids?"

"Sierra, I know I don't have to spell it out to you. You're smart. Adrian is ready."

"Ready for what?" I asked all wide-eyed. I had felt for a while that Adrian had reached that point where he wanted marriage. I just needed confirmation for my speculation.

"For marriage."

"How do you know?" I asked.

"I see it in his eyes. It's the eyes, Sierra. It's also a man thing."

"Really?" I said, rolling my eyes at Chi. "Anyway, if he does decide to go there, I'm ready." I knew I shouldn't have said that. Chi started to freak out like I had told him that Jesus had come again.

"Baby girl wants to get married. My Sierra. Oh, Imma cry," he said wiping his eyes. He then gave me a serious, thoughtful look. "I'm glad that you found love, Sierra. You deserve to be happy, and I'm pretty convinced that Adrian makes you happy. Just as long as I'm the gentleman of honor." Chi just had to ruin the moment with that comment. I laughed in spite of myself.

"What the hell is that?"

"You know I can't be the maid of honor. So we're going to have to modify it a bit."

"Suppose I hadn't planned on asking you to be in my wedding?"

"Yeah, whatever, Sierra. If I'm not in your wedding, there's not going to be a wedding. I'll kidnap the minister. I'm not playing with you. Weren't you my best person?"

"I'm just kidding, Chicago. Of course, you'll be my gentleman of honor, but don't you think we're getting ahead of ourselves? Adrian hasn't proposed yet."

"It's imminent," Chi said and winked. "Anyway, isn't ya'll's one-year anniversary coming up?"

"Yeah. Damn, I can't believe it's been that long already. Adrian is planning something big. He told me to take a couple of days off. I don't know what to get him, though. I was thinking about that jet ski he's been meaning to get."

"How much is it?" Chi asked thoughtfully.

"Too much, but I want to make him happy. That definitely will have him on cloud nine. It's not like I can't afford it. I haven't touched the money in the mutual fund that my grandparents left for Savaughn and me. Savaughn used his to build his and Lisa's house—excuse me—mansion.

"I want to use it for something worthwhile. Something my grandparents would be proud of."

"Why don't you open that library you've been talking about? Two-and-a-half million dollars is certainly enough to do it with."

"I know, but if it's nonprofit, it's going to take a lot to keep running."

"I'm sure the government will be more than glad to help you with funding, and all these private organizations around here."

"I'll start some research, maybe after this weekend."

"Yeah do that. Your grandparents would definitely be proud of that. I loved them like my own grandma. I remember the day they won the lotto. It was wild." Chi's eyes sparkled with distant memories. It had been wild, too. It was a shame that they both passed before they could enjoy their winnings. My grandfather had a stroke and died. Three weeks later my grandmother had a heart attack. They left their winnings to their only grandchildren, Savaughn and me. They had always made me feel like I was someone special. I missed them still.

Our conversation was cut short when Chi said, "Look who's entering the building." I turned around to see my brother. He waved at us and headed toward us. When he got to our table he shook hands with Chi and kissed my cheek. I cared for my brother, I really did. I just didn't like him. That may sound like an impossible contradiction but it's not.

"Chicago, where have you been hiding yourself?"

"I've been in court mostly," he said as he took a sip of his coffee.

"Heard that you have some political aspirations."

"Maybe," Chi said uncommittedly.

"If you do, I know a few people who can give you some direction."

"Thanks for the offer," Chi said. Savaughn then turned his attention to me.

"You're looking well," he said pulling a lock of my hair. It was something that he always did because he knew I didn't like it. "I haven't seen you around lately, either. The boys have forgotten they have an aunt."

"I've been off the island a great deal lately."

"I'm sure Adrian can't be pleased with that. Speaking of Adrian, I saw him the other night at Café Renaissance. He was with your friend. What's that girl's name? The one with the long, long hair? Kayla?"

"Mikayla," I supplied. I wasn't the jealous type. So normally news like this wouldn't bother me, but the feeling I had gotten when I was around Mikayla was one that I didn't like.

"That's it, Mikayla. Yeah they were there. Anyway, I've got to go. Lisa is waiting for me. I hope to see you soon," he said to me and left. He had done what he had set out to do. He had planted the seed of doubt and insecurity, suspicion and mistrust in my mind. All the way home I wondered what Adrian and Mikayla could have been doing together, having dinner at Café Renaissance of all places. Would Adrian cheat on me? That was the question that took hold of me? He didn't seem like the cheating type. Looks could be deceiving. Wasn't that what I had told him once before.

When I got home I called Adrian, but he wasn't home. That wasn't unusual for him since he worked until all hours of the night. Still, I let all types of scenarios form in my head. I saw visions of Adrian and Mikayla making love on his desk. I commanded myself to stop my foolishness. Adrian had never given me any reason at all to doubt him. I wouldn't start because of something my asinine brother said. On that thought, I rolled over and went to sleep.

I wasn't working like I was supposed to be doing. I had on my headphones and I was jamming to the sounds of *The Best Man* soundtrack. Lauryn Hill and Bob Marley's duet was my favorite track and I had it on repeat. "Turn the Lights Down" was the jam. Lauryn's words moved me. I'm a big fan. I like Lauryn not only because of her music. She's obviously a gifted young woman, but I also like her because she showed the world that you don't have to be the Li'l Kims or Foxy Browns to make it in the music industry. She is a grounded, God-fearing, independent, beautiful black woman who didn't succumb to the pressures of showing ass and tits. I have much respect for Lauryn Hill. I like to think that we're a lot alike.

My jam session was interrupted when Mr. Vaughn made

his way into my space. I hadn't seen him in a while, not since he got his promotion. I wondered what brought him out of the woodwork.

"Mr. Vaughn, please come in and have a seat."

"Sierra, you've treated me badly. Haven't even come to visit me. I'm hurt."

"I'm sorry, but I've had my hands full."

"I bet you have," he said with his characteristic smirk. We talked about the job for a while, and then his true intentions were revealed. "So what are you doing after you leave here?" he asked. I was going to Adrian's place, but I had no intention of telling him that.

"I have plans," I said smoothly.

"What about tomorrow?" He was relentless.

"Got plans then, too." Didn't he get it? I was never, ever, ever going out with him.

"I'm sure that those plans all include Mr. Quant." I gasped. Few people knew about the extent of my relationship with Adrian.

"Mr. Vaughn, I don't think that's any of your business," I said getting upset. I forced myself to remain calm. No there was no use getting upset with the boss man.

"I know that you two spent a couple of extra days in Barbados when you were sent there on business." I was boiling. "Before Mr. Quant came on the scene the reason you gave me for not going out with me was because of our work relationship. That didn't seem to stop you from fucking Mr. Quant."

"Hold the fuck up!" I said not able to contain myself anymore. "I don't appreciate being talked to like that. What I do and with whom I do it is none of your goddamn business. My decision not to go out with you was my decision, regardless of what grounds they were on. I told you that story to spare your feelings, but it seems as if you can't understand English. I don't like you. I can't stand you, and I'm never going out with you," I said, all in one breath. I exhaled. "Please leave."

"You'll regret this, Sierra. Brushing me off is the biggest mistake of your life," he said angrily. 'You'll pay and it'll hurt. I guarantee that."

"Whatever. Get out of my office," I said and slammed the door behind him.

Chapter Six

Adrian sat alone in his office at a quarter past eleven. A mountain of papers surrounded him. He had sworn that he would get to the bottom of this mystery. It just didn't add up. He had discovered a while back that someone had been stealing money from dormant accounts. It all started when he got a call from a friend from NYU. She had told him that her grandaunt had died. She had several offshore accounts since her husband had been some kind of business mogul in Texas, probably oil. He wasn't sure. The aunt had died, and Angela, a lawyer, was trying to get all her assets in order. Everything was going fine except when she checked the account in the Bahamas at National the balance read zero. Angela's aunt had been dead for almost two years, and the withdrawal was made after her death. The only person that had access to the account was the dead aunt. Even Angela didn't have access to it.

This all left Adrian with a lot of question marks, which prompted him to check other accounts. Some accounts, which had been dormant for years, suddenly had large withdrawals. Others were just like Angela's situation. The ac-

countholders were all dead and withdrawals had been made
after their deaths.

What did all this mean? This meant that someone inside
the bank, someone who knew the inner workings of the system, was embezzling the money. Who? That's the answer
Adrian was looking for. Sierra hadn't complained about his
late hours at the bank, but he felt guilty nonetheless. He just
couldn't let this go, though. Adrian picked up the phone and
dialed Sierra's number.

"Hey, babe," he said into the receiver.

"Adrian?" Sierra questioned groggily.

"Who else would it be? I'm sorry that I didn't make it by
your place, but I had to work late."

"I understand. I've had to pull a few all-nighters before,
too."

"I don't deserve you. I love you. You do know that,
right?" Adrian murmured into the phone. Suddenly he had
visions of Sierra in bed wearing nothing but a thong. His
groin tightened and he forgot about work. Sisqo's "Thong
Song" played in his head.

"I love you, too," Sierra was saying while Adrian's imagination ran away with him.

"Since you're up now, how about I come over?" Adrian
asked. Immediately Sierra was wide awake.

"Why would you want to come over at such a late hour?"
she asked in a seductively low voice.

"I can tell you a few reasons, but I don't want to make
you blush," Adrian laughed.

"Okay, bad boy, come on over." Sierra laughed, too.
"We'll see who's going to be the one blushing."

"I hope that's a promise," Adrian said. "I'm leaving now.
So I should be there in thirty."

"Okay, I'll see you then." Adrian hung up the phone and
started to get ready to leave. Just as he was logging off his
computer Mikayla walked through his office door.

"What the hell are you doing here?" he asked not even trying to hide his annoyance.

"I came to see you. I figured you would be lonely," she said as she crossed the room to stand in front of him.

"I'm about to leave," Adrian said as he pushed Mikayla aside and headed to the door. Mikayla was faster than he was because she was at the door blocking his way.

"I thought I told you that I have a girlfriend whom I love very much. I'm not into you, Mikayla," Adrian said shaking his head.

"Really?" Mikayla said as she walked closer to Adrian. Her mouth was inches away from his. Before Adrian could protest any further her lips were on his, forcing him to accept her tongue, and he did. Her kiss left him feeling giddy, like he was drunk. Mikayla had always had that effect on him, and he was powerless to her sexual appeal. Mikayla quickly undid her blouse and gave Adrian a view of her bare chest. His heart was already pounding, his hands were trembling, and he was ready to take her.

Mikayla knew that she had Adrian exactly where she wanted him. She had realized a while back that Adrian would never love her, not the way he loved Sierra. He would go to his grave loving Sierra Allen, but she would be damned if theirs was a match made in heaven. She was determined to break them up. If she couldn't have Adrian Quant, then no one else was going to have him. So that's when she had hatched this plan. Mikayla knew her power over Adrian. He had never been able to say no to her. She was going to make love to Adrian and make sure Sierra knew about it. Looks like her plan was working.

Adrian had long ago stopped thinking. Right after Mikayla had undid the buttons on his shirt. Right after she had trailed kisses down his lean torso. Then she had gone down a little farther. Her lips sent shivers up and down his spine, making his body convulse. Then his boxers were gone and she had taken him between her lips. He had closed his eyes and moaned Sierra's name. Sierra! Logic returned. This was not Sierra. This was that tramp Mikayla. He pushed her away from him and scrambled to put his clothes back on. Adrian refused to believe that he had almost done what he had done.

"Get out!" he yelled at Mikayla. "Get the hell out," Adrian repeated and Mikayla was stunned into motionlessness. "Get out before I . . ."

"Before you what?" Mikayla sneered. "Don't threaten me, Mr. Quant." Mikayla said with a smirk.

"That's not a threat, Mikayla. That's a promise, and if you even try to mention this to Sierra you won't have a job, a house, a car, nothing," Adrian spat out.

"You can't do that."

"Try me and we'll see. Now get out!" Adrian yelled again. Mikayla left without another word, and long after she had left Adrian sat at his desk wallowing in self-condemnation. He was guilt ridden. Something nagged at him, urging him to tell Sierra. They'd always been honest with each other. He had to tell Sierra. She'd be mad. She'd be beyond mad. She'd be hurt, too, but hopefully she'd understand. She had to. He couldn't live his life without her. Adrian cursed under his breath. How could he have let this happen?

Adrian had said that he would be at my place in thirty minutes. An hour had passed and he still wasn't there. I had started to worry. I had told Adrian long ago about the route he took to my house. He claimed it was shorter, but I knew that people often got robbed and even killed on that road. Especially if that person drove a Lexus like Adrian's. Finally, at ten minutes after, I heard Adrian's car pull into my driveway. I got up to open the door for him. As soon as the door swung open Adrian was in my arms, kissing me, holding me as if he didn't want to let me go, with an urgency that almost scared me.

"I'm so sorry I'm late, but I got held up in the office, trying to log off. You know how that system goes."

"Shh," I said as I led him to my bedroom. Once there I took off Adrian's shirt and I couldn't help but notice the scent of Elizabeth Taylor's White Diamonds, a scent I didn't like and never wore. I pushed doubt aside. I had promised myself that I would always trust Adrian. I felt the tenseness in his shoulders. I knew that he had been working way too hard lately. I couldn't wait until the weekend when we would be leaving for California. I massaged away the tension and I heard Adrian moan his appreciation.

"That's enough," Adrian said as he turned around and took my hands in his. He kissed the palms before telling me how much he loved me. Then his lips touched mine and his tongue played with mine and he tasted like coffee, which he never drank. There's a first time for everything, I reasoned. Adrian quickly undressed me before undressing himself, and right before he slid off his boxers that's when I saw it. It was the evidence that would incriminate him. Lipstick was on his Carolina blue boxers. A rich-pink-colored smear of lipstick. I thought that maybe my eyes were deceiving me. While Adrian made love to me like it was the last he would do so I prayed that my eyes had deceived me. I felt an urgency and desperation in him that he had never displayed before. It was real and not imagined. This time it did scare me. Before Adrian succumbed to sleep he said to me, "Always know that I love you. Remember that."

As soon as Adrian was asleep I got up to inspect the boxers. I couldn't help it. I really couldn't. It was the nosey part of me that drove me to do it. Yup, it was lipstick alright. So Adrian had let some other chick do the do to him. Why else would there be lipstick on his boxers. I hated to jump to conclusions. I believed in getting answers rather than drawing assumptions. I had to ask Adrian. I refused to believe that he would hurt me like that until I heard it from his own lips or saw it with my own eyes.

I stood by my bedroom window, looking out at the morning sky. I felt Adrian's presence behind me. He wrapped his arms around me and kissed the nape of my neck. It took everything in me not to melt into his arms. I figured that there was no time like the present, so I might as well get it over with.

"Adrian," I said.

"Mm."

"Last night before you came here where were you?" There, I had asked him. It wasn't the right question. I knew that, but I couldn't just come out and say, "Who have you been screwing behind my back." I had some tact.

"I was at the office. Why?"

"Alone?" I pressed. Adrian hesitated before he answered me.

"Yeah," he said and I didn't believe him. He had never lied to me, but I knew that he was lying then. "Right before I left, Mikayla came over." I shrugged out of Adrian's embrace. I turned to face him. There was something in his eyes. It was guilt.

"And?" I prompted.

"I never intended anything to happen."

"But something did happen?" I questioned, much calmer than I ever imagined I could be.

"Yes, but I didn't sleep with her," Adrian said quickly. "There's nothing there. Nothing at all."

"Except that you wanted to?" I sneered.

"No. Sierra, I love you. Mikayla came after me. I never pursued her."

"Damn it, Adrian!" I was quiet for some time and Adrian's eyes pleaded with me to understand, but I couldn't. I looked at him. I tried to rationalize this, but the betrayal was too real. "You made me fall in love with you. How could you do this to me?" Agony was evident in my voice. I was on the verge of tears but I refused to let him see me cry.

"I'm sorry," he said with his head hung down in shame.

"Sorry?" I asked. "I fell in love with you, Adrian. Don't you understand that? I love you more than I love myself." The tears began to flow. I couldn't stop them. "Adrian, I would die for you. I love you. I trusted you not to screw up and hurt me," I sobbed as anguish embraced me. "No amount of apologies is going to change the fact that this hurts. It hurts."

"Sierra, I'm hurting, too."

"Why the hell are you hurting?"

"I don't want to see you like this," Adrian said reaching for me.

"Don't touch me," I hissed, eluding his grasp. "If you didn't want to see me like this you never would have done this. *You* did this!"

"Sierra, we fell in love. You . . ." Adrian started, but I couldn't let him finish.

"We fell in love," I questioned him. "We didn't fall in love. I fell in love. Okay? It was just me. I can see that now."

"Sierra, how could you stand here and say that to me. You know that I love you."

"I don't know any such thing. If you loved me so much how could you do something like this? Huh?" He fell silent. Adrian had no defense.

"Get out, Adrian! Get the hell out!"

"Sierra," he pleaded with me to hear him out. I didn't want to hear anything else he had to say. There was nothing more that he could say. We were through. There was no more Adrian and Sierra.

"Good bye, Adrian," I said with finality.

Chapter Seven

I sat in front of my television with it on mute while Toni Braxton sang one of her songs about love and betrayal. I was in the depths of despair. Before, I had always joked about being in the depths of despair, not knowing what a painful place it was. I had probably listened to every sad love song that was ever written and I had related to all of them. I felt Mary on "I'm not Gonna Cry" and I heard what Karyn was saying on "I'd Rather Be Alone" I experienced every emotion after Adrian had left. I cried like I hadn't cried since I was a kid. I cried because he had hurt me. I cried because I had lost him. I cried because I had failed. I blamed myself. I thought that I hadn't loved him enough. I wasn't good enough. I hadn't satisfied him. I wasn't what Adrian Quant's girlfriend was supposed to be. I was angry. I was angry with Adrian for not loving me enough to not let lust tear apart our relationship. I was angry with him because he had torn my heart into a million little pieces. I was depressed. Depressed because I knew that I couldn't go back to him. I would never give him the chance to hurt me again, ever. I loved him, but that wasn't enough to make me feel secure, to make me feel like it could work. So as I sat there holding on to one of his T-shirts, the tears ran down my face and I was saying goodbye not only to Adrian, but also to love.

Adrian sat in front of Mr. Vaughn and refused to believe the words that were leaving his mouth. When all else had failed, Adrian had gone to Mr. Vaughn about the missing monies. The two had worked on finding the culprit for almost two days. That morning, Mr. Vaughn had come to Adrian with a list of suspects. Adrian was more than surprised to see Sierra's name on that short list. Even if her name was there, that didn't mean that Mr. Vaughn really thought that she did it, but he did.

"Adrian, if you would just put aside your personal feelings you would see that Sierra is the thief," Mr. Vaughn reasoned with Adrian.

"Come on. Sierra is the most honorable person I know. This is totally out of character for her. Maybe you made some kind of mistake."

"Adrian, the evidence is all here. Sierra may be smart, but she's not smart enough. She used her own security password to get access to those accounts. She forgot that the computer records it along with what activity she carried out while on-line. Then, to top it off, she has about five savings accounts, a fixed account, and an offshore account. None of them with National, of course. Let's not forget that nice gift she got you. Ever thought about how she could afford that?" Mr. Vaughn put in for good measure. Adrian had wondered about that, but the thought had passed. There had to be a reasonable explanation for a $10,000 gift.

"She lives in the big house and drives the Explorer," Mr. Vaughn continued. "All of this on her salary? Come on, Adrian."

Adrian didn't like to admit it, but Sierra did look guilty. Adrian didn't doubt her, though. He had to give her the benefit of the doubt. He had not fallen in love with a greedy, materialistic thief. Sierra's parents would give her anything she wanted, and they could afford to. It didn't make any sense.

Adrian looked across the desk at Mr. Vaughn and there was a strange look in his eyes. Before Adrian could consider it, the look had vanished; nonetheless, Adrian got the impression that Mr. Vaughn was not to be trusted. This all smelled like a setup to him. It was too perfect. Still, though, there was a "why" Adrian had to figure out. Why would someone do this to Sierra? Snatches of conversations with

Sierra replayed in his head. Mr. Vaughn had been sweating Sierra since her first day on the job. Everyone knew that, but she had turned him down time and time again.

After an hour and a half of trying to convince Mr. Vaughn to wait awhile before he went to the authorities, Adrian gave up. The man had made up his mind. He wasn't even going to confront Sierra first.

As soon as Adrian left Mr. Vaughn, he went by Sierra's, but she wasn't home. Adrian left message after message, and none were returned. Then when he called her at ten minutes after one, and she still wasn't home he figured that she was out, getting on with the getover.

As Adrian drove to work the next morning, Sierra was heavy on his mind. In the five weeks since their breakup there wasn't a day that went by that he didn't want her. It was evident to him that she was his destiny. He had decided, though, to give Sierra some time. If she needed to date someone for a while like she had probably done last night, then so be it, but in the end she would be his. When her time would expire he would let her know that he wanted to spend the rest of his life with her. He hoped she realized that he was for real.

Eric and Ed, 100 Jamz's morning crew, interrupted Adrian's thoughts.

"So you think she thought she was going to get away with this?" Kirk Smith, the newsman, asked the duo.

"Of course, she did. Why else would she have done this? To get caught?" Eric laughed.

"Twenty million is a lot of money," Kirk commented.

"It was that much? You think she hid some of that somewhere? Like in the Caymans," Ed asked.

"If she was smart," Eric said. Adrian had the sinking feeling that they were talking about Sierra. He needed to get to work. Adrian looked around him at the bumper-to-bumper traffic on Shirley Street. So close, yet so far. He took out his cell phone to call National. After a series of recordings he got Sierra's voice mail. He then called Mr. Vaughn's office, and his worse fear was realized.

I was so mad I could hit someone. You could imagine my shock when I was greeted at my office door by two uniformed police officers. In my life I had only had bad experiences with the police, so I was prepared to give them attitude whatever the reason for their visit.

"Sierra Allen?" the taller, younger officer asked. I glared at him suspiciously before I answered him. I wondered what they wanted with me. For a minute I thought something bad had happened. I prayed that Adrian (of all people) was okay.

"Yeah," I answered as I opened my door.

"You need to come with us," the same officer said. He then grabbed my arm and slapped handcuffs on me. We don't have that Miranda business in the Bahamas. So the police don't have to say anything to you except "you're coming with us."

"Hold on one damn minute!" I yelled. "Are you arresting me?" I asked.

"Is it that obvious," the other officer said smartly. I cut my eyes at him.

"For what?" I yelled at the man in disbelief. I may have done some not-so-nice things in my life, but none of them merited my arrest.

"For that Explorer you drive and that fancy house you live in. And how could I forget those million-dollar bank accounts you have," he answered smartly. I wanted to slap that smug expression off his face.

"Look, unless you show me a warrant I'm not going anywhere with you," I said confident that this was some kind of mistake, but when he did show me a warrant reality sank in. I had been arrested for stealing, theft, embezzling, or whatever the hell you want to call it. I, Sierra Simone Allen, was being dubbed a criminal. For a quick minute tears threatened to flow, but I was too angry to cry. Somebody was playing games, but when I was finished with them it would be the last game they would play.

The drive to Criminal Investigation Unit in Oakes Field was all a blur. How could they do this to me? I didn't even get a phone call like in the movies. I was asked the same stupid questions over and over again for the next twenty-four hours. My answers were always the same. I guess they hoped to catch me in a lie but there was no lie. The truth was that I didn't know what the hell they were talking about.

I sat in that dank, musty cell and thought about my life. What had I done that was so bad that I had to go through this? I decided to put all the negativity aside. It wouldn't help me. It would probably drive me to insanity. Instead, I thought of all the sermons I had heard my father preach. He was actually a very good preacher. I knew that God would never put more on me than I could bear. If Jesus could withstand the persecution that He went through, then certainly I could get through this. No one's life is without trials and tribulations. It was just a test and I had never failed at anything; therefore, I prepared myself to beat this thing.

A day and a half had gone by, and then, of all people, Savaughn came to rescue me. My brother was the last person I expected to see at Her Majesty's Prison. I had imagined all the bad things that he and my parents were saying about me. I knew that this probably was the last straw for them.

"Looking good, babe," my brother said while looking at my dingy off-white linen pantsuit. I had been wearing it for almost three days. It was not in good condition, and neither was I.

"Ha. Ha," I said. "So what brings you here?"

"We came to bust you out." He smiled.

"We?"

"Yes, me, dad, and mum. Chicago is here, too. He's going to represent you in a bail hearing or whatever these legal people call it."

"The parents are here?" I asked in total incredulity. "Both of them?"

"Yeah, you sound like you didn't expect us," he said as a prison officer came to let me out. I was fortunate enough to not have to share a cell. That was strange due to the fact that the prison was overcrowded. The guard followed closely behind us as we started toward the exit.

"The last couple of days have been hectic. The media is all over the place out there. So you're going to have to deal with all that, but if you don't want to talk I'll tell them no comment or something to that effect. If you don't want to go home, you can stay with us or with the parents." Savaughn just went on and on and on until we got to Chicago and our parents. I couldn't believe it. This was not what I expected from my family.

As soon as my mother saw me she ran and hugged me. She nearly knocked me over.

"Sierra," she cried. I mean literal tears. "I've never been more happy to see you. You can imagine all the thoughts that went through my mind. Are you okay? Tell me the truth now."

"I'm fine, Mum," I said, trying to take in everything that was going on around me. My father gave me a hug, too, but didn't say much. He looked really anxious and worried. I had never seen my parents like this.

"Okay, Sierra," Chi spoke up. "We've got a long battle ahead of us. I'm not even gonna lie and say that this is going to be a win because it doesn't look good for you." I had known that much from the attitude of the police detectives that questioned me. I could only manage to shake my head. "Change your clothes and let's get this show on the road," Chicago said.

Bail was set at $75,000, which wasn't really high. It wasn't like I was a mass murderer or anything like that. My parents paid the bail and I was released into their custody. Just as I was leaving the courthouse in downtown Nassau, I saw Adrian and my heart stopped. Our eyes connected and I felt what I had always felt for him, an overwhelming love, but only for a moment. Then reality sank in and I remembered that he had done me wrong. So I turned away from him before he could say anything.

As we drove to my house, Chicago, Savaughn, and I, I thought about Adrian. My mind wasn't even on all the drama that was going on around me. Chi and Savaughn had taken turns filling me in on what had gone down. I had a strong suspicion that it was all a setup and I knew exactly who was behind it. I just couldn't figure out how I would prove it. Despite my urgency to devise a plan to take Mr. Vaughn down, I daydreamed about Adrian. I still loved him. I couldn't run from that no matter how hard I tried. I just wished that this didn't have to happen, any of it. I want my happily ever after, but this was real life and we don't get those.

We got to Samana Drive, the street I lived on, and couldn't get through because of all the cars. Every newspaper, radio station, and the lone TV station were out there. I didn't want to confront the media right at that moment so I decided to crash at my parents' house. I hadn't stayed there since I had moved out five years before and I rarely visited. We had a lot of mending to do. I just didn't want to make the first move for fear of rejection.

My parents' home was a two-story colonial style house that we had moved into when I was about six years old. My room had a beautiful view of the ocean even though we lived quite some way from the beach. I loved my old room. My mother had decorated it in baby blue because it was my favorite color. The side of my room that faced the ocean was nothing but windows. On a cool day the breeze was heavenly. I strolled around my room looking at pictures of me at different stages in my life. Nothing had changed. It was exactly the way I had left it.

I decided to take a bath. I wanted nothing more than this nightmare to be over with, but I had a long way to go. After my bath I decided to take a nap but sleep eluded me. I had too much on my mind. I didn't know what to do with myself. Then I took out a pen and a piece of paper and did something that I hadn't done in ages. I wrote.

I Wanna Be. . . .

Society dictates to me
What it takes for me to uncover life's mysteries.
You're too short to be a model,
Too fat to be an athlete,
Too poor to be a lawyer,
Too smart to be ordinary,
Too woman to be Prime Minister.

Society dictates to me what I should do and who I can be.
You can't be yourself.
No, that's too Black.
You're too smart, too beautiful, and too intelligent to be
Just another face wandering on the streets.

Mom wanted me to be a doctor.
Daddy wanted me to be a politician.
Everybody was telling me, yelling at me what they wanted
me to be.
They didn't realize that success can't make you happy and
money
Can't buy you everything.

So, Society, guess what.
There's a list of unending possibilities.

I could've been a doctor, a lawyer, an astronaut, a
politician, an
Entrepreneur, a writer, anything.
What you failed to realize was that the choice was mine.

As I sit here listening to the dogs barking and the babies
crying
I know that my dreams and aspirations depend on me and
only me
But thing I wanna be most depends on you.
On that Society can't dictate to me who my heart should
beat for eternally.

I read over my poem and thought that it was actually pretty
good. It was a combination of two constant conflicts in my
life—my parents' dictations and my love life. Before I could
philosophize with myself any further, someone knocked on
my door. It was my mother.

"Hey, baby." My mother hadn't called me baby since I
was a baby. What was going on with everybody? I knew that
I faced some jail time, but, hey, they were scaring me.

"Yeah," I said.

"Are you up for seeing anyone?" she asked and I kinda
just shrugged at her. My mother came into my room and
took a seat on my bed beside me. She had that "let's talk"
look in her eyes. I really wasn't in the mood for talking. I already had so much on my plate. The last thing I needed was
an argument with my mother, but we did need to get a few
things out in the open.

"Sierra, you do know that I love you?" my mother asked
me, and I knew the answer was yes. I didn't feel it though. I
never had.

"I don't feel like it," I said quietly, honestly. A pained
look clouded my mother's face. She got up and walked over

to my window wall. I knew that she was preparing to bare all.

"I was hard on you coming up. I know that, but it wasn't because I didn't love you. It was because I knew that the world wouldn't give you anything. You'd have to work damned hard for everything you had.

"And you were so different. I wanted a baby girl more than anything in the world. When your brother was born I was a bit disappointed, but then you came along. I had someone to dress up and take to ballet lessons. I had someone to give everything that I never had, but you didn't want those things. You didn't want to be a cheerleader and cheer the team on. You wanted to be on the team. You didn't want to date the doctor. You wanted to be the doctor. You weren't the Ms. Bahamas contestant I wanted you to be. Not because you weren't pretty enough, but because you wanted the world to know you for something more valuable than your looks, your brain. You are an independent black woman. I am proud of you." I couldn't believe it. I sat speechless, in awe, in shock. My mother had said the words I had been longing to hear.

"How come you never said this to me before?" I asked. My mother laughed but there was no mirth in her laughter. It was kind of bitter.

"To tell the truth, I was jealous of you." My eyebrows shot up disbelievingly. "Sierra, believe it or not, you are everything that I wished I was. Instead of becoming the teacher that I wanted to be, I married your father and became the preacher's wife. I'm not saying that I regret the decision that I made because I don't. Your father has been the best husband a woman could have.

"It's just that I somehow lost myself in him along the way. I stopped being Nikki and became just the preacher's wife. That can never happen to you because you are so secure in who you are and where you want to go with your life." My mother had stopped talking, but there was so much more that I wanted to know. More that I had to know.

"Why are you telling me all of this now?"

"Why?" My mother laughed again, and this time it was real. "People are all over town saying all kinds of lies about you, and I've had to defend you. While telling people about you, I realized how lucky I was to have a daughter like you. That's all. I figured that I didn't tell you often enough so I should start now."

"I appreciate it," I said getting choked up. I was up on embezzling charges, my father was a minister of the gospel, and my perfectionist mother was going around defending me. That had to be a dream.

"Well, I'll let you get some rest now," my mother said moving toward the door. I ran behind her and gave her a big hug, like I used to do when I was a kid.

"I love you, Mummy," I said.

"I love you too, baby. We're going to have to invite that Mr. Quant over some time. Maybe I was too prejudiced in my judgment of him." My mouth dropped open. I had to be dreaming.

"That won't be necessary. We're not together anymore."

"Why?" my mother shrieked. "That's one fine boy." Oh, no. The woman was getting out of control. I had never heard my mother refer to anyone as fine. She'd usually say "good looking." I burst into uncontrollable laughter. If this was a dream I didn't want to wake up, even with the jail time and all that drama.

"Out!" I yelled. "I can't believe you said that. I have to lie down now." I laughed.

"Well, he is," my mother said and left the room.

Chapter Eight

Adrian was nervous. He wouldn't even lie to himself and say that he wasn't. A lot was riding on this conversation. Adrian turned into Skyline Estates and drove into Mr. Vaughn's driveway. Adrian couldn't prove it, but he was certain that Mr. Vaughn was the one framing Sierra for this fall. He had been thorough and had covered up all his tracks neatly. The one thing that Adrian had learned about Mr. Vaughn in the year and change that he had worked with him is that he loved to brag. He just had to get him talking and he would have a confession. Adrian wasn't sure if he could pull this off, but he knew that he had to try for Sierra.

Adrian was ushered into Mr. Vaughn's den by a Jamaican housekeeper. He glanced around at the decor of the house and knew that something was amiss. Before he was promoted Mr. Vaughn held Adrian's position, and he sure as hell knew he couldn't afford the kind of artwork that lined the walls of this man's home.

"Adrian, what brings you to my neck of the woods," Mr. Vaughn asked as he took a sip of brandy. Good, Adrian thought to himself. He was already halfway drunk. His tongue should be loosened pretty well already.

"I've been stressing about this whole thing," Adrian said as he took a seat. Mr. Vaughn raised an eyebrow at him.

"Why is that?" he asked. Adrian exhaled and sighed.

"I mean Sierra was right under our noses and she got away with all that money. I feel like a jackass. I didn't see it."

"Yeah, she sure strung you along." Mr. Vaughn was falling exactly where Adrian wanted him. "She had your nose wide open and pulled the rug right from under you."

"She sure did," Adrian agreed. "I wouldn't want anything like this to happen again."

"No, we wouldn't," Mr. Vaughn agreed.

"That's why I think we should beef up security around National. Rework the system so it will be impossible if someone tries something like this again." Adrian said, ready for Mr. Vaughn to put himself out there.

"There's really nothing wrong with our system per se," Mr. Vaughn said.

"If there wasn't, Sierra wouldn't have been able to do what she did. It was rather simple," Adrian pretended to muse to himself. "I figured it out you know, but Sierra was dumb. If she were really smart she would have changed the names on her accounts. She would have used somebody else's security password. She had access to all of them."

"In other words, she would have pinned this on someone else?" Mr. Vaughn cheesed.

"Yeah, if she were smarter, like myself or like you. I'm sure that you would have done things differently, and I'm sure that you would get away with a whole lot more than ten million dollars."

"If I were smart?" Mr. Vaughn said.

"But you're not smart," Adrian said and Mr. Vaughn's smile dropped. "No, you are not a smart man, Mr. Vaughn. If you were smart, I wouldn't have figured out that you are the one, and not Sierra." Adrian laid all his cards on the table. He was bluffing, but he had to give it a shot.

"I hope you have facts to back up your accusations," Mr. Vaughn sneered at Adrian. Suddenly he wasn't in such a good mood anymore.

"Facts? I've got 'em. The accounts, the houses all over the U.S., and your mistress. I've got more than enough proof." Adrian had found out about Mr. Vaughn's illustrious living from Mr. Vaughn himself. He loved to brag about where he had traveled and what gifts he had bought his wife and girlfriend. At first Adrian thought that this was money that he had won gambling. It was no secret that Monty

Vaughn was a big-time gambler. Then, when this whole thing with Sierra happened, things started to make sense. Adrian remembered Sierra telling him about Vaughn's promise to make her pay for rejecting him. This was payback if it ever was.

"I don't have to go to the police, though. We could settle this without the law," Adrian said slyly.

"What about your girlfriend?" Vaughn asked.

"What about her? We're talking money here, lots of it. So what do you say? How about a cool fifteen million or I turn over everything I found out to the police and you go to jail?"

"'Fifteen million! Hell no, Adrian! I'm not giving you fifteen million of my money."

"Your freedom isn't worth fifteen million? You'll have a lot more left. Come on, Monty. May I call you Monty? I know that the guys aren't too nice to white collar convicts at Her Majesty's Prison."

"Ten," Mr. Vaughn tried to bargain.

"No negotiations. Fifteen or nothing." Adrian could sense that Vaughn was exactly where he wanted him. He didn't want to go to jail, and he would do anything to prevent that. For a split second Adrian thought that Mr. Vaughn would try to kill him, but he was a punk and probably didn't want to get any blood on his clothes. So Adrian thought better of it.

"Okay," Mr. Vaughn agreed slowly. "I didn't go through all the trouble of getting one hundred million to let your greedy ass take it away from me."

"I'm glad you're seeing things my way, but you shouldn't have told me that it was one hundred million. I didn't know that it was quite that much. I might want more than fifteen million. How did you pull this off?"

"It was easy. The OB division was in the rut for so long that National wasn't paying any attention to it. I really didn't have to work hard at all. I didn't snatch the money all at once, but over the course of several years. I had to get them back. I was worth more than they were paying me, and it took me almost ten years to finally get a promotion. They had this coming. They'll never get this money back." Mr. Vaughn laughed at his cleverness, but he wasn't clever enough.

"You're giving me ideas. So you'll transfer this money to this account by tomorrow at 8:00 A.M. If it's not there, I'll go to the police with everything I have. Understood?" Adrian said handing Mr. Vaughn a slip of paper with an account number on it.

"Understood," Mr. Vaughn said.

"It was real nice doing business with you. I'll see you around. And don't even think about leaving town," Adrian said before he stood to leave.

Adrian didn't dare take his tape recorder out of his jacket pocket until he was in the privacy of his own home. He played the tape back and heard Mr. Vaughn's voice crisp and clear. He got right on the phone and called Detective Clement Webber, Sierra's cousin, at the Criminal Investigation Unit. Finally, this nightmare was coming to an end for Sierra. Then maybe they could get on with the rest of their lives.

Chapter Nine

I sat in the silence of my bedroom and thanked God for my freedom. Freedom was something that we definitely took for granted, but when you're faced with the reality that you may lose it, you appreciate it more. That's what had happened to me. My impending imprisonment was real. It wasn't a bad dream. It wasn't my imagination. I thought I was going to jail. As smart and as brilliant a lawyer as Chicago is, he couldn't fight the evidence, and it all was pointing at me. I was scared. I had never been that scared before in my life, but my family was there for me. Their support is what made me want to fight and not just lie back and give up. They were behind me all the way, and it was good to have them there.

I sat in my room and watched the flicker of the flame from a candle, and then I did something that I hadn't done in a long time. I prayed. I had said, "Thank you, God," but that wasn't enough. I sat there and had a one-on-one talk with God. The way I used to when I was a little girl. Suddenly a peace came over me, and I knew that I would be alright. I would achieve everything I set out to do, and God would be with me always.

I wouldn't let myself to talk to God about Adrian. I didn't want to admit it, not even to God, that I wanted him. I wanted him to be a permanent part of my life. Adrian had proved to me that he wanted to be with me for the long run. I don't know many men that would have gone to the lengths that Adrian did to prove it, either. He was just like in all those fairytales that we read. He was my Prince Charming and he rescued me. He may not have ridden in on a big, white mare, but he came through for me, nonetheless. When I least expected it, too. He was the one. I knew that. I allowed myself to open up.

"God, just give us one more chance. I just want a chance to show him that we can live happily ever after."

As you can probably guess I wasn't too hot on the idea of going back to National. I really didn't like people gawking at me. Grown folks know how to be extremely juvenile. I took a leave of absence and decided to leave the island for some time. Nassau may be paradise for some, but for a native it's home. I needed to get away. So I decided to go to my parents' place in Eleuthera.

I had hoped for two weeks that Adrian would come knocking on my door and I would let him in. He would say beautiful things to me like in those romance novels and we would ride into the sunset. Reality check. This is real life. It doesn't happen like that. I guess he moved on. Now I had to, too. It wouldn't be easy, but I convinced myself that I would get over Adrian Quant. Yeah right.

I put off packing for as long as I could. It was what I hated most about traveling. Almost as much as I hated unpacking. So I was doing everything except packing. I even ironed my nightclothes. Finally, there was nothing left to do and I had to pack. I resigned myself to the chore, comforting myself with the thought that in two days I would be away from it all. Drinking piña coladas, basking in the sun, and reading Omar Tyree's new joint. Now that sounded like paradise.

Just as I put the first article of clothing into my suitcase the doorbell rang and I couldn't have been happier. It was an excuse to stop the packing process. I figured it was Chicago because he had promised to bring me some dinner. I didn't even like to eat my own cooking. It wasn't Chicago at the door, though. It wasn't my brother or my parents. It was the person I least expected to see two days before my month-long vacation, but it was. It was Adrian standing there in the flesh. I wanted to pinch myself to make sure I wasn't daydreaming again, but when I opened the door and he spoke I knew that this wasn't a figment of my imagination.

"Hello, Sierra," he said in that voice that he knew drove me to insanity. Oh, how I had missed him. I thought that I would melt right there on the spot. I didn't know what to say so I just smiled at him like I was some kind of idiot.

"You mind if I come in?" he asked, a bit unsure of himself. He thought he had work to do. I'd let him think that. I didn't want to make it too easy for him. Besides I still had my reservations about this whole forgive and forget thing. I didn't know if I could do it.

"Sure," I said and led him to my living room. We had never spent much time in that room. Adrian didn't waste any time. He got right to the point of his long overdue visit.

"Sierra, I have a lot to say and I don't want you to interrupt me." He meant business. I couldn't help the smile that curved my lips.

"Go ahead," I said. Adrian took a deep breath before he spoke.

"When I first met you I wasn't looking for love, but I found it anyway. You became my world and I didn't even realize it. I've never begged for anything in my life, but I'm begging now. I need you. I love you with every fiber of my being. Please, Sierra, I need for you to give me a second chance. If you do, I will never do anything to hurt you again." I could see the tears in Adrian's eyes. They stirred my soul. I was about to mist up myself.

"Adrian, I can't explain to you what you put me through. Unless you went through it you'd never understand the pain I felt."

"Sierra," Adrian said grabbing both my arms and the first tear slid down his cheeks. "Don't you understand that I'm hurting, too? It hurt me more than anything when I saw you crying and to know that I put those tears there made the pain that much worse. When you walked out of my life my heart broke, too, and it was my own fault.

"I didn't want to fall in love. I didn't want to feel what I feel for you, but I do. I love you more than I've ever loved anyone in my entire life and that includes myself. I've come to terms with that. Sierra, I want to spend the rest of my life with you. I want to make you laugh, not cry. I will do whatever you want me to do and I will be whomever you want me to be if you take me back." By this time the tears were streaming from my eyes also. No one had ever said anything like that to me before. This man loved me. I could see that, and I loved him. He didn't love Mikayla. She was a nonissue. The real issue was trust. Could I trust Adrian again? I looked in to his eyes and he touched a part of me that had never been touched before. I reached up and wiped away his tears. I smiled. I smiled because I was relieved. This is what I had been waiting for all my life. He was the one I had dreamt about all my life. All my life. I could trust Adrian. I saw it there in his eyes. I knew that he would love me for however long I let him.

"You won't mind that your girlfriend will be in hiatus for a while?" I joked.

"Fiancée," Adrian corrected.

"Fiancée? I haven't heard any proposals," I was smiling from ear to ear. Adrian went down on his knee and asked the only question I wanted him to ask me.

"Sierra Simone Allen, I love you and I want to spend forever and a day with you." He laughed and I laughed along with him. "Will you marry me?" Hearing those words from his lips left me speechless. God did answer prayers.

"I would love to," I said. Adrian stood up and we looked into each other's eyes, and we smiled. He took my face in his hands and kissed my lips softly without taking his eyes off of mine. My eyes drifted shut as Adrian deepened the kiss. I felt butterflies floating in my stomach and I became giddy with love. I knew right then, at that moment, that this was as perfect as it got.

More Sizzling Romance from
DONNA HILL

MORE ROMANCE FROM
ANGELA WINTERS